Something Real

Books by J.J. Murray

RENEE AND JAY

SOMETHING REAL

Published by Kensington Publishing Corporation

Something Real

J.J. Murray

KENSINGTON BOOKS
http://www.kensingtonbooks.com

KENSINGTON BOOKS are published by

Kensington Publishing Corp.
850 Third Avenue
New York, NY 10022

All Kensington titles, imprints and distributed lines are available at special quantity discounts for bulk purchases for sales promotion, premiums, fund-raising, educational or institutional use.

Special book excerpts or customized printings can also be created to fit specific needs. For details, write or phone the office of the Kensington Special Sales Manager: Kensington Publishing Corp., 850 Third Avenue, New York, NY 10022. Attn. Special Sales Department. Phone: 1-800-221-2647.

Kensington and the K logo Reg. U.S. Pat. & TM Off.

Library of Congress Card Catalogue Number: 2001099488
ISBN: 1-57566-865-3

First Printing: August 2002
10 9 8 7 6 5 4 3 2 1

Printed in the United States of America

For my sisters,
Janet and Jill

Acknowledgments

Sheree Williams, who kept me straight on all the gospel music and helped provide jump rope rhymes with Shemeka Childress, Ashley Jones, and Tonya Brown; my agent, Evan Marshall, for keeping my fingers crossed; my editor, John Scognamiglio, for helping me write "deeper" than I've ever written before; my parents for making me the way I am; my freckled sons for "helping" me write with all their glorious interruptions; and my wife for loving me . . . just because.

Something Real

Prologue

I never should have married the motherfucker.

I know I shouldn't curse. I'm a Christian woman. But sometimes I believe that God makes mistakes, because when he made Jonas Borum, he made a six-foot-two, one-hundred-and-sixty pound pile of dog shit that even other dogs wouldn't sniff. It's as if God took a dump, and I happened to step into the pile.

For fifteen years.

I know, wasn't I conscious during that time? I thought I was. But when you smell anything—even shit—long enough, you don't smell it anymore.

And now I know what alone is all about. Alone is loss. Alone is by yourself in the basement folding sheets for a bed you haven't had sex in for over six years. Alone is rereading the same verse in the Bible twenty-five times at four in the morning wondering if the sun is really going to rise or if your husband is really going to come home. Alone is hearing the echo of your angry words to him—"You're the biggest asshole I've ever known!"—and the echo of his calm, cool reply: "You married me, so what does that say about you?" Alone is losing most of your friends, all of whom you see every Sunday at church, who treat you like you have AIDS because you divorced their preacher.

That's right. I divorced the great man of God, Reverend Jonas Borum.

And I *still* attend his church, playing the organ at every service because it's *my* church, too. I put fifteen years of my life into that place as the preacher's wife and over twenty years as the organist. And it's not like our divorce can forbid me from attending church. I lost quite a bit in the settlement because most of our shit was in Jonas's holy name, but I didn't lose my church membership. I've had that membership since I was baptized at twelve. Besides, when folks attend Antioch Church in Calhoun, Virginia, at the corner of Vine and Twelfth now, they'll see the great Reverend Bore-'em and his ex-wife Ruth Borum because I am keeping his name to keep folks scratching their heads. We'll be up there, side by side like always, and folks are just gonna have to wonder . . . What the hell is going on here?

I have lost so much.

I just hope I can hang on to my sanity.

And my faith.

PART ONE

It's Me, Oh Lord

One

I've been playing organ since I could reach the pedals, and I don't wear the heavy shoes some organists wear. My fat feet are heavy enough. And I never had any lessons. When I hear a tune, I can play it. That's my gift. God blessed me with a musical ear. Don't show me no notes, don't show me no hymnal, and leave the sheet music at the store. You hum it or sing it, and I can play it.

"You have a gift," Grandma told me when I was very young. "And gifts get given. No need to get paid for having a gift from the Lord." As a result, I have never gotten paid for all those services, baptisms, and receptions. When I was younger, I didn't care. I just liked to play. I loved to be *heard*. I loved all the compliments I got, loved the attention. But later I learned that Grandma was wrong about the payment part. Grandma never had to hold the same note or play the same sad chord for ten minutes till Reverend Hamlin, Antioch's preacher before Jonas, was satisfied that enough folks had fallen out, come forward, or felt guilty enough for being one-day-a-week Christians. Grandma never had to repeat the choruses of "I Prayed About It," "He's Able," or "Hallelujah" forty times because those were the only songs anyone seemed to know. Grandma never had to play "The Wedding March," "Always," or "Endless Love" several dozen times a summer. At least at a wedding I sometimes got some form of payment, usually a crummy corsage or maybe a ten-dollar bill in one of those tiny thank-you note cards.

Though I can't sing for shit (trust me), I know all the words. "I Want To See Him," "His Eye Is on the Sparrow," "I Still Have Joy," "No Ways Tired," "That's Love"—just a few of my favorites. Till the divorce. The Sunday after the divorce became final, I played "It's Over Now" instead of "Take It to the Lord in Prayer" during Jonas's altar call. I wonder if anyone even noticed the significance. Now the only song that can get me through the day is "My Life Is in Your Hands." And it is. It has to be. I've been praying non-stop for something, anything good to come out of all this, and when I play the organ, I feel good. I don't feel the glory I once did, but at least I feel something. It surprised me that the church board at Antioch let me keep my unpaid "job" at the organ, and at first I took it for a sign from the Lord. God was still letting me give my gift.

Fact is, cheap asses at Antioch just didn't want to have to pay anyone to replace me.

Antioch Church. Where do I begin? Antioch is a male-dominated, y'all-womens-better-stay-at-home, and y'all-working-womens-better-keep-quiet kind of place. Jonas, of course, has used this defect in our church to his advantage, telling his version of the divorce which is about as close to the truth as white is to black. "She has become mentally unbalanced," he told the deacons, "and, sadly, anything the poor woman says is a lie." And being the big-lipped, thimble-brained carp that they are, the deacons swallowed his story hook, line, and sinker. They then passed the story on to their ignorant stay-at-home wives who care only about decorations for the next "Ladies' Social." That makes about two-thirds of our church population who no longer know how to or even want to speak to me. In a church of five hundred, I have never felt so isolated. If it weren't for Tonya Lewis and Naomi Baker, two of the dearest friends that I've ever had in my life—and my need to be a weekly object lesson to Jonas's flock of ignorant sheep—I'd be gone from this persecution.

But where could I go? Calhoun is a small Southern city with a gossip streak as long and wide and shallow as the muddy Calhoun River. Can't *nothin'* happen in Calhoun without someone knowing about it and puttin' their mouth in it. Small minds, large mouths, houses too close together, too many folks fanning themselves on porches putting more hot air into the humid sky, and ain't nobody got cable. Naturally, *everybody* knows about the woman who divorced the preacher, and I can't even set them straight because everything I say *must* be a lie because the great Reverend Borum said so. Tonya and Naomi know the truth, and that's all that matters to me. To the rest of them, I say, "BAAAA! Go on and be good sheep while your good shepherd takes out his rod and plows many a valley. Surely goodness and mercy ain't gonna follow none of you—Dr. Bone-'em's bad ways is gonna haunt y'all all the days of your lives."

Right now, I'm just trying to keep my head above water. I've been nearly drowning in court-appointed this, that, and the other. I had a court-appointed divorce orientation (complete with videos) that told me what I already knew: "Divorce is shitty." I had a court-appointed mediator who told me what I already knew: "You ain't gettin' shit." I had a court-appointed psychologist who told me what I already knew: "Your brain is for shit." And I even had a self-appointed court clerk goddess white bitch who told me that my handwriting and typing were for shit. They all did everything in their power to further victimize me because they were taking such major pains to protect Jonas's career.

Fact is, Jonas wouldn't have a career if it wasn't for me because *I* wrote the damn sermons, nearly every last one of them. Oh sure, he wrote the rough drafts, and that's all you would have felt in that church as much feeling and spirit he put into them—rough drafts of *dull* air. "Today's sermon is on the love of God," he'd write. "Please turn with me to . . ." I'd scratch that out and write, "People, (pause and take a deep breath), the Lord has brought me safe thus far (wait for an 'Amen,' Jonas), through many dangers (wait for it), toils (wait), and snares (wait); and what did He use to carry me? (pause; take a deep breath) I say, what did my (loud) glorious Savior use to carry me? (pause; another deep breath) He gave me His love. (If they don't 'Amen' here, Jonas, repeat 'He gave me His love' till they do) . . ."

I gave those sermons fire, I gave those sermons depth, I gave those sermons feeling, and the church grew from thirty old, brave souls who met with us in a drafty, crumbling building ready for the condemned signs to five hundred and climbing in a totally remodeled, warm building. But did I get any credit for even one of those seven hundred sermons? You kiddin'? Since our divorce was finalized last month, the man's been recycling *my* old sermons, and he *still* ain't waitin' long enough for folks to say "Amen." I should have copyrighted those sermons so I could at least get a cut of the offering.

Everything I have tried to do since all this began is to protect myself. During the separation, I hired another psychologist, a hopefully impartial white female psychologist, to reevaluate me *and* Jonas this time. The tests were brutal invasions of my privacy, but I took them and tested as being reliable, dependable, practical, reasonable, conventional, loyal, and flexible. That's me. Faithful as a puppy dog. I felt

vindicated, especially when Jonas tested as being narcissistic and extremely self-centered. But somehow, this cold bitch psychologist with
an ego the size of the North Pole ignored Jonas's shortcomings because "large numbers of people in Reverend Borum's profession share
these characteristics." In other words, I married a stuck-up man, and
preachers, as a general rule, are stuck-up people. I paid a thousand
dollars (in addition to my attorney's retainer) for this ridiculous evalu-
ation which only supported the court-appointed psychologist's claim
that only I, Ruth Lee Childress Borum, was dysfunctional.

Because of all this shit, I've been seeing a psychiatrist. I know most
black folks don't do that, but they have their mamas and their families.
I don't. My white daddy left the scene before I was born, and Mama
died of a stroke when I was ten. I have no brothers, no sisters, no
aunts, and no uncles, not even a second cousin twice-removed. My
grandma, who raised me, passed twenty years ago, also from a stroke.
And now, thanks to Dr. Holt, I am chemically fucked up. I don't know
if I'm going or coming . . . and I definitely ain't doin' any coming.
Something about my drug "therapy" has destroyed my sex drive. Dr.
Holt says that will come back (I doubt it) as he's weaning me off one
drug while weaning me onto another drug which takes three to six
weeks to see if it works. I'm trying to sleep, but it ain't easy. I'm on a
new sleeping pill that leaves a metallic taste in my mouth. Taking one
is like sucking on the lid of a four-day-old, unrinsed Spaghetti-O's can.
But it gets me five whole hours of sleep, and I can handle the shitty
taste, because five hours beats none.

When JonASS and I first separated, my attorney advised me to do
two things: get a job, then get disability insurance, you know, the kind
of policy that protects your income in case you can't work due to ill-
ness or disability. I knew why I needed a job: so I could pay my damn
attorney. I could always cut and style a mean head of hair, so I found
me a job at Diana's, a little two-chair salon just around the corner from
my one-bedroom apartment on Vine. That's right. I live within spitting
distance of the church I helped rebuild. But my "fame" nearly cost me
a chance at the job. *Shit,* I bet the owner, Diana Poindexter, was thinking during the interview, *I can't hire the bitch I been talkin' about! Weather
in Calhoun ain't that interestin' to talk about all damn day!* I had to convince her that I could turn my friends into regular, paying customers.
Diana, who's pushing fifty and who still wears a Diana Ross 'do and
has posters of Diana and the Supremes all over her walls, asked, "Will
they come weekly?" I had laughed just then because that's exactly

what Jonas used to do. That was also one of the reasons that we didn't have any children. One "Dear Jesus!" or a "Yes Lord!" and he was through, leaving me blinking at the cobwebs on the ceiling. "Yes," I told her, "they'll come here regularly," and I got the job. And Tonya and Naomi did become regular paying (and tipping) customers because that's what true friends do. They chip nails on purpose or home perm their hair too long so I can have a job . . . to pay my attorney.

Six months of that, and I have money. Not much, but enough for a single forty-year-old divorced mother of none living in a single-celled apartment to survive on. Enter the disability insurance. "Why do I need this insurance again?" I asked my attorney. "Because you're under a doctor's care." So I got the insurance, and, sure enough, they have some of *my* income, and now they're protecting it for all *they're* worth.

I tried to get some of my income back when I had my first breakdown and just couldn't get out of bed for two weeks. Depression is the heaviest motherfucker on earth, and it hit me so hard and fast after a Sunday service that I had trouble even breathing. I had just played "He's Working It Out For You" for folks to walk out to when—BAM—I felt so low. It felt like one of those dreams where you can't move, and you know someone's behind you grabbing at you, but you can't move, and whoever it is will strangle you or stab you or rip your head off. It was like claustrophobia and that other phobia, that fear of heights thing, at the same time. I was boxed in and falling.

Somehow I filled out forms and gave them to Dr. Duckworth, my family doctor since I was born, and to Dr. Holt. They filled out the forms. The insurance people called me and asked me the same damn questions that were on the forms, they called Dr. Duckworth and asked him the same damn questions that were on the forms, and they called Dr. Holt and asked him the same damn questions that were on the forms. That was just so my "claim form" could go from Medical Review to being assigned a caseworker. How nice of them. Next, they took five to seven business days to pick daisies and their asses. They plucked off the petals and chanted, "She's sick, she's not sick. She's sick, she's not sick." At the end of that period, I got an official proclamation that my "claim" was approved. By that time, I was feeling better and could leave the apartment without feeling small and dizzy, so I went back to work and became undepressed. Just being around other people and solving heads of hair helped me through.

I have still not seen a *single* penny of this income of mine that they're protecting. I'm sure cutting a check will take at least three months because they have to have a review committee approve procedures for using scissors. If they're anything like the church board at Antioch, which once took six months to decide on *whether to decide* to paint the lines in the church parking lot, I will never see my money again. Thank God I have lots of credit cards and big credit limits. You'd be amazed at how much these credit card companies are willing to risk on a preacher's ex-wife, like I'm better able or more likely to pay since I'm so godly. I had to buy so much shit for my apartment. It was like starting completely from scratch: a table, chairs, dishes, silverware, glasses, and curtains for the kitchen; a sofa, chair, coffee table, curtains, and lamp for the main room; a bed, dresser, and night stand for the bedroom; a shower curtain, towels, toilet brush, cleaners for the bathroom. I have a feeling that my godly credit rating will go to hell by the time this divorce is finally over.

If the divorce ever ends, that is. Dearest Jonas—who never gave me birthday presents, who never gave me anniversary presents, who never gave me Christmas presents, and who never even gave me one measly card—sent me an anniversary card for what would have been our fifteenth anniversary. In it, the prick graciously included a check for the hundred dollars he shorted me in spousal support that month. It was the single largest gift he had given me in the history of our marriage, and he probably had to raid the offering plate to get it. At the bottom was a simple note: "Could you please return my ironing board and iron?" That he rarely used. That I slaved over with the Niagara starch. Nearly every night. For fifteen years. I returned them. I had to. They were part of the settlement . . . and now they're part of the big oak tree out in front of his house. He'll never be able to get up to that iron, though I'd like to see him try. I think it's wrapped around a branch and a power line. The ironing board I couldn't throw as high, but I doubt he'd want it now since the birds have pecked the padding out of it for their nests. All the settlement said was that I had to return them. The settlement didn't say in what condition.

I should have married my senior prom date. Stuart Hart, a poindexter, an egghead, asked me to the prom in his squeaky geeky voice, and I accepted because no one else asked me. No one else had *ever* asked me to any dance. I was just that big-boned church girl who could play the organ, that light-skinned girl with the lightning smile and thunder thighs. Grandma told me that I was born big "with a head the size of a pumpkin." I am kind of pumpkin-colored—imagine an almost new penny—with naturally reddish hair and orangeish freckles because of my daddy. I'll bet he was Irish, which might explain my temper. I recently heard that Stuart is now a full partner in an Atlanta law firm, the corporate attorney for a big movie studio and a couple cable networks, easily making a half million a year. But (sigh) he's married (happily) with five kids and a dog. Five kids. What I would do for just one child.

But . . . There was no room in our marriage for a child or a dog, because we already had both, but I didn't know I did till I married Jonas Borum.

T*wo*

Reverend Ebenezer Hamlin was retiring after fifty years as Antioch's good shepherd, mainly because the congregation had dwindled from two hundred to thirty during his final wheezy, gravel-voiced years. The church board, which made up half of the remaining members, urged him to retire, while secretly, I'm sure, wishing the old fart would just go on and die.

Reverend Hamlin refused to die, said he'd "go on a-preachin' to his grave," said "Jesus never retired—He was just sent home early," said "God will call me home in God's good time." Which *He* did, taking Reverend Hamlin home the week after Christmas while folks were returning gifts at the mall. Folks said that God was just calling Reverend Hamlin to *our* rest, not his. Yes, old "Hambone" died in his sleep, most likely saving another generation from dying in *theirs* every Sunday morning.

After three consecutive Sundays of only singing and testifying, candidates to take Reverend Hambone's place began preaching at us, trying to win us over. It was quite a show, too. All of them were young, fine black men who preached hellfire and brimstone, who strutted and pleaded, who sweated all over the threadbare carpet.

They weren't hired.

Then Jonas showed up. Boring as lint. Dry as hot sand. Dull as a butter knife. Tedious as watching dust settle.

Jonas was hired.

During his first sermon, we had to listen hard since we had no idea what he was talking about. He quoted something from Dante's *Inferno*, and I could hear someone in the choir whisper, "Dante Who?" and someone else replying, "Oh, that's Mattie's sister's nephew's boy." He quoted from *Pilgrim's Progress*, "by that great writer John Bunyan," and another whispered, "Bunions? What he talkin' 'bout bunions for?" Finally, he quoted from C. S. Lewis's *The Screwtape Letters*, and I started looking it up in the Bible. *Let's see . . . Letter to the Corinthians, Letter to the Galatians, Letter to the Ephesians . . . but no Letter to Screwtape.* "These famous quotations will be illuminated by the end of our discussion of sin." There was no illumination during that sermon. The man lost us from the first "thee-thou-thy" and had us scratching our heads at his constant reference to someone he called Wormwood. Still, it was different, a change of pace from Reverend Hamlin, and it really made us pay attention . . . so we could have some shit to talk about *after* the sermon.

Back then, the choir outnumbered the congregation most Sundays. Antioch's music was and still is a blessing to all who attend. Folks seem to come for the music like some folks attend football games to watch the halftime show. Naturally, we had a bigger budget for choir robes than for the building fund. Jonas, to his credit, noticed this discrepancy and approached the music committee, which back then was just me and Mrs. Edna McKinney, the choir master.

Mrs. McKinney was a bitch's bitch, cruel and demanding, requiring Wednesday rehearsals past midnight if necessary, screeching, "Louder!" and pounding her fists if she heard a stray note. She was also the best damn choir director Antioch's ever had and probably ever will. At only four feet seven (if that) and maybe eighty pounds, Mrs. McKinney could make even the most tone-deaf person sing like an angel. Unfortunately, I was never an angel. "Ruth, you just hum, softly, please, in your *head*, please," she'd tell me. I miss her a lot, because the new director, Cedric Lee, a sweaty man who closes his eyes to sing every damn song, has made himself into the featured soloist and probably thinks he'll be a star someday with his little towel and glass of water.

Jonas approached Mrs. McKinney and me and asked, rightly, that we put off buying robes for a year to get Antioch's roof reshingled. "It's in really bad shape, Sister McKinney," Jonas said.

"No," Mrs. McKinney said quickly.

"Kinda hard to keep singing if rain's comin' down on you, Sister McKinney."

"There will be showers of blessing, Reverend."

"Be right cold, too."

"The Lord will provide, Reverend."

Jonas shot his eyes at me, and I shrugged. "It's not something that can be patched, you know. The shingles up there now were put on over seventy years ago."

"They've held up thus far," Mrs. McKinney said. "I don't see any leaks. And, Reverend, the Lord *surely* wouldn't let it fall."

"I'd hate for anything to ruin those nice robes y'all have, Sister McKinney. Such beautiful colors. The blood red of Christ and the electric blue of heaven." Which matched absolutely *nothing* in the church. The choir looked like a bunch of folks from an old roller derby team. Thankfully we have golden robes that match everything now. "Who picked out those colors, Mrs. McKinney?"

"Why, I did, Reverend," Mrs. McKinney said, her hand to her chest. He was getting to her.

"You have a keen eye, Sister McKinney," Jonas said with a smile. "A keen eye and a keen ear. You have created the best choir I've ever heard, too. Y'all ought to travel, to compete." Oh, how that man could talk from those thin-ass lips under a thin-ass moustache, thin-ass nose, and thin-ass eyebrows. He put his thin-ass fingers on Mrs. McKinney's bony little hand. "Take it to the Lord in prayer, Sister McKinney."

Mrs. McKinney seemed a little out of breath. "Well, we *could* put it off for six months . . ."

Jonas smiled then, but not at Mrs. McKinney. He smiled at me. "Wonderful. And then maybe we can get the piano tuned, the organ fixed up a bit . . ."

Antioch's roof reshingled, the piano tuned, the organ a little less dusty, and Antioch started to change. Jonas ordered two offerings taken per service, stressed the hell out of tithing, and even siphoned off some of the flower fund from old Miss Paula, Antioch's self-appointed flower arranger who never met a lily she couldn't tape somewhere. Pews were replaced or refinished, windows replaced or scrubbed clear of eighty years of filth, grimy railings cleaned or sanded and painted. A new neutral carpet appeared under our feet. If nothing else, Jonas Borum was a practical man for a practical people. Jonas helped Antioch bloom again. We had chosen well.

On Easter Sunday, Jonas was, as usual, as dull as a wait at the doctor's office, but he got the service started on time (10:30) and ended the service precisely at noon. That had never happened before. I had noticed that the services were getting shorter and shorter over his first three months, but to pull off an Easter Sunday miracle like that? A ninety-minute Easter service at a *black* church in the *South?* Unheard of! Miss Paula told me afterward, "Christ for *sure* be comin' back this evenin'. I'm goin' home to pack."

But word got out. There's a black church in Calhoun that isn't on Colored People's Time? It starts on time and ends on time? What, I can get home in time to catch the *beginning* of the *first* football game? Wait, you mean I can get out of my heels and serve Sunday lunch before *four* o'clock without rushing? Hold on here. You mean, I won't have to beat my kids in the pews during the service because they can't sit still? Where is this heaven of a church?

Normally empty pews started filling. Clock and watch watching became all the rage. Alarms beeped all over the sanctuary at 11:59. Jonas even removed his wristwatch and laid it on his Bible before every sermon, and every service ended precisely at noon. Mrs. Mc-Kinney remarked, "You could time a pound cake to that man."

More folks turned into more money turned into new sidewalks, new front steps, new oak front doors, and new light fixtures . . . Antioch was reborn.

At a church board meeting in October of Jonas's first year, the board voted to give him a raise. They also hinted, and they said it almost exactly like this, that he should "perhaps, um, well, in order to be able to more fully do your duties as spiritual leader of Antioch Church, maybe, um, well, this is so delicate, but, um . . . You should *marry* . . . and, um, perhaps, well, we don't like to say these things, and we normally wouldn't, but it's just that, well, you know . . . Your further *tenure* here could depend on it . . . so you take it to the, um, the Lord in prayer, Brother Jonas."

I was shocked. What nerve! All that he had done in just nine months, and he was being threatened with marriage? The church board proved to me that there wasn't a generation gap at Antioch—it was a generation *trap*. The old ways hadn't passed away like the verse says, and nothing was new.

I lingered after the meeting and found myself alone with him for the first time. I waited at the front of the sanctuary till the last crusty board member left before saying, "They have got some nerve, huh?"

He shrugged. "I understand their concerns."

"Don't mean you have to listen to them," I said. "Or do what they say. I mean, telling a grown man to marry to keep his job after all the wonderful things you've done? You've quadrupled the daily attendance, tripled the membership rolls, fixed this place up, and made it shine, and they tell you that you need a wife to keep your job? That is so wrong."

"It's their right, Sister Childress. They're the board. They were here before I got here, and they'll be here long after I'm gone."

"Reverend, if they suggested as much to me, I'd be out the door."

He sat in the first pew and sighed. "I don't have that luxury, Sister Childress."

"And please call me Ruth. That 'sister' business is as old-fashioned and stale as the bow tie Deacon Rutledge wears."

He smiled. "Ruth." He sighed again. "You know just about everybody here, don't you?"

"Yes. Born and raised in this church."

He squinted. "Why haven't *you* married?"

I dropped into the pew on the other side of the aisle. *What a question!* "I've, um, I haven't found the right man, and I wasn't exactly blessed with beauty."

He didn't answer right away. *Doesn't he know that I'm fishing for a compliment?* "Inner beauty lasts forever," he said eventually. *So I ain't pretty, but I got pretty innards. Thanks a lot.* "You know something, Ruth? I like watching you play. Watching your feet marching, almost dancing, your hands flying. You are really talented. I know you could be playing for a different church, a bigger church, on a nicer organ, most likely making a nice salary. But you stay here. Why?"

Now, those are compliments. "This is my home. I love this old building, that dusty old organ, the dusty old people." I laughed. *Quit your babbling, girl.* "I wouldn't dream of going anywhere else."

"Hmm," he said. "Building, organ, people. No mention of the preachin'."

Oops. "Well, to be honest, Reverend, you're, well—" I looked at him, and he seemed very interested. "You're sometimes too . . . logical, like maybe you're more of a teacher or a professor than a preacher. It's like we're all in school or something."

He dropped his head. "I'm boring."

Least the man knows the truth about himself. "Well, I didn't say—"

"No no," he interrupted. "I've heard folks talk. 'Bore-'em Borum,' they call me. 'Least he gets us out in time for the kickoff,' they say." He rubbed his hands through his thinning, neatly groomed hair. "Guess I need a little fire, huh?"

Boy, you need a flamethrower, a blowtorch, and a bolt of God-honest lightning. "Well, there are a few things you could do to spice things up, but not too much at first. Gradual-like. Antioch isn't a place for drastic changes, you know."

Then he looked me dead in my heart, I swear, and asked, "Would you help me, Ruth?"

Damn right I did. I helped him with those sermons, lighting a match or building a fire here and there, and eventually the amens came, the hands started to rise, folks started to sway, the testifying lasted longer, the singing came from the heart, and we sang that extra chorus like we really meant it. Jonas compensated by shortening his sermons, and, I swear before God, Antioch became warmer all over and under and everywhere in between.

And so did I. Working next to that man, and being able to tell folks that I had a "date" with a preacher *every* Saturday night (I didn't tell them what for), and, God forgive me, listening to "my" sermons *all the way through* each Sunday—I thought I was getting closer to God. I even prayed that Jonas would think I was truly beautiful on the outside, too.

One evening we were tackling I Corinthians 13, the so-called love chapter in the New Testament, when he touched my hand for the first time. I froze. Then he said with the most serious eyes, "I've never been in love, Ruth."

My meaty hand had never felt better, and I felt a tingling in another place, too. *Damn, gettin' moist in the pastor's study.* "Never?"

He shook his head. "How can I preach *on* love, Ruth, if I've never been *in* love?"

I tried to pull my hand away to point at the Bible, but Jonas wouldn't let go. "This chapter is about God's love, right? You know all about God's love, Reverend."

He let go, leaving traces of his warm, skinny fingers on my hand. "Yes, but . . . I want to make it relevant." Jonas firmly believed in the adage, "If the congregation can't apply it, don't try it." He stared into my eyes. "Have *you* ever been in love, Ruth?"

My eyes popped. "Me?" Oh, I had some lusting crushes on some traveling singers, a guest pastor or two, once on a pianist who played so beautifully one Sunday that I was in tears. But he never came back. Probably because the piano was out of tune then. I looked at the man I prayed to God for every night and, trying to remain calm, said, "No, I've never been in love."

Jonas moved closer. "Well, maybe, Ruth . . . Maybe we can discover love . . . together."

My freckles were threatening to sweat off; I was blushing, breathless, my heart pounding. *What a beautiful thing to say!* "What . . . What do you suggest?"

He shrugged. "I don't know. It's all new to me. Would you like to see if, maybe, we're a possibility?"

I was twenty-five, had but one date in my life, was a tall, plump, unmarried woman the color of a penny, and the holy man of a growing church was asking *me* to discover love? I tried not to sound too anxious. "Would *you*, um, like to see if we're a possibility?"

He smiled. "Yes."

After several silly moments, my eyes and stomach dancing up and down, I said, "I'd like that . . . Jonas."

I should have asked him if he had ever been in lust before. If I had known that Jonas needed a quiet, homely "show wife" to accent his career, that he needed a wife to praise his holy name daily, that he needed . . . damn, a religious slave, I never would have given him the chance. But I did. And I thought the whole time that he was the answer to my prayers.

After just four months of courting without a single kiss, hug, or held hand, we were engaged to be married. It bothered me some that he didn't show any affection toward me, but, damn, I was so fat and he was so skinny. He probably couldn't reach his arms around me. The folks at the church used to smile at us with pursed lips and nods, and for the first time in my life I was getting attention from people for something other than my playing the organ. We didn't go on "dates" during our courtship, exactly. We visited sick folks in the hospital or at their homes together, sometimes went for walks, and once got some fish sandwiches from Dude's Take-Out Soul Food on Vine. It wasn't very romantic at all, but at the time, it was wonderful. He never said he loved me, and I never said I loved him; yet there we were. Engaged.

The first time I kissed Jonas was after "You may kiss the bride." *Damn,* I thought at the time, *his lips taste thin, too.* We had us a potluck dinner in the church basement afterward, with Tonya and Naomi taking pictures. Yeah, it was a cheap-ass wedding since I had no family to help pay for it, and his family was a bunch of skinny, gray cheapskates from Maryland who didn't say a damn thing to me and barely even spoke to Jonas. I asked him why they were so cold, and he said, "That's the way they've always been." I've sat on toilet seats that were warmer than his family.

We went on our honeymoon to Hotel Calhoun, a very expensive

hotel, but for only one night. I was nervous, scared, excited, worried, proud, and happy (and even a little guilty at all my sinful thoughts) all at the same time. I slipped under the covers wearing a sinfully slinky nightgown, a gift from Tonya. When Jonas came out wearing some maroon-and-gold pajamas, I nearly laughed. *Who wears pajamas anymore? And plaid? Man looks like a sofa.* Before we finally got down to business, Jonas led us in a prayer. A long prayer. A prayer so long my coochie dried up. He said, "Amen," turned off the light, and went to work. After some difficulty on his part with his pajama pants and my draws, he got himself in, did his business for about twenty seconds, whispered, "Yes, Lord," pulled out, and went to sleep, snoring on the other side of the bed while tears spilled out of my eyes. *I waited twenty-five years for this? The pre-sex prayer lasted a hundred times longer! Your wedding night ain't supposed to be a prayer meeting! What about foreplay? It's in, it's out, it's over? Ain't there supposed to be a wet spot? I had wet dreams that lasted longer, and there was definitely a wet spot in my bed in the morning!* I stayed up most of that night listening to the sounds of cars on the nearby interstate blend in with Jonas's nasty snoring. Man even smacked his lips and ground his teeth.

The next morning we went to church as husband and wife and got all those knowing nods and smiles again, especially from the old biddies who probably hadn't had none since World War II. I wanted to scream, "YES, I HAD SEX WITH THE PREACHER!" but I didn't. Their little biddy hearts would have stopped.

Tonya cornered me downstairs after the service. "So?"

"So what?" I replied.

"Was it good?"

"Was what good?"

Tonya's smile flipped to a frown. "Damn. I told you that man would need a two-by-four tied to his ass. Bet he fell in. He skinny down there, too?"

"Shh, Tonya, we in church."

Naomi joined us. "How are you this fine morning, Sister Ruth?"

"Horny," I said.

"Shh, Ruth," Tonya cracked, "we in church."

Naomi took my hand. "It'll get better."

"How you know, Naomi?" Tonya asked. "You still a virgin."

"I have some knowledge of these things," Naomi said.

Tonya flipped a hand in Naomi's face. "You ain't gettin' it; you just don't get it." Tonya turned to me. "Did he warm you up?"

"No," I said. "He stayed on his side of the bed."

"I didn't mean it that way," Tonya said, shaking her head. "Did he meet your man in the boat face-first?"

I reddened even more. I was so naive back then. "Please, Tonya."

"We are in the house of the Lord, Tonya Lewis," Naomi said. "Act proper."

Tonya stepped in front of Naomi. "You tell that man of God if he want a piece of your heaven, he got to row row row your man in the boat. No licky, no sticky. He don't lick the coochie, you ain't no hoochie."

"I'm not listening to any of this on the Lord's day," Naomi said, and she walked away.

"Um, thanks for your concern, Tonya, but we're new at all this. We'll just have to take things slow, I guess."

Tonya hugged me. "Don't just take what you can get, girl. You gotta learn to *get* what you can *take* . . . till you can't take it no more. All that man needs is a little schoolin', and you is his teacher. Hell, he little enough. You just wrestle his little pointy head down there, and don't let up till you satisfied."

I laughed. "I can't do that to the good reverend."

"You want a nice sex life?"

"Of course, but—"

"Take that man to school."

I didn't do what Tonya suggested, but . . . We made out okay. And as Jonas's sermons warmed up, so did he. It was all so new and exciting, gettin' some just about every other night! My man in the boat was a little lonely, but at least Jonas put my ocean in motion. I almost felt guilty Sunday mornings still thinking about the night before or the morning *of* (those were rare), but in my joy I played the hell out of that organ. I always wondered if anyone knew that I pulled out all the stops on Sunday mornings after a good humping by the good reverend.

And then . . . I got pregnant. Jonas was so happy, the church was happy, Tonya and Naomi were happy, I was glowing, we started planning the baby's room—

And I miscarried after only two months. My placenta just . . . collapsed. I wept, Jonas wept, the congregation wept, Tonya and Naomi wept. I felt like a failure till—

I got pregnant again not two months later, and Jonas announced the news from the pulpit to glorious applause. We painted the baby's room, even put up a wall border full of little animals peeking out of the forest. This time I took more precautions, got more rest, ate right, took my prenatal vitamins like I was supposed to, saw Dr. Duckworth once a week, slept as much as I could—

And miscarried again, this time at three months. They called it a spontaneous abortion and never told me why it happened. It just did.

Folks in church looked at me like I was a sinner, looked at me like I wasn't holy enough to hold a child to term. "Fuck 'em," Tonya told me. "I'll pray for you," Naomi promised. Jonas? He mourned for seven straight days . . . then went right back to work, and another month later, I was pregnant again.

Dr. Duckworth put me on bed rest once I made it to three months, even made house calls or called the house to check up on me. He checked me for infections (negative), anemia (negative), lupus (negative), diabetes (negative, though I got a warning about my weight), and fibroid tumors (negative). I was cleared to have this baby. Jonas, to his credit, waited on me hand and foot, putting up with my complaints for his weak-ass, no-salt-or-pepper cooking, letting Tonya and Naomi visit whenever they could, even putting that crib together by himself with only a little fussing at the directions. It felt so wonderful to show a little pumpkin poking out of my stomach at five months, knowing I was having a little boy who we'd call Jonas, Jr., so fulfilling to see my bellybutton pop at six months—

Jonas, Jr., was stillborn at six months. We didn't even put an obituary in the paper, didn't have a funeral, and I almost didn't have a husband. I'd hear Jonas weeping in the baby's room, crying out to God. I tried to cry, I really did, but I couldn't. I think I was too scared to cry, maybe too ashamed to cry. I had let this marriage down again.

Dr. Duckworth recommended me taking a break after nearly a year of being pregnant, and Jonas agreed. I was, after all, the size of a house, my titties the size of watermelons, just one of my legs as thick as Jonas's whole body. I wasn't much to sleep with at the beginning, but now . . . Jonas tried to stay with me in our room after that, but he said he couldn't sleep and ended up sleeping on the couch downstairs.

I couldn't sleep either. My husband downstairs for the last two months, my baby's room empty, my heart aching, my body bloated. That's when I finally cried—alone—and decided it wasn't my lot in life to be someone's mama. It just wasn't God's will. Then Jonas, for whatever reason, made a visit to my bed, unspeaking, did his business, and left.

And got me pregnant again.

This time, we took absolutely *no* chances. The church raised money to put me up in the hospital when I reached six months. I spent nearly ninety days in there, visited, I think, by every member of the church at least twice, flowers on every available space. They even held mini prayer meetings around and over me, we got two of the night nurses to join the church, and I felt the spirit of the Lord moving in me. Tonya and Naomi finished the baby's room and brought me snapshots, and Jonas stayed with me till visiting hours were over every night—

The baby, a boy, was born full-term by C-section . . . with an Apgar score of one. He didn't cry out, didn't make a sound, never opened his eyes, and died while I was in the recovery room.

I cannot explain what I was feeling back then without using the word "empty." Lying empty in recovery alone with my hands empty because Jonas was taking a walk to grieve, I almost thought of taking my own empty life. One little, empty bubble in the bloodstream into one of those tubes, and that would be it. One little, empty pocket of air to fill my empty heart. I cried silent, empty tears and refused to be consoled by anyone, their words as empty as my two arms.

Once again, we didn't name the baby or have a funeral because Jonas didn't want our shame to be in the paper or paraded in front of the church. That shame lived with me at home. I had no words to comfort Jonas, and only Tonya and Naomi were there to comfort me. But when they left, the shame was still there, taunting me from the unblinking face of my husband, cursing me from the empty crib, haunting me in dreams where I would hear a child crying . . . and could never find the child.

Twenty months pregnant and nothing to show for it. I felt cursed. I closed the door to the baby's room one day, and I vowed never to open it again. Jonas returned to his couch, me to my tears, and another one of my children . . . to God. Four children I should have had. I didn't like God that much. I felt betrayed and abandoned because He was taking much more than He was giving. I turned to Psalms for comfort and only heard David's cries to the Lord. I tried to pray, but the words that left my lips had too much venom, too much hate.

My body was a hot air balloon with two ham hocks for arms, round floppy breasts, a tight shiny face, all on a set of long heavy legs.

Huge. I became huge. The wife of skinny Reverend Borum was as big as God's house, filling the organist's bench. Oh, I tried off and on to lose what genetics and four pregnancies had put on, and Jonas tried off and on for the next five years to make us another child; but all those potluck dinners, those weddings . . . I ate my way through a depression that never ended. I'd see a child, any child, and feel the weight. I'd play the organ and feel the weight of all those eyes on my back. I'd pass that closed door next to ours and feel heavier.

And . . . That's when it started. Seven years into our marriage, Jonas got the itch. I know that's cliché, but once he got it, he had to scratch it. At the church. Every night. With his new secretary. A divorced woman. A slut. A harlot. A ho. Who shall remain as nameless as the children I should have had.

After yet another night of "I'm working late at the church," I hired me a private investigator named Joe Beverly, a white man who only charged if he got results. He brought me those results only a few days later. I paid Mr. Beverly two hundred dollars, and he gave me twenty-four snapshots. "I'll keep the negatives," he said. "Unless you'd like them, too, for, oh, five hundred more?"

"These will do," I said, and I looked at the pictures in angry wonder. *He never made that face with me! Where'd he learn that position? Damn, the man looks right funny with that bony ass of his. But up in the window of his study for all the world walking by to see? How'd Mr. Beverly get these pictures of them right in Jonas's study? What part of the Bible they studyin' anyway? Sodom and Gomorrah?*

I confronted his ass with the pictures that very night. "How could you? You call yourself a man of God, and you're nothing but a mother-fuckin' hypocrite!"

"It's not me," he said with a straight face.

It felt like someone had punched me in the stomach. "So it's just someone else who looks like you fuckin' the church secretary in *your* study?"

"That's not my study."

I held up the one with the two of them at the window. "And that's not the watch I gave you for Christmas?"

"No. It's not me, Ruth."

"You a lyin' son-of-a-bitch, *Reverend!*" I held up the one with her in his swivel chair and him with his head between her legs. "That ain't the computer you use? And that ain't your banker's lamp? And that ain't the birthmark you got on your ass?"

"Like I said, that isn't me, and that isn't my study."

I balled up my fist and looked at it for the longest time. It was big as Jonas's nearly bald head. *I could push it right on through that pointy nose and make him have to walk backward the rest of his life!* "Get the fuck out my house."

He tried to hug me, but I stepped back. "This is all a big misunderstanding, Ruth."

"What the fuck don't you understand about 'get the fuck out my house'?"

"You're overreacting, Ruth. Those pictures could be of anyone. With the right equipment, someone could have superimposed faces that look like ours doing those sinful things. Do you really think that I'm capable of doing those things?"

"As many times you been in my bed lately, *hell no!*" I waved the picture of him munching the secretary's coochie. "And you ain't *never* done this to me! But now I know why you ain't been draggin' your ass to fuck me, and pretty damn soon, Antioch gonna know who you fuckin', too." I shook the pictures in his face. "These will go right nice up on the announcements board!"

His eyes dropped. "You wouldn't do that, Ruth. It'll make you look bad, too." *Say what?* He puffed up his chest. "Look at what that fat woman reduced our poor reverend to. It's a shame he married a bitch in disguise."

"What the—*Bitch!* I got your bitch right here, mother—" And that's when I hit my husband dead in the chest with a fist as big as his head and knocked his skinny punk ass across the room and over the couch. Shit, Muhammad Ali didn't have nothin' on me. I rushed in for the kill, but he was too quick, getting off the floor and scurrying like the cockroach he is through the kitchen and out the back door.

I immediately called Tonya. "What should I do?"

"Kill him," she said. "No, wait. Stone him. That's what they do to adulterers in the Bible, right?"

Naomi, as usual, said the opposite. "Pray about it, Ruth."

"God ain't been listenin' right to me, Naomi," I said. "I asked for a good man and got this motherfucker."

"You'll be in my prayers, girl."

I decided not to kill him, and we were secretly separated for two months with him sleeping in his office at Antioch. We kept up appearances ("For the sake of the church," he begged me), me at the organ playing as loud as that old organ could, him at the pulpit practically whispering his sermons, afraid to even look at the congregation. Eventually, his sermons started to cool off without my help, the board met to talk to him, and he told them that I had kicked him out of the house for *no good reason*. He blamed *me* for his weak-ass sermons!

When the board called me in, I had the pictures in my purse and was fully ready to air out all of Jonas's dirty draws. "Please reconsider, Sister Borum," Millard Rutledge, the head deacon, said.

"Reconsider what?"

"Think of the effect this separation will have on our church, your church, this community," Deacon Rutledge said. "So far, we've kept a tight lid on this thing, but all it takes is one person and . . ." He folded his hands in prayer. "We cannot have this scandal. Whatever has come between you and Reverend Borum must be resolved, and the sooner the better."

"Or what?"

They didn't have a ready answer for that question. They looked at each other, they looked at their hands, and they looked to heaven for the answer. Deacon Rutledge sighed and said, "Or your husband will be out of a job, and by extension . . ."

I'll be out on my ass, I thought. *Can't get spousal support from an unemployed man, now can I? And it ain't like the want ads are full of openings for adulterous black preachers.* "Don't y'all even want to know *why* I kicked him out?"

"That is not our concern," Deacon Rutledge said. "The marital problems you are experiencing are nothing each of us hasn't encountered." *I doubt that.* "I imagine your, um, difficulty in childbirth may have had something to do with it." *Say what?* "At any rate, we have to think of the future of the church. That is a much more important concern."

I shot my hand into my purse . . . then slipped it out. *God,* I prayed, *if I show them these pictures, this church will be ruined, my husband will be ruined, and I'm sure in a twisted way that I'll be ruined more than I already am. Please, I'm askin' . . . Please help me make the right decision.*

"Mrs. Borum?"

"I'm thinking." I looked at their leathery, wrinkled faces. *I've got gossip material in my purse to last y'all till Jesus comes back.* "I'll take him back, but only under one condition."

Deacon Rutledge sat up straighter. "Name it."

"Fire the secretary."

They blinked at each other for a while and asked that I leave the sanctuary while they "considered" my request. An *hour* later, they called me back in. "The board has decided," Deacon Rutledge said, "that it will ask for the secretary's resignation. If she refuses to resign, I'm afraid that there's really nothing the board can do. You see, we hired her in the first place. Firing her would reflect badly on us."

Oh, we wouldn't want that. "If she isn't fired by noon tomorrow, I will send several revealing pictures of the reverend *you* chose and the secretary *you* hired to a local TV station making it *very* clear that *this* board hired her."

Another blink-fest. I could almost feel little puffs of wind coming off their wrinkled eyelids.

"Don't worry. I'll make sure they spell your names right."

Another hour of waiting. "The board has decided," Deacon Rutledge said, "to offer the secretary a generous severance package—"

I cut his ass off. "You gonna pay off the *bitch* that's been *fucking* my husband in the pastor's study right *upstairs* in this very building?!" I pulled out a pen and a scrap of paper while flies buzzed around all those open mouths. "I got to write this shit down." I scribbled a series of loops. "*This* information and *my* pictures on TV . . . Y'all is *toast!* There will be headlines in the paper for weeks."

They fired the secretary that very evening, and I let Jonas come back into *my* house despite Tonya's warning ("Dogs always return to their vomit, girl"). Naomi, of course, was glad. "All things work together for good, Ruth." But I had some rules for Jonas, my "Ten Commandments," that he had to follow or else: "One, you clean up after your damn self. Two, you cook for your damn self. Three, you wash your own damn clothes. Four, you iron your own damn clothes. Five, you do your own damn dishes. Six, you put the *goddamn* seat down every *goddamn* time you use the *goddamn* toilet! Seven, any of your shit left lying around, I throw it out in the street. Eight, you sleep in the damn basement. Nine, you will be home from that church or whatever duties you have before the sun goes down. Ten, you will never cheat on me again or I will cut your little dick off and nail it to the altar."

For six months, *I had it made.* I treated that man like the shit that he was and liked every bitchy minute. I'd hover around him as he cleaned up the kitchen or the bathroom, whispering, "You missed a spot, Reverend Bone-'em . . . Bet you didn't miss any of that ho's spots . . . Bet you put the love of God up into every one of her nooks and crannies . . . Scrub hard—sin don't come out with just a little Dutch cleanser . . . Wasn't your last shitty sermon about sins being leopards with all them spots that just don't come out?" I knew it was a cruel thing to do, but Jonas had to be held accountable in some way. The church board wasn't gonna do shit, so I had to.

And then . . . I softened up. It takes *work* to be a bitch, and I wasn't a very good one. I was out shopping with Tonya and Naomi, and we stopped to eat at a little restaurant in the mall.

"How are you holding up?" Naomi asked.

"Fine."

"You still workin' his ass to death?" Tonya asked.

"Every second of every day. He's supposed to be cleaning that house all day today. I just love to see that man down on his knees."

"That's the way, girl," Tonya said. "Treat a dog like a dog."

Naomi threw her napkin on the table. "Now, that isn't the way, and both of you know it." She turned to me. "Haven't you punished that man enough?"

"No."

"What gives you the right?" Naomi asked.

Tonya slapped the table. "She got *every* right! Man of God or not, her husband still a man, and he been a dog."

"He made a mistake, a bad mistake," Naomi said, "but I'm sure he's asked for God's forgiveness. And last time I checked my Bible, it isn't up to any of us to punish anyone. 'Vengeance is mine, saith the Lord.'"

"You'd be talkin' differently if it had happened to you, Naomi," Tonya said. "Why you always got to be holy anyway?"

"It's the right way to be," Naomi snapped. "It's the only safe way to be."

Tonya rolled her eyes. "And that's why you the oldest virgin in Calhoun."

"And it's why you aren't, Miss Sleep-With-Any-Man-Who'll-Buy-The-Pizza!"

I had had enough. "Stop!" I pushed my plate to the side. "I'm no good at being mean, y'all. Bein' a bitch makes me feel good, but only for a moment. I go to bed every night sad. I don't want to be sad no more."

When I came home, I decided not to be evil anymore. The house was spotless. Even the refrigerator where all his drips used to be . . . Spotless. And the space behind the toilet seat that collected his pubic hairs . . . It sparkled. I even opened the door to the baby's room. I peered in and saw a completely dustless room, the scent of lemon wax in the air. Jonas had been keeping it up, keeping it prepared. *He still thinks we can have a child.* He had a nice meal of pork chops, greens, and rice cooking. He smiled at me. "How was your day?" he asked.

And I forgave him. My heart just burst, and I forgave him. And when I did, bony Jonas Borum started to look *good.* My coochie got moist, and I grabbed his bony ass with both my hands. "Upstairs," I whispered, and we left all that food simmering on the stove, humping till the chops burned, the greens became mush, and the rice turned to plastic. We did it a second time till the smoke alarm came on, and were at it a *third* time (a record for our marriage) when the neighbors came to our door, saying that they'd seen some smoke. "Are y'all all right?" they asked.

"Which window was the smoke comin' from?" I asked them while Jonas played with my ass out of their view.

Oh, the days and nights that followed! But no child. We did it every way possible, even read up on how to know the best time for conception. Still no child. I had Dr. Duckworth check me out. I was in perfect working order. Then we checked Jonas. *Low sperm count?* How was that possible? His sperm were hitting on all cylinders before! "Take cool showers instead of hot baths," Dr. Duckworth advised him, "and wear boxers instead of briefs. Hot and tight is not the environment for one's seed to be properly planted."

Jonas told me all this in bed, then added, "And Doc Duckworth also says I should 'marshal my resources,' you know, save it up, only do it once in a while."

I kissed his pointy nose. "Long as you service me in between."

We were like newlyweds, doing foreplay for days at a time. All the stops were sticking out on that organ at church . . . but Jonas's organ was barely making a squeak.

I talked to Dr. Duckworth about it. "Is there anything *else* we could be doing?"

He ticked off a list: "Intrauterine insemination, artificial insemination, in vitro fertilization, gamete intrafallopian transfer, intracytoplasmic sperm injection."

"Which has the best chance?"

"One I didn't mention."

"Which is?"

"Donor insemination."

I had to sit down after that one. "Donor, as in somebody else, not Jonas?"

"Yes. Success rates can be as high as sixty percent after five or more attempts."

I couldn't believe what I was hearing. "What exactly are you saying?"

"He didn't tell you?"

"No."

"Well, um, I can't tell you if he didn't. You'll have to ask him."

And I did. At the dinner table later that night. While we were eating spaghetti and meatballs. "What did Dr. Duckworth tell you about your sperm, Jonas?"

He choked. "Please, Ruth, not while I'm eating."

"He wouldn't tell me, but it has to be bad. Are you . . . Are you sterile?"

"No," he said with authority. "Just low sperm count. And remember, all it takes is one sperm and one egg. As long as I have that one sperm, we'll be fine."

Without saying it, Jonas was telling me that he had been shooting blanks. I even read up on the whole sperm thing and found that men today have lower sperm counts, poorer quality of sperm and semen than ever before, and up to half of all miscarriages are from bad chromosomes. My eggs were fine. *His* shit was bad. The two miscarriages, the stillborn boy, the boy who died at birth—*they weren't my fault!* At first I was relieved, but then . . . I was pissed. I had spent over seven years grieving silently for something that I didn't cause to happen, and Jonas had been letting me take all the blame. Jonas's weak-ass sperm just couldn't complete the job.

Instead of confronting him with this like I could have, I started hinting at adoption. "Who wouldn't think we were good candidates, Jonas? I mean, we're the perfect candidates. Who would deny a preacher and his wife from adopting a baby?" I showed him all the literature. "So we can't *have* one of our own. Least we can *make* one our own. There are plenty of children waiting for a good home. I mean, we have that room upstairs all ready to go, and—"

"I'd rather keep trying."

I touched his hand, and he pulled it away. "Jonas, it just wasn't meant to be. We have to accept that this is God's will—"

"No!" he thundered. "We'll keep trying!"

And we did, nightly till either he or I started crying from the sheer pain of the act itself or the heartache from the futility we felt. He eventually drifted away, started staying out later, had lame excuses for being late—and I didn't care anymore. I didn't care for the next six years, and I didn't want to care. I didn't care to care. Every Sunday I put on my fake smile and made the world think I was happy and fulfilled by standing at his side and shaking hands, but inside I was lost in sorrow. Though I was fertile, I was barren, and Jonas wouldn't even put an adopted baby into my arms, our lives, or that empty room.

I received a phone call late one night, while Jonas was out who knows or cares where, from Joe Beverly, the private investigator I had hired before. "Got some information for you about your husband from another investigation of mine. You interested?"

"No."

"You oughta be."

"I'm not. Please, just—"

"You'll need to get an AIDS test."

Oh . . . no. I managed a weak, "What?"

"I been followin' this other guy around, can't tell you his name; but I catch him with this other guy who you know *very well*, and they ain't exactly been drinkin' beer and playin' cards, if you know what I mean."

Oh . . . God . . . no . . . this . . . isn't . . . happening. I let the phone fall from my fingers to the floor. Cold. Dizzy. A voice saying "if you'd like to make a call, please hang up and try again." Hands shaking. That alarm sound from the phone. The front door opening, the little moan in the hinge Jonas promised to fix giving him away. Steps. A skinny hand reaching to hang up the phone. Light from the bathroom. Water running. My feet running to the bathroom, hands tearing at the shower curtain, nails scratching flesh, fists pounding bone till blood streamed down the drain. . . .

"Get out," I heard my voice crying. "Get out," it echoed again and again till I was alone in the bathroom, splashed by the shower, sucking on bleeding knuckles, a whale of a woman wailing away. I stayed there all night and much of the next day till I found the courage to stand. I looked down at my legs, and they held me up just fine. I looked at my fists, and they looked like they could go a few more rounds. I felt my body, and though there was a lot to feel, at least it *felt*. I called Tonya on the phone. "Tonya, I'm divorcing the bisexual preacher I married," I said with a firm voice.

"Daa-em. No wonder this neighborhood has gone to hell," she said.

"Can you go with me to get an AIDS test?"

"Oh, no, Ruth . . . sure. I'll pick up Naomi, and we'll be right over."

I offered my knuckles instead of my arm to the doctor at the free clinic, but he stuck me in the arm anyway. "Results could take as long as three weeks," he said.

"I'll manage," I said.

And I did.

And I have.

And I *will*.

Three

I didn't have HIV or AIDS and wasn't dying. At the time, I didn't count it as a blessing. I wanted to die so I wouldn't feel so hollow, so alone, so empty, so lost. To top it off, the new "me" fit in well in the neighborhood around Antioch. I thought I knew everything there was to know about Vine Street, living here as long as I have, knowing most of the folks because of the church, but I don't. I've missed out on so much being a preacher's wife, like I was above it all somehow. I just haven't noticed shit, like the low-riders cruising by rattling manhole covers with rap rhapsodies till all hours of the night, like the scarcity of green grass on lawns, like the absence of adults when children are out playing and often wearing nothing but dirty diapers, like the abundance of little girls with no hips pushing strollers carrying their babies. Tonya and Naomi, who have lived on Vine next door to each other since the day they were born and even work side-by-side at the phone company, have had to set me straight often. It's strange, but I simply do not know the people I've tried to serve all these years. But now we have something in common—we're all lost on Vine Street now.

On a hot, sticky July afternoon just ripe for gossip, we were sitting in rickety old green lawn chairs, the kind that maybe last the summer before splitting, on the porch of my apartment house, an old Victorian someone thought would be worth more if it housed six skinny apartments with no water pressure and healthy roaches. Whenever we'd see someone out walking, Tonya and Naomi would give me the low-down between sips of sweetened iced tea.

"Who is that man, and what is he doin' with that jar?" I asked. I nodded at a skinny dark man sitting under a tree with a Mason jar covering one ear.

Tonya leaned in. "Don't know his name. We just always called him Jar-Man. Man is the stankest thing you've ever smelled. Too many forties of Old English and too much of this." She rubbed a finger in the crook of her left arm. "Man has *got* to be the oldest living heroin addict in Calhoun. Walked by him once, and girl, it was spooky. Heard him sayin' somethin' about 'why we got sea gulls 'round here when we ain't got no sea?' "

I've always wondered that, too. They get blown here by a hurricane or what? Calhoun is at least two hundred and fifty miles from the Atlantic.

"I tried witnessing to him back in the day," Naomi said. She has always been the most religious among the three of us, leaving tracts everywhere, even putting "Do You Know If You Are Saved?" on top of the tip she leaves when we eat out together. "And I got an earful. The man said he had a booger he just couldn't flick, said that his addiction was a child he didn't whip now to chase later."

A booger I can't flick . . . a child I don't whip now to chase later. Jar-Man was a genius in disguise. He could have been describing my depression . . . or my ex-husband. *Yeah, I'd like to whip the boogers out his ass.*

"Heard he showed up over at Slim Reaper's wake and gave a big speech," Tonya said.

That gave me a jolt. "I was at that wake," I said, remembering. "I know him." More like I knew *of* him.

Slim Reaper was a local punk who got killed a couple years ago by his girlfriend, a sweet little member of our church named Danielle Owens. Danielle was a bright girl, a good student, so pretty—in other words, everything I wasn't when I was her age—but when she found out Slim was messing with a rich white girl, she emptied a gun into his belly. Never knew what she saw in Ty "Slim Reaper" Williams, the boy who hung out at the corner of Vine and Fourteenth selling crack. Heard Danielle gave birth to his child in prison. Out of shame, mostly, and my duty as the wife of a preacher, I went to Ty's wake. "But Jar-Man, or whatever his name is, wasn't all stank then. He was wearing a suit." I squinted at the man. "He looked like anybody's granddaddy. I even thought he was Ty's granddaddy at the time."

"What'd he say?"

Fact is, the man wouldn't shut up. "What *didn't* he say. He told Ty's entire life story, said Ty was born with a splintered spoon in his mouth, called his mama, who was right there grievin', he called his mama a big ol' bag of bones and moans."

"That's cold," Tonya said.

I rolled my eyes. "But it was true. She didn't give a shit about her boy till the day *after* he died when she got to go on the TV." I have never understood that. Her own boy's out there dealing, being a player, and she didn't do a thing to stop him. Saw her on the TV saying that she tried to beat the streets out of him, but it wasn't the streets that killed him. It was his pecker. "Jar-Man said something like 'Ty played musical stares on the corner,' said he 'profited without honor sellin' bags of fix.'"

"Jar-Man soundin' like a poet," Tonya said.

He was, at the wake anyway. "Sometimes you get what you stray for," he had said, and I had taken that to heart. *You either get what you pray for or you get what you stray for.* I prayed for a man . . . who ended up straying.

"Heard he got thrown out of the wake," Tonya said.

I nodded. "Man ended his speech, least I think it was the end, with 'ain't nobody here gonna miss Slim Reaper's narrow ass one damn bit.'"

"That's a bit much," Tonya said, "but I ain't missed him, have y'all?" Neither Naomi nor I answered. A neighborhood boy, only nineteen, dead, and nobody missed him. "You heard about what happened to that Myers boy last month, right?"

"I saw the blood on the sidewalk myself," Naomi said. "Over on Fifteenth. I hear he's still in a coma."

"Isn't he called Guitarman or something?" I asked.

Naomi sighed and nodded. "He was real good with a guitar."

"Probably thought he was the second coming of Jimi Hendrix," Tonya said.

Naomi frowned. "You remember how he used to play for the Christmas show when he was little?"

"He only knew 'Silent Night,' Naomi." Tonya hummed the song badly.

"But he played it beautifully. He is a good kid, Tonya."

"Pul-lease," Tonya scowled. "Boy had lung dung from all those blunts he smoked. I spoke to him once. I said, 'Hi,' and he says, 'I wish *I* was.' Boy was just beggin' in the street, gave us all a bad name."

"Jesus had a soft spot for beggars, didn't he?" Naomi asked. Tonya looked away. "And I knew Kevin Myers, knew his mama, Nicole. She raised him right, tried to keep him in Sunday school at Antioch, tried to keep him in school, tried to get him a job. I watched that woman dragging him from the street many times." She turned to face Tonya. "All the boy ever did was play that guitar and get change from folks, Tonya. Somebody cut up that boy for some change, for a little bit of silver. It isn't right for *anybody* to get beat up for a song."

As hot as it was, I was starting to feel cold. "Ain't no one in this neighborhood who isn't dead or in a coma? What about Evangeline?" Evangeline was a woman who sat on a bus bench and read fortunes. "She seems full of life."

Tonya smirked. "That overdressed wench who works roots on folks? She ain't nothin' but a junkie. She think she some voodoo child with all them extensions. They say she even got plaited breath, and her real name Betsy Johnson."

"How you know so much?" Naomi asked.

Tonya looked at her hands. "Well, I asked her for some numbers this one time, and . . . They hit."

Naomi waved a long finger at Tonya. "You told *me* you got a raise."

Tonya smiled. "Well, in a way, I did. Right?" She laughed. "Evangeline be right about seventy percent of the time—"

"You've gone *back?*" Naomi shouted.

"Dag, Naomi. How you think you got your last birthday present? Shit."

"That watch broke, Tonya. Bet you got it from Soapbox Sam."

I smiled. Soapbox Sam Harris stood on an old milk crate at the corner of Eleventh and Vine preaching most days—and selling whatever he could sell at night. "I like him." Tonya and Naomi raised their eyebrows. "What? He's funny, got a nice smile, and he always says hello to me. And he's a better preacher than Jonas will ever be."

"He a crook," Tonya said. "He a fence or something, and I bet he even sellin' crack." She waved her hand toward the street. "He got himself at least four, five chaps running loose around here."

"I can see why," I said. "He's a handsome man."

Naomi grabbed my arm. "Hold on, now, Sister Childress. It's too hot to be horny over a sixty-year-old man."

"I ain't horny," I said. "Just bein' honest." I nodded toward a whisper-thin child spinning around a thin, leafless tree in front of a brick two-story across the street. "That one of his children?"

Tonya squinted. "Think so. Angie something-or-other. Think she kin to Deacon Rutledge in some way. She's so skinny, if she turns sideways, she disappears. She's so skinny, if I cough from over here, she'll fall down over there."

I ignored Tonya's laughter. "She's pretty." Thin legs, dark skin, bright eyes, a blue bow in her hair. "Bet she has Sam's eyes."

"But Sam don't do for her like he should," Tonya said.

"He does more for her than that Donnie Smalls did for his daughter, Teresa," Naomi said, and I shiver at the mention of those names. Donnie Smalls had killed his wife, Evie, with a shotgun not two blocks from Antioch one hot August night . . . with his seven-year-old daughter's finger stuck in the barrel. Teresa had tried to stop it—with just one tiny finger—and her finger got blasted right through her mama's chest.

"Let's not talk about that," I said. "I'm tryin' not to be depressed, y'all, and you ain't helpin' me a damn bit."

"Yeah we are," Tonya said. "Lots of folks out there ain't got shit, got it worse than you, while you at least got us."

"Some comfort."

Jar-Man. Guitarman. Evangeline. Soapbox Sam. Angie. Teresa. Six souls completely untouched by their neighborhood church . . . but they were getting by just like me. I stood and stretched my back and looked up Vine toward Dude's Take-Out and Hood's Grocery. Lying in front of Hood's was a man holding a plastic bag.

"Lord Jesus," I cried. "Bag Man's fallen out again."

"He'll be all right," Tonya said. "He just drunk."

I turned to Tonya. "On a day this hot, he shouldn't be out lyin' in the sun." I moved toward the stairs. "Y'all comin'?"

Naomi stood, but Tonya kept her place. "I'm tellin' you," Tonya said, "the man is just drunk as usual."

While Naomi and I race-walked to Hood's, I remembered other days Bag Man (a.k.a. Larry Farmer) had fallen out. He wasn't a drunk. He just didn't eat right. I bet he had diabetes or something, and coffee and cigarettes ain't enough to live on. He collected empty soda and beer cans from the dumpsters around Vine and recycled them down the way into a cup of coffee and a smoke. I had found him a few times over the years lying out in front of the church. A glass of iced tea or a mug of hot cocoa would bring him around, and he'd be off limphopping down the street with his carefully tied plastic bag of dripping cans and bottles.

Sweat rolled off me by the time I got to Hood's and looked down at Larry, who had to be pushing seventy, maybe even eighty. His face was creased red-raw by the sun, his smile uneven, teeth green-brown and gapped, his legs shaking, his chafed hands reaching out. This was a man in need, yet folks were still walking in and out of Hood's, walking around him, even crossing the street before they came to him, like he was nothing more than a puddle of mud.

"You all right, Mr. Farmer?" I asked.

He stopped shaking for a moment. "That my Penny?"

He always called me that, saying that "a good penny always turns up." I smiled. "Yes, Mr. Farmer."

"I been better, Penny." He started shaking again.

Naomi knelt next to him and held his wrist, shaking her head slightly. "We'll probably need an ambulance this time, Ruth." She unbuttoned the top button on his red flannel shirt and fanned her hand around his face.

"Be right back, Mr. Farmer," I said, stepping into Hood's where it wasn't much cooler. I addressed Mr. Hood, the white owner who charged too much for everything he sold to the folks in the 'hood. But since most folks couldn't get out without taking a bus or a cab—few folks owned reliable working vehicles on Vine Street—they had to pay his ridiculous prices. "Y'all call an ambulance yet?"

"What for?" Mr. Hood said. If any man on earth looked like an overgrown billy goat, it was Mr. Hood: white hair parted down the middle, tufts of hair jutting from his chin and ears, the smallest little mouth with the smallest little teeth. Man probably ate rusty cans for breakfast and asked for seconds.

I pointed through the front window. "Don't tell me you can't see Larry Farmer lyin' out there."

"Who?"

"Larry Farmer. That's his name."

"You mean Bag Man."

"Whatever."

"He's done it before."

"Well, he ain't liable to get up this time."

"He'll be all right. Just buy him a soda."

Buy him one? Some people have no souls. "He gonna need more than a soda today, Mr. Hood." I tapped the counter. "You make that call." Mr. Hood only rolled his eyes. "Be a shame if that *black* man died outside your door, Mr. Hood. Wouldn't be good for future business with your *black* customers, now would it?" He reached under the counter and pulled out a phone. "Think the number's nine-one-one." I waited till he pressed those three buttons and asked for an ambulance before returning to the hot sidewalk.

"Ambulance is on the way, Larry," I said.

"Oh, y'all goin' through too much trouble."

"You need to see a doctor, Mr. Farmer," Naomi said. She pointed at his legs, and I nodded. It looked like he had gangrene or something, the skin all blotchy and tight on his ankles.

"Jes' gimme a drink, an' I'll be on my way, Penny."

I squatted down and put my hand on his forehead. "Not this time, Larry." He was as hot as an iron, but he wasn't sweating. *Lord Jesus, he has heat stroke.* "We gonna take care of you."

Larry looked up at me and smiled that gap-toothed grin. "I guess I could use me a little rest. Thank you, Penny." Then his shaking stopped, and his eyes closed.

I looked at Naomi, who still held his wrist. "Is he gone?"

She placed her hand on his chest. "I think so."

I closed my eyes, and when I opened them, I saw more of my people weaving around us. That's when I lost it completely. "Do you not know that you are your brother's keeper?!" I shrieked at an old crow who walked away a little faster without looking back. "You *better* not look back! You'd turn into a pillar of pepper!" A pair of shoppers, two old biddies, were staring at me from the front step of the store. "What you two good Samaritans lookin' at?" They scuttled into the store like two little blue crabs.

"Ruth, please," Naomi pleaded, tugging on my arm.

Mr. Hood stuck his goat head out the door. "Why are you screaming at my customers? You should be ashamed, scarin' 'em like that!"

I shook Naomi away and stalked toward Mr. Hood. He wisely shut the door and locked it. "Oh, we wouldn't want to be *scarin'* no one!" I yelled. "Nah, we can't have *that* on Vine Street, can't have *that* in front of Hood's Grocery!" I pounded on the door, making Mr. Hood jump back.

Naomi dug her nails into my arm this time. "Please, Ruth. Let's get out of this heat."

"Nah, we *can't* have no *yellin'* on Vine Street!" I shouted as she led me across Eleventh. "But we *can* have black men *dyin'* in the street!" I whirled toward the crowd that had finally formed around Larry Farmer. "Oh, *now* you see him! Couldn't see him before, huh? You all ought to be ashamed!" Naomi grabbed at my arm again, but I swatted it away. "If any of *you* decides to fall out in front of *my* house, I'm gonna call the sanitation department and have your motherfuckin' asses hauled away!"

"Ruth," Naomi whispered, "let it go."

"Nah, I know. I'll call the po-lice and have your asses arrested for trespassin'!"

By the time I got back to the apartment, I was shouted out. I felt like two hundred thirty pounds of steamy sweat. Naomi and Tonya ran me a bath to cool me off, and I soaked for a time, sipping some more iced tea. I heard the ambulance when it approached, sirens blaring, but I didn't hear it go away. *Larry's really gone. Man never hurt no one. All the man needed was a little drink of water, and here I am sippin' tea in a cool bath.* I poured my tea into the tub. Then I caught pieces of whispered conversations from the bedroom . . . "another breakdown . . . her doctor . . . which pills? . . . a shame."

A shame. World's goin' to hell, folks have no souls, I'm on drugs, I'm a prime candidate for diabetes, stroke, heart attack, already got a broken heart, Larry's on his way to the morgue . . . "LORD JESUS, WHY DON'T YOU DO SOMETHING!"

Tonya and Naomi peeked in. "You all right?" Tonya asked in the smallest voice I've ever heard come out of her big-lipped mouth.

"I been better," I said, and I stood, water cascading off me. They both looked away. "Don't you avert your eyes from me!" I got out of the bath tub. "Skinny-ass bitches! If I sneeze from here, y'all both gonna go down like dominos."

Naomi looked up and held out a handful of bottles. "Which one do you need, Ruth?"

I looked at the puddle forming on the floor, then stared her down. "*All* of them."

Naomi snatched her hand back to her chest, her hands and the pills shaking. "Oh, come on now, Ruth—"

I held out my hand. "Give them to me."

"She trippin'," Tonya said.

I took a step forward, my foot slapping on the linoleum floor. "Just one of my legs outweighs the two of you combined, and if you want me to break bad on you, *you* trippin'. Give me the pills."

Naomi handed them to me. "Ruth, please don't—"

I held up a hand. "Now, I want y'all to watch."

"I'll go call an ambulance—" Tonya started to say, but I cut her off with a grunt.

"Bitch, just shut the fuck up and watch."

I opened the first bottle, the nasty sleeping pills, and rattled them around . . . then poured them into the toilet. "Don't need y'all no more. I'm gonna sleep just fine from now on." I heard Naomi and Tonya sighing behind me. I opened the next bottle, something for my nerves, and dumped them into the toilet. "Don't need y'all no more. I want to feel *every little thing* from now on." I opened the next two bottles and watched them plop into the sea of pills. "I don't even remember what y'all are for, but I hope it wasn't for my memory. I don't need y'all no more." I looked at the label of the last bottle, the one for my high blood pressure. I opened it, dumped it, and tossed the empty bottles into the trash. "Don't need y'all no more neither. I'm gonna get back to normal without you."

I turned to my friends. "Come here." Both of them had tears running down their cheeks. "I said, come here." They slipped over, Tonya stepping around the puddle. "Put your hands on my hand." They did. "Now help me flush this shit." We pressed down on that lever together, then watched the pills go round and round till only crystal clear Calhoun city water was left in the tank.

"We just fucked up about a million rats," Tonya said as Naomi tried to hug me.

"Don't you skinny bitches be huggin' on me yet," I said, walking past them, still naked, to the kitchen. I stood in front of the refrigerator, took a deep breath, then yanked open the top and bottom doors. I stared at the food that I loved that didn't love me back: the pork chops, the ham, the ground beef, the fatback, the ice cream, the sour cream, the cheese, the sodas. *Y'all got to go.* "Stand back and get ready to catch."

I emptied that bitch of a refrigerator in less than five minutes, leaving me some celery, some lettuce, a couple carrots, and a pitcher of water, while Tonya and Naomi ran around behind me filling garbage bags and grocery bags. I closed the doors. "Don't y'all *ever* let me buy this shit again. Promise?"

"Promise," they said together.

I tore off some pizza coupons taped to the refrigerator door. "This shit either."

Tonya smiled. "Glad you're back."

I let Naomi hug me. "It's good to be back. Now get your narrow, no cellulite, never-had-a-stretch-mark asses out of my sight. You makin' me feel bad."

After they left, I wept . . . and ate some stale-ass, rubbery celery. And I loved every shitty bite.

Four

But in the morning, I was weeping in pain and could not move. My stomach and chest felt like they had lead weights on them, I had trouble breathing, and my heart was pounding. I thought I was having a heart attack. I managed to call Naomi, who called Tonya, and the two of them showed up in a hurry—but I couldn't get out of bed to answer the door because of the pain.

"Break down the damn door!" I yelled, but they went and found the supervisor in apartment one, who opened the door for them. And that's when I pooted and felt so much better.

Shit. I ain't dyin'. I just got me some gas.

"Oh, my Lord!" Naomi yelled as she raced into the bedroom and grabbed my wrist.

"It ain't my wrist that hurts," I said, pulling my wrist away. "It's my stomach."

Tonya felt my forehead. "Girl, you got a fever, too. I already called an ambulance."

"What'd you do that for? I just got some bad gas is all."

"You're probably having a heart attack," Tonya said.

"Or a stroke," Naomi added. "Just like your grandma and mama, girl. They say it runs in families."

"Ain't nothin' runnin' down there, y'all. I just got me some gas." I let loose another string, and they winced. "See? It's all that old celery I ate last night. Call off the—"

"Comin' through!" a male voice yelled.

"Oh, shit," I said, and in seconds, two paramedics and two firemen, all white, burly, and sweaty, came stumbling into my bedroom with all their gear, and me wearing two-day-old bloomers, footies with holes in the toes, and a gray T-shirt that read "I'M TIRED, I'M CRANKY, LEAVE ME ALONE." I had died and gone straight to hell in my own apartment.

"Look, y'all—" I tried to say, but one of the paramedics attached a blood pressure sleeve to my arm while the other took my pulse. *Hmm. Man holdin' my wrist kinda cute. Do I mind if a white man holds my wrist? Just hope I don't poot. Lord God, please keep all my gas inside till they leave!*

"What's your name, ma'am?" wrist-holding paramedic said.

"Ruth. What's yours?"

"Bob." He looked like a Bob. Kind of the generic, all-American white boy with blond hair and bushy eyebrows. "Do you have a history of heart trouble, Ruth?"

"Yeah, but it don't have nothin' to do with my body." Blood-pressure-pumping paramedic stopped squeezing that little bulb. "I just have some really bad gas, fellas. Honest. When I called my friends, it felt like a heart attack. It's just some gas from some bad celery."

"Pressure's kinda high," BP-Boy said.

"Cuz I'm overweight and black," I said. "You have to believe me. I'll be fine."

BP-Boy shrugged at Bob. Bob shrugged back and pulled out his stethoscope. "You mind if I listen?"

Do I mind if an all-American white boy puts his strong, hairy hand inside my shirt? Decisions, decisions. "No, just warm up that thing first, Bob."

He put the metal part on me . . . but not under my shirt. *Damn!* He bounced it around a bit before shrugging again. "Sounds fine."

That was when the biggest poot escaped, and I felt ten pounds lighter. "Told you that was all it was." Tonya and Naomi left the room laughing. The firemen left the room laughing. The paramedics, though, left the room gasping. *Damn, what just a little bit of bad celery can do!*

Naomi returned with a table fan, the kind that turns back and forth, and set it on high. "Won't do no good," I said, finally able to sit up without pains shooting into my gut. "Girl, that celery is just cleaning out my colon or something."

"That's all you ate?"

"That's all I had. Shit, I probably got food stuck up in me twenty years old. You'd be stank, too, if you was locked up inside someone's intestines for twenty years."

Tonya breezed in fanning the air in front of her, a huge I-just-got-a-phone-number smile on her face. "Guess what?"

"You got one of the firemen's numbers," Naomi said wearily, opening the window wider.

"*Both*," Tonya said. Nobody spoke for the longest time. "What?"

"Girl, haven't you got any pride left?" Naomi moaned.

"What's pride got to do with it?" Tonya said. "Those two boys is *paid*, and I hear they only work three days on, four days off, and I intend for one or both of them to be on me when they're off."

"They're white," Naomi said. "You'll only get hurt. Again."

"You ain't my mama, Naomi," Tonya said.

"Remember the last one?" Naomi asked. "The one who made all those promises?"

Tonya bounced up and down on my bed. "So?"

"Wasn't he married?"

"And your point is?"

I stared at both of them (while stifling another poot) and wondered how we all ever became friends: Tonya the sexy she-devil who sometimes came to church, Naomi the black nun who got none, and me, the black Cinderella, the pumpkin girl who would never be changed into a beautiful carriage because she was already the size of the carriage. All it took was a young adult Sunday school class twenty years ago to bring us together.

I decided to let that poot fly to shut them up, and it was the squeaky kind, like lettin' air out of a balloon real slow. "That's what I think of y'all, now get the hell out."

"But—" Naomi said.

I stood and shut her up with my hand. "Bringing four sweaty men into my apartment when it's lookin' like shit with me lookin' like shit, Naomi, it just ain't Christian. And you know they'll charge me for the visit, and I ain't got the money. Gonna show me some Christian charity then?" I stared at Tonya. "And hookin' up with two white firemen cuz I got some gas—you *ain't* got no self-respect, Tonya. Now, I'm gonna take a shit, and when I get out, y'all best be gone."

Tonya rolled her eyes. "I'll, uh, just take the battery out of the smoke alarm."

Naomi smiled. "And I'll call the gas company and tell them that there isn't a leak. It just smells like one."

Another poot rolled out, and they scattered.

One thing I can say for gas—it'll prove who your friends are every time.

PART TWO

The Storm Is Over Now

Five

All of that happened just yesterday, and now it's a new day. Any day is a good day to start over. Check that: *every* day is a good day to start over. I'm through being where I've been. Got my comfortable traveling shoes on, gonna start a new journey. Don't know where, don't care. Long as I'm going, I'll be fine, just fine. This day, unfortunately, is another typical Sunday at Antioch Church with Reverend JonASS Bore-'em in the pulpit, so my journey begins with a little mountain to climb.

In the Amen Corner, wrinkled brown men in freshly ironed black suits yell "Tell it!" to the Fan Ladies in flowered and laced hats toe tapping in the first pew next to Tony Richards, the pianist, caressing the keys, his eyes closed, a thin black tie dangling from his starched collar, in front of the swaying choir of women in golden robes singing "When We Reach the Blessed Homeland" while I add the bass (and an occasional poot) as Jonas hops and struts like a stiff white man behind the pulpit, the microphone pressed to his thin-ass lips, children standing on the pews in the middle rows, their parents wide-eyed, hands in the air, shouting "Yes Lord!"

The people of Antioch Church *know* that God is in the house this morning. All their tears have been wiped away. They're running and winning that blessed race, calling and falling out, these, the fire-baptized and sanctified, testifying of God's miracles, shouting, "Hallelujah, Jesus!"

It makes me want to puke, but I play (and poot) on.

Then a heavyset white man blasts through the oak church doors,

stumbles down the aisle, and slumps over the altar-call railing. Silence
fills the sanctuary save the weeping of the white man.

This shit has *never* happened before. I cannot remember a white
man, much less a white person, entering this church during a service.
Oh, sure, they come on other days of the week to collect overdue bills,
but they never come during a service. I keep holding my chord, even
pull out a few more stops, and in a moment, my chord is the only
sound in the sanctuary . . . except for the white man's weeping. Damn,
that weeping sounds familiar. It's the echo of my own these past few
months.

Jonas looks at me like he used to when something went wrong. I
shrug my shoulders and roll my eyes as if to say, "It ain't my church
no more, JonASS. I just play the organ, Little Man. You still playin'
with yours?" He turns to the congregation, mouths, "Sing something,"
and joins the man at the railing. They kneel together, heads touching,
Jonas's bony arm barely reaching around the man.

Mrs. Winnifred Poindexter, the oldest Fan Lady with the largest
hat, begins to hum "Ain't Nobody Can Do Me Like Jesus," and I start
to play along with her. I'll bet that old Winny is also worrying that the
man crying in front of her will later be double-dipping his celery into
her onion dip, using his finger to gouge the icing off her famous
devil's food cake, or worse, eating her secret-recipe chicken with a fork
at the potluck following the service. Old Winny thinks that only people of color have proper table manners.

One by one, the other Fan Ladies join in humming, blending alto,
contralto, and soprano, each probably wondering why the man's wife
let him go out of the house wearing a wrinkled blue suit, scuffed
brown shoes, and white tube socks. Tony finally finds the right key,
and I know he's staring hard at the man's no-name-brand shoes, his
Sears polyester suit, and his K-Mart blue light special maroon-and-
black paisley tie. Mr. Otis Saunders, lead Amener from the Amen
Corner, adds a deep rumble of bass, most likely hoping that the man
will get himself straight with God soon since Otis is planning to testify
a long, long time today like always. His record is forty-five minutes,
leaving Jonas with only a seven-minute sermon on the topic of sin. The
choir swishes and sways, each woman, like me, astonished at the
man's uneven, shaggy hair, my own fingers twitching with the need to
either edge him up or shave him bald.

The soloist standing next to me, Mrs. Beverly Williams-Jones,
sings, "He healed my body, and He told me to run home," and the

congregation clears its throat and repeats "told me to run home." And by the last phrase of the verse, even the children sing, "He's my friend."

The congregation adds more verses, each sung louder and faster and in a higher key, hoping that speed, volume, and a higher pitch can get this man vertical. As the song reaches a stained-glass-shattering crescendo (if we had any stained glass, that is), Jonas helps the man to his feet. I don't know how. Man could barely lift a finger around the house, and that white man has to outweigh me.

"He's all right!" roars Otis, fishing for his three-by-five testifying card.

"He's all right," purrs Winnifred, probably still worried about her damn frosting.

"He's all right," sings Beverly, staring hard at the man.

"He's all right, the man is all right," bellows Jonas. That man *never* could sing.

And then, everything goes wrong.

The white man, who has the softest brown eyes set in the most innocent boy's face, turns to Jonas's smiling face and somehow turns whiter. I didn't know that was possible. He faces the Fan Ladies, and his pretty brown eyes bulge out. He glances at the Amen Corner and actually commences to tremble. He whirls and looks up at me and the choir and begins to hyperventilate. "He's going to fall out," I say to myself. *Lord Jesus,* I pray, *please don't let that white man fall out in front of this church. I mean, Lord, I know how he feels. I've been to the place where he is obviously at. You saw me the other day in the street, right? Give him the strength You gave me and please lift him up—*

But instead of falling out, the white man bolts wildly down the aisle and out of the church, the heavy oak doors slamming behind him, their echo jarring us all back into the presence of God. *Thank you, Lord. I owe You another one.* But Jonas, the prick, actually doubles over laughing at that, and the rest of the congregation joins in. Then Jonas raises his arms to heaven and says, "Jesus musta done healed him and told him to run home!"

I look out on the congregation, the one I helped create, and feel shame as they laugh and slap hands with each other. A sorrowing soul has just left us in a time of his deepest, darkest need, and they're in here laughing. I also feel shame for me. In the old days, I would assist Jonas at the altar, but my heavy feet stayed on the bass notes. I prayed for that white man, yes, but I really didn't help him.

Yes, I say to myself, trying not to shake with rage, *the people of Antioch Church know that God is in* their *house.*

I could have left, I could have followed that man out of the church, could have helped him, should have helped him. Instead, I turn on my bench and look out at the folks in the sanctuary, a nice sanctuary that's big enough to swallow brides like me and so many others. Ushers do their jobs, whispering greet nothings to the folks nearest the aisles during the offering. Deacon Rutledge makes a prayer stand on end, and Jonas numbs us with another sermon, saying something like "when you're asleep, you don't know you are till you awake." I bet he had to think all week to come up with that lame line. He's back to being a professor. The choir sings the benediction a cappella, and the folks I was watching while I'm sure they were watching me instead of Jonas— the congregation, my congregation, vanishes . . . into *sin* air.

I think about and pray for that white man the rest of that day. He had to be desperate to stumble down the aisle and weep in a church full of black folks. That man must have been in a heap of trouble. I pray for the Lord to lift him up and keep him there.

And in doing so, I have the most pleasant Sunday afternoon I have had in years.

Six

After a month of pleasant Sundays in mid-August just before school starts in Calhoun, I am *thirty* pounds lighter (Hallelujah!) and sleeping like a baby. I'm under two hundred for the first time since I was in high school and can finally wear anything in my closet. I cry for joy at the silliest things: being able to trim my toenails without grunting, not needing two towels to dry my body, watching a shirt billow out from my stomach because of a breeze and not my fat stomach, seeing wrinkles in my once tight, shiny face. I may look like a forty-year-old woman yet. Even got a little touch of gray goin' on at my temples.

And all it took was limiting what I've eaten to fruits, vegetables, and skinless chicken. I couldn't do one of those diet plans you gotta pay for. I cannot understand why folks spend so much a week to lose weight. Shit, just buy less and eat less. I only drink water or fresh-squeezed lemonade (without any sugar), don't snack, and keep myself busy cleaning the apartment or walking or working. I've tossed out the television—it only got one channel to come in good anyway—so I don't have anything to sit in front of to snack. That's what I used to do. Watch, eat, mess with the antenna, eat some more. I shouldn't blame the TV for my size, but when I don't have anything to watch, just sitting and eating without any entertainment ain't all that fun. I still have dessert since I haven't had my sweet tooth taken out, but I don't have cake, pie, ice cream, brownies, or cookies. I suck on sugarless candies or chew sugarless gum instead.

I'm also staying away from Dude's. I just loves me some greasy-ass food that goes straight to my ass. I've been walking a different way to work so I can't smell all that . . . delicious, satisfying, greasy food. Gives my nose an orgasm just thinkin' about it, but I've been good so far. In my mind, if you're fat, don't eat no fat—be Jack Sprat.

Yeah, I'm cranky as hell, but my body likes me again. And I think the lady I see in the mirror every morning is gettin' fresh with me. The way she looks at me when I'm naked . . . Ooh, child, it's absolutely sinful.

Today my skinnier self is plaiting Mildred Overstreet's hair at Diana's, the only salon on Vine Street that's usually open on Monday. I untie Mildred's salt-'n'-pepper hair every Monday at eleven o'clock on the spot, finger combing it in the sunlight sneaking through the big front window, steady, sure, listening to what Mildred has to say.

"It used to be down to my ass," Mildred says, leaning forward in her wheelchair. "Back when I had two good hips."

"How your hips doin'?"

"They ain't," she says, and I laugh, continuing to unwind years of hair. Usually, she tells us stories of Vine Street back in the day ("Vine Street used to be the shit till the white folks came!"), or her children (five sons and four daughters long since passed), or her lovers (too many names she always mixes up *much longer* since passed). "Don't do me like my great-grandmama did!" she warns me with a trembling finger. "She used to pull my hair too tight, make me look Injun. I got Cherokee in me, you know."

"Is that a fact?" I plait her hair every Monday, and by the next Monday, her plaits are gone. I know she comes just for the attention, probably pulls out the plaits around the corner before rolling in. I'm just amazed that she's still able to live on her own. "Sure you don't want me to trim these ends, Millie?"

"Winter's comin'," she says. "Got to have my hair to keep me warm."

I nod, straightening as much as I can, tightening as much as I dare. "All through."

She rolls toward the door with just one push. "Just put it on my bill."

"I will."

I roll my eyes to Diana after Mildred bangs out the door. Mildred never lets us help her with the door. I tried once and got the most vicious stare.

"That woman owes us at least a thousand dollars," Diana says while working on Mrs. Simpson, who never speaks. Never. Most folks come to Diana's to talk . . . and maybe get their hair done. Not Mrs. Simpson. Do her hair, don't engage her in conversation, and maybe you'll get a fifty-cent tip and a half smile.

"Can't start the week without Mildred," I say, and I see two light-skinned children, a boy of maybe four and a girl of about six, lingering outside the door.

"Looks like more school cuts," Diana says. "You want one or both?"

"Both." I love doing children's hair. Really. I don't mind the squirming, the sudden movements, the questions, sometimes the tears, the kicking feet, or the funky smells. I motion them in, and the little girl pushes open the door, pulling the little boy behind her.

She marches right up to me and stops. Her hair flies every which way, though someone has attempted two floppy braids held by red ribbons, and his hair . . . Lord, what a mess! It's a spider's web four inches high. They both have good hair and a few freckles, and I can tell they are brother and sister. Clean faces, clean but wrinkled clothes, no dirt under their nails, the soft scent of Dial and baby shampoo drifting up to me. They are beautiful children, maybe what I might have had.

"'Scuse me," the girl says. "My daddy sent us in here." She holds out a crumpled twenty.

I squat down in front of the boy. "What's your name?"

"He don't say nothin'," the girl says. "His name Dee. I'm Tee."

"Tee and Dee," Diana says with a laugh. "Ain't that a touchdown?"

I ignore Diana and smile at the boy. "Hello, Dee. I'm Ruth, but you can call me Penny if you like."

Tee pulls Dee closer to her. "My daddy wants us both to have haircuts." She puts the money in my hand. "Dee gotta go first, and I gotta hold his hand."

"Gonna conk that, girl?" Diana asks.

"No," I say, lifting Dee into my chair.

"He lookin' like Malcolm X, Jr."

"Diana, stop." I run my fingers through his hair. *So soft!* "Okay, Mr. Dee, I'm going to edge you up, shave the sides, and leave you some curls on top. Is that okay?"

The boy only blinks.

"I'll take that as a yes, Mr. Dee." I look at Tee. "Your daddy outside?"

"Uh-huh," she says, gripping Dee's hand tightly.

"Why didn't he come in?"

Tee shrugs. "I dunno."

I don't like cutting any child's hair without a parent present because, technically, no child owns his or her own hair. Mama and Daddy and Grandma and whoever else have a lock on that child's locks. "Wait here," I say, and I go to the door, stepping out and looking up and down the sidewalk. All I see is a rusty white pickup parked around the corner. "Your daddy have an errand to run?"

"No," Tee says.

"Did he just drop you off?"

"Nuh-uh. He's takin' a nap in the truck."

I look back at the truck and don't see a head on the driver's side. "A white truck?"

"Uh-huh."

I walk toward the truck, feeling strange about creeping up on a man taking a nap. Let sleeping dogs lie, right? I get to the passenger side and look in—

It's the white man who nearly fell out at Antioch three weeks ago. What the hell is he doing here ... with two mixed kids callin' him "daddy"?

I want to praise the Lord, but ... Dag, he's taking a nap in a busted-up pick-me-up truck on Vine Street wearing dusty overalls and a white T-shirt at noon on a Monday! Even *my* people have more pride than that!

I hold my breath and try to back away quietly, but I step on an empty beer can next to the curb. *If Larry were still here, Lord, this street would be clean. Why You had to take away the only man who tried to keep Vine Street clean?*

The man opens one eye, then the other, and sits up, blinking his eyes. "Hello."

He looks so young with his baby face. What is he, thirty, thirty-five? I can never tell with white folks. "Hello."

He rubs his eyes. "Musta dozed off." He checks a little black clock taped to the dashboard, and I notice he doesn't wear a wedding ring. "They done already?"

"Uh, no. Just came out to see what you want done."

He shrugs. "You see what I done already?" I nod and smile. *At least he tried, and, Lord, is his voice country. He definitely from back in the hills.* "Do what you gotta do. Is, uh, twenty dollars gonna be enough?"

"More than enough."

"Okay." He smiles, and little dimples form in his cheeks. *Such a cute baby face!*

"Uh, okay," I say, and I return to Diana's feeling like a giggly school girl who just had a cute boy smile at her for the first time. I breeze over to my station, pick up a hand mirror, and place it in Dee's little hand. "Hold this, Mr. Dee, so you can watch my magic." He takes it but doesn't make faces into it like other children usually do. He just stares at himself with the blankest set of sad eyes. It makes my heart hurt. I blow hairs out of the electric clippers and put on a number three guard instead of the number two, just in case. Don't want to bald him with his daddy lookin' so cute. "Ready?" I say to Dee, but only Tee nods. *Talk to one, the other answers.*

When I turn on the clippers near Dee's ear, he tears his hand from Tee, leaps from the chair, and runs out the door. "Not *again!*" Tee cries, and she follows him out the door. *What the hell is going on?*

"You certainly got a way with the boys, Ruth," Diana says.

I step outside and see both children in the truck, their daddy hugging and holding Dee close. I approach the driver's side, and Dee shrinks away from me. "All I did was turn on the clippers."

The daddy (I wish I knew his name!) laughs. "Same thing happened when my mama and I tried the other night. Hoped it wouldn't happen here, but . . ." He kisses Dee on the forehead. "It's okay, big guy. I got ya."

"Uh, Mr. . . ."

"Baxter. Dewey Baxter."

Dewey? I cannot say that redneck name without laughing. He ain't from the hills—he from back in the holler. "Hi, Mr. Baxter, I'm Ruth, and I can give Dee a haircut with just the scissors." I hold out my hands. "Come to Penny, Dee."

"Penny?" Dewey says. "I thought you said your name was Ruth."

"Penny's my nickname." *Given to me by a dead man.* I reach out to Dee again. If anything, Dee tightens his death grip on Dewey's neck. "I won't use the clippers, promise." No movement. "Just some nice ol' scissors." That boy ain't movin' for nothin' in this world.

"I'll bring him in, Daddy," Tee says.

Dewey holds Dee out from him. "You go with your sister. I'll be right here if you need me."

"You're more than welcome to come in." Please come in so I can look at your whole body. It ain't every day I see a man my size.

"Thanks for the offer, uh, Ruth, but I, uh . . . I kinda feel out of place." You got that right, Dewey. You might have to walk into Diana's sideways. "I'll, uh, just wait out here."

"You sure?"

"I'm sure."

"Okay."

I walk back into Diana's. "You scare 'em away?" Diana cracks.

"No."

"What's the daddy look like? Is he fine?"

"He's all right, a little too light-skinned for your tastes." Diana swears by "the darker the berry, the sweeter the juice." If a man don't have a blue shine to his skin, she won't even look at him. She even wants to get a tanning bed for the salon "because black folks around here should be darker than they're gettin' to be." I think she really wants it so she can darken me up, but I'd never get into one of those contraptions. It might only freckle me more.

Tee leads Dee to the door, Dee's head bowed like he's going to the electric chair. I hold the door, and they walk under my arm to the chair. I hand Dee the mirror, and we begin again. "You both have such pretty hair." I grab a section of Dee's hair and snip. Dee's eyes widen slightly, then return to their dull gaze. I know there's a little boy in there somewhere. "Wish I had me some hair like this."

"My mama used to say that, too," Tee says.

Used to? Grab, snip. "She cut y'all's hair?"

"Uh-huh," Tee says, and even Dee nods.

I don't want to pry, but . . . Hell, I'm in a beauty salon. "She doesn't cut your hair anymore?"

Tee shakes her head, and so does Dee. Maybe they're twins who share the same thoughts. No, Dee's much shorter.

"Mama's in heaven," Tee says.

I stop cutting and let out a long, slow breath. Poor kids! And that's maybe why Dewey visited Antioch that Sunday. I want details, and I see Diana leaning in to hear them; but I don't pry any further. "You must miss her."

Only Dee nods. Whoa. Tee doesn't miss her own mama?

"My daddy tried to do our hair like Mama, but he ain't got a clue," Tee says.

"I don't know," I say, continuing to cut. "He did all right." I smile at Tee. "He pulled your hair back so the world could see your pretty face." *They both have such big eyes and high cheekbones, Lord. You can make Yourself some beautiful people when You want to.*

"Daddy's tryin' real hard, though."

I even everything as best I can without clippers and put my face next to Dee's as we look in the mirror. "What you think?" Dee shrugs. "You're a handsome little man." I take the mirror and replace it with a sucker, but his eyes don't dance at all. He hops down and sits on a chair in the waiting area, hands together, blinking. He doesn't even open the sucker.

Tee is already in the chair. "I'm ready, Penny."

"How short you want it?"

She reaches a hand to mine. "Short as yours."

"You like my hair?"

"I dunno. I like your sprinkles, though."

My what? "My sprink—oh, you like my freckles."

"Uh-huh. Mama called 'em angel kisses. Mama's an angel now, so I hope she kisses me lots." She smiles up at me. "Your mama musta kissed you a lot of times."

I have to blink a tear back and clear my throat after that. I miss my mama, too. Not as much as I used to. Mama got me through the first ten years, and Grandma saw me through puberty and the next ten; but Mama was so strong, so tough. And the Lord saw fit to give her a weak body. Oh, she was a proud one, though. I remember the day we went into a carpet store to do what Mama called "Dream Shopping." A tall white lady jumped us as soon as we entered and asked, "You here to buy remnants?" My mama went off on her. "Remnants? What, you think cuz we black we only here for remnants? I'm here to carpet a whole damn house!" I had giggled because we were living in the Dixon-Oxford projects then. When the white lady recovered, she led us to the cheapest carpet in the store, but my mama walked over to the Laura Ashley carpet instead. "This what we want," she said, and my mama, to get back at that racist saleslady, ordered a whole house of Laura Ashley carpet . . . that we never intended to buy. I wish I was that strong. I mean, I have a strong body. Just wish I had my mama's mind.

I need to change the subject so I can cut this child's hair without sobbing. "Where do y'all live?" I unravel her snakelike braids.

"On Sixteenth Street in apartment D, just like the name of my brother." Just five short blocks from me. I've got to change my walking route to include Sixteenth.

I start combing and wince when I think I'm pulling, but Tee doesn't complain. "Why," I whisper, "why doesn't Dee speak?"

"Daddy thinks it's cuz he saw Mama die," she whispers back.

Why did I ask that? Here comes that tear again.

"It was a car wreck. Dee was in there till they cut him out with those *RR-rrr* things."

The Jaws of Life . . . which sound just like the clippers. I turn away and let the tear fall as I get a vision of that child maybe hanging upside down in a car seat, crying his eyes out for his mama who is dying maybe an arm's length away. A child should never have to see that.

"I wasn't in the car. I was at Nanna's." Which explains why Tee isn't as broken up inside as Dee is. "Nanna lives on a farm far, far away from here with apple trees and a pig and everything. Dee likes it there."

So Dewey Baxter is a farm boy, a real-live, big-boned, corn-fed redneck . . . with mixed kids. My God, life on the farm has certainly changed.

For the better.

"But Daddy's job at the steel place is here. He loads up the trains."

Calhoun Steel. Good pay, has a union, nice benefits. Why ain't he workin' on a Monday?

"He took a day off today," Tee says. "We're goin' out to buy school clothes next."

I steady myself with a hand on the chair. This child can read my mind. I slide my fingers from the ends of her hair to the lobe of her ear. If I was this child's mama, I wouldn't want that much cut off. There's so much you can do with good hair like this. "You sure you want short hair, Tee?"

"I dunno. Mama said she wanted to let it grow and grow till it reached the floor!" She giggles. "But I'd trip and fall down if it was that long."

"You sure would." I look her right in the eye. "Tell you what, Miss Baxter. I'm gonna—"

"I'm not Tee Baxter," Tee interrupts. "I'm Tee Jones. That was my mama's last name."

Dewey and *Miss* Jones? Twice? This is getting as complicated as the head of hair I'm looking at. So they weren't married, she dies, he gets the kids? That might put any man on his knees at a church. "Okay, Miss *Jones*, I'm gonna trim your ends and make 'em even, and then I'm

gonna style this head of hair so nice that your daddy won't even recognize you."

"He won't?" She widens those eyes so wide. *Lord, I am falling in
love with this child. You doin' this on purpose?*

"Oh, he'll know it's you." I lean in and whisper, "But he'll think
you're *so* much older."

"He will?"

"I guarantee it." I happily start trimming her ends. "What grade
you goin' into?"

"I'll be in first grade at Avery Elementary School."

I smile, mainly up at God. *You certainly are trying to tell me something, Lord. And I don't know if I like what You're saying just yet, but at least
You're talking to me again.* "I went there."

"You did?"

"Yep."

"About a million years ago," Diana cracks.

"Hush, Diana," I say, and I really think about it. It was only . . .
dag, *thirty* years ago? "You know who your teacher's gonna be?"

"Not yet."

"I remember my first grade teacher, Mrs. Steck."

"Don't see how," Diana says.

I stop cutting. "Miss Jones and I are having a conversation, Miss
Poindexter. So if you don't mind." Diana zips her lips with a hand to
her mouth, and Mrs. Simpson's right eyebrow twitches. Diana ain't
getting that fifty-cent tip or that half smile today. "You'll have lots of
fun in first grade, Tee. Is, uh, is Dee going to school?"

"Uh-huh. He'll be at Avery, too."

"He's in kindergarten?" He seems so small.

"Nope. He'll be in that other building."

The prekindergarten program. I nod, then smile at the ceiling.
Starting me all over again, huh, Lord? I was a paid teacher's aide in that
program at Avery before I married Jonas, but gave it up to be his wife.
I should never have given that up. I loved that job so much that it wasn't
a job anymore. They were my children, each and every one of them.
Jonas thought I wouldn't have enough time playing organ, attending
meetings, visiting sick folks at their homes or in the hospital . . . and
tending to our own children. "Besides," he had said, "I don't want you
to go into that neighborhood." Yeah, it's a rough neighborhood, but
Avery is the oasis in the middle. Principal Carter runs a tight ship, and

it's about time I got back on the boat. Didn't I get something in the mail about volunteering there? I could rearrange my schedule to get Tuesdays and Wednesdays off since those are slow days. . . . *Lord, You're being mysterious as usual, but I like Your mysteries. It's nice to have a purpose again.* "Um, when does your daddy work?"

"He goes to work when we go to school and picks us up after." So I'll be able to see him after school twice a week? Hmm. I smile. But nine to three? Only six hours a day? That's only a thirty-hour week— "Oh, and he works all night Friday and comes home in time for cartoons on Saturday. Nanna stays with us then. She's a really good cook."

Dewey's a real-live working man. But working a split shift on Friday night into Saturday morning? Least he's around for his kids, and I bet he don't get enough sleep. Napping in that truck is just what he needs.

After trimming, I plait Tee's hair as tightly as I can, and she doesn't complain a lick. "Mama used to do it that way."

I spin her in the chair. "You like it?"

"Uh-huh." But she's not smiling, rather getting that faraway look like her brother. Maybe I've done it *exactly* like her mama used to do? This is too much drama for two little kids' haircuts.

I hand her a sucker, and she takes it reluctantly, still looking at her pretty face in the mirror. "No thank you, Penny," she says, handing the sucker back to me.

"Keep it for your brother."

"No thank you."

"Give it to your daddy, then."

She stares at the sucker, a cherry-vanilla one. "He likes grape."

I fish out a grape sucker. "Last one."

Tee almost smiles. "Thank you."

"Let me get your change." I slide the crumpled twenty into the cash register and pull out a crisp ten. I'm shorting myself a few dollars, but I really didn't do much cutting. "Here you go."

Tee takes the ten, takes Dee's hand, and the two of them walk out of Diana's . . . taking my heart and soul with them.

"Better make sure they get to their daddy okay," Diana says with a crafty smile. "Wouldn't want 'em gettin' lost."

I check myself in the mirror. I'm still so big! I flick some of Tee's hairs off my smock and stride down the sidewalk, stopping at the passenger window. Dewey's eyes are as big as soup bowls. "What do you think?"

"Wow," he says. "I almost don't recognize them." I wink at Tee, and she winks back.

"You could use a cut, Mr. Baxter."

"Uh, well, I usually go to a barber."

"Where they thin out your hair too much. You got a fine, thick head of hair. All it needs is a little edge-up. And I'll do this one on the house." I am being so charitable today.

"No, I, um, well—"

"Never been in a salon, huh?" I interrupt.

"No."

"I'll cut you out here. Got some battery-operated clippers. Won't take but a second."

"Thanks for the offer, Ruth, but—"

"Daddy," Tee says, "you lookin' all ragged."

Dewey looks from Tee to me and back to Tee. "I'm lookin' ragged?"

"Mama wouldn't want you in the house with you lookin' like that," Tee says, sounding infinitely older. "Penny *got* to cut that wig of yours."

"I'll get the clippers," I say, dashing into Diana's.

"What's wrong?" Diana says when I bust through that door.

"Nothin'." I snatch the clippers. "I'm cuttin' the daddy."

She checks herself in the mirror. "He comin' in?"

I put a clean comb and some scissors in my smock pocket. "No."

"Why not?"

I walk to the door. "Cuz he a man, that's why. I'll be back."

When I get outside, Dewey is sitting on the bed of the truck, the tailgate down, Dee and Tee dancing all around him. Now that is a picture worth a thousand words. "How am I gonna cut you?"

"Oh," he says, and he slides down to the pavement. A little taller than me, about as wide, nicely proportioned, with big hands and feet. Dewey Baxter is just my size. "You have to be able to get behind me, right?" That's not what I had in mind, but oh, the wicked thoughts rolling through my head right now.

I nod. "You just sit on the edge there, and I'll work around behind you."

"Okay."

I hoist myself onto the bed of the truck and kneel. That shit hurts my knees, so I slide directly behind him and flop a leg to either side, Dee at my right shoulder, Tee on my left. Now *this* is a picture worth a *million* words. Folks driving by on Vine are sure to be crossing that center line for the next fifteen minutes.

"Do I look that ragged, Ruth?" Dewey asks.

"Uh-huh," I say. I drink in his Dial scent and some kind of cheap peach-scented shampoo and start to trim the hairs on his neck. "Seen mops lookin' better." He laughs, but he doesn't jiggle like the Santa Claus he could play in real life. "Keep still, Mr. Baxter, or you'll get cut." I place my left hand, which holds the comb, on his back while cutting with my right and find a solid wall of muscle. Dewey must load the trains all by his damn self. He *is* a front-end loader. I feel Dee's breath on my neck and turn to him. "How am I doin'?"

Dee shrugs.

Tee points at the little rooster tail dangling from the nape of Dewey's neck. "You gonna cut that off, Penny?"

"Definitely."

"Good," Tee says.

"Cut what?" Dewey asks.

"This little ponytail you got growin' back here." I snip it away, and Tee smiles. "Turn to your left." When he turns, I look closer at his face: smooth-shaven, not a single wrinkle, kind of ashy, chubby ears, pretty full lips for a white man. I edge around his ears, hair falling and flying back with the breeze. "You want your sideburns?" He ain't exactly Elvis, but he's pretty close.

"Not really."

"Good," Tee and I say together. I trim them off. "Your Elvis days are over."

"You don't like Elvis?"

What's to like? He's dead. "I like his music all right." I tug softly on his right ear. "Turn to the right."

When he turns, I feel his weight on my legs. "Sorry," he says, and he leans away from me.

"It's all right," I say softly. It ain't, though. It felt nice. My thighs haven't tingled like that in a long time, and when my thighs tingle, my body tingles. I act like I can't reach his other sideburn and pull on his shoulder so his weight returns to me. "One more snip, and . . . no another, and . . . No, that part's not quite right. I've just got to . . . there."

I push him gently off my legs and stand. "How much you want off the top?"

"How much do I need?"

If that was my hair, it would be about a year's worth. "A couple inches."

"You're the boss."

"You got that right," I say, and I start sectioning and cutting, sectioning and cutting, till Dewey Baxter is once again presentable to the world. I ruffle his remaining hair to dislodge as much cut hair as possible and wipe the hairs off his shoulders. Solid as a rock. Nanna is a *good* cook.

As he turns around, I stand on the edge of the tailgate. He reaches up two hands to me. "Let me help you down, Ruth."

"No, I can manage."

"Come on," he says. I lean forward, and he lifts me off the tailgate, his hands gripping my arms, my legs completely in the air, and sets me down gently. I am utterly speechless. He lifted me! And he didn't even grunt! "How much I owe you?"

I cannot find my voice. "Like I said," I say, almost whispering, "no charge."

"You sure?"

"I'm sure." I look at Dee and Tee. "Just keep bringin' these beautiful children by at least once a month."

"Okay." He runs his hands through his hair. "Feels right nice."

It does, indeed. *A man lifted me!* I can't remember any man being able to do that. Jonas could barely lift even one of my legs. Damn. I can't remember if a man *ever* lifted me, since I know my daddy never did. I can only remember being lifted by women.

"And, um, you stay away from the barber."

He smiles. "Guess I'll need a trim about once a month, too."

"Your hair grows fast, Mr. Baxter. Better make it every three weeks."

"Sure." He smiles. "Ruth."

Oh, my heart! "Well, y'all take care." I turn to Tee and whisper, "If you need to have them plaits tightened, you stop by anytime."

"Okay, Penny," she whispers.

I rub Dee's head. "Goodbye, Little Man."

Dee rolls his eyes and jumps into Dewey's arms.

"You take care, Ruth," Dewey says, loading his children into the truck. As the truck rumbles away, Tee leans out and yells, "Bye, Penny!"

I walk back into Diana's whistling "All Things Are Working."

And they are. My heart and soul are alive again because a man and his children have swept me off my feet!

Seven

The following Tuesday, I walk to Avery to sign up to be a volunteer. I didn't go that first week since I know how crazy the first week of school can be. And I also know the Bible says to wait on the Lord, so I did; but sometimes you just can't do that for very long. God's been talking right loud to me from the very second I saw those children. Is this "God's will" for me? I don't know. I've always had trouble with that phrase. Whenever we had a funeral at Antioch, I'd say "It was God's will, brother," or "It was God's will, sister" till I wasn't hearing what I was saying anymore. How can anybody know God's will since *He* owns it? There's an apostrophe after His name in that phrase, right? I believe you can only pray so much to know His will. After that, you gotta get up off your knees, put on your traveling shoes, and go.

I take the long way to Avery, walking by the apartments on Sixteenth. Just to see. No harm in that. I pause just long enough to count the doors since none have letters on them. The place looks like a hotel almost with all the doors facing the street. Four floors, four doors per floor . . . daa-em. They have to be one-bedroom efficiencies, those "shotgun" apartments with just enough room to turn around in. Dewey and family aren't exactly living large (like I am, right?), but at least they're close to me. But for Dewey and two children to live there? They're boxed in like I am. Least they got a bottom floor, corner apartment, so the only folks to bother them are upstairs or to their right. Folks in the middle must go crazy, surrounded by noises on all sides. And those metal stairs going to the other floors look right rusty. Wouldn't want Tee or Dee to be climbing on those.

I cut over to Fifteenth, pass the spot where Guitarman's blood still stains the sidewalk, and head to Avery, an all-brick relic from back in my day. I walk into the office which looks so much smaller every time I go in. I stop at the counter and freeze. Mrs. Holland is *still* the secretary. She was ancient when I was here as a child and has to be pushing ninety. And it even looks like she's still wearing the same awful clothes she wore thirty years ago: frilly white blouse, gray skirt to her shins, black pumps right out of the '40s. She totters her hunched body off her chair and groans, approaching the counter with a squint. "If it isn't Ruthie Lee Childress."

"How do you know it's me?"

"I never forget a face." She looks at me and smiles, but her eyes are sad. "You were hard to forget when you volunteered here, and you were definitely an unforgettable child."

I drop my eyes and fidget with my hands. Mrs. Holland was the one who told me my mama had died, and I had pitched an unholy fit in this very office, telling Mrs. Holland that she was wrong, that I had just spoken to my mama this morning, that someone had told her a lie. But somehow that old lady had held me right over there on that shiny bench till it had sunk in.

"I've never, uh, apologized for that," I say. "I'm sorry, Mrs. Holland."

She waves a hand. "I'd have done the same thing. Your mama was *young*, too young to be havin' a stroke." She pulls out a sheet of paper and writes my name at the top. "You're here to volunteer, right?"

"How'd you know—"

"Because I seen the look in your eye, girl. Saw the same look, what, fifteen, twenty years ago when you used to work here regular. You are here for the children."

Just one in particular, actually. A little boy.

"How many days can you serve?"

"Two, Tuesdays and Wednesdays."

She places two check marks on the sheet. "Any preference?"

"Pre-K."

Mrs. Holland's furry little eyebrows arch. "You sure?"

"Yes."

"It's all day now, you know, not half a day like the old days."

"I'm sure."

"*Twenty* four-year-olds in the *same* room *all* day."

"Uh-huh."

She looks at me hard. "Don't you 'uh-huh' me, Ruthie Lee. You got somethin' cookin'." I don't reply. "You got a child in mind already, don't you?"

Damn, she's good. She should hire herself out as a lie detector. "Yes."

"Some little boy or girl stole your heart." I nod. "Good. We need more folks like you. Sorry we can't hire you as an aide. Our funding got cut again. Sign here." I sign the form "Ruth Borum," and Mrs. Holland blinks. "That the name you still go by?"

"I have my reasons."

"Didn't you—"

"Yes, we're divorced," I interrupt.

"Ruth Lee Childress is a much prettier name."

I know it is. "Like I said, I have my reasons."

She shrugs and takes the paper, stuffing it into an overflowing file cabinet. "Well, you are still Ruthie Lee to me." She turns and winks. "Now get your little bubble butt to class, young lady."

"Yes, ma'am," I say cheerfully, and I nearly skip through the first-grade hall. I pause at a few windows and look for Tee but don't see her. I do find her locker and see a pretty picture of a tree taped to it. I know we'll see each other. Avery isn't that big of a school. Maybe we'll do lunch.

I walk outside and enter what we kids used to call the tunnel, the roofed section that leads to the pre-K building. I crack open the purple door and see . . . twenty four-year-olds in every color of the rainbow, even a couple white kids, running all over the place. I also see oozing, snotty noses, scores of untied shoes, shirttails hanging out, and dirty fists and fingers, and I hear high-pitched voices giggling and shouting and screaming. Though it is bedlam, I smile. They are so full of life, so alive, every emotion etched on their faces. Sometimes I think children are the only real humans. They still tell the truth (because we adults haven't fully taught them how to lie), and they complain out loud, cry out loud, fart out loud, burp out loud, walk out loud—*live* out loud.

Except for Dee. He sits by himself at a table away from the rest of the children and stares out a window, completely uninterested in the circus around him. *Lord Jesus, give me a heart big enough to capture Dee and bring him back to life.*

There are two other adults in the room, one obviously the teacher since she's white, her clothes are old-fashioned, her hair has wilted already, she wears a name tag that reads "Mrs. King," and she's yelling,

"Circle time!" at the top of her lungs. The other adult is probably someone's mama, and neither of them can get these soaring, racing children into a circle taped on the floor in the center of the room. Circle time? More like circle the wagons, padner, these Injuns is on the warpath. I step inside and grab the nearest track star and loop an arm around a tiny boy writing on the wall in crayon.

"Let me . . ." the tiny boy starts to say, but when he's airborne in the crook of my arm, he swallows that "go." I carry him and the other boy to the circle and set them down. Then I approach Dee. Though his jeans and red shirt are wrinkled, his face is clean, and his hair still looks good. He looks up at me, his little lips a thin, straight line. I offer him my hand, but instead of taking it, he slides off his chair, steps around me, and sits at the edge of the circle.

So that's how it's gonna be? *Lord, give me patience.*

"Hello?" Mrs. King says in a nasal voice behind me.

I turn and smile. "Hi. I'm Ruth, but I'd like the kids to call me Penny." Mainly because it's easier to say. I don't want to be called "Roof."

"And you're here because . . ."

"Oh, I'll be helping y'all out Tuesdays and Wednesdays."

"I wasn't aware of this."

Aware of it or not, y'all need me. "I only just signed up—"

"Okay, class!" she shouts as she spins around, cutting me off. Wench. "Today we're going to read a story about a little boy named Jack."

I reach out and touch her elbow. "Mrs. King, what do you need me to do?"

Mrs. King sighs and turns to me slowly. "For circle time?"

No, for your hair. Another blond white woman with dark-ass roots. "Yes, ma'am."

"Just guard that side of the room and keep them in the circle."

"Yes, ma'am."

I slide in behind Dee and flop out my legs. Any child who tries to escape gonna run into a barricade of light brown flesh. But surprisingly, the children are quiet and almost still during the story about a little white boy who makes cookies with his blond-haired mama. Couldn't she have read a story about a little brown boy or girl? I'm sure that there are stories like that out there.

Mrs. King shuts the book. "Wasn't that a good story?"

Nineteen nods. Dee hasn't stirred a bit. If I was him, I probably wouldn't like the story either. The wound is just too fresh. His mama will never be able to make cookies with him again.

"Kind of makes me hungry," Mrs. King says, rubbing her caved-in tummy. "Does it make you hungry?"

Nineteen loud yeahs. Dee only blinks.

"Well, later today, we'll all make cookies together."

A loud shout. Dee hasn't budged.

"But first, I want us all to talk about our mothers." No response. "Um, your *mamas*."

Nods all around, and I almost laugh. Ain't a child in here who calls his mama "mother."

"Who'd like to tell us about his or her mama?"

Nineteen children raise their hands, some jumping to their feet and waving their whole bodies.

She points to a child closest to her. "Britney."

Britney? She as black as coal. What's a white name doin' on a charcoal-colored girl?

"My mama makes the best chocolate cake in the whole wide world!"

Over the next few precious minutes, we learn that Stuart's mama works at KFC and brings home chicken every night, Ashley's mama has fingernails as long as Ashley's arm, Desiree's mama likes to watch TV, and Chuckie's mama is nine feet tall. Every child says something wonderful about his or her mama, and I feel the pangs inside me, like hunger pangs only more painful. What would my children, had they lived, say about me now? She's nine feet wide, she plays the organ, she cuts hair, she walks, she eats rabbit food?

Mrs. King focuses on Dee, and I tense up. "Dee? You didn't raise your hand."

The bitch *has* to know, and I almost say something. It's almost cruel what she's doing, but I'm too curious to interrupt. Maybe he *will* talk about his mama. Hell, maybe he'll just talk period.

But Dee doesn't even look up.

"Dee, why don't you tell us about your mama?"

I inch closer to Dee. If he does speak, it'll have to come out as a whisper. I wish I could read minds like his sister, Tee. What is going through this boy's head?

Mrs. King frowns. "Dee, everyone else has said something about his or her mama. Just tell us one thing you remember about her."

Oh . . . shit. What the *fuck* is this lady trying to do? Now nineteen children know Dee don't have a mama. I put up with that shit during junior high and high school, and it wasn't any fun at all. "What'd you get your mama for Mother's Day, Roofie Pee?" they'd ask. "Another flower for her grave?"

"Dee? I know you heard me."

Dee shifts his weight. *Lord Jesus, please make that ho leave Dee alone!*

"Was your mama a good cook perhaps?"

Dee's head comes up, but his eyes—daa-em. Those eyes are burnin' holes in Mrs. King. I inch even closer.

"Was she pretty?" She opens the book to the page with Jack and his mama putting the cookies in the oven. "Did you ever make cookies with her?"

Dee stands, his eyes never leaving Mrs. King, and takes two steps closer to her. He seems to be looking at the picture . . . Then he grabs that book and flings it across the room where it collides with a vase of flowers on Mrs. King's desk, water spilling all over the papers on her desk. Nice arm. The other children yell, "uh-oh!" while Mrs. King grabs Dee's arm and drags him down the hall to another room. The other children get real calm now. *One of our own is in big trouble,* I'll bet they're thinking, *and we could be next.*

"Where?" I mouth to the other aide, a short, plump chocolate woman with what looks like her short, plump chocolate daughter on her lap.

"Time out," she mouths back.

They still use that shit? Time out? Like a child understands the concept. I get to sit alone in a small room with no one else around me? Shit, adults could use that. And time out is probably what Dee wants anyway. Mrs. King is actually giving Dee a reward.

Mrs. King shuts the door and returns to us, fixing her hair and applying that fake-ass smile. "Now, children, we'll go to our tables and—"

THUNK, THUNK, THUNK.

Daa-em. Little Dee has a temper. I start to get up, but Mrs. King stays me with her hand. "Ignore him."

THUNK, THUNK, THUNK.

Eyes pop all around me. I hope he's just banging the door with his fist.

THUNK, THUNK, THUNK.

Mrs. King's smile vanishes. "Dee must learn, as must *all* of us, to behave. We don't throw books. Say it with me. We don't—"

POOM!

That wasn't no fist! That was a little boy's head! I stand despite Mrs. King's flailing hands and race down the hall, Mrs. King following behind me saying, "What do you think you are doing?"

I open the door and save Dee from another head butt to the door. He falls forward and thunks my leg instead. "Puttin' this boy out of his misery."

"We have procedures, Miss, uh—"

I take Dee's wrist, and he doesn't resist. "Why I gotta be a 'Miss'?"

"Well, I just assumed—"

I pick Dee up, and he drops his little head onto my shoulder. "Just cuz I'm an older black woman don't make me a 'Miss.'"

"Well, I—"

"And you can stick your procedures where the sun don't shine." I rub Dee's head. "I have this boy's head to think about."

"Mrs., uh—"

"Borum."

"Mrs. Borum, I don't think you're qualified to—"

"You got children of your own?"

"Well, uh, no, but—"

"I ain't got any either." I hold Dee closer. "So who's qualified? You punish the child, and I hold the child. Who's helping who?" She doesn't answer. "Dee and I gonna go outside and have us a little chat."

"That's not allowed. I have to get advance permission from Principal Carter, and if I don't, I can get fired."

I smile. "I'm only a volunteer. They can't fire me."

"But—"

"Look. You want to have to explain to Principal Carter or this boy's *white* daddy how this boy got bruised fists and a knot on his head?" That finally shuts her up. "Come on, Mr. Dee. Let's go for a walk."

We leave Mrs. King punching a few numbers on a phone and go for the quietest walk I've ever been on. We leave the school campus, walk to a nearby park, and sit on a bench, watching squirrels scurrying about swishing their tails. "That squirrel over there be lookin' like Mrs. King," I say. "Runnin' around chatterin' like her head been cut off." I look at Dee out of the corner of my eye and see the beginnings of a smile. "Old white lady shouldn't have been talkin' 'bout your mama. You don't want to talk about her, it's *your* business, not hers." His face twitches.

I squeeze his hand, but he pulls it away to his lap. *Lord, slow me down.*

"My mama died when I was ten years old. Found out the news right here at Avery, and I pitched a fit, let me tell you. Took four, five, six teachers, the principal, *and* Mrs. Holland to hold me down." It's only a little fib. Mrs. Holland is worth six teachers and a principal to me. He raises his cute little eyebrows, his long lashes flashing. "Makes me sad to think about my mama, but I still think about her every day. I'll never stop missin' or thinkin' about my mama."

That tiny, grimy hand leaves his lap and slides oh so slowly to mine. *Lord, please hold back my tears.* He turns my hand over and sizes his up in mine. "Your hand is about half as big, huh?" He lays it in mine, but I don't squeeze. "Don't worry. You gonna have big hands like your daddy one day, I just know it."

We sit there a spell, a breeze cooling the sweat between our hands. "Don't expect you to apologize to Mrs. King. I wouldn't. But will you try not to throw any more of her books?"

Dee nods.

I squeeze his hand, and he squeezes back. "Good. And I don't want to ever hear of you goin' to that room again, okay?"

Dee nods again.

"Mrs. Borum?" a male voice behind us says.

I turn and see Principal Carter, as wide as he is tall, as black as the darkest night. "Principal Carter." Man *still* scares me whenever I hear thunder. "We were just—"

"I know," he says, and he slides onto the bench next to me. "Fine day to be just . . . doing this."

"Sure is."

"Too beautiful to be spent in a classroom."

"I agree."

He chuckles. "Mrs. King is all bent out of shape. She wants me to reassign you."

"She does?" He nods. Bitch needs to be reassigned her damn self.

"She says you need psychological counseling."

I laugh. I haven't had the need to see Dr. Holt in months.

"Says you disrupted the unity of her class."

The unity? I roll my eyes. "What are you gonna do?"

"What I like to do in situations like this: nothin'. Absolutely nothin'. That okay with you?"

I smile. "Fine with me."

"Good." He leans forward and smiles at Dee. "Hear you got a good arm, young man." Dee tenses. "I'm gonna write your name down so I can remember it in a few years when you're Dee Jones, star quarterback at Webster High. That okay with you?"

Dee looks at me first, then nods.

"Time for my lunch, y'all," Principal Carter says. "Wish I'd have brought it with me. This is a nice spot for a little picnic." He stands and stretches. "I got to get out that office more often. Y'all comin'?"

I turn to Dee. "Ready to go back?"

Dee nods, but I can tell he isn't ready. "In a little bit," I say. "When does Dee eat lunch?"

He checks his watch. "In about half an hour."

"We'll see you in the lunchroom then."

Principal Carter winks at me. "Good to have you back, Ruthie Lee."

"Thank you."

Dee and I walk around the park for the rest of our "time out session," watching smaller children swing on swings and slide down slides while their mamas gossip. Maybe they think we're a son and his mama just like them. It'd be a nicer feeling if it was true, but it's still a nice feeling. We walk around under trees watching squirrels climb, his hand never leaving mine. "You ever climb a tree, Dee?"

He nods with a smile. He can smile! And it's as cute as his daddy's smile with the same little dimples.

"Was it a big tree?"

He points at the biggest tree in the park.

"As big as that one?"

A bigger smile.

"*Bigger* than that one?"

A big nod.

"Wow. I don't think I could climb a tree as big as that. Were you scared?"

He shakes his head.

"Where'd you climb such a big tree?"

He doesn't respond.

"I'll bet you climbed it at Nanna's."

He nods.

"I'd like to see that tree some day. You promise to show it to me?"

He nods.

"Let's shake on it." I squat and shake his hand. "And maybe you can teach me how to climb it. Okay?"

He nods. I want to hug this child so bad, but I don't. Hugging his hand will have to be enough for now.

Mrs. King doesn't say a word to either of us the rest of the day, leaving us to do whatever we want. We share a fairly decent meal of corn dogs and fries in the lunchroom where we don't see Tee (the first graders eat later), then sit at a tiny-ass table in tinier-ass chairs watching the other children make cookie dough—with their hands. That is so nasty. Fun, but nasty. Mrs. King and the parent, Miss Hayes, had inspected each child's hands carefully and had even wet-wiped a few; but there is no way that I am going to eat those cookies, and there is no way that I am going to let Dee eat them because they all keep licking their fingers, fingers that have been digging in their draws and noses.

"You like cookies?" I whisper while Dee uses a blue crayon to draw something vaguely dog-shaped on a thin piece of gray paper.

Dee shrugs and colors in the dog.

"Me neither."

I look at his drawing, and I know from experience not to ask who or what it is. If I say "what a cute dog" and it turns out to be Grandma, I'll be in trouble. He takes out a black crayon and puts four circles on the dog. Oh, it's a car. But the wheels are wrong because . . . They don't touch the ground. I bite my lips together to keep them from trembling.

He's drawing what happened to his mama. He's drawing the car upside down.

He looks at me and cocks his head back to the picture.

"Is, um, is that what happened to you and your mama, Dee?"

He nods and draws an arch over the car.

"It happened in a tunnel?"

He nods rapidly and chooses a light blue crayon, drawing wavy lines farther into the tunnel.

"There was water in the tunnel."

He nods and drops the crayon.

"Your mama drove into the tunnel and didn't see the water." When did this happen? And why wasn't this all over the news? Oh, yeah, a black woman in Calhoun, Virginia, died in a car accident. Had she been murdered, she still wouldn't be front-page news, but I would have heard or read about it. There's only one tunnel near Vine Street, the one all the trains go over, and it is a dangerous tunnel. Too narrow, always potholed, floods even in a light rain, not enough overhead lights. It might have rained and flooded, and any car even going the speed limit would have had trouble staying under control.

I turn the paper over. "Will you do something for me? Will you draw me a picture of your mama?" I want to see what my competition looks like.

He fingers through the section of brown crayons in the box, choosing something called "mocha." This child has an eye for color. He draws a balloon-shaped head with a tiny neck and shoulders, then adds eyes that nearly fill the balloon.

"Your mama had big brown eyes, huh?"

He nods and adds a tiny nose and a big smile. He colors the eyeballs dark brown and the teeth white.

"She had a pretty smile, too?"

He nods. So far I'm two for two. I don't have a skinny neck, though.

As he works, I notice he's panting more than breathing—and so am I. A miracle is happening right before my eyes. This child is "speaking" to me using some crayons! He pulls a black crayon toward him and grips it tightly. He adds curls to her forehead and long, straight spaghetti-looking things that hang almost down to her shoulders. Extensions? Well, extensions are spaghetti-looking things sometimes. This child has talent. He drops his crayon. Sweat beads on his forehead.

Mrs. King chooses this moment to cruise over. "What a beautiful drawing, Dee," she says. "Who is that? Is it Mrs. Borum?" Dee's eyes become two little dots. Oh shit. I move the crayons to the other side of the table out of his reach. Crayons may be small, but the sharper ones could put an eye out.

"It's a picture of his—"

"I *know* who it is," Mrs. King interrupts.

"And on the other side—"

She scowls at me and picks up the drawing. "I think we should put this one up on the big board, Dee. It's very good."

I look under the table and see two little fists pounding two little legs. Something bad is about to happen, and I want it to happen. I want Dee to go off. I want him to scream, to break shit, to throw the unholiest fit in the world, to let it all hang out like I did the day Larry died in front of Hood's. Too much rage and hurt been building up in this little boy, and this lady is about to bring it out. All she has to do is say the magic words. The *wrong* magic words.

"But what about the rest of her?" she says with a frown. "Where is the rest of your pretty mama?"

Those are the magic words. Dee's hands slide up under the table, palms up. He stands, kicks his chair back, and heaves the table up till it flips over with a crash, flattening the crayon box. Whoa. This child has his daddy's shoulders. Then he just stands there, his eyes wild, his body stiller than still. The room is silent. The cookie factory is temporarily on a work stoppage.

I don't want to look at Mrs. King because I'm afraid I'm gonna bust out laughing. I imagine her pouty red lips forming the most delicious little O. "Dee Jones, that just wasn't necessary. Mrs. Borum, I hold you responsible for this little outburst."

Lord God, please keep me from killing this woman. I turn to her and keep my voice calm. "Dee drew that picture of his mama for me. If you will look on the other side, you will see a drawing of the accident that took her life. She doesn't have a body because her face was probably the last thing Dee saw of her." Either that or he doesn't want to remember the rest of her.

She turns the paper over and stares. "Well, Mrs. Borum, why didn't you tell me all this?"

God, You still there? I'm about to say some vile things. Go work on that Middle East thing for a while. I stand and tower over Mrs. King. "I tried to tell you, Mrs. King, but you interrupted me. You've done that to me often today. Is interrupting people another one of your procedures?"

"Excuse *me*, Mrs.—"

"Nah, *bitch*, you excuse me." I wave a finger in her face, and the room is so quiet that I swear I hear a couple children poot. I have just said the B word. "This child has just spoken to the world with these drawings, and it's a breakthrough for Dee; but you can't get your ashy, brunette-rooted head out of your skinny tight ass long enough to see that. Must be hard breathing with your head up your ass, but somehow you do it, cuz all you doin' is talkin' shit."

Mrs. King's lower lip bobs up and down.

I snatch the drawing from her. "This drawing ain't goin' up on no big board. This child's pain ain't gonna be on display for the world to see. It's going home to his daddy . . ."

My voice trails away when I notice tears welling in Dee's eyes. *God, come back. I'm gonna need You. I didn't mean to make Dee cry.*

"You sendin' us to the office, Mrs. King?" I ask.

Mrs. King's eyes drop to her nasty open-toed shoes. "I, uh, no. That won't be necessary."

I scoop up Dee. "Well, *I'm* sendin' us to the office." I wipe away Dee's tears, whisper, "Let's go, Little Man," and we leave the pre-K building. By the time we get to the office, Dee's tears have dried, like his body has sucked them back into his face. I set him on the bench and sit beside him. Two children, probably third or fourth graders, stare at us from the hall, and I stare back till they scamper off. Yeah, we bad.

Mrs. Holland stops filing and leans on the counter. "Is this . . ."

I nod.

Mrs. Holland smiles, creeps around the counter, and stands in front of us. "We heard the whole thing," she whispers. "Principal Carter and I heard the whole thing."

"How?"

She points at the loudspeaker on the wall. "Those are all two-way, have been since Avery was built. Probably to root out the Communists way back when. We can listen in on any class we want to, but you didn't hear it from me. We got your back, Ruthie Lee."

"Thank you."

She waves a wrinkled hand at us. "Don't mention it. One of the many and various perks of the job." She winks at Dee and creeps back to her file cabinet.

Principal Carter's door opens, and he steps out. "IN MY OFFICE NOW, YOU TWO!" he thunders.

Both Dee and I slip off the bench, eyes down. Dee grabs my hand, and I grab it back. Daa-em, my first day, and I'm in the principal's office. We walk by Principal Carter, who slams the door behind us and storms to his huge chair behind his huge desk.

"WHAT AM I GOING TO DO WITH YOU TWO?" he shouts. He points to two chairs and whispers, "Just relax and have a seat."

Say what? Principal Carter is possessed!

"THAT'S TWICE TODAY THAT YOU'VE UPSET THE CONTINU-ITY AND TRANQUILITY AND UNITY OF THIS SCHOOL!" he shouts again. He points at the drawing and whispers, "Let me see that." I hand him the drawing with a shaky hand. "This is very good, Dee," he whispers. "Maybe you'll be an artist *and* a football player." Oh, I get it. Principal Carter is the good cop and the bad cop all at the same time. It's scary, but it's effective. He hands me the picture, then slams his massive hand on the desk. "TWO WEEKS' IN-SCHOOL SUSPENSION FOR BOTH OF YOU!" He smiles and whispers, "You only work Tuesdays and Wednesdays, right?" I nod. "OKAY, IF THAT'S THE WAY YOU WANT IT, FIVE WEEKS!" He shakes with laughter and whispers, "On Tuesdays and Wednesdays only, that is."

I squeeze Dee's hand. "Mr. Dee," I whisper, "you're gonna see a lot of me every Tuesday and Wednesday. That all right with you?" He shrugs, nods, and almost smiles.

"NOW, GET OUT OF MY OFFICE AND SIT ON THAT BENCH OUT THERE TILL THE LAST BELL RINGS! AND YOU THINK HARD ABOUT WHAT YOU TWO HAVE DONE!" He checks his watch and whispers, "Bell rings in five minutes. Sorry for all the yelling. Have to keep up my rep. And try to, um, regulate your choice of words in the future, Mrs. Borum."

"I'm sorry, I just—"

"Woman makes me curse, too," he interrupts. "But I don't say it in front of twenty four-year-olds."

Ouch. I nod. "It won't happen again."

He smiles. "I bet it will." He's probably right. "And try to look guilty while you're sitting out there, okay?"

"I understand," I whisper, making a gruesome frown. "Dee, you frown, too." Like he needs to be asked. The corners of his little mouth droop, and we leave looking like two sad little puppy dogs.

While we sit on that bench looking guilty, I think back to all the times I heard Principal Carter yelling at someone in his office. You could hear it all over the school, and it made everyone, even a few teachers, tremble and shake. And now, I wonder how many of those kids didn't get punished at all.

"Dee's daddy picks 'em up at the yellow curb out front," Mrs. Holland says. "But he is *never* on time, so Tee and Dee wait in here till he arrives." She chuckles. "Y'all start lookin' more pitiful now. Bell's about to ring."

I step to the counter, folding Dee's picture and sliding it into my pocket. "Mr. Baxter is *always* late?"

"He's been late every day so far."

I don't know if I can abide a tardy man. Jonas was always early— particularly in bed—but I hate being late for anything. It may be in my culture, but it ain't in me. "How late we talkin'?"

She flips open a notebook filled with dates and times, sliding her finger down the page. "Ten minutes . . . fifteen minutes . . . twelve minutes . . . twenty-two minutes . . . eight minutes yesterday." She shuts the book. "He hasn't been on time yet this year."

"Did," I whisper, "did their mama pick up Tee last year?"

Mrs. Holland nods. "She came to Tee's room last year with Dee, and the three of them walked home together. Every day." Mrs. Holland's eyes twinkle. "Nice day for a walk, huh?"

I bite my lips to hide the smile. "Sure is. But Mr. Baxter might panic if his kids aren't here when he gets here." I know that I'd panic if I was their mama.

"So you *know* Mr. Baxter."

I drop my eyes. "Not really."

"Uh-huh." The bell rings, and children fill the halls.

I look at Mrs. Holland. "Really. I only cut some hair. That's all."

She looks around me to Dee. "You do nice work."

"Thank you."

Tee skips into the office and goes right to Dee. "I hear you been bad, little boy," she says in that older voice of hers. She jumps onto the bench and smiles at me. "And I hear you been bad, too, Penny."

I clasp my hands and hold them at my waist. "Yes. I've been very bad."

Tee giggles. "Daddy's gonna be so mad at you two!"

I wince and look at Mrs. Holland. "Uh, help me out here."

"I'd go for your walk," Mrs. Holland says, "but don't leave campus. Walk by Tee's classroom first, then stop by the playground out back. I'll smooth things out with Mr. Baxter and send him to you."

"Thanks." I turn to Tee and Dee. "Why don't you show me your classroom, Tee?"

"But Daddy's gonna pick us up soon," Tee says.

"I'm sure your daddy won't mind. Mrs. Holland will tell him where we are. We may even play a bit on the monkey bars."

Tee shrugs. "Okay, I guess." She takes Dee's hand. "Come on, bad boy, we goin' for a walk."

As we walk out, Dee latches on to my hand, and the three of us swing arms down the hall. *God, if heaven is anything like this, I'll never want to leave.*

We stop at Miss Freitag's room, and Tee sticks her head in first. "Good. She's not here."

"Well, I don't think we should go in if your teacher's not here," I say.

Tee pulls me in. "Come on." I let her pull me in and am surrounded by colorful everything: numbers, letters, pictures, drawings, and handprints. She points at a little desk and chair. "That's where I sit." Right next to the teacher's desk. How awful, unless . . .

I see a chart with children's names on it and notice five red blotches next to Tee's name. The rest of the children have greens and yellows. Tee been bad, too. Daily. "What do these red marks mean, Miss Tee?"

Tee shrugs. "I dunno. Wanna see our gerbil, Penny?"

I check out the gerbil, and Tee taps the glass and makes faces. "Tee, don't those red marks mean you have been misbehaving?"

Tee shrugs again. "I guess." She smiles at me. "Just like you, Penny." She got me. "Oh, wanna see something *really* neat?" She pulls me to an aquarium full of goldfish and presses her nose to the glass. "You do it, too, Dee," she says, and Dee flattens his nose on the glass. The fish swarm around their cute freckled noses.

"Why do they do that?"

"Don't know," Tee says, her lips scrunched up on the glass.

"May I help you?"

I turn and see a white woman who couldn't be more than sixteen, five feet tall at most with bushy eyebrows and stubby hands. This must be Miss Freitag, and she looks pissed. "Uh, I'm just watching these children till their daddy gets here. I'm a volunteer. Hope you don't mind. You have such pretty fish, and a pretty room, too."

"Tee," Miss Freitag says in the highest-pitched voice. Girl sounds like Minnie Mouse. "You know I don't like you doing that."

Tee rolls her eyes at me and pulls me and Dee away from the aquarium. "The fish like it, Miss Freitag," she says, and she keeps pulling us out into the hall.

"Nice to meet you, Miss Freitag," I call out (though I don't mean it) as I'm pulled by both children to the doors leading to the playground. This is a ride I can get used to!

Once we're outside, they release me, tear to the jungle gym, and are swinging from the monkey bars before I can blink. I feel a little sadness—I could never even climb the *ladder* to the bars without difficulty—but shake it off as a new emotion grabs me by the throat. Fear. "Y'all be careful now," I say, walking under their flailing arms and legs. If just one of these children falls . . . *God, keep Your angels handy. These children are defying Your gravity today. And while we're talkin' here, why didn't You make the ground softer? It's much too hard on my feet.*

Happily they quit swinging through the air and climb up and

shoot down the slide. I try to talk to them, but they ain't havin' it. I don't blame them. They probably go from here to the apartment . . . and that's all the activity they get till lights out. I find a bench and sit, smiling in the sun. Bet Mama's kissing me right about now.

So this is what watching your children play is like: catching your breath when it looks like one of them is about to fall, laughing as they laugh, clapping when they've done something miraculous—and worrying the entire damn time, your butt barely on the bench, your legs ready to leap to the rescue. Daa-em, they givin' me a workout, and I ain't even the one playing.

They're both at the top of the slide, Dee in front of Tee, ready for their twentieth descent in the last two minutes it seems, when Dewey appears suddenly to my left. "Hi, Daddy!" Tee calls. "Watch this!"

They slide down together and spill onto the sandy ground, Tee giggling, Dee smiling ear to ear. They jump to their feet and race each other to the ladder.

"Where do they get their energy?" I say to Dewey. His coveralls are one big black stain, the circles under his arms darker black, his Chicago Cubs hat tipped up, dark smudges under his eyes. He wears shit-kicker boots, the kind with five-pound metal slabs in the toes, and carries two book bags. Oops, I forgot about the kids' book bags. I smile. "You gonna sit and rest a bit, Mr. Baxter?"

He sits, setting the book bags on the space between us, sighing heavily. "Feels good to sit." He groans, stretching out his legs.

I get a whiff of his stank body, and it is *ripe*. "Your children are somethin', Mr. Baxter."

"Yup."

"Oh," I say. I take out the picture, unfolding it in front of Dewey. "Dee spoke to me today."

"He did? That's wonderful! What'd he say?" Dewey's face is beaming, and he isn't looking at the drawing. Oh shit.

"Uh, I shouldn't have said 'spoke,' Mr. Baxter. He drew those pictures for me, and they *told* me a lot." Dewey looks carefully at both sides, nodding his head, his face beaming no longer. "That child sure can draw."

Dewey folds it quickly and stuffs it into his shirt pocket. "Never could draw myself. Takes after his mama."

That's it? No reaction to the drawing at all? "What do you, um, think of his drawing?"

"I've, uh, I've seen it before." Seen it before? How could he have seen it before if Dee just drew it today? He stands. "Come on, y'all. Time to go home."

Tee groans, and Dee shoves his hands into his pockets, but both children come running.

"Dee drew those pictures *today*, Mr. Baxter."

He nods. "And yesterday and the day before. I have a collection of a hundred of these at home."

Damn. That child is reliving that nightmare daily... and I just helped him to do it today. This day isn't ending the way I want it to end. "Mr. Baxter, I could watch 'em for a while, even walk 'em home if you like. I'm sure you'd like to get cleaned up, take a load off."

"Maybe some other time," he says in a soft voice. "Thanks for the offer." He straps a book bag on each child. "Nice to see you again, Ruth."

I watch them walk away till they disappear around the side of the school and feel all mixed up. Dewey called me by my real name, which is wonderful, but not to take me up on my generous offer? He could have gotten himself cleaned up, maybe gotten a long nap. Dag, I didn't mean to interrupt his daily routine. I should have just handed the drawing to him without saying anything. That man wants his boy to speak again in the worst way, and I just built him up and let him down.

I bury my head in my hands. *I know, Lord Jesus, I know. Slow down, Ruthie Lee. All in Your good time, love takes time, healing that little boy takes time ... But couldn't You maybe just once speed things up for me? I ain't no spring chicken anymore. You know I would be a good mama to those children, and I feel something for that man. It's Your love, but it's something more, and I want it to be something more, stank as he is.* I laugh. *But it's a good stank, Lord. It's a working man's stank, and I like it.*

I stand and drift toward the monkey bars. *And ain't I been waitin' long enough for something good to happen to me? I ain't never asked You what I did to deserve Jonas and the miscarriages. I know I cussed You, and I'm sorry about that. But You invented language, right? And all through this shit (sorry), I have never questioned why it's happened. Ain't I been a good and faithful servant? When will all those showers of blessings rain down on me?* I stop at the bottom of the stairs. *Tell You what, if I can go all the way across these monkey bars, something You know I have never done before, You have to bless me quick. Deal?*

I look around before climbing the ladder. I don't want no audience. I don't see anyone. So far so good. I lean out and grip the first bar with both hands and drop, my feet almost touching the sand. My shoulders immediately scream in pain. *Lord Jesus, You said if I had the faith of a mustard seed, I could move mountains. Well, here I am, Mount Penny, and I'm tryin' to move.* I loosen my right hand to reach for the second bar . . . and fall flat on my ass, sand flying up into my face.

I crunch the sand with my hands and sit a moment. *Couldn't lose that bet, could You? I know, never put the Lord thy God to the test.* I stand and dust myself off. Serves me right. I spent twenty-five years waiting for the first one, and here I am expecting another in a week's time. Dewey doesn't even see *me* yet. He sees Penny, an overweight hair stylist who volunteers at an elementary school. He might call me Ruth, but he doesn't see Ruth yet.

I have faith, Father, but I just don't have enough strength, enough beauty.
But I know how to get it.
And some skinny-ass bitches gonna help me, starting tonight.

Eight

"Shouldn't you go see your doctor first?" Naomi says. "That's what they always say, you know. Always consult a physician before—"

"I know what they say, Naomi," I interrupt, munching on a carrot that tastes like every other carrot I've ever eaten. They ought to flavor carrots with chocolate or something. I mean, if they're so good for you, spice 'em up so more people will experience that goodness. I pull the phone cord as far as it will go, but I can't reach the refrigerator. It's a phone company conspiracy to keep overweight women from the fridge. I know I could buy a longer cord, but all it would do is get tangled up. I want to get at those low-fat, bite-sized Peppermint Patties I've been craving all day. I keep a bag of them in the freezer to at least give me the feeling that I'm eating ice cream. "I've lost over thirty pounds, I walk every day, my heart feels fine, and I'm even getting some tone to my legs. Can't y'all take me as a guest just to see how I'll do?"

I had called Tonya earlier, and she had no problems. "Just don't wear any Spandex, girl," she had said. "Wouldn't want you bustin' loose and killing my step aerobics class." Naomi, though, as Christian as she is, just cannot be seen at her health club with the likes of me.

"You know I have a very rigid and demanding workout, Ruth," Naomi says. I roll my eyes. Tonya says that Naomi's workouts are her substitute for sex and that they're punishing on her body because she's so hard up to get some. Naomi isn't much different from those holy men who whip their backs bloody. Her body is a temple for the Holy Spirit, and for the Holy Spirit alone, which is a damn shame because she is so much prettier than I'll ever be. "I don't want you to think that you have to keep up with me."

"I ain't gonna keep up with you at all," I say. "I'll just do what I can and get a good sweat goin'. And I promise to stay out of your way."

"Okay," she says finally. "We'll pick you up in a few."

I search my closets and find a sweat suit that hangs off me every which way. I look like a gray shar-pei. I don't have a sports bra, and I doubt they make one big enough for me anyway, so I put on my tightest bra, the one that pushes my titties up the most. Hopefully the men at the club will be looking at my titties instead of at my stomach and ass. Sweat socks, my walking shoes, a bottle of water, and a white towel wrapped around my neck later, and I am ready to get toned to the bone.

When Tonya and Naomi roll by in Tonya's Mustang, I see them laughing before the car even stops. "What you two laughin' at?"

"Shit, girl," Tonya says as she giggles, "put you on a big white head band and some wrist bands. Be *completely* accessorized."

"I bet you even have high striped tube socks under there," Naomi says.

"Forget you both." The tube socks aren't that high, and the red stripe looks nice. I check out their colorful Reebok outfits with their matching colorful shoes. Even the little balls on their footy socks match their outfits. "Y'all just jealous cuz I can make whatever I wear look good. And I bet I get more attention than both y'all combined tonight. Y'all cookie-cutter workout bitches, a dime a dozen. *I* am unique."

"You'll get attention all right—from the fat-ass men who come in to work out and look at *us*," Tonya says. She turns off Vine Street toward the county since there's no such thing as a health club in the 'hood. Just staying healthy is enough for most folks on Vine Street. "They'll come up to you and ask for phone numbers, all right—*our* phone numbers."

"Better watch what you say, Tonya," I say. "What goes around comes around."

"In your case, around and around and around," Tonya cracks. She turns to Naomi at a stop light. "They got three-wheeled exercise bikes for Ruth, don't they?"

"Ha ha," I say, and I look ahead at the bright neon lights of Jeffries Gym, a two-story building with lots of windows. Anyone can see you working out? That can't be good for my self-esteem. I'll have to stay away from the windows.

Before we go in, Naomi says, "Just take it easy, okay? If you get tired, sit down and rest."

"Hell, I'm tired already," I say. "Tired of both y'all's mouths. I'll be fine."

Half an hour later, I am not fine. I am soaked. My socks slosh in my shoes, and even my ears are sweating. My ass hurts and probably has blisters. Every joint in my body hurts. Even my eyelids hurt.

And all I'm doing is riding a damn stationary bike. That's all I've done the whole time: pedal a bike, drip sweat, and watch the little TV attached to the handlebars. Alone. Away from the windows and away from everybody else. No one has gotten on the bikes to either side of me, but I don't blame them. This bike ain't goin' nowhere, but my sweat be flyin'. I don't look around me and stare like so many others do. Folks who come here, like Tonya and Naomi, are obviously here to be seen with their little radios and headphones and expensive work-out shoes and clothes. I don't want to be seen. I just want to survive. Wish this bike would go someplace else.

I look at the odometer. I have just reached two miles. In half an hour. On a bicycle. I could have walked faster. I'm about to give up when I see Naomi wading through all the equipment, some of which reminds me of a trip to the gynecologist's with all the straps and stir-rups. She wipes her forehead with a towel that, of course, matches the blue of her sports bra and her tight, if-she-had-a-freckle-on-her-ass-you'd-see-it shorts. I start pedaling again, though my knees cuss me up and down as they go up and down.

"You doin' all right?" she says with a lazy smile.

Daa-em, girl looks like she had a workout orgasm. All I got are the wet spots. "I'm fine. This seat, though. This seat wasn't made for our people. You ought to talk to the management of this place about that. This seat was made for skinny-ass, anorexic white bitches."

She hits a few buttons on the little computer in front of me. I didn't mess with any of them mainly because I was afraid the bike would pedal itself faster. "Let's see, you've burned . . . a hundred calories." She frowns. "That can't be right. You've been out here for thirty minutes."

"I've only gone two miles," I say.

"Oh," she says, checking her fancy sports watch with a blue strap. "Time for my step class. Want to watch?"

"I'll just cruise around for a little while more thanks."

She presses a button on my little TV screen, and a room full of skinny-ass bitches, most of them white, fills the screen. Anorexia in motion. "You'll see me in there in a few minutes. That's just the intermediate class. What you'll see is the advanced class."

As soon as she skips away, I turn off the little TV. I don't want to see anything except the soft mattress of my bed. Wish I had me some headphones so I couldn't hear all the grunts and groans . . . that are coming mainly from me. Think my left knee's squeaking a high D. Maybe I'd do better if I was listening to some gospel. Maybe if I heard "No Ways Tired" I'd get a second wind. I laugh and stop pedaling. *"I Surrender All" of this nonsense, Lord, and hope there's still some "Balm in Gilead" because this is "More Than I Can Bear." You better "Wash Me Lord" because when I get off this thing, "It's Gonna Rain" some Ruth-sweat all over the—*

"Hey, Ruth!" Tonya shouts from somewhere close by.

I try to play it off as she bounces over. "Just taking a little rest." I stare my knees back to their pedaling, then look up at her.

"Guess who's here, girl?"

Oh, how I hate when she does this. "Just tell me."

"I'll give you a hint. He's thin, bony, and runs Antioch Church."

"Deacon Rutledge?"

She turns my head to the side. I see Jonas pulling down on a bar attached to some machine, and the bar is winning. "Your ex is here, girl."

"So?"

"So? Look at him."

"I'm lookin'. So?"

She leans in and whispers, "He's only working out with twenty pounds." She massages my shoulders. Oh-that-feels-so-nice-please-don't-stop—She stops. "Why don't you go over there and show him up?"

I point at my other shoulder. "Massage this one first." She only gives me one weak squeeze. "I'm late for step." She, too, turns on the little TV. "You can watch me if you want to."

I snap it off. "No, I don't want to watch you bouncing off the walls with a bunch of anorexic white bitches, and no, I do not want to outlift my ex-husband." I tap the bike. "Me and this here bike are doing just fine."

"Suit yourself." Tonya bounces away, and every man in the place watches her ass bounce by. I ought to tell 'em all that she's pushing thirty-seven . . . though the bitch still somehow looks like a teenager. *God, You are a funny creator.*

"One more mile," I whisper to my knees, "just one more mile and then we'll go soak someplace. And we'll even sleep in tomorrow. Promise."

"Still talking to yourself, I see," JonASS says behind me.

I don't answer and see the speedometer go up two miles per hour. My knees are burning in pain, but I ain't slowing down.

He gets on the bike next to me, hits a few buttons, and starts to pedal. "Looks like you've lost some weight, too. You look good, Ruth."

I am in no mood for this, so I concentrate on the odometer. There's another tenth of a mile. Nine-tenths to go.

"I joined here to *gain* weight, can you believe it?"

No. You joined so you could pick up stray men and slutty women skinnier than you. Two-tenths done . . . eight-tenths to go. My knees, thankfully, are now numb.

"But I can't seem to get anything to stick to me."

A truer statement has never been spoken. Jonas Borum, a living, breathing nonstick surface. The Teflon preacher.

"Guess you spoiled me with all that good cooking."

Seven-tenths to go. A compliment? All the man ever did was grub and get on, leaving me with the dishes and the leftovers.

"So how have you been?"

Six-tenths. I am flying! Daa-em, if he sits there all night, I might shrink down to Tonya's size. The "Hate Your Ex And Lose Weight Diet" works!

"I can understand your reluctance to talk to me."

No you can't. You never even understood me. Hell, you don't even understand yourself. Halfway there. This isn't so bad. All I needed was some practice. I am one with this bicycle. We are—

"I'm sure you've heard about my engagement."

Jesus, Your Daddy is playing with me again! Make Him and the asshole beside me stop! To a man or a woman? I almost ask, my speed increasing another mile per hour. Four-tenths to go. Keep your eyes on the prize, girl. Ignore the petty man to your left. He's already got a nice cozy room waiting for him in hell . . . but he's already engaged?

"We're planning to be married sometime in October, and, well, since you're the church organist, naturally we'd like you to play at our wedding."

I am numb from my head to my toes. Even my hair seems to freeze. He wants *me* to play at *his* wedding? I didn't even play at *our* wedding!

"I was against it, for obvious reasons, but Junie was insistent that you play."

Junie? Junie Pruett?

"She says that you can't have a wedding at Antioch without Ruth Childress at the organ."

Junie Pruett, second row, right side, always comes early and alone, never testifies, sings too loud, skinny as a switch, has to be at least fifty, sometimes uses a cane. *That* Junie Pruett?

"I don't expect you to give us an answer right now. I imagine it will take some prayer on your part."

Junie Pruett, who visited me in the hospital all those times, who brought over those wonderful casseroles when I was resting in bed, who has been complimenting me on my music after nearly every service for as long as I can remember? *Her?* I look at the odometer. I am two-tenths over my goal.

"If you could give us an answer by, oh, the end of September, we'd really appreciate it."

I slow and stop the pedals. My knees are dark gray splotches of sweat. I wipe streams of sweat from my face. I want to cuss him, I want to hurt him, I want to take his arm over my leg and snap it in two. Why aren't I reacting? I should be. No woman on earth would agree to this, and no amount of time on my knees should make a difference. I am *not* going to play at their wedding. I bet even Miss Manners would say that Jonas and his new bride-to-be are trippin'.

"So we'll hear from you?"

I nod, my eyes blank, and he leaves. What the hell just happened?

I struggle to the locker room and sit on a bench near Tonya's and Naomi's lockers. Some skinny-ass women go giggling into the shower . . . and I follow them. Fully clothed. They cover themselves, which isn't a hard thing to do when you're as thin as a dime, as I go to a corner, direct two shower nozzles toward the corner, and sit. They're gone before I can settle my sore ass onto the tiles. The water is only lukewarm, and I know my hair is gonna be for shit, but I don't care.

I should have said something. I should have told him that he had a lot of damn nerve asking me. I should have said that he and his senior citizen wife, who'll have to use a walker to get down the aisle, can call someone else. I should have cussed his ass for being such an ass.

I said nothing. I just kept pedaling. *What You tryin' to teach me here, Lord? This silence is not part of my culture! You made me; You know what I'm capable of. What'd You do, grab my tongue? How dare You! And here I am, my sweat mixing with these showers and runnin' down the drain while he's engaged to be married—*

I look up. Showers. Showers of blessing. I scratch at my hair with both hands, lumpy locks falling over my eyes. *How is what Jonas said to me a blessing, Lord? If I play at their wedding, I see a man I loved marrying someone else. I actually help them do it! That ain't no blessing . . . is it?*

Another skinny-ass bitch walks in, sees me, and scurries out. I smile. "Y'all still outweigh her, don't you?" I say to my legs.

Okay, let's say I don't play at the wedding. I am a proud woman. No one could blame me for not playing. I mean, even Naomi, who'll probably sit her skinny ass down near Your right hand, Naomi will agree with me. It's just not done, Lord! A man's ex-wife does not play the organ or even attend the wedding of her ex-husband! It shouldn't be done!

A trio of towel-wearing white women sticks their heads into the shower. "You all right?" one of them asks.

Just arguin' with God. Does no good. He always wins. "I'm all right." But I am soaked to the bone. I stand and have to grab at my sweatpants, holding them up by the drawstring. I slosh past them, smiling, and drip water all the way to Naomi and Tonya, who are freshening up at their lockers.

"You took a shower?" Tonya says.

"No. This is from my workout." With God, the ultimate personal trainer. I let my sweatpants drop to the floor with a loud thwack. "I know I lost at least twenty pounds. How 'bout y'all?" I peel off my sweatshirt and ring it out over a little drain in the floor.

"Ruth," Naomi hisses, "stop embarrassing us."

I act like I'm covering myself. "Oh, sorry." I sit on the bench and pull my sweatpants off over my shoes and wring them out as well. "Any of y'all got a change of clothes for me?"

"I don't believe this," Naomi says, slamming her locker shut. I am wide-eyed with wonder. I have never seen Naomi lose her temper before. I like it. Makes her more like the rest of us heathen.

"Well, believe this," I say, sliding off my shoes and emptying the water down the drain. "Good old Jonas just asked me to play the organ at him and Junie Pruett's wedding." I strip off each sock, wringing them together over the drain.

"Jonas and Junie Pruett are engaged?" Naomi asks.

"Yep."

"And he asked you to play at the wedding?" Tonya asks. I nod. "What a complete asshole!"

"And that's why you were in the shower?" Naomi asks, her voice changing back to nice, concerned Naomi. I liked Naomi the Bitch better. I don't need her pity.

I look down at my bra and bloomers. I think I'll leave them on, spare the world that particular sight. "I went into the shower to cool off. I'm cool now, almost cold." I rub my arms. "Can I borrow a towel?"

Naomi spins the dial on her combination lock and pulls out two towels, draping one over my shoulders, the other over my legs.

"You're not gonna do it, are you?" Tonya says.

"Don't know," I say.

"Don't know?" Tonya says. "Girl, there is only one answer to that question: no. No motherfuckin' way."

"I have till the end of the month to think about it," I say, drying the water out of my ears. I sniff a laugh. "I can't believe how calm I am, can you?"

Naomi sits next to me. "Normally, Ruth, I'd say to pray about it."

"Done that." Kept getting interrupted by skinny, naked white bitches, though.

"But this time . . . This time I agree with Tonya. It just isn't right, not only for him to ask you, but for you to actually consider doing it."

I shrug. "Maybe it ain't a question of right or wrong. Maybe it's a question of which decision is more right. Yeah, it's a shitty offer, but . . . Maybe I ought to do it anyway. It might give me some closure." I know "closure" and a bunch of other talk-show words. "Maybe seeing him end it with Junie will start something with me."

Naomi pats my hand. "Ruth, dear Ruth, believe me when I say this, but that's just pure bullshit."

My mouth drops to the floor, and for once, Tonya doesn't say a single thing. Naomi the Perfect just cursed! *Lord, I think that seat at Your right hand is vacant now.*

"Forgive me, Lord, but it's true," Naomi says. "Folks at that wedding will see a scared, defeated woman, a woman who's still under that man's power, a woman who has no kind of self-respect, a woman—"

"Who can really fuck up his wedding," I say with a smile.

Naomi starts to say something and stops. "No, Ruth," Naomi says real slow. "Oh, no, not that."

"Yes," Tonya says with a broad smile. "Yes! That's perfect! Damn, I wasn't gonna crash it before, but now I want to be in the front row! I mean, even if you don't fuck it up, it'll sure make those two paranoid. When the preacher gets to 'speak now or forever hold your peace,' all eyes will be on *you*, Ruth. Now, that's some motherfuckin' power."

I smile. "I'd have to practice what to say, of course."

"Of course," Tonya says.

"And I could sing 'Nobody Knows the Trouble I've Seen' instead of 'The Wedding Song,' huh?"

"You could," Tonya says. "Even though you can't sing . . . but that would be even better!"

"No, Ruth," Naomi says. "Doing that would be wrong."

"Wronger than him having the living gall to ask me or wronger than not playing at the church where I've been the organist for over twenty years?"

"Ruth, I—"

I put a finger on Naomi's lips. "No sense in discussing this now. I'm gonna do what you always say to do, Naomi: I'm gonna pray about it."

"But in this case—"

I press my finger harder on her lips. "And when the time comes, Naomi, I'm gonna make the decision all by myself." I pull my finger away. "Now, do you, or do you not, have a change of clothes for me?"

"No."

"Fine." I unroll the sweatpants and slide into them. "You know I ain't ever comin' back here." I squeeze into the sweatshirt and decide to carry my shoes and socks.

"Why not?" Tonya asks. "It looked like you were having a good workout."

"Oh, I had a good workout. Know I lost some weight, too. I just think I can get a better one somehow without my ass gettin' blisters. Thanks for inviting me, though."

"You invited yourself," Naomi says.

"Well, thanks for not saying no."

And all the way home I think about it: if I hadn't gone, I wouldn't have seen Jonas. Oh, I'm sure he would have asked me to play at his wedding eventually, but for that monkey of a man to ask me the same day I fall from the monkey bars? This *has* to be God's will.

I just hope I can figure out what to do about it.

I don't want to move even my pinkie toe in the morning, but I have to go for my walk and then go to Avery to flirt with Dewey through his son. I know that's twisted, warped, even foolish, but how else am I going to get to that man? I could invite Dewey to church, but I doubt he'd come. Everyone would remember his last visit. I could ask him out, but where to? What do redneck country boys do for fun that doesn't involve hay, killing a defenseless animal, or cars driving in circles? Maybe I can simply offer to baby-sit for him. I don't want to stalk this man by walking by his apartment every day, but I don't only want to see him for a haircut every three weeks either.

Lord, help me out here. If there have ever been two people who need each other, it's me and Dewey. Those children need me, and I need those children. I know that's selfish, but at this lonely time in my life, I have to be selfish. Just give me an opening today.

I prop myself up on my arms, swivel my hips out of bed, and stand. So far so good. Both knees cuss my ass, so I cuss 'em back. I take small steps to the bathroom and turn on the hot water. Cold water comes out for five minutes before I give up. So glad the cost of the hot water is included with the rent. I soap up a washcloth and scrub every place on me that has odor, dry off, and look at my hair. I have turned into a Rastafarian overnight.

Today is hat day.

I stuff as much hair as I can up under a visor, ease into some jeans and a blouse, and put on my walking shoes. They're still wet and will have to remain that way. I had them propped up against a fan all night, but Calhoun is just too humid. I eat a bagel for breakfast (no butter, no jelly, no cream cheese . . . no flavor), drink my first eight ounces of water (and only seven more thrilling glasses to go), and leave the apartment, my knees creaking more than the stairs.

I walk as fast as my body will allow, but I'm still an hour late to Avery. I enter the office to sign in with Mrs. Holland. "Dee isn't here today," she says.

"What?"

"Tee's here, but Dee isn't."

"Did you call home?" Mrs. Holland always calls every absent student's home. It's another one of her many perks.

"Not yet." She writes a number on a slip of paper. "Why don't you make this call for me?" She waves me around the counter. "Dial nine first."

I dial nine and pause before dialing the number because . . . Here's the opening! *That was quick, Lord!* I'm about to talk to Dewey, if he's there, and now I'm nervous. Should I be professional about this? I want him to know I'm concerned, but I don't want to gush. I close my eyes. *You with me, Lord?* I dial the rest of the number. After two rings, Dewey answers. "Hello?"

I take a breath. "Uh, hello, Mr. Baxter. This is Ruth Borum from Avery. How are you doing today?" Damn, I sound so white!

"I'm all right."

"I'm calling about Dee. Is he sick today?"

"No. He has a doctor's appointment."

"Will he be attending at all today?"

"I'm not sure. I'll try to get him there if the appointment ends early."

"Okay. Thank you, Mr. Baxter."

"Thanks for callin'." *Click.*

Oh, that went well. Dewey is a man of few words, and I'm a woman of too many.

I look over at Mrs. Holland, who is flipping through a file. "Says here that Dee has all his shots. Has to have 'em to be able to attend. Had a checkup less than a month ago." She closes the file. "But I'm not supposed to tell anybody that, so you didn't hear it from me."

"Um, Mrs. Holland, does that file say how old Dee's daddy is?"

She peeks inside. "Maybe."

"Well?"

She writes on a Post-It and sticks it to the counter. "You didn't hear it from me."

I look over and see a ... question mark. "You didn't write a number."

"How old you think he is?"

"Thirty, thirty-five."

"Close."

"Thirty-seven?"

She smiles, and my heart leaps a little. A ten-year age difference might be too much, but only three? I can handle that—"Thirty-four."

Six years. Hmm. Gonna have to think on this. The man needs me, if only to be more punctual. Those kids need me, him dressin' them like he does. Got to shine them little pennies. Dewey ain't too good lookin' for me. Just my size. And I bet he'll be potent. Bet he hasn't had none since before Dee was born. Whoo, a little bump in my hump, a bunch of buff in my stuff, will make me feel at least six years younger—and then we'll be the same age practically. Ain't that why older women go to younger men? Yes, Lord, I'm an older woman in need of a little fountain of youth. I need me someone to wax this booty till it shines . . . This big booty of mine, Dewey's gonna make it shine, this big booty of mine—

"Ruth? You still here, girl?"

"Sorry. Just doin' the math." Dag, my upper lip's sweatin'. I definitely still want this man. My upper lip ain't sweated in years.

Mrs. Holland giggles a little, then squints. "Wonder what kind of doctor's appointment that boy's having. You have any ideas?"

Plenty. "He's probably taking Dee to see a psychologist."

Mrs. Holland nods. "Yep. You're probably right. That's what white folks do when their kids aren't functioning properly."

Some black folks do it, too.

"Just hope they don't drug him up. All this ADD and ADHD and Ritalin is just too much, if you ask me. I have a regular pharmacy locked up in the drawers of my desk. Children just need more healthy, continuous, strong doses of love."

I agree. "Well, I best be gettin' to Mrs. King's class." I wince as I move around the counter.

"You walkin' like you need to be oiled, Ruthie Lee. You okay?"

"Took a bike ride last night, and I'm a little sore."

"Well, you go on home."

"I'd like to do nothing better, but I'm here to volunteer."

She shakes her head. "How can you today? Your 'class' isn't here. You were supposed to spend all day with that boy, right?"

"Right."

"He isn't here, so there's no reason for you to be here. I'll call you if he shows up, okay?"

"Okay." I sign out. "My knees thank you."

I pass by the playground and see girls jumping rope, doing double Dutch and singing out the rhymes that never go out of fashion:

> *"Cinderella, dressed in yella,*
> *went upstairs to kiss a fella,*
> *made a mistake*
> *and kissed a snake,*
> *how many kisses will it take?"*

I count along with them, and that little girl, who couldn't be more than six, is still counting it out as I walk away.

I could always jump me some rope; I mean, I only had to get an inch or two off the ground, right? Just because I was big didn't mean I didn't have the rhythm necessary to jump in. Oh, and I could turn me some rope, let me tell you. Used to go so fast the skinny girl at the other end would complain I was hurting her arms. Kind of took a little pride in trippin' up some of my scrawny friends. I got me some rope-turnin' arms, yes sir. And jumping rope ain't that hard. It doesn't require much skill, just timing.

And a high ceiling.

My apartment has a high ceiling.

I could jump me some rope to lose me some weight. I look back at all the skinny girls bouncing off the pavement. I could jump myself skinny.

But what about the folks below me? They are sure to complain once the plaster starts snowing down on them. But if they're not at home . . . like now . . .

Wait. Forty-year-old women do not jump rope. They don't even *think* of jumping rope. They watch. They say the rhymes. They count. They clap. They don't jump in. Their knees just can't take it; their flat feet just will not accept jumping up and down repeatedly. Jumping rope is just too childish.

But like a child, I take a bus out to the mall, go into one of those sporting goods stores, and walk out with a brand-new jump rope and a little jump rope workout guide that says I can burn ten calories a minute doing crossovers and ankle touches. That's three hundred calories every half hour.

That bike seat is never gonna bite my ass again.

I'm-a gonna jump my weight off, and if the folks downstairs don't like it, they'll have to kiss my . . . toned, muscular ass.

Nine

After changing into some maroon sweats and moving the couch, I center myself in the sitting room and start to jump, nice and slow, crunching my butt between swings of the rope. I have to change that "Cinderella" chant just a bit:

> "Cinderella, dressed in sweat pants,
> waited years to get some romance,
> made a mistake
> and kissed a snake.
> How many more years will it take?"

I fall out laughing on the couch and try to think back to something less depressing, and all I can remember is "Teddy Bear":

> "Teddy bear, teddy bear,
> turn all around, teddy bear.
> Teddy bear, teddy bear,
> touch the ground, teddy bear.
> Teddy bear, teddy bear,
> tie your shoes, teddy bear.
> Teddy bear, teddy bear,
> now how old are you,
> are you one, are you two . . ."

I only make it to seven—I wonder if I'll *ever* make it to forty—but I'm surprised I can still do this, and after five minutes, I'm feeling it all over. My knees still cuss and fuss, my calves are crying out, and my shoulders burn, but I'm still turning the rope, my stomach and titties bouncing up and down. Didn't have this tittie problem when I was little. I'm about to give myself a black eye. I'd give myself two if the left tittie was as big as the right tittie. I need to invest in a tight sports bra. And sweat? I closed all the windows and the blinds before I started, and the apartment is an oven. I may need to put some towels on the carpet to catch my drips. The workout guide, which has pictures of a Nubian princess with a six-pack stomach and come-hither thighs going through the moves, says I only have to jump five minutes a day, three times a week to "stay in shape." I think I can spare an hour a day every day and burn at least three thousand calories every week. And all it costs me is fifteen bucks while Tonya and Naomi spend that much every week at that gym. Don't need the fancy clothes. I can wear what I want and work out when I want (as long as the folks downstairs aren't around, that is). Don't even need any of them fancy machines. I am my own machine, thank you very much, and I don't need to wait in line to use me.

I'm taking a break in the kitchen with my second glass of water when the phone rings. Oh shit. I'm all stank, and Dewey's brought Dee back to school. "Hello?"

"Hello, Ruth? This is Junie Pruett. How are you this blessed day?"

I cover the mouthpiece of the phone and curse Jonas. He's so impatient for an answer that he's got his new wench calling. I uncover the mouthpiece. "I'm fine, Junie."

"That's good, that's good. Just wanted to call and ask you if you've decided yet."

I've had no time! "Jonas told me I had till the end of the month to decide, Junie. He only told me just last night."

"That can't be right. He told me he had talked to you last month about this."

He's lying to her already. But . . . They've been engaged for over a month? The ink on the final divorce decree was still drying! "Trust me, Junie. The first I heard about any of this was last night."

"Why would he tell me . . . Oh, well. So you haven't decided?"

"I'm still praying about it, Junie."

"I want it to be a beautiful wedding, Ruth, and with you playing, it will be beautiful. Every wedding I've been to at Antioch has been beautiful, and you played at them all." Except for one. Guess *my* wedding wasn't beautiful. "I just want my day to be so perfect."

I grip that phone like it's Jonas's scrawny neck. "I know you do, Junie."

"Is there anything I can do or say that will help you in your moment of decision?"

My moment of decision? This ain't no altar call! Well, I guess it sort of is. "Like I said, I'm praying—"

"Perhaps we should talk, you know, woman to woman. Are you free this afternoon?"

I check the clock. It's almost noon. I doubt Dee will be going back to Avery. My first visit to Dr. Holt took four hours. "I'm free now."

"You are? Wonderful."

After giving her directions to my apartment, I open all the windows to air out some of my funk, wash the few dishes in the sink, and make my bed. Then I wait by the window overlooking the street till I see Junie coming down Vine dressed like she is in church: black skirt, black hose, black-and-white-striped blouse, black purse. The kids at Antioch have nicknamed her The Virgin Widow, but I know that Junie has never been married. Maybe we should be talking outside on the porch. What would folks think about that? Do I want folks to know that Junie Pruett, my ex-husband's new bitch, and I are on speaking terms? Should I care? I sniff the air in the apartment, decide it's still too funky, and meet her on the porch.

"Thought we'd talk out here, day as nice as it is."

"Certainly," Junie says, sitting on the edge of one of the lawn chairs. I sit in a chair next to her, and we say absolutely nothing for three solid minutes. I don't start the conversation because I am only here to respond. Junie fumbles with her hands and looks out toward the street often, occasionally smiling my way.

"Well," she says finally, "let's talk."

"Yes."

"I'm sure you, um, have mixed feelings about all this. I certainly do." She has doubts? Good for her. "I have always considered you a friend, Ruth. I have so few friends, you know, and you've always been friendly to me, always spoken to me. I . . . I just . . . I just want us to remain friends. I don't want any of this to come between us."

"It already has."

She jumps a little. "Yes, I know, I know, and I can't say that I know how you feel—"

"No, you can't," I interrupt.

"Well, certainly, of course. But . . . Look at me, Ruth. I'm almost fifty-one, and . . . and I've never . . . I've never . . ."

"Been in love before?"

"Yes." She smiles at her hands. "Yes, that's right. I've never been in love before."

It's beginning to sound like an old, familiar script. Jonas finds the loneliest woman in the church, wins her heart, and makes her see a golden future that will surely tarnish at the first signs of a storm.

She looks at me with two sad eyes. "I don't know why I never . . . married. I had a few offers. I just wasn't . . . ready. I'm ready now, at least I think I am. Do you understand?"

I nod. I can't hate this woman. I can pity her, though. I rub the callus on my ring finger where my wedding band used to be before I put it in the offering plate. "Has Jonas told you why we divorced?"

"Oh, no. That's none of my business. That's between you and him."

And the other woman. And the other man. And the church board. And God. "Aren't you the least bit curious?"

"Well, um, no." She doesn't want anyone to burst her bubble. "I heard the rumors about it like everybody else."

This should be good. "What exactly did you hear?"

"Well, that you had become, um, mentally unbalanced." She shoots a quick look and a smile at me. "But I didn't believe those rumors. Anyone who can glorify God like you do at that organ can't be mentally unbalanced."

I smile. "Thank you."

"I just . . . figured it had something to do with . . ." She stops. "I want you to know that I cried for every one of your children, Ruth. I grieved, oh, how I grieved. I am not . . . able to have any children, and, in a way, I was hoping . . . maybe to be Aunt Junie or something. I don't know."

Aunt Junie? If I had any children, she'd be stepmama Junie in a few months. "It wasn't about the children, Junie."

"It wasn't? I was so sure. Why, then?"

Should I tell her? Jonas won't. Do I have a right to? Yes. Ex-wives are *supposed* to badmouth their ex-husbands. Is it a divine right? Probably not. *Lord, give me the words because I simply do not have them.* "I'd be wrong if I told you that the loss of those babies didn't affect our marriage. It did. But the marriage survived that." And a slutty church secretary. "I don't want to worry you about Jonas, but . . . Jonas is a very complex person."

"Oh, I know. He's so intelligent."

That isn't the word I'd use. Confused, controlling, contemptible—anything that begins with "con." I sigh. "Yes, he is an intelligent man, but that's not what I mean by complex. He has some . . . issues." This is not going well. Where are the rest of my talk-show words? "Junie, I don't want to be the one telling you any of this. You should be talking to Jonas about it."

"What issues? I want to fully know the man that I'm marrying."

I blink. Who wants to know everything? The less you know . . . will have you ending up like me. I stare her down. "How much do you want to know, Junie?" I ask in a deadly tone.

She literally shivers. "Um, well . . . I'm not so sure I want to know now. It's something bad?" I nod. "Something unmentionable?" I nod again. "Oh. Oh, my."

I hear Naomi's words echoing in my head and say them: "I'm sure he's asked the Lord for forgiveness, Junie, and I'm sure the Lord has forgiven him."

"Have you forgiven him, Ruth?" Junie asks in a shaky voice.

I have to be honest. "No." I watch two teenaged boys across the street throwing rocks at each other. Don't they have anything better to do? Where are their mamas?

"Why not? Why haven't you forgiven him, Ruth?"

I stand and go to the railing. "I don't know." I forgave him the first time, but that second time . . . no. I haven't forgiven him for that. But if I forgave Jonas for that ho, why can't I forgive him for the "other man"? Is it because I could have gotten AIDS? Or is it something else? *Lord, why haven't I forgiven Jonas for sleeping with that man? I know sin is sin, but come on now. Some have to be worse than others.*

"Well, if the Lord has forgiven him . . ." Junie says, and I cut her off with a stare. "I'm sure Jonas prayed about it. He is one praying man."

And a *preying* man, too. *Am I supposed to warn her here, God? Is this where I rescue her from Jonas?* "Yes, he's a *preying* man all right."

"Do you think the Lord has healed him of his affliction?"

A spotted leopard jumps into my head. "You'll have to ask Jonas about that."

She stands, her hands clasped in prayer in front of her. "Indeed, I will." She looks directly at me, but those sad eyes give her away. She won't ask him. She's afraid, like I was, to know the truth about Jonas. "Thank you for talking to me, Ruth. If I was in your position, I don't know if I could."

I'm constantly surprising myself these days, aren't I, Lord? I place my hands on hers. "Thank you for coming, Junie."

"Will you *please* play at my wedding?"

I release her hands. "I'll let you know, and sooner than the end of the month."

"Promise?"

"I promise."

"Thank you."

I watch her walk away and feel a peace that like the Bible says, passes all understanding. The things I could have said to her, maybe should have said to her, maybe even had a *duty* to say to her—I didn't say. God's angels are wrestling with my tongue again. Got the one scaring the shepherds and the one standing at the tomb all up inside my mouth.

As I open the door to my apartment, I hear the phone ringing and race to answer it. "Hello?"

"Ruthie Lee, Mrs. Holland."

"Is he there?"

"Dee or Mr. Baxter?"

Busted. "Dee, of course."

"Dee isn't here. Mr. Baxter just called to tell us that his mama would be picking up Tee today." Daa-em. That's one long first visit to the psychologist. I hope everything's all right. "She did it once or twice last year. Real nice lady."

I check the clock. If I shower quick and jog, I can make it to Avery by the last bell. I start shedding my clothes. "Can you, um, hold her there till I get there?"

"Hold her? I'm sure she's got things to do."

"Please. I just want to see her."

"You mean you want to meet her, right?"

"No."

"Ruthie Lee, I can't hold up someone's grandma just because you want to take a gander at her."

I'm stark naked in the kitchen. "Just do what you can."

I hang up and run to the bathroom . . . and get no hot water again. I fight the icicles stinging down on my body, giving myself a half-assed once-over with the soap. I put on a fashionable pair of khakis and a multicolored sweater and realize that I am still wearing my visor. I can't meet Dewey's mama looking like this!

I turn on all three of my curling irons and touch them repeatedly till one gets hot. What's up with that? They should all warm up at the same damn speed! I steam and press more than style my hair into something almost regal, stacking my hair as high as I can since I know the humidity outside is gonna knock it all down. And why am I wearing a sweater? It's at least eighty degrees outside!

I finger through my closet and come up with a refined white blouse, but it's long-sleeved. Don't I have any short-sleeved blouses? Why don't I—oh, yeah, I have reverse biceps. Always been trying to hide them. I pull on the long-sleeved blouse, tuck it in, roll up the sleeves to my elbows, and—I need a belt. I drop to the floor and start pulling out belts, looking for the brown belt that matches the flats— wait, I'll be walking, and those flats will kill my feet. My walking shoes! Damn, they're still wet. Shit!

I close my eyes and collapse against the closet door. What am I doing? I'm dressing up for a woman who I'm really only going to look at, not meet. Why am I killing myself like this? I look at the clock on my nightstand. I have ten minutes to get there, and this morning it took me close to thirty. I'll never make it in time.

But I've got to try.

I put on the flats and go beltless out the door, walking as fast as my knees will allow. I cut over to Sixteenth, though taking Fourteenth would be quicker, just on the off chance that—

I stop at the corner of Sixteenth and Vine. Dewey's truck is parked in front of the last apartment to the right. He's home? What's he doing home? My heart flutters. Maybe Dee had a bad time at the psychologist's. Maybe they've already put Dee on medication. That poor boy! I was a zombie that first day and couldn't function for at least two more days. Should I say hello or keep on?

Another truck, a blue, dusty, dented something from *way* back in the day, turns into the lot and parks beside Dewey's truck. I see a tiny woman wearing a blue flannel shirt and jeans get out, and a moment later I see Tee racing around the back of the truck. So that's Nanna. Sturdy little thing. Spry, even. She lifts Tee off the ground all in one motion and carries her to the door.

I race-walk closer and am almost even with Dewey's door when the door opens. Dewey walks out shushing everybody, his finger to his lips. Dee's asleep. Good. Boy's probably bushed. Dewey holds the door for them, they enter—

And Dewey looks right at me. He isn't smiling. He isn't frowning. He's just . . . looking.

I look down at the sidewalk and see that I'm not moving anymore. Why have I stopped? I cannot play this off by looking for something on the sidewalk. I look up, smile, and wave.

At a closed door.

Ten

I can't help thinking about the significance of that closed door as I tear into a greasy fish sandwich from Dude's (where they have oil in the vats as old as me) and gulp a twenty-ounce root beer. I know I shouldn't be eating anything greasy or drinking so much sugar, but I can't be properly depressed on an empty stomach. If I had a half gallon of rocky road ice cream, I could be depressed in style.

I just can't get that scene out of my mind. I know Dewey saw me. He had to. There isn't anything else to look at on the other side of Sixteenth except for a vacant lot full of broken bottles and the remains of a house. It's possible that he saw me but didn't recognize me with my hair up, but . . . I should have waved sooner, maybe even should have crossed the street to speak to him. No, that would have been too obvious.

Lord, how am I gonna get to know this man?

I dial Tonya since she knows white men better than Naomi does. "Hey, girl," she says. "What you up to?"

"Nothing. You busy?"

"Not as busy as I want to be."

Girl always has sex on the brain. "No firemen tonight?"

"No," she says with a pout. "They're all on call."

"All? As in more than two?"

"Yes."

I will never understand this child. "Listen, I need your advice."

"Why don't you come over? I'll get Naomi over here, and we can pop some popcorn, play some cards."

I start to salivate. "Will the popcorn be buttered?"

"It always is."

Damn. I've already set myself back a week with the fish sandwich. "I shouldn't."

"Come on. The walk over will work it off before you get here."

Gee thanks. Feels like I've walked to West Virginia and back already today. I hang up and change for the fourth time into some ratty jeans and a T-shirt. They'll give me shit for my outfit, but I'm used to it. I'm sure they have a special section in their closets for "popcorn-eating and card-playing clothes."

I will myself five blocks down Vine and climb Tonya's steps. Both she and Naomi got nice old places, red-brick four-squares built back when Vine Street was a beautiful place. Wide porches, porch swings, plants hanging everywhere, pansies spilling out of box planters, even green strips of lawn out front dotted with more pansies. I tap on Tonya's screen door and enter, the aroma of popcorn drawing me to the kitchen where I find Tonya standing in front of the microwave.

"Naomi here yet?"

"No." She eyes me up and down.

"Don't you say a damn thing."

"I wasn't going to say anything."

"Yes you were."

The microwave beeps. "No I wasn't." She takes out a bag of popcorn and shakes it. "Not this second anyway." She pours it into a bowl. "I plan to wait till Naomi gets here to tell you how tacky you look. I'll have to close all the drapes."

"Thanks a lot. But till she gets here, I need your advice."

"On what?"

"On men." She smiles like I knew she would. "On white men."

She blinks at me, and the smile disappears. "You interested in a white man, Ruth?"

"Yes, but you can't tell Naomi."

"Why not?"

I lean against the counter. "You know how she feels about you messin' with them, and she acts like she's my mama half the time, so I just don't want her to know."

She hops up on the counter and sits Indian style. *Lord, if I could do that again, I wouldn't need to have this talk with one of Your fallen angels.* "What do you want to know?"

"Everything you can tell me."

"Everything?"

"Everything."

"Are you sure?"

"Positive."

She points at a portable phone. "Gimme that."

I hand it to her, and she hits redial. "Naomi, girl, I'm PMS-ing like a bitch. Tonight isn't a good night . . . Yeah, I already called Ruth . . . I'll be all right. See you tomorrow." She hands the phone to me. "Okay, let's get started."

"You just lied to your best friend!"

She shrugs. "I do it all the time. That's what best friends are for, girl. C'mon, let's get cozy."

I follow her into this interesting little room that has no windows, a low ceiling, and a love seat. She calls it her "necking room." A man cannot escape her in this room, and I almost check the love seat for stains as I sit down next to her, the bowl of popcorn between us.

"So who is this man, Ruth?"

"Someone I met."

"He got a name?"

I wince. "Dewey."

She laughs. "Dewey? He got two brothers named Louie and Huey?"

"Not that I know of."

"Sounds like a real country boy."

"He is."

"He's big, then."

"Yep."

"Big feet and hands?"

I know where she's going with this. "Let's talk about the sex part later. I just want to know how to get him to notice me."

"Where's he work?"

"What has that got—"

"I am the expert here," she interrupts. "Now, where does he work?"

"Calhoun Steel."

She grabs a handful of popcorn and shakes it in her hand like dice. "Doin' what?"

"Loading and unloading trains."

"Yeah? Is he ripped?"

"He's strong. Built like an ox. But what does—"

"Shh," she says. "I know a few guys who work at Calhoun Steel, and they will do anything for me."

"Huh?"

"All I have to do is to tell one of *my* guys to tell *your* guy—"

"That is so childish."

She tosses a few pieces of popcorn into her mouth. "But it works. Men never outgrow that junior high shit. They hear a lady is interested in them, and they jump."

Will Dewey jump? I can't see that man getting off the ground. "What if he don't jump?"

"You don't think Dewey will jump?"

"No."

"Well, that means he ain't married. You don't *ever* want one of those."

This child amazes me. She can be so smart sometimes. "How you know Dewey ain't married?"

"Cuz married men jump the highest, the farthest, the fastest, that's why. They tired of the same old pussy, want something fresh."

"You nasty."

"Just keepin' it real, girlfriend," she says, waving one hand and snapping her fingers.

"Real nasty." I eat a single piece of popcorn, letting that buttery taste roll around my mouth till the piece dissolves. I will eat these one at a time . . . nah. This shit tastes too good. I stuff my face full and talk while I'm chewing. "Far as I know, Dewey has never been married, but he has two kids with some sister he had been kickin' it with."

"Well, that's in your favor, Ruth. He already has a hunger for dark meat."

"Why you gotta put it that way? Maybe he loved her."

"He didn't marry her, did he?"

"No." I wonder what the story is there? He seems like a sweet, sensitive man. "But lots of folks in love ain't married." And lots of married folks ain't in love. "Anyway, he's now raising these two children by himself."

"Cute kids?"

"The cutest."

"And you want in."

"I want in."

"You want to kick it with a country-ass white man who likes chocolate women and has two Oreo kids."

The way she puts things! "Yes. And they ain't Oreos. They look just like me, freckles and all."

"Two little pennies, huh?"

"Yes." Big Penny and her little pennies. I like the sound of that.

She flicks a piece of popcorn onto the couch. "You ain't just after some dick?"

I blush again. "No." She stares at me. "Really." She sucks her teeth. "Okay, okay. Some dick would be nice, but I want more than that."

"More than some dick?" I nod. "Oh." She munches on a handful of popcorn. "Then, this is serious."

"Yes."

"How old is he?"

I look away. "Thirty-four."

"A younger man?" She whistles. "Daa-em. You tryin' to take my action?"

"No." I turn back. "I just want some action with this one man, Tonya. Just him."

She whistles again. "I don't think I can help you, Ruth."

"What you mean? You claim to know everything about white men."

"I do, but not when it comes to kids." She pulls her knees to her chest. "I ain't goin' down that road ever."

"Why not?"

She kicks out her legs and rubs her hands down her chest and sides. "And ruin this? Uh-uh, honey. I want to be this size for as long as I can." I growl. "No offense."

"Offense taken." I sigh. "Well, tell me what you *do* know."

She smiles that wicked smile of hers, her tongue lightly licking her bottom lip. "I know how to satisfy them, know how to make them beg for more, know how to make them want me more than anything or anyone they've ever wanted."

"That's what I want, too, but I ain't got the body you been blessed with."

"Maybe he likes big women. You know what his ex-girlfriend looks like?"

From Dee's drawing, she looks right pretty. "No, but she ain't his ex-girlfriend no more. She died a few months back."

Tonya doesn't move a muscle for the longest time. "You're in love with a country-ass, thirty-four-year-old widower?"

"You can't be a widower if you weren't married, Tonya."

"Same thing." She crunches on some popcorn. "Damn, girl, you really know how to pick 'em."

"Thanks."

"Bisexual preacher, then widowed, younger, redneck father of two mixed kids. There ain't a talk show on earth that couldn't have a show devoted just to you."

I start to get up. "If you ain't gonna help—"

"Hold on, now, girl. I have an idea."

"What?"

"You could invite him to church with his kids."

I could just bring the kids, but . . . "Remember that white man who came in a while back? That was one of the few services you've been to lately."

"Remember him? Man had absolutely no fashion sense. He wore tube socks, for God's sake. And if his suit jacket had been any shorter, you know we'd have seen us some butt crack." She laughs and looks at me, and I ain't laughing. "Oh shit! *That* was Dewey?" I nod. She smiles. "You two were made for each other. Neither one of you can dress yourselves for shit, but maybe if you dressed him and he dressed you?" I throw a handful of popcorn at her. "I have just *got* to get you this hookup, Ruth. What you done so far to get him?"

I tell her about the haircuts and my volunteering at Avery, and she nods often. "I just ain't gettin' anywhere with the daddy, though."

"You've made a good start, girl. Gettin' the kids to love you first seems like a good plan. I'd never do it, but it could work. You ain't gonna be the baby-sitter he messes with, are you?"

"No."

"Heard that can work. I know, you could cook for him."

"Out of the blue? 'Scuse me, Mr. Baxter, but here's your dinner."

"Not like that. He's new to the neighborhood, right?"

"Pretty new."

"You'll just be the Welcome Wagon."

"I live five blocks away from him. We ain't exactly neighbors." She rolls her neck. "Do he know that?"

"No." This might work. "No, he doesn't. But what do I fix?"

"For a white man? You fix meat and potatoes and more meat and potatoes with a side order of meat and potatoes and for dessert—"

"More meat and potatoes, right?"

"Right. Don't make him no casserole with noodles, and don't make him anything he can't pronounce or identify. Just give him a slab of steak medium rare and a pile of fried potatoes and onions."

I can do this. I could cook it up tomorrow after my shift at Diana's and take it over tomorrow night. But what if Nanna's already done the cooking? "I don't know. His mama might be cooking for him." I tell her about Dee's problems.

"That's so sad. Maybe you should make some cookies or a cake. I know, make him one of your famous pound cakes."

"I would, but the oven at my place don't cook 'em even. Half of it is cooked, and the other half is gooey."

"Cook it in my oven, then." She jumps up. "And I probably got everything you need already here, girl."

"You got flour, eggs, milk, sugar, sour cream, three sticks of real butter, vanilla, and lemon extract?"

"Yeah."

She's joking. "You even got a cake pan, a sifter, and a mixer?"

"Yeah."

Say what? "You don't bake, Tonya. Hell, you barely cook."

"I know. I just want folks to *think* I do. Gotta put *something* in my cupboards so folks don't talk bad about me." She pulls me off the couch. "Besides, I've always wanted your recipe."

"Ain't no recipe. I just make the cake."

"I'll take notes, then."

So, I make a pound cake with Tonya writing everything down that I let her see. This is, after all, *my* recipe. No skinny-bitch heifer gonna steal the recipe to my trademark cake. While the butter gets soft in a large bowl on top of the warming stove, I sift the flour into one bowl, then separate the whites from the yolks into a second bowl, dropping the yolks into bowl number one.

"Why you do that?"

"I just do. Now be quiet and write."

"Put yellow parts on flour," she says as she writes.

"They're called yolks."

"Whatever."

I add the sugar and the sour cream (and a couple drips of milk

Tonya can't possibly see) to the second bowl and mix that bowl till it's creamy.

"How much milk did you add?"

"I don't know."

"C'mon, Ruth."

"Really. I don't know. The spirit just moves me."

"Estimate."

"A couple drips." I add the softened butter to bowl number one and mix it up. This is the longest, messiest step, and Tonya steps back.

"Why not mix it all together in one bowl?"

I turn off the mixer. "You like my pound cakes?"

"Yes, they're delicious."

"Then, don't criticize the process."

"Dag, I was just sayin'."

I pour bowl number two into bowl number one and add a few dabs of vanilla and lemon extract into the mix. Tonya actually counts the number of drops out loud. Then I blend it all together till it's smooth.

"That's it?"

"What do you mean, that's it?"

"It only took you ten minutes."

"So?"

"I thought you spent all day making those."

I hold up a beater and flick a gob of batter at her. "I make at least two every time I bake, girl."

"Still, that'd only be twenty minutes."

"Cookin' ain't all that hard if you know what to do."

I pour the batter into the round cake pan and smooth out the top, putting it into the oven at three hundred fifty degrees for ninety minutes.

"Why so long?" she asks.

"I don't know. Grandma always cooked it that long back in the day."

"Cook for ninety minutes cuz Ruth's grandma says so," Tonya says as she writes.

We return to the necking room. "I know you've had your share of white men, Tonya, but did you ever have any feelings for a white man?"

"Once, but that was a long time ago."

"The married man?"

She nods. "The man was fine, kind, and I thought he was mine. I never met a more decent person."

"How could he be decent? He cheated on his wife."

"Except for that, he was decent. He sent me flowers, called me at all hours, visited whenever he could get away from his wench of a wife. We never went out, of course, so we spent—"

"Why didn't you go out?"

"He was married, girl."

"So it wasn't because he was white and you were black?"

"No."

"You sure?"

"Yeah, I'm sure."

I don't know if I believe her. "Who ended it?"

"I did."

I don't believe her for a second. She was so broken up about the whole thing, her depression lasting a week. I had made a pound cake for her then, too, and the bitch ate the whole thing and still didn't gain an ounce. "That's what you told us, Tonya, but that ain't the truth."

She sighs. "He's the one who ended it, but don't tell Naomi. I got back into her good graces when I told her that I broke it off."

"*How* did he end it?"

"He just came over one last time and gave me a goodbye fuck. Said he had decided to try to make his marriage work, no hard feelings, I'll have a bunch of nice memories, see you around. After that I swore that I'd never mess with another married man, and I haven't." She frowns. "Just wish there were more men my age that didn't have any baggage, physical or otherwise. Last week at the bowling alley, this man who had to be at least sixty started hitting on me, tried to buy me a beer, asked me for my number."

Tonya and Naomi bowl in a league every Wednesday night, and they say even the holy bowlers flirt with them, their holy wives sitting right there watching. "What'd you do?"

"Told his ass off, and I'm glad I did. Naomi tells me he has *sixteen* children, ten of them older than me. The youngest four are, get this, two, four, five, and seven years old, and each one of them has a different mama." She stands and stretches. "Yeah, that bowling alley is a regular meat market. You ought to come out some time and see it for yourself."

"I don't bowl."

"Judging from our team scores, neither do we. It's just for fun, girl. Some of the folks are serious, but we ain't. We just there to tease and please."

"I thought Naomi was a good bowler."

"She is, but the rest of us ain't. Shoot, I bet you could bowl better than at least two of our team members. I should add you to our team."

I shake my head. "I'd only embarrass y'all." But I've never really been to a meat—or did she mean "meet"?—market like that. It'd be nice to get some attention. "But I *will* come to watch."

"Good. I'll pick you up at five-thirty tomorrow."

After ninety minutes, I open the oven and see a beautiful, brown pound cake. "Girl," I say, "it's late, and I know I'll have a lot of hair to cut tomorrow. Let this cool off overnight, then dump it carefully on a tray or something flat in the morning. Wrap it up tight in aluminum foil and bring it with you when you pick me up."

"You want to drop it by his place before we go to the alley?"

"Yeah. And don't bring Naomi."

"Okay. But you're just going to drop it off and say 'bye'?"

"What's wrong with that?"

She crosses her eyes. "Nothin'. It just ain't very romantic."

She's right. "How do I make it romantic?"

"Put a note in with it."

"I hardly know the man."

She takes a pad of paper and a pen from a drawer. "If you don't write it, I will."

"Gimme them," I say, and I write Dewey a note:

Mr. Baxter,
    I hope you enjoy the cake, and I hope Dee is doing okay. Welcome to the neighborhood.
                                                    Ruth Borum

Tonya grabs it from me and sucks her teeth. "You about as romantic as a fish, Ruth." She hands it back. "Put some more life in this."

I tear off another piece of paper and write:

Mr. Baxter,
    I made this cake for you. I hope Dee is doing okay. Welcome to the neighborhood.
                                                    Ruth Borum

I hand it to Tonya, and she sucks her teeth again. "C'mon, girl. You can do better than this."

I really don't know how. "Well, what would *you* write?"

She raises her eyebrows and writes for almost a minute. "Something like this." I take the notepad, and my eyes pop out:

Dewey,

    I made this cake <u>especially</u> for you. I hope you enjoy eating it as much as I enjoyed making it. I hope Dee is well enough to attend Avery soon, because I <u>really</u> miss him. If there's *anything* I can <u>ever</u> do for you or your family, <u>please</u> give me a call (555-6467).

Ruth

"I can't be givin' out my number, Tonya!"

"How else you expect him to call you?"

True. I want that. "And why'd you underline so much?"

"So I could write it louder."

I have to admit that it's a nice letter. It says what I want to say and says it better than I can say it. "You don't think it's too pushy?"

"I don't think it's pushy enough. We should put a few drops of perfume on it."

"Might ruin the taste of the cake."

"Might, might not. Least he'd know you want more than just to feed him."

I don't give her another objection and rewrite Tonya's letter in my own somewhat sloppy handwriting. "Just put it in an envelope first, okay? The cake might be moist, and the words could get smudged." I feel a tingling inside, like I've already made contact with Dewey. "I better be going. Thanks for everything."

"Any time."

When I get home, I pick up that jump rope to rid myself of the fish, the root beer, and the popcorn. While I'm jumping, as softly as I can on a square of carpet, I remember one of those hand-clapping chants and whisper it loud:

    "Went downtown to see James Brown,
    he gave me a nickel, I bought me a pickle,
    the pickle was sour, so I bought me a flower,

the flower went dead, and this is what he said:
peanut butter, peanut butter, peanut butter, peanut butter . . ."

I collapse onto the couch, giggling like the little girl I'm becoming. *Lord, it feels nice to giggle again.*

Eleven

The next day, I stand in one place, cut hair, and get some badly needed rest for my knees and my forty-year-old body. I can't act like a child every day. What was I thinking? In the past forty-eight hours, I've tried to cross the monkey bars, ridden a bicycle, jumped rope, and walked several miles. I need a day off *at* work.

As soon as I'm done with my first customer, I call Avery to check on Dee, and Mrs. Holland says that he isn't there again. I resist the urge to call Dewey (I don't want to wake Dee), and I am so lost in thought about the man who'll be eating my cake tonight that I almost leave Mrs. Blackwood's perm in too long. Heifer probably wouldn't have noticed anyway. She's about bald as it is.

"Girl, you look like you're walking in a dream today," Diana says.

"Just had a busy day yesterday." But I am sort of walking in a dream, and maybe this time the dream will have a happy ending.

Diana sends me home early since we're not as busy as usual. I really think it's because I sing "Understand It Better By and By" all day long, and she just does *not* like good gospel music sung by someone who *can't* sing. I rush home to get ready and stare at the clothes in my closet. What do you wear to a bowling alley if you're only watching? Do I dress up? Folks shouldn't be looking at me. They should be looking at the pins. I put on some jeans and a blue sweatshirt and wait on the porch. I can't wait to see Dewey's face up close again. I can't wait to see those children again. I can't wait to see Dewey smile again. I can't wait to see—

Then I see Tonya and *Naomi* show up in *Naomi's* car! It was just supposed to be me and Tonya! How we gonna pull this off without Naomi figuring it out?

"Hi y'all," I say as I get in. "Got the cake, Tonya?"

"Yes."

"Who's the cake for?" Naomi says.

Does Naomi already know? "Just for some new folks in the neighborhood," I say.

Naomi turns to Tonya. "You cooked it last night?"

Tonya looks at me. "Yeah."

"I thought you were PMS-ing," Naomi says.

"Oh, yeah," Tonya says. "I needed something to take my mind off it, so I called Ruth. She talked me through it, and it came out as if Ruth made it herself." Tonya is the best liar I know.

"That's so nice of you two."

So Naomi doesn't know. I can relax. I direct her to Sixteenth Street. "Pull in over there."

She pulls in to the parking lot, but I don't see Dewey's truck. Is he even here? Then I see Nanna's truck. Okay, Dewey's out, and Nanna's in. He's probably at work catching up on his hours. I'll just give her the cake and go.

"This isn't your neighborhood, girl," Naomi says.

Tonya hands me the cake through her window after I get out. "I'll only be a minute."

"Hurry," Naomi says. "I don't want to be late for shadow bowling."

"For what?"

"Practice, Ruth. We get fifteen minutes of practice."

"Oh."

I take only one step toward that apartment door and get nervous. Why? I'm just dropping off a cake. That's all. I did it all the time as the preacher's wife. No sweat. Then, why are my hands sweating little rivers? The light's on in the window of Dewey's apartment, so maybe I can even see Dee and Tee. I knock, and Nanna opens the door.

"Hi, I'm Ruth, and I just wanted to welcome y'all to the neighborhood with this cake." That sounded so . . . lame.

I hand her the cake, and she smiles, the many wrinkles in her face disappearing. Nanna has a child's face when she smiles. Dewey has her pointy nose, brown eyes, and light brown hair, only her head is half as big as his. "That's so nice of you," she says with the same country twang. She acts like she's weighing the cake. "This is a real pound cake, ain't it?"

"Yes, ma'am."

"You make it with sour cream?"

"Yes, ma'am."

"That's the way. Won't you come in?"

Naomi chooses this moment to blow the horn. "I'd love to, but my friends are waiting. How's Dee doing?" Nanna squints. "Oh, I volunteer at Avery and work with him two days a week. Is he feeling any better?"

She steps out of the doorway and closes the door behind her. "No, he ain't better at all."

BEEP. I turn to the car and mouth "in a minute." I turn back to Nanna. "Is it the medicine?"

"Yep. It's wearing his little body out. All he wants to do is sleep."

BEEP. Naomi, you wench! "Could you tell Dee, next time he's awake, that Penny said hello?" Nanna blinks. "That's my nickname."

"I'll tell him."

"Oh, and say hello to Tee, too. Is she behaving any better in school?"

"No. The child is an absolute terror. Four more fish today."

"Four more fish?"

Nanna blinks her eyes rapidly. "The child likes to feed the fish when they ain't supposed to be fed."

I want to laugh, but I don't. BEEP. "I better go."

"Surely. You take care, and thanks for the cake."

"You're welcome."

Naomi beeps one more time as I'm getting in the car, doesn't say a word to me, and drives like a bat out of hell to the bowling alley. Tonya turns to me and smiles, but she doesn't say anything either. We wouldn't want to piss off Naomi any more because she's late for shadow bowling.

After cussing the management of Mountainside Lanes for having too few parking spaces, Naomi parks illegally in front of a dumpster, gets out, snatches her bowling bag from the floor behind her seat, and runs to the side door of the alley.

"Girl takes her bowling seriously," I say, following Tonya to the door.

"Nah. All the girl needs is a thick, stiff dick." I'm beginning to agree with Tonya. Naomi is just too tightly wound sometimes. A good stiff dick might loosen her up. "Was that Dewey's mama at the door?"

"Yeah. She's nice."

"She only about four feet tall. Dewey's daddy must have been a giant."

Inside Mountainside Lanes, the noise is deafening, the air thick with cigarette and cigar smoke, the tables loaded with pitchers of beer and plastic cups, every one of the forty lanes swarming with people, balls flying down the lanes, pins crashing. There's even a certain rhythm to the noise, like a drummer is playing boom-ditty-ditty-ditty-CRASH continuously. Tonya stops me at lane thirty-four where we find us an empty table. I immediately notice that the folks from lanes one to twenty are white, and the folks from lanes twenty-five to forty are black. Segregation, Calhoun style.

"This the black bowling league, huh?" I say to Tonya as she puts on her bowling shoes.

"Uh-huh. A few sisters bowl in the other league, but not many."

While Naomi rolls a few practice balls, Tonya, who wears the tightest little miniskirt and T-shirt, introduces me to her team. "We're called NYTBM," she says, "and it don't stand for 'naughty young thing bowel movement,' though we bowl like it sometimes. We naughty, we pretty young, and sometimes the pins is constipated. NYTBM is just our initials." She points at a very tall black woman rolling a practice ball. "That's Yvonne. She bowls all right if she don't fall down."

"She falls down?" I didn't think bowling was a dangerous sport.

"Least once a night. She says the floor is too slippery."

"Is it?"

"Sometimes it's too oily, but not that oily. She just tall and clumsy." She points at an older black man, short, almost stumpy, with big arms and flecks of gray at his temples, waiting for his turn to bowl. "That's Bill. Believe it or not, he's married to Yvonne, and they have six children all her size. If he's on his game, and he ain't on most nights, we have a chance." She looks around. "Mike ain't here again? If he do show, he'll either be drunk or high or both. Boy barely breaks a hundred. That's why we need you to bowl with us, Ruth. When he don't show, we have to use his shitty average *minus* ten pins. I *know* you can bowl higher than a ninety."

"I've never bowled before." At an all-night bowling party for the teenagers at Antioch years ago, I had contented myself merely with keeping score back when you could keep score. They got these computers doing it now.

"It ain't hard. Just roll it down the middle. We could put you on as a substitute, and whenever Mike don't show, you get to bowl."

"Like tonight?"

"Why not?"

"I'd rather watch tonight if you don't mind." I see lots of folks lined up to roll practice balls now. "Ain't you gonna practice?"

She smiles and stretches, putting her head on one knee. "And miss my grand entrance?"

Some unintelligible voice crackles from the loudspeakers, and the bowling alley becomes silent. Blue screens above the lanes flicker on, and in less than a minute, the balls start flying down the lanes again.

Tonya bowls first for her team, and she is definitely a distraction. She picks up her ball and shines it with a towel so slowly, smiling that little smile of hers with her tongue on her lower lip. She is so nasty. She takes up her position and wiggles a long time before stepping toward the pins and releasing the ball. While the ball is rolling, she poses, sticking her ass out as far as is legally allowed in public in this state. I check the men all around us, and they are *all* staring. She only knocks down five pins, but I know she knocked out quite a few more eyes.

For the next half hour, I watch some of the most anal behavior I have ever seen in my life. Bowlers are a funny breed: they shine their already shiny balls, they tighten their already tied shoes, they blow on their fingers, they squat and do strange exercises, they talk to the ball, they talk to the pins, they sometimes use a different ball to pick up a spare, they cuss the floor, they cuss their scores, they cuss their shoes, they cuss the ceiling. One elderly gentleman even cusses his beer.

I focus on a woman about my size a few lanes down to see how she does it. She picks up her ball with both hands and inserts her fingers into the holes. She takes a deep breath and brings the ball up to her chest. She kicks out her right foot and takes a long step, then pitter-pats toward the pins before hurling her ball—into the gutter. She looks good, though. Hell, even I could do that.

NYTBM loses the first game by over a hundred pins, and Naomi won't speak to anyone, not even me. She had a nice game but kept fussin' because she didn't get any strikes. Tonya rolls her eyes a lot at Naomi, and the other team makes fun of Bill whenever he gets a split, which is right often. Mike, who showed up just in time to take his turn, bowled a measly eighty-seven but smiled and hooted like he had bowled a good game, giving and getting dap from anyone he could reach, including me.

"We suck, don't we?" Tonya asks as she reties her shoes for the tenth time. I think she does it so she can stick out her ass between turns.

"Yeah," I say. "The BM fits. Y'all take a rest break now?"

"You kiddin'? As soon as the scores are cleared, we start all over again."

During the second game, which is a replay of the first with NYTBM falling way behind, I smell beer breath at my ear and turn. A wheezy, wrinkled man with gold-rimmed teeth and Coke-bottle glasses smiles at me. "Why ain't you bowlin'?" he says as he sways.

Lord Jesus, an eighty-year-old, drunk, blind man is hittin' on me. The meat at this meat market is gettin' rancid. "I just came to watch."

He sits next to me, his knee getting cozy with mine under the table. "I haven't seen you here before."

I shift my chair away from him, his stank breath, and his nasty knee. "This is my first time."

He reaches over and squeezes my arm. "This feels like an arm just *full* of strikes." He releases my arm. "Bet you could *break* you some pins."

Is that a compliment? "Oh, I don't know."

Tonya comes to my rescue. "Reverend Moore?" My eyes pop. This geezer is the good Reverend Henry Moore? "Reverend Moore, your wife is *that* way."

Reverend Moore looks in the direction of Tonya's hand, then focuses on Tonya's titties. "I know that." He turns back to me. "Just getting acquainted with your friend here."

"Isn't it your turn to bowl, Reverend?" Tonya says.

He looks down the lanes. "It certainly is." He stands and shuffles away.

"That was Reverend Moore, Reverend Henry Moore from East Baptist?" I ask.

"Scary, huh?"

"But he all shrunk now." I see Jonas and his prune Junie in my mind ten years into the future and shudder.

"He thinks he's still the ladies' man. He hits on anyone new."

"I'm so flattered."

She laughs. "You havin' fun?"

"Not really."

"That's why you should be bowlin'." She hands me a few dollars. "Go get us some drinks, and make sure you get the bowler's discount."

I weave through the tables past the main desk to the "white" side of the bowling alley where the snack bar is. Figures it'd be on their side. While I'm waiting in line, I look at all the white men lookin' all serious as they bowl. They high-five each other instead of giving dap, wear these wrist-guard things, and make the meanest faces. Dag, y'all, it's just bowling. It ain't like you're out to save the world or nothin'. Lighten up.

I focus on the back of one of the white men in lane eighteen, kind of a beefy fellow, the ball lookin' like a toy in his hand. He and the rest of his team wear Pittsburgh Steelers jerseys and hats. His body is perfectly still, and then—whoa! He charges toward them pins and rockets that ball, the pins literally exploding and flying all over the place! He claps his hands together once, turns, and—

It's Dewey.

"Ma'am? May I help you, ma'am?"

I turn back to the girl behind the counter. "Uh, yeah. Three Cokes." I turn to see Dewey sitting down at a table not ten feet from me pawing through a basket of fries. He's here? What's he doin' here when he got a sick kid at home?

"What size, ma'am?"

I turn back. "Hmm?"

"I said, what size drinks?"

I see the cups and the prices attached to a wall. "Medium." I look back at Dewey and wonder about this man. I know Dee's probably sleeping, and I know it can't be any fun to be cramped up in a little apartment for two days with a sick kid, but choosing to go bowling over minding your own child?

"Here you go." I hand her the wad of dollars. I bet he needed to get out, to get away for a few hours. He just needed to get away from his troubles for a spell. Nothing wrong with that. Should I speak to him? Dag, Ruth, you on the white side of the alley. What would that look like?

"Here's your change, ma'am."

"Oh, did I get the bowler's discount?"

"Yes."

"Thanks." I collect the change and the drinks, and in getting out of the way of a little girl running by, I find myself standing next to Dewey. Really. I was just getting out of the way of the child. I don't mean to be standing here. I watch him finishing the last of his fries and notice that he's sipping water instead of beer. I'm about to leave him be when another child brushes by, my grip on the drinks slips, and I slam all three drinks down on his table, one of them almost spilling over.

Talk about a grand entrance.

"Oh, sorry about that," I say to him as he jumps back in his seat while I corral the drinks.

"No problem," he says, looking at me. "Ruth, right?"

I love a man who remembers my name. "Mr. Baxter. How you doin'?"

He points at his score. "Not too good."

I look at the numbers, and he has the second-highest score for his team. "Looks pretty good to me." And so do you, Dewey, but you got a little ketchup in the left corner of your mouth. If I had a napkin, I could just dab it off—

"I just can't concentrate tonight."

Neither can I—now. I want to sit down so bad, but I don't because I haven't been invited to sit down. "Thinkin' about Dee?"

He nods. "You know anything about Ritalin?" He pulls out a chair. "Have a seat."

My little heart. "Thank you." I take a deep breath as I sit. I know a lot about antidepressant drugs but nothing about Ritalin. "I don't know much about that stuff."

"Supposed to help him, but I don't see it doin' much good. Makes him hyper for a bit; then he just falls out. Gonna take him tomorrow to get the dose changed." He looks down at my shoes. "You ain't here to bowl?"

I lie a little. "I'm a substitute on my friends' team. They all showed tonight, so I'm just a spectator."

"How heavy a ball you throw?"

Gulp. I don't know shit about this. "Think it's a ten."

"A ten? That's awful light." He looks up and stands. "My turn. Wish me luck."

"Luck," I say, and I watch him go to work, charging toward those pins like a bull; but he's light on his feet, almost graceful. The pins explode again, and a turkey flashes on the screen. Dewey Baxter can bowl. Maybe he'll give me lessons.

"Girl, where have you been?" Naomi hisses in my ear. "We are waiting for our drinks."

I hand two of the Cokes to her. I ain't gettin' up from this chair for nothin' in this world now. "Here they are."

She takes the drinks from me. "Why are you sitting way down here?"

The view is *much* better down here. "Talking to a friend."

She looks around. "Who?"

Dewey returns to his chair and smiles at Naomi. "Howdy."

Naomi doesn't even say hello (how rude!), blinks at me, and leaves. The ride home probably ain't gonna be as quiet as the ride here.

"Three strikes in a row," I say to Dewey. "Where'd you learn to bowl like that?"

He tilts his head down toward the "black" end of the alley. "Got my start in your league 'bout five, six years ago." *My* league? I don't know if I like the way that sounds. We are in the twenty-first century everywhere but Calhoun, Virginia. "But I was terrible then. Tiff helped me out."

"Who's Tiff?" And as soon as I ask it, I know.

"Dee's and Tee's mama." He didn't say "girlfriend." How . . . impersonal. "She was kind of like my coach. Had me lining up my feet right, watching the arrows instead of the pins, getting me to approach in a straight line, even getting me to use a heavier ball. You sure you only use a ten?"

I shrug. "I really don't know. I don't bowl all that often."

"Bet you could use a thirteen, maybe even a fourteen. Get a lot more pin action that way."

And if I bowl, I'm gonna get me some pin action. *Sorry, Lord. I know You sent those running children to move me closer to Dewey; but a girl's got needs, and this man is right up my alley! And I haven't had a strike in my alley in so long!* It's almost his turn to bowl. "Does Dee like to bowl?"

He smiles. "Loves to. They put up the bumpers in the gutters, and he and Tee have a ball." He nods. "I should take them to do just that on Saturday, get them out of the apartment for a while."

"Sounds like a lot of fun."

He turns and looks at me with those soft brown eyes of his. *Please, please, Lord Jesus, please let him ask me to go along!* "Yeah. It's a lot of fun."

My heart droops a little, but I'm not sad. I mean, the man hardly knows me. Maybe when he gets home and reads the note—that his mama's probably reading right now! Oh, Lord, what will she think of me? And will she even show it to him? "Well," I say as I stand. "Better get back to my friends."

"Yeah." He stands. "Thanks for stopping by."

I nod and walk away feeling happy and sad and worried, but when I reach the table on "our" side, I am more happy and less sad and less worried because I got the chance I had been praying for. I've got an "On Time God."

Tonya joins me. "We lost again. Only by seventy pins this time." She touches my hand, and I jump. "Girl, where you been?"

"I was talking to Dewey," I whisper.

She smiles. "Yeah?"

"He's bowling on the other side."

"Which lane?"

"Eighteen."

"Be right back."

I grab her arm. "Don't you be goin' down there," I hiss.

"Girl, I'm just gonna test him. If he don't look twice at me, it means he ain't interested in small, thick, sexy sisters." She pulls her arm away. "Besides, I wanna see if *you* got any taste in white men."

I turn to see Naomi staring holes in me from the semicircle bench near the lanes. Why she always gotta be pissed? Sometimes I think the more religious you are, the meaner you are, the more sour your facial expressions, the tighter your ass. Naomi is just too heavenly minded to be any earthly good sometimes . . . like I was when I was married to Jonas.

Tonya returns and slumps into a chair. "Your man didn't even notice me."

Good. "What you think of him?"

"He big."

"So am I."

"He all right." She puffs out her lower lip. "But I don't like being ignored. Maybe I should gain some weight."

"Girl, you got weight in all the right places." I got all the weight— it's just everywhere I *don't* want it to be.

She stands and groans. "Maybe. But when I can't even turn the head of a chubby white man, something's wrong." Dewey ain't chubby. He's just . . . husky.

NYTBM loses all three games and the overall score by over two hundred and fifty pins, and the only person smiling is Mike, who fi-

nally broke a hundred in the last game. Naomi jams her shoes and ball
into her bowling bag and walks out before Tonya can even get one
shoe off.

"Why she so mad?" I ask Tonya.

"We lost."

"I thought you always lost."

"We do. Just not this bad."

But that isn't all Naomi is mad about, and I get an earful all the
way home. "So, who was your *friend?*" Naomi says "friend" like it's a
nasty word.

I decide to spill it all, and damn her if she can't handle it. "His
name is Dewey Baxter."

"I know who he is."

No, she don't. She just sayin' that to piss me off. "He is the father of
two children, Tee, who's six, and Dee, who's four. Their mama—"

"Died in a car accident this summer," Naomi interrupts.

Daa-em. "So you know him?"

"Yes."

"So why didn't you speak to him? That was so rude."

"It's *because* I know Dewey. I also knew Tiffany, and I know you are
wasting your time."

Do I want to know any more? "Well, it's my time to waste, and
nothing you can say—"

"He ruined that girl, Ruth."

That takes my breath away. "What you mean, ruined? He gave her
two beautiful children."

"Who he did nothing for till the day *after* she died."

Boom. "How you know that?"

"Don't tell me you don't remember Li'l T."

Li'l T? What kind of name is that? "Li'l T, who?"

"You don't remember." She shakes her head. "You wouldn't because back then your head was so far up Jonas's butt you wouldn't
have noticed her."

I still can't remember. "You gonna tell me?"

"Li'l T, also known as Tiffany Jones, used to come to Antioch till
her mama died. She drifted away, dropped out of school, ran the
streets, got arrested a couple times."

"Sound like that child was ruined long before Dewey," Tonya says,
which is just what I was thinking.

"The story isn't over, Tonya. I got Tiffany to come back to church after she got out of prison, and she was doing fine. Had a job, had her own place, she was going somewhere. Then Dewey got her pregnant."

"And Tiffany had nothing to do with that," I say.

"Let me finish."

"You can't blame one person for another person's life, Naomi," Tonya says.

"Just listen. Tiffany expected Dewey to marry her, but he wouldn't and wouldn't even give her a reason why. He quit coming around, but when she had Tee, he showed up again. He wanted to see what he made."

"Tee is a beautiful child," I say.

Naomi sighs deeply. "Anyway, Tiffany told Dewey to beat it and tried to get her life back in order, and for two years, she did. She got her job back, raised her daughter right, started attending church more regularly. And then your friend Dewey snaked his way back into her life."

"She had to make the decision to take him back, Naomi," Tonya says. "She had a choice."

"Maybe."

"What you mean 'maybe'?" Tonya snaps. "Girl could have held her ground and showed him the door again."

"Tiffany wanted something more. She wanted a marriage. She loved Dewey, and then he got her pregnant again. Same story, second verse. No marriage, no help, no Dewey till Dee is born. She almost named that child Dewey to get that man to be a man; but she didn't, and I am sure glad for that." She turns onto Vine Street.

I don't know what to say. "He said Tiffany taught him to bowl."

"Yeah, taught him so well that he won't bowl in our league anymore. He barely even speaks to anyone." She parks in front of my apartment. "Ruth, the only reason that man is being a father to his children is because Tiffany is dead. If she didn't die, he wouldn't be their father. You understand? You saw how messed up Dewey was the day he came to church. You sure you want to get to know a *friend* like that? That man isn't ready to raise any children."

"He's got his mama helping him."

She rolls her eyes and sighs deeply. "His *mama* is probably the reason he wouldn't marry Tiffany in the first place."

Another boom. That kind, little woman . . . is a racist? "You don't know that for sure."

"Come on, girl. You know how white folks are when it comes to us."

I have to get inside to do some thinking. I let out a long, slow breath before answering. "Naomi, I'm not quite sure why, but the Lord seems to be leading me to this man." She scowls, so I decide to throw her words back in her face. "And the last time I checked my Bible, it isn't up to any of us to punish anyone." I get out and shut the door, but I don't slam it because at least *I* have some self-control.

"I'm not punishing him, Ruth," Naomi says through the window. "I'm just telling you the truth about that man."

I put my hand on the roof and lean down. "I remember *someone* who was happy I took Jonas back, and look what happened."

"Ruth, please listen—"

I hold up my hand. "You're my friend, Naomi, and all you can do is give me advice. You've given it, and I aim to think on it; but I'm not going to dismiss the thought of me and that man because of all that shit in the past, his shit *and* my shit. I'm through with the past, too, or haven't you noticed?"

"I've noticed, it's just that—"

I hold up the other hand. "Maybe God's bringing us together to start us both over, Naomi. You ever think of that? Maybe we're both gettin' a second chance." I smile at Tonya. "See you later, Tonya."

"Bye, Ruth."

"Good night, Naomi."

Naomi doesn't look at me. "Night, Ruth."

Once inside, I sit down on the couch with my bag of Peppermint Patties and think (I always think better with sugar running through my veins) and realize that I ain't in it yet. I can always fade away, no harm, no foul. I'll still work with Dee, though. Maybe that's what I'm supposed to be doing all along. I have to find a way to get that boy to speak. But all these little coincidences with Dewey are too hard to ignore. He shows up at my church the day after my gas attack which was the day after I flushed the pills and decided to eat right. A few weeks later, he shows up with his kids at Diana's. A week after that, I volunteer again at Avery and latch on to his child, who latches on to me. I go to a bowling alley for the first time in over ten years and nearly fall into his lap. He has my phone number and could call at any minute. . . .

I pick up my bag and sit at the kitchen table. Dag, I hope these

Peppermint Patties don't give me the runs. I got to get me a cord long enough to reach the bathroom.

So Dewey was a bad father. I never knew mine at all, so at least Dee and Tee know him and have him now. Better late than never, I say. So he wouldn't marry Tiffany. Maybe they weren't compatible. He seems the strong, silent type, and maybe she was a little too "street" or "ghetto" for him. She *had* been to prison. How the hell did they even meet? There's so much I don't know. Maybe he thought she had tried to trap him by getting pregnant. Here was a girl right out of prison looking for a hookup. She tried to trap him, and he wouldn't go for it. But hooking up with her a *second* time? What was he thinking? Or was he thinking at all? Maybe Naomi got it wrong and *Dewey* wanted to make it work after Dee was born, and she died too soon for it to happen . . . though in four years, it should have been a done deal. Maybe he just wasn't ready to settle down. So what if his mama was against the two of them getting together. What mama of any race thinks any other person of any race is good enough for her son? Besides, Dewey Baxter is a grown man. He probably made up his own mind about it, and that was that.

I stare at the phone. "Ring," I say.

And it does.

I look up at the ceiling. *Lord, what You up to?* I cradle the phone and try to speak calmly. "Hello?"

"Ruth, it's Naomi." Damn. "I just wanted to apologize for the things I said. I had no right to judge you or anyone you're interested in. It was so rude of me to . . ." And she talks on and on and on. I never know how to stop her. Folks who work for the phone company are like that, and religious folks who work for the phone company are *worse*. I pop a few more Peppermint Patties into my mouth, watch the clock, and wait for her to take a breath. ". . . I want you to be happy, Ruth—"

"So do I. And you'll make me happier if you stop apologizing."

"I'm sorry."

"You did it again."

"Sorr—Thanks for understanding."

"I understand, and I thank you for your concern. Now get off the phone. I don't have call-waiting, and I'm expecting Dewey to call."

"How'd he get your number?"

"I gave it to him."

"At the bowling alley?"

"No. In the cake. Call Tonya if you need an explanation. Bye." I hang up. I look at the bag and find it empty. I am going to be dreaming in brilliant color tonight. I look at the clock. If I had a TV, I could be watching some late-night talk show, but since I don't, I pull out the jump rope and jump for a while on my little piece of carpet chanting:

> *"Dewey bear, Dewey bear*
> *call me up, Dewey bear.*
> *Dewey bear, Dewey bear,*
> *call me now, Dewey bear.*
> *Dewey bear, Dewey bear,*
> *pick up the phone, Dewey bear.*
> *Dewey bear, Dewey bear—"*

I sigh and look at the clock. Midnight. I toss the rope on the couch. "Have sweet dreams, Dewey bear."

PART THREE

You Can't Make Me Doubt Him

Twelve

So Dewey didn't call last night. I can handle it. He didn't call for the first forty years of my life, right? So what. I can return to my little world of cutting hair and jumping rope and still keep smiling, even if the weather is changing outside. Fall is falling, and I'm going to be another one of the orange leaves skipping along Vine Street.

And thinking about that man.

Thursday is so slow I spend most of it sitting on a folding chair just outside the door at Diana's watching the world go by. Huddled figures, wrapped against the cold and the wind like I am, walk briskly to Dude's to raise their cholesterol or to Hood's to get ripped off. The street corner pharmacists dance in place, hands in pockets, waiting for the pay phone to ring or another foolish soul to drive by to get a fix. Soapbox Sam's words appear in the air in rapid bursts of mist, brown leaves swirling around his milk crate. Evangeline's place on the bus bench is as empty as I feel. Haven't seen her around since the first frost. She must be a fair-weather fortune-teller. I wish Larry Farmer could come back again. As dead as Vine Street has become, at least he had given it some life and kept it clear of bottles and cans. That man was always busy, always moving, always doing something—

"Hey," a soft voice says.

I turn and see no one around me. I stick my head inside Diana's. "You call me, Diana?"

She looks up from her chair and pauses from sharpening her claws with an Emery board. "No."

I look up and down Vine. *Lord, if it's You, it's polite to call a person by*

name. And anyway, I didn't know You were Southern. Sayin' "hey" instead
of hello. Oh, yeah. That other word has that other place in it.

"Hey," the soft voice says again.

I look all around me and still see no one. Someone is trying to play
a trick on me. "Hey yourself," I say toward the corner of Diana's
where an alley starts. "What you up to?"

"Nothin' much." A young man's voice. Probably one of the corner
druggists getting out of the wind to count his money.

"How you doin'?"

"Aw-ite. Yourself?"

"Aw-ite," I say, mimicking him. "How's business?"

"So-so. Y'all busy?"

"Nah. Weather's keepin' folks away."

"Tell me about it." A pause and a laugh. "Got time to give me an
edge-up?"

Cut a drug dealer's hair? Why not. It'll give me a chance to give
him an earful. "Sure."

"How much you charge?"

Like it really matters. The boy probably got more in his pockets
than I make in a month. "Depends."

"On what?"

"On how much edging I gotta do."

A head pops out from the corner for a second, then disappears.
"How much for that?" he asks.

"I didn't see enough of it, boy. Come here for your estimate."

He comes around the corner . . . carrying a guitar case. It's Kevin
Myers, Guitarman himself, and I can see why he was hiding; but it's
not because his hair is all nappy. His dark brown face is crisscrossed
with white scars. One scar starts at the bridge of his nose and ends at
his hairline, and another begins at his right ear and ends under his
chin.

"Well, if it isn't Kevin Myers," I say as I stand. *Lord Jesus, I will never*
understand the cruelty of Your people toward each other.

" 'Lo, Mrs. Borum."

I fold up the chair. "C'mon in, Kevin."

I follow him in and point to my chair while Diana mouths "Oh, my
God!" Kevin sets his guitar case to the side of the chair and sits while
Diana disappears into the back. Diana has a weak constitution. I
nicked the ear of a customer once, and when Diana saw the little speck
of blood, she nearly passed out.

I loop a towel around Kevin's neck, then fasten the gown. "That ain't too tight, is it?"

"Nah."

I start to trim and try not to stare at all the scars covering his head, but it ain't easy because they are everywhere I look. I had heard that he had to have sixty stitches in the back of his head alone. Concrete sure can do some damage. I don't ask him why he isn't at a barber's. From what I hear, the barber shop is often a worse place for gossiping than a hair salon is. "So how you been?"

"Aw-ite. Just got out of the hospital a few days ago."

Four *months* he was in the hospital, part of it in a coma. "Bet your mama's glad you're home."

"Yeah. I guess. She ain't too happy about all the bills, though." I can't even imagine how much that would have cost. "I'm supposed to be looking for a job today, but . . ."

"But what?"

He turns to look me in the eye. "Would you hire me?"

I stare back. "Don't know. What are your qualifications, Mr. Myers?"

He smiles. Lord, they even messed up his teeth, two broken, a few missing. I doubt even a fast food place would hire this child. "I play guitar." He turns away. "Least I hope to be able to play like I used to."

"What you mean? You been playin' that thing as long as I can remember."

He pulls his hands out from under the gown and holds them up. "Soon as these heal all the way."

I don't see a thing wrong with his hands. "They look fine to me."

He hides them again under the gown. "Yeah. But when I got my head smashed in, I had some seizures, and now . . . Sometimes I can't stop my hands from shaking long enough to finish a song. My brain knows what to do with my fingers, but my fingers just ain't gettin' the message all the time. The doctors say I have some nerve damage or something, say it'll be a while till I get it all back, maybe it'll work itself out."

That is so sad. To lose the one gift you have, for any length of time, is tragic. I don't know what I'd do if I couldn't play the organ. "I'm sure it will work itself out, Kevin. Just give it some time. And you know that I'll be praying for you."

"Thanks." He nods to himself. "Bet you already been prayin'."

"Yep."

"You still playin' the organ?"

"Sure am."

He smiles. "Always liked to hear you play. Used to run up to the balcony after Sunday school so I could see your fingers better. Right hard to see 'em from the pews down below." He shifts toward me. "Bet you could play some guitar, Mrs. Borum. You're good with your fingers."

"My gift is the organ, and you have to have nails to play the guitar, right?" He nods. "Never could get mine to grow." I stand in front of him to make sure his edges are even. "Did I take off enough?"

He pulls one hand out and runs it over his head. "Yeah. Thanks."

I remove the gown and towel. "Tell your mama I said hello."

He stands and reaches into a pocket, coming up with a few wadded bills, his hand trembling just enough to notice. There but for the grace of God go I. "How much I owe you?"

"Consider it a welcome back haircut, Kevin."

"Nah. Here." He puts a wad of one-dollar bills in my hand, but I put it right back in his.

"I'd rather you paid me with a song." I nod at the guitar. "Play something for me."

He shoves both hands in his pockets. "Nah, I—"

"Nah I nothin'! I haven't heard you play in years. Last time I heard you play was when you was little."

" 'Silent Night.' " He toes the ground with a boot and flashes a look at me. "Don't know if my fingers remember that one."

"Only one way to find out, boy."

"Yeah." He squats, opens the case, and pulls out a shiny guitar. Instead of finding a chair, he sits cross-legged right there on the floor of Diana's and strums "Silent Night," playing it slow but with steady hands and fingers. He plays it almost like it's a love ballad, and if you think about it, it is a love ballad—for a little baby named Jesus. I sit in my chair and hum along, and eventually Diana comes out of the back to listen.

Kevin finishes, and I clap while Diana busies herself at her station, her back to us. "Your fingers haven't forgotten that one, Kevin," I say.

He packs up his guitar. "Guess they haven't."

And then I get a wonderful idea. "Tell you what. We got us a nice spot right outside this place on that sidewalk, a nice *safe* place, and lots of folks come in here or come by here; so why don't you—"

"Ruth," Diana interrupts.

"What?" She motions me to the back. "Hold on, Kevin. Don't you leave, now."

"I won't."

I join Diana near one of the sinks where we wash hair. "That boy is *not* playing out in front of this place," she whispers.

"Why not?"

"You saw his face."

"Scared the shit out of you, didn't it?"

"Yeah. And if it scares me, it'll scare our customers, too."

Oh, Lord, we wouldn't want that. "Girl, we already got us some scary customers, or haven't you noticed? They come in scary, and sometimes they leave *scarier*. I know I'm scary, and when you haven't had your coffee, *you're* scary. What's one more scary person to welcome them in and give them something to do while they're waiting?"

"I just . . . We can't have him playing out there. What if someone comes by and messes with him again?"

I make a fist and a face. "Then we kick some ass, go out with some Golden Hots and return the favor, burn some scars into *their* thick heads."

She almost smiles. "I ain't been in a fight since the second grade, girl." She points at a bicep. "I just ain't made for that shit."

"You could be." I point at her hands. "Those nails of yours could do some damage."

She shakes her head. "I just don't want that kind of attention, girl."

"Sure you do. Think what folks will say. Will you look at that? Diana has given Guitarman a job serenading customers. Wasn't that nice of her? Why, she must be doing pretty well if she can afford him doing that."

"I ain't payin' him!"

"Maybe not you, but I will. His mama must owe over a hundred grand for his hospital bills. Every little bit helps."

"I don't know, Ruth. I mean, we might lose customers."

I nod. "Yep."

"And that doesn't bother you?"

I shake my head. "Not in the least, because we might even get us some more customers."

"How?"

"You heard him play. Wasn't that beautiful?"

"Yes, but—"

"Name another hair joint in Calhoun that offers live entertainment."

She freezes, her face blank. "Does he know any Motown?"

I walk to the front. "Know any old Motown music, Kevin?"

He nods.

I whisper, "Boy, this is your audition."

"Huh?"

"You want a job where you can use your gift, right?"

"Yeah, sure."

"Well, open that case and play us some Motown."

He opens the case. "What should I play?"

"Diana is named after Diana Ross, boy. You've seen her hairstyle and the posters on the walls. What you think?"

"Oh." He pulls out the guitar. "Um, name some of her songs."

" 'Baby Love,' 'Come See About Me,' 'You Keep Me Hangin' On,' 'Someday We'll Be Together.' " He shrugs. Oh, Lord, this child is so young. " 'You Can't Hurry Love'?"

He strums a chord. "Does it go something like 'I need somethin', somethin' to grease my mind'?"

Not even close. "Yes."

"Know that one."

"Let's hope so."

I step back and motion for Diana. Kevin taps the back of the guitar to simulate the opening drum beat . . . then plays the *hell* out of that song. By the middle of the song, Diana is humming along and eventually doing a little lip-synch in front of her mirror with a brush for a microphone, one arm spread wide like her namesake. Kevin has just gotten himself a job.

Kevin finishes. Diana drops the brush into her smock pocket and turns from the mirror. "Um, that was pretty good, Kevin."

"Pretty good?" I say. "Boy has that song down, girl."

"You know 'I Hear A Symphony,' Kevin?"

Kevin shakes his head. "Nah." I clear my throat. "I mean, no, ma'am. But I'll go home tonight and have Mama teach me. She got a crate of old forty-fives."

I raise my eyebrows to Diana. "He got a good ear, girl."

Diana scrunches up her lips, rolls her eyes, and sighs. "Okay. Be here when we open tomorrow, eight o'clock sharp. But wear a hat, okay?"

"Diana!" I shout.

Kevin laughs. "No, it's aw-ite. I understand."

"And any tips you get . . ." She pauses and looks at me. I shake my head slowly. She had tried to pull the same shit on me when I first started, telling me that we were gonna split all tips. I had to set her straight with the same slow shake of the head. Diana sighs. "And any tips you get you can keep, provided you sweep up, do some cleaning, take out the trash, that kind of thing, and you better not be late, and you *better* not be high."

"I won't be." He packs up his guitar and stands. "Anything else?"

"Just one more thing," Diana says, staring at the floor. "If, um, if it's too cold out there, you're welcome to play in here." Diana can be nice? I didn't know she had it in her. "But no weird shit."

He smiles. "What you consider weird?"

"Weird is any song no one here has ever heard, like any song after nineteen seventy-five, and definitely no country."

"Geez, Diana," I say, "you think anyone who come in here gonna request them some country?" Besides Dewey.

She shrugs. "Who knows? We got us some scary customers, right? Hell, we might even be gettin' us some white customers now. Because of Kevin, we gettin' right she-she."

"She-she?" Kevin says to me. "What's she-she?"

"It's Diana's word for chic," I say. He shrugs. "Means we're getting fashionable, cool, hip, far out."

"Oh." He starts for the door and turns. "So it'll be okay if I play some James Brown, then?"

"Oh, I don't know about him," Diana says. "Our clients might get too wild, throw out a hip or two."

"Well, James Brown is pretty cool, hip, and far out, isn't he?" Kevin is catching on fast.

"We'll see," Diana says. "Long as you play whatever you play slow and slower. Don't want to set off any pacemakers."

"Okay."

I walk Kevin outside, and the wind doesn't feel as cold as it did before. Something about doing nice things for people makes cold days warmer. He turns to me and shakes his head. "I don't know how you did it, but . . . thanks, Mrs. Borum."

"Don't thank me, Kevin. Thank the Giver of the gift." I point to the sky, and Kevin nods. "You go on home and learn them forty-fives now."

"I will."

"And you get to church, hear? Want to see you up in that balcony watching me play."

"Sure. Mama would like that."

I give him a hug. "So would I." I hold him in front of me. "Maybe we can work up a duet for a service."

"I don't know."

"Think about it. God likes to hear you play, too." It's at this very moment that I decide to play at Junie's wedding. I mean, here's Kevin, a struggling musician with a gift he has trouble giving because his brain's still healing, a guitar player who has no place to play. I don't have any trouble playing, and I have a steady place to play. And I'd like to think that God likes to hear me play, too.

"Thanks again, Mrs. Borum."

He turns to go, and I get another idea. "You know 'The Wedding Song,' Kevin?"

"No."

"I think sometimes it's called 'There Is Love.' Your mama might know it. Work on it for me."

"Who's gettin' married?"

"My ex-husband, Mr. Borum."

He blinks. "Damn. A whole bunch of shit happened while I was gone."

"You're tellin' me."

"So that's why you're, uh," he says, pointing at Diana's.

"Yeah."

"Pays pretty good?"

"Enough. And I tell you what. I'll try to make the wedding a pay-ing gig for you. You do that right in front of a whole bunch of people, you might be playing at weddings for a long time."

"Hmm." He scratches at his chin. "Be nice to play in front of a packed house." He smiles, nods, and walks toward the corner of Diana's, turning down the alley as Naomi pulls up in her car for her weekly lunch-hour edge-up and gossip session.

"Wasn't that Kevin?" she says as she gets out of her car.

"Yep."

She follows me in and sits in my chair. "How you doin', Diana?"

"Fine, Naomi, fine." She laughs. "Ruth tell you what we gonna start doing?"

Naomi looks at me as I drape a gown over her. "*Please* tell me y'all are gonna start doin' pedicures."

I shudder. "I ain't gonna do no one's crusty toes."

"My toes ain't crusty!" Naomi shouts. One thing I've noticed about Naomi: whenever she comes into Diana's, she talks just like everybody else. Something about this salon that makes folks more real or something, like they can let down their hair while they're gettin' their hair done. Either that or college-educated Naomi just wants to fit in with the likes of us lowly high school graduates.

"If I do your stank toes, Naomi, I gotta do everybody's stank toes, and that just ain't in my job description, is it, Diana?"

Diana doesn't answer right away. Oh shit, she's thinking about it. "I don't know, Ruth. Maybe we ought to start. I mean, now that we got us some live music, maybe doin' toes won't be so bad."

"Yeah, they'll be toe tappin' to Kevin, then spreadin' that funk on me. No thank you."

Naomi grabs my arm. "Kevin's gonna play here?"

"Starting tomorrow morning."

Naomi beams. "That is so nice of you two. Y'all payin' him hourly, right?"

I turn to Diana. "Yeah, what *is* the minimum wage these days, Diana?" I only get paid a percentage of each cut, perm, or manicure. I been paid under the table from the get-go.

Diana throws up her hands. "Y'all are tryin' to get me in trouble with the IRS. I ain't gonna be fillin' out forms for the government. I'll just pay him like I do Ruth." She grabs her coat. "I'm goin' to Dude's. Y'all want something?"

"A fish sandwich," Naomi says, "and a bag of fries."

"I didn't know you ate that shit," I say.

"It's for you," she says. "My treat." The girl is *still* trying to apologize. It would be better if she apologized with a salad.

"Diana, make sure that my fish is fried in oil from *this* decade."

"I'll try."

As soon as Diana leaves, I get to work, but there ain't nothing to be done. There never is. I know Naomi trims the back of her own head at least once a week, so mostly I trim a hair here and there and maybe comb it out. Today I find a gray hair and snip it away without telling her. No sense in depressing her.

"Did Dewey call?" Naomi asks.

Now *I'm* depressed. "No. Maybe tonight."

She doesn't say anything, which is good, but I know she's thinking

"I told you so." I play with a tiny hair till it stands up, then snip it. "All done." Fastest cut in history.

Naomi feels the back of her neck. "Just right." I whisk her off, and she stands. "Want to play cards with me and Tonya tonight?"

"No thanks." I want to wait by the phone all night watching it *not* ring.

"You sure?"

"Yeah."

She hands me a twenty. I tried to give her the change the first time she came in with only a chipped nail, but she wouldn't take it. Must be nice to be single and paid. "What are you doing tomorrow night?"

"Haven't decided. I'll call you."

"Okay."

And with that, she's gone, and it happens the same way every week. She drops in during her lunch hour, gets four or five hairs snipped or rearranged, invites me to do something, pays way too much for no work, then leaves if Diana isn't around to sling some gossip because I'm just no good at gossiping.

And after Naomi, no one else comes in. Diana and I eat our sandwiches, then stare out the window. A pregnant girl walks by. "There go Teresa," Diana says.

"Teresa Smalls?" The little girl who put her finger in the barrel of her daddy's shotgun is all grown up?

"Uh-huh. She a whole lot more eye than meets the ear now, huh?"

"What a shame. Who's the daddy?"

"Who knows? She already got one child and another bun in the oven."

"She can't be more than, what, fifteen, sixteen?"

"She's seventeen."

All that happened *ten* years ago? *Where the hell have I been, Lord?*

Diana tenses. "Oh shit. Here come Mrs. Goody Moo-Shoe Gai Pain in the neck herself."

I see Mrs. Wilomena Monroe, a member of Antioch, waddling in our direction. No matter how you cut her hair, it's wrong. She brings us pictures of women from *Essence,* and we do our best to recreate the styles; but some styles just do not look right on Willie's round, fat head. Diana says that we should staple the pictures to her nose. "Her hair looks okay to me."

Diana dashes to the front door, locks it, flips the open-closed sign, turns out the lights, and runs to the back. "Come on, Ruth!"

"I bet she don't stop this time."

Diana groans, but she still won't come to the front. "She will, Ruth. You know she will. She is just one big ol' mound of flesh out to take some of mine."

"Wind ain't messing it up at all," I say as Willie waddles closer. "Looks like this one worked. You should be proud." Willie stops in front of the window, waves at me, then waddles on. "She gone, Diana."

"Really?" She sneaks up behind my chair. "She didn't stop?"

"Only to wave." I check the clock. "Nothin' happenin' today. Mind if I leave early?"

Diana tiptoes to the door and looks out. "She really didn't stop. It's a miracle." She turns to me. "Sure. You can go. I'll hang out for any strays."

While I walk home, I think about all the "strays" on Vine Street. If I could somehow collect them all and put them to use . . . Nah, I'm just an organ player. I ain't no Pied Piper. Besides, it ain't like an organ is portable. Folks got to come *to* the church to hear me play.

I stop at the corner and listen to Soapbox Sam for a bit. If Jonas had this man's thunderous voice, Vine Street couldn't contain Antioch Church. It would grow out to the suburbs for sure.

"Y'all upty-ups!" he shouts. "You doctors of dull! Y'all who scritch and scratch in your newspapers, who snitch and snatch on the TV!" He looks down from his milk crate at me and tips his nonexistent hat. "Good day, Miss Ruth."

"Good day, Sam."

"Listen here, you hypo-critic, demo-critic, hippie-critic, arrog-ANT arroGENTS!" He turns to me again. "Am I comin' on a little too strong here?"

"No, Sam. You're sayin' it right."

He winks. "Y'all best unprint the printed, unsay the said, unwrite the wrong, and write the right!" He smiles. This man *should* be a preacher with that smile. He'll have all the biddies gettin' moist in the front row. He's giving me chill bumps right now. "There's just too much lead and not enough eraser, too much ink and not enough White-out, just too many words darkening the truth!"

"Amen, Brother Sam," I say, and I continue home. I'm almost there when I see Jar-Man sitting in the yard next to my apartment house, that Mason jar stuck up to his ear. "What's the good word, Jar-Man?"

He doesn't look up and says, "Condoms need born-on dating in big bold numbers."

I laugh. "You got that right." Someone ought to write down the shit he says and send it to *Reader's Digest*. "You warm enough?" He's only wearing a thin windbreaker. "I got a heavier coat you could use inside."

He shakes his head. "Nah. I'm just waitin' on the po-lice."

I move closer. "What for?"

He looks behind him. "Ain't I trespassin'?"

I shrug. "Folks who live there are already trespassin'. Think they all got evicted."

"Damn." He stands, but the jar never leaves his ear. I've always wanted to know why he uses the jar, but I can't bring myself to ask. "Where you live?" I point at the apartment house. He stands and walks over to my yard. "*Now* am I trespassin'?"

"You actually *want* the po-lice to pick you up?"

"Damn straight. It's Salisbury steak night, and if you hadn't noticed, it's cold as shit out today."

I can't fault his logic. "I could cook you up something."

"You got any Salisbury steak?"

"No, but I could get some."

He shakes his head. "It won't be the same. They got some good gravy down there at the jail." He pauses and "listens" to the jar.

"You *want* me to call you in for trespassin'?"

He smiles. "If you would be so kind."

"Are you sure?"

He frowns. "You don't call me in, I start doin' a little Josephine Baker number out here, and I ain't wearin' no underwear."

Gulp. "I'll call it in."

When I get inside, I dial 911. After identifying myself and giving my address, I say, "There's a strange man trespassin' in the yard wearin' only a windbreaker." No response. "I invited him in to get warm, but he didn't wanna come." Still no response. "I mean, it's cold outside. Can't you send someone to pick him up?"

"He can go to a shelter, ma'am."

"Look, he's old. It ain't like he's gonna be walkin' anywhere tonight, and I don't want him dying in my front yard."

"What is the man's name?"

"I don't know. Folks around here just call him Jar-Man."

"Jar-Man?"

"He puts a jar to his ear, you see, and—" I am getting nowhere. "Uh-oh, he's takin' off his clothes." He isn't, but a little lie might get Jar-Man a warm bed to sleep in tonight.

"He's doing what?"

"He doin' a striptease! With children out there playing! They shouldn't be seeing something like that! And he ain't wearin' any underwear! You gonna do something?"

"We'll send someone right over."

I hang up and open the window. "Jar-Man?"

He turns to me mumbling something about "this 'hood ain't placed on hold; it's placed on mold." He smiles. "Yes?"

"They on the way. You might wanna do that Josephine Baker number now."

"Are you serious? As cold as it is?"

I lean on the sill. "Look, you don't strip, you don't get no Salisbury steak."

He takes the jar off his ear and sets it on the ground, unzips his jacket, and unbuttons his shirt. "Shit, woman, didn't you tell them I was trespassin'?"

"Yeah. But they weren't gonna come till I told them you were gettin' naked."

He shakes his head. "It's gettin' to be that trespassin' ain't enough to get you arrested on Vine Street." He kicks off his shoes. "What this world comin' to?"

He piles his clothes on the ground and snaps that jar to his ear. A minute later, a police car shows up, and instead of Jar-Man waiting for them to come to him, he picks up his clothes and runs to them. A black officer, one of the few I've ever seen in Calhoun, wraps a thick blanket around him and helps him into the car. Jar-Man turns to me and smiles as the car speeds away.

"That man is crazy like a fox," I say as I shut the window and try not to look at the phone. Grandma always said that a watched pot never boils. So, I spend the evening not watching the phone and cleaning up instead. I sweep and mop the kitchen and bathroom floors, wipe down all the baseboards, scour the bathtub with Dutch Cleanser, and shine my toilet till it blinds my eyes.

When I'm done, it's only seven. The phone hasn't rung, and I have nothing left to clean except my clothes. I look at the pile on the floor of my closet and decide to leave it for another day . . . of waiting for the phone to ring. I could call Junie to tell her that I'm going to play at her wedding, but I don't want to tie up the line. Surprised she hasn't called already.

I have nothing to read, don't own a TV anymore, and only have a little radio (that works when you smack it on something) to entertain me. So after a quick trip to Hood's, I sit on the couch and snuggle up with a friend—a half gallon of rocky road ice cream.

Even if it is a "Silent Night," it's so good to spend time with an old friend, don't you think?

Thirteen

In the morning, I feel guilty for eating the entire half gallon of rocky road. The chocolate, nuts, and the marshmallows kept me up most of the night, and when I did sleep, I dreamed of Josephine Baker doing a striptease at the corner of Vine and Eleventh. Don't ask. I feel too bloated to eat my bagel and decide to eat nothing all day as punishment. Yeah, I'm fasting . . . and praying that my stomach calms down.

When I get to Diana's at quarter to eight, I see our Friday morning regulars milling around like the cattle they sometimes resemble, but I don't see Kevin. It's early, but I say a prayer for him anyway.

"How y'all doin'?" I say, and I take up my place near the door. The four ladies (Mrs. Johnson, Mrs. Coles, Mrs. Thompson, and Mrs. Phillips) grunt and nod, holding their places in line, hands in coat pockets, and don't make any eye contact. Maybe it's bad luck to look the stylist in the eye, I don't know. Either that or they're pissed because they have to wait. Shit, I have to wait, too. I've asked Diana to give me a key since she's always late, but she says she'd rather be the only one with a key. I don't think it's a matter of trust. Diana is just too cheap to have another key cut.

As the chilly wind burns my face and tightens my jaw, I remember another cold morning waiting in front of a glass door. Grandma had just died, and because I was only twenty, there were some problems with the transfer of Grandma's house to me. I got to the courthouse a little after seven A.M. and saw a bunch of white women behind the counter inside chomping on biscuits, sucking down coffee, laughing, and giggling. I tapped on the door and waved at the woman closest to me, but she pointed at her watch and mouthed "Seven-thirty." So I waited, stamping my feet, blowing on my hands, turning away from the wind, hoping I wouldn't die of frostbite. At about quarter after, a white woman joined me at the door, and Miss Gotta Eat My Biscuit opened the door. Fifteen minutes I waited, and she opens it the *second* a white woman showed up. "Who's first?" she asked. "Who you see?" I wanted to ask, but all I could do was gasp and stop moving. When I did, Miss Biscuit waited on the other lady first. Two women with white daddies, but only one of us got decent treatment. Twenty years ago it happened, and I can still remember. Cold, windy days like this always bring back the day I lost my grandma's house at the courthouse.

At five till eight, Kevin straggles around the corner and freezes when he sees us. Bet he never had a crowd like this over on Fifteenth. I smile at him, but he doesn't smile back. Stage fright. Bet his hands are gettin' sweaty. I feel my own, and they're a bit moist, too. Guess I'm nervous for him. He eventually slips through the crowd and joins me.

"Mornin', Mr. Myers." I tug on the bill of his New York Yankees cap. It hides the scars on his head but not on his face. The ladies don't seem to notice yet.

"Mornin', Mrs. Borum."

"You ready?"

"Hope so." He blows in his free hand. "Pretty cold today."

I put my arm around his shoulders. "And it's your job to warm us all up." I turn to the ladies. "Y'all know Kevin Myers, right?" More grunts and nods, but at least they didn't turn away or grimace. "Kevin's gonna take y'all's requests, play some music while you're gettin' your hair done, so y'all be thinking up songs for him to play."

"Will it cost extra?" Mrs. Thompson asks. Bitch never tips and holds on to her money that extra second so you have to tug it away from her.

"No, Mrs. Thompson," I say. "It's all part of the service. You have a request?"

"I do," Mrs. Coles says. "I'd like to request that the damn door open at eight like it says so on the door." Grunts and nods.

I turn to Kevin and whisper, "You know that song?"

"Which song?"

"The one called 'The Damn Door Should Open At Eight'?"

He finally smiles. "No."

I lean in closer. "Better play some James Brown, then. You know 'Hot Pants'?"

"Yeah. All four parts."

"Good." I got to dance me off some ice cream, and when you play any James Brown song, you get a workout. He ought to come out with a videotape called "The Godfather of Soul Workout." Dag, some of his songs are thirteen minutes long.

Diana shows up at five after, and the stampede begins, Mrs. Johnson in the lead. I put out an extra folding chair for Kevin since the waiting room (all two chairs' worth) is full. Kevin opens his case, looks at the chair . . . and sits on the floor between my chair and Diana's.

"You could sit in the chair," I say to him.

"I'm all right," he says, beginning to tune his guitar.

"You're liable to get right hairy," Diana says, throwing a gown on Mrs. Johnson while I do the same for Mrs. Coles.

"Already am," Kevin says, and Mrs. Johnson smiles. I have never seen Mrs. Johnson smile before. She's a lemon-colored lady who looks like she sucks on lemons twenty-four-seven, her lips all wrinkly and tight.

"You have a request for Kevin, Mrs. Johnson?" I ask.

"What about me?" Mrs. Coles whines.

"Mrs. Johnson was first in line."

"Ho always gotta be first," Mrs. Coles huffs.

Mrs. Johnson's lemon face returns. "I do have a request, but I doubt that he knows it," she says loudly. She thinks she has to be loud since she wears a hearing aid and can't hear herself speak.

"Try me," Kevin says.

" 'Oh, Girl' by the Chi-Lites."

Kevin starts the intro . . . and it sounds *just* like the Chi-Lites. Kevin hit them forty-fives *hard* last night. "I don't have to sing along with it, do I?"

Mrs. Johnson's head moves to the beat. "No, child. You just keep playin'." She turns to Diana. "You remember the Chi-Lites, right?"

"They was all Afros and moustaches," Diana says directly into Mrs. Johnson's better, right ear.

"I remember how stylish they were with their wide-lapel shirts, fancy suits, and handkerchiefs," Mrs. Johnson says.

Mrs. Coles grunts. "They were wearing leisure suits, girl. Didn't your husband wear leisure suits up till the day he died?" She's always trying to start something, and I don't mean to be cruel, but a bulldog has a cuter face than Mrs. Coles. Better teeth and breath, too.

"They were stylish," Mrs. Johnson says with a nod. "And the Chi-Lites were clean-cut boys, always smiling. Not like these rappers today."

"Bet you liked the Dramatics, too," Mrs. Coles says with a sneer.

Mrs. Johnson smiles. "Yes, I did."

"You would," Mrs. Coles says. "They looked like rejects from a marching band."

"They did not!" Mrs. Coles snaps.

"Did, too. White buck shoes, vests, stripes down their pant legs. All they needed was the fuzzy hats and the batons."

"What's wrong with that?" Diana asks.

Mrs. Coles grimaces. "Nothin'. Just sayin' what I thought they looked like, damn. Don't mind me. I'm just entitled to my own damn opinions, that's all. Shit."

Kevin finishes the song and looks up at Mrs. Coles. "You got a request?"

Mrs. Coles smiles and looks at Mrs. Johnson. "Yeah. Play me some James Brown."

He looks at me and winks. " 'Hot Pants'?"

"Nah, boy. Play Mrs. Johnson's theme song." She sucks in a deep breath and yells, "It's called 'Talking Out Loud And Saying Nothing'!"

"Oh, I just love that song," Mrs. Johnson says.

"Don't play that one, boy," Mrs. Thompson says from her chair in the waiting area. "Play 'I'll Be Around' by the Spinners."

The woman next to Mrs. Thompson, Mrs. Phillips, the quietest, most ancient woman around with a thick shock of white hair, starts cackling and tapping her skinny feet on the floor, her ankles no wider than my pinkie.

"What you laughin' at, Emma?" Mrs. Thompson asks.

" 'I'll Be Around'? You already *been* around, Anita. Ain't no 'I'll Be' to it. Ain't a man on Vine Street that don't know Anita Little Johnson."

Mrs. Thompson stands and puts out two bony fists in front of Mrs. Phillips. Oh shit, wrinkled ladies about to rumble. "I told you never to call me that!"

"It was your nickname back in the day, wasn't it?"

Mrs. Thompson slaps her hands together. "You ain't too old to be slapped, old lady!"

Mrs. Phillips cackles again. "Don't you be buckin' at me, Anita Little." She turns to me. "Anita Little Johnson here used to get a whole lotta—"

"Shut your mouth!" Mrs. Thompson takes a wide swing and misses Mrs. Phillips by a foot.

"Everybody know you can't fight without kickin', scratchin', and dislocatin' somethin', Anita. Sit your black ass down."

I turn to Kevin and whisper, "Boy, you gotta play something to calm these wenches down."

"What?"

"Shit, boy," I say as Mrs. Phillips rises from her chair. "Play some damn Barry White!"

Kevin breaks into "Can't Get Enough of Your Love, Babe," and both ladies turn to him, smile, sigh, and sit back down. I blink at Diana, and she blinks back. Dag, they ought to be playing some Barry White over there in the Middle East. Can't no one do nothin' but some lovin' listening to Barry.

Kevin plays a medley of Barry White songs till the ladies leave (and mean ol' Mrs. Thompson even tips him!), and Diana calls a meeting. "Kevin, you just play what you play from now on, and if anyone got a request, everybody in here got to agree on it. Okay?"

"Okay by me."

"And any time you want to play some Diana Ross, you go on and do it."

Kevin looks past me to the window. "Got a customer."

I turn and see Soapbox Sam himself, hat in hand, bald head shining, just cheesing and pointing at us. I dust off my chair with a towel. Then he steps in and practically leaps into my chair so it spins once around. "Sam," I say, "you ain't got no hair."

"Sure I do, sure I do," he says. He points to a few sprouts of gray hair just above his left ear. "Here they are."

"There ain't but ten, maybe twelve tops."

He smiles. "They need to be cut." He rubs a completely smooth part of his head. "Got to be aerodynamic, you know, especially in the dark."

"You nasty, Sam," Diana says.

He puts his hand over his heart. "I wasn't bein' nasty, dear lady. I have to be aerodynamic to make my narrow escapes."

"From who?" Diana asks. "The po-lice?"

He winks at her. "You play your cards right, it might be *you* to-night, Miss Diana."

"Get over yourself, Sam Harris," Diana says. "I ain't your type."

"And what is my type?"

"Young and dumb."

He nods. "Well, in your case, I'll settle for one out of two."

Diana's mouth drops open. "Oh no you *didn't* just say—"

"You look so *young,* Miss Diana," Sam interrupts.

Kevin packs his guitar away and walks to the door. "Where you goin', boy?" I ask.

He turns and smiles. "It's gettin' right thick in here." He flexes his fingers. "Need a break anyway."

"Okay," Diana says. "You can start your second set when you get back."

I pull out a straight razor and a can of shaving cream. "You sure you want it all cut off, Sam?"

He eyes the razor. "Just make sure you keep that thing above my neck." He smiles at Diana. *"Now* I'm bein' nasty, Miss Diana."

"Hope we have an earthquake while she's cuttin' you," Diana says. "You could use a little slowin' down, *Preacher."*

"The Lord said to be fruitful and multiply," Sam says as I spread the shaving cream on his head. "I'm just doing my small part to bring beauty into the world."

"Like Angie?" I ask.

His head snaps to me. "Which one?"

I blink. "You have more than one daughter named Angie?"

He shrugs. "Doesn't everybody?" He laughs. "I'm just messin' with you. Yeah, Angie's mine. She's Deacon Rutledge's granddaughter."

"Really?"

He nods. "Now, there's a man who needs a good spanking. He hasn't spoken to his daughter, Paulette, since Angie was born. Why you probably ain't seen her comin' around to the church."

I shave off Sam's hairs all in one stroke. "Y'all ought to come to Antioch this Sunday. I'll play something special for you." I smile. "Like 'Jesus Loves the Little Children.' "

"Why, Mrs. Borum, are you invitin' *me* to Antioch?"

"Yes."

"Will it be a date?"

"Puh-lease," I say. "I'm much too old for you, Sam."

"True."

"And I want you to bring Paulette and Angie, too. The good deacon sits on the right side, third row, and the row in front of him always has room." I wipe off the extra shaving cream. "No one wants Deacon Rutledge lookin' down that pointy nose of his at them during the service."

Sam rubs his hands together. "Service is at ten-thirty sharp, right?"

"Right."

"We'll be there." He steps out of the chair. "What I owe you?"

"Nothin', Sam. Just your presence in church Sunday with . . . with one of your families."

He stands taller. "Ain't enough room in that church for all my families, but we all part of the family of God, right?" He steps up to Diana. "You want to be part of my family, pretty lady?"

"Already am," Diana says with a groan. "Shakura Barlow is my cousin."

He squints. "Y'all blood-related?"

Diana nods. "I ain't interested, Sam." She nods at me. "Seen what a hypocrite preacher can do to a friend of mine."

He slumps and pouts. "I'm no hypocrite, Miss Diana. I practice what I preach. I preach lovin', and I do me some. Nothin' hypocritical about it." He bows to us. "Good day, ladies. Got to go back out there and preach some more lovin'."

"Dag," Diana says. "Kevin was right. It *is* gettin' right thick in here."

He pulls his hat over his head. "Ladies, it's been a pleasure. Just remember this: it's a God eat God dyslexic world out there." He leaves.

"What the hell did he just say?" Diana asks.

"I haven't the slightest idea."

Customers stream in steadily during the day and early afternoon, and Kevin makes 'em all smile, hum, sing, or do little chair dances— and no one throws out a hip. The boy has talent, and whether he's playing some Luther Ingram or some Aretha Franklin, his expression doesn't change. Guess he lets the music do that for him. Kind of like me. All folks see of me is my back while I play. Kevin and I let the notes give us our personalities.

Tonya calls Diana's late in the afternoon. "Y'all busy?"

"Full house," I say. "What you need done?"

"Just my nails."

"You got a date?"

"Nah. Givin' my coochie a rest. Why don't you come over tonight?"

Dag, two women who are prettier than me are gonna be home on a Friday night? "I'm beat, girl. Gonna go home to my bed."

"Anybody waitin' there for you?"

"No."

"Just checkin'. See ya."

We have to stay open past seven since the Calhoun Civic Center is having one of those black folks shows running, you know, the ones with singing and gospel and a title like "Stop the World Cuz I Wanna Get Off Since Mama's Mad at Everybody." Can't have one of those shows unless "Mama" is in the title.

I feel light-headed on my walk home in the dark since I haven't eaten all day and have to rest before going up the stairs to my apartment.

"Hey," a voice says.

I turn and see Jar-Man camped out in the yard next door. "You trespassin' again?"

"No. Pork and beans at the jail tonight. Beans taste like rubber, sauce has too much sugar."

"So . . . you're just sittin'?"

"Tried to get inside, but evicted folks is right conflicted. They been kicked out, but they won't let anyone else in."

"You could stay with me. My couch is free."

"Nah. Just need me a basement or something, something close to the ground." He pulls the glass off his ear. "Can't hear God if I'm too high in the air. Got to be close to the earth."

I get all sorts of chill bumps. Jar-Man's jar . . . is his direct line to God? "What's God tellin' you today?"

"Havin' trouble today. Too much interference from all those damn satellites up there."

I try not to smile, but I can't help it.

He scowls. "Didn't expect you to believe me."

I move closer to him. "No, I do believe you, Jar-Man. Really."

"Fred."

"Huh?"

"Name's Fred."

I squat in front of him. "Hey, Fred." The man has some serious funk, but his scowl is gone. "We got a laundry room in our basement you could use. Ain't no one doin' any laundry on Friday night." Except for maybe me, but I'm too tired to do it. "No one will bother you."

He smiles. "You got any Salisbury steak?"

I stand, pains shooting into my hips. My squattin' muscles is for shit. "No, but I know I could whip up something quick."

"Okay. I guess I can settle for whatever you got."

I lead him to the laundry room, which really ain't a laundry room. Yeah, it has a washer and a dryer (each at least thirty years old), but there isn't a place to fold your clothes, there ain't no hot water for your whites, and the heating element in the dryer needs to be replaced. Your clothes get dry in a couple hours, but they come out all cold.

He hands me the Mason jar. "Mind cleanin' and fillin' that with something?"

"No. Iced tea okay?"

"Is it sweet?"

"A little."

"Is it fresh?"

"Made yesterday."

"Okay, but not too much ice."

I leave him to get comfortable and fix him a salad plate because that's all I have. When I hold the plate and his jar out to him, he shrinks back. "That's rabbit food, woman."

"Rabbits live in the ground, don't they, Fred?"

He knits his eyebrows together. "Yeah, they do." He takes the plate and munches on a carrot. "Not bad."

I hand him the jar. "Just bang on the pipes when you're done."

"Okay." He takes a sip of the tea. "Too sweet."

The nerve! "I'll make the next batch with less sugar."

"You do that."

I return to my apartment, fall out on the couch, and laugh. Lord, what a day. I had Kevin at my feet, Sam in my chair, and now Fred's in my basement. *I been surrounded by men all day, Lord. When You gonna make my phone ring?*

And then, the phone does ring.

I race into the kitchen and grab the phone. "Hello?"

"Ruth, it's Junie. You made a decision yet?"

I make a face at God. "Yes, Junie. I will play at your wedding."

I have to hold the phone away from my ear as Junie whoops it up. Geez, I'm just makin' everybody's day but my own today. "Thank you *so* much, Ruth. God bless you!"

Don't bless me yet, Junie. "And Kevin Myers will also be playing."

"Kevin . . . Myers?"

"Yes. Nicole Myers's boy. He's an absolute genius with the guitar, and—"

"But I just want you, Ruth," she interrupts.

Hmm. "Well, if you want me, you gotta have Kevin, too. We are a package deal."

"Oh. I'll have to speak to Jonas about this."

"Why? It's *your* wedding, right? It's *your* day."

Junie doesn't say anything. "You're right. Um, what will he be playing?"

" 'There Is Love.' You know that one?"

"Yes. It's pretty. Will Kevin be singing it, too?"

I get a wicked idea. What would it be like if *I* sang that song to Jonas and Junie? Oh, the cringing in the pews. And I wouldn't even have to sing it. I could just say the words. "We'll let you know, Junie."

"I'm so excited, Ruth!" And now, so am I. "Oh, how do you want to be listed in the program?"

Another wicked idea. "As Mrs. Borum, of course."

"Um, well, Jonas prefers—"

"I know what he prefers, but it's what I prefer. My name is still legally Mrs. Borum, and we wouldn't want to print a lie in something folks are going to read in a church, would we?"

"Why, no, of course not."

"You take care, Junie."

"Oh, I will. I'll let you know when we're rehearsing."

"Thanks."

"And, Ruth, I just know God's going to bless you something wonderful for this."

I hang up and shout, "When?"

A moment later, the pipes rattle from down deep in the house.

I put a pot on to boil and get the tea bags ready. "Lord Jesus, I just don't know if I can handle all these blessings. Slow Your holy roll now. I don't want to get blessinged out."

Fourteen

The phone wakes me before sunrise the next morning.

I think it's a wrong number and growl, "What?"

"Ruth? This is Dewey."

What time is it—5:38! *Lord, Your on-time status is in jeopardy. This just ain't the time!* "Hi, Dewey."

"Um, the kids and I are goin' bowling later today," he says. I hear Tee's voice in the background saying, "Ask her, Daddy! Ask her!" Tee's up, too? What the hell's goin' on over there? "They want you to go along with us."

They want me to go along. Hmm. What about the daddy? And what's he doing gettin' his city-born and -raised kids up at the crack of country dawn? "When y'all goin'?"

"Well, the kids are awake now, so as soon as Mountainside opens at eight. We'll be leavin' here about a quarter till."

So "later today" means when the sun finally rises, and I have to walk over to his place to participate. This obviously isn't a date. "I'll be there by then."

"Good. Well, uh, we'll see you. Bye."

I sit up and stretch. My feet are killing me, my knees are achy, and my hair looks like the ink-blot tests that bitch court psychologist showed me. I have no clean, casual clothes except for a black sweatshirt and sweatpants, I'm about to take an ice-cold shower, and I'm also about to go bowling for the first time in my life . . . with a man who could have called *two days ago so I could be ready to do this shit right!* What did the biblical Ruth do to get a hookup with Boaz? Her mother-in-law said something like "take a bath and put on some perfume,

homegirl, and wear your finest threads." Something like that. I flip
through my Bible and find the passage: ". . . wash thyself therefore,
and anoint thee, and put thy raiment upon thee, and get thee down to
the floor: but make thyself known unto the man, till he shall have done
eating and drinking."

Don't see him till he's had his breakfast. I use star-sixty-nine to call
Dewey back since I can't remember the number from when I called
him from Avery. "Dewey, have y'all eaten?"

"Yeah. We had us some Captain Crunch with those little berry
things."

"Crunchberries."

"Yeah."

"Y'all have juice?"

"Nope. Just the milk."

"Oh." He has eaten and had some milk. "Just checkin' to see if I
needed to bring y'all anything."

"We're fine."

"Okay. See you in a bit."

Guess it's time to get me down to the floor (of a bowling alley?)
and make myself known to this man.

I brave the shower first. I turn it on and get wet; then I snap it off
and soap up. I am shivering something fierce and decide not to rinse
off. I ain't too young to have a heart attack, and this shower just ain't a
blessing this morning. I towel off most of the soap and realize that I'll
just have to be itchy and ashy today.

I tackle my hair next. I am probably the only hairstylist on earth
with shitty hair. It's possessed. One day it lays almost right, and the
next day it sticks straight up and out. This morning, it does the opposite of what I want it to do. I lift, it falls. I press, it springs up. I roll it
and hold it for a minute, and it doesn't do a damn thing. It just ain't
awake yet. Maybe I can trick it. I could fake like I'm about to lift it and
press it instead . . .

It's hat day. Again. I hope it's dark in that alley, because my navy
blue visor does not go with black sweats.

I slip into the sweats and notice lint. Lots of lint. Black sweats are
lint magnets. I don't have a lint roller, so I sit with a roll of masking
tape . . . and make a damn fool of myself. Now I have stripes about a
half inch wide. I am going bowling as a zebra.

I take a whiff of my walking shoes before I put them on. They reek.
I spray some of the bathroom air freshener in them, so now I'll smell

like "Country Meadow" all day. I "anoint" myself with perfume, but I still smell that country meadow. Least there ain't any cow patties in my meadow, and to make sure of that, I don't eat breakfast. I ain't gonna leave no clouds behind me when I bowl.

I look at my face carefully. I still have smooth, almost silky skin on my freckly face, but according to Tonya, "It ain't got no definition." She showed me once how to highlight my eyes, nose, and lips with a few simple strokes (and hide most of my freckles), so I attempt to do the same. Mascara, lipstick, lipstick pencil, moisturizing base . . . This ain't gonna work. Who adds makeup to sweats and a visor? I end up looking like a black vampire. "I vant to zuck zum face," I say to my reflection, and I wipe that shit off. I do use some of the fancy oatmeal milk facial cleanser Tonya bought me for my birthday. Who figured that a bowl of cereal would be good for your face anyway? Someone out there has too much time on his or her hands. I sit back and stare at the woman in the mirror. She stares back, then starts cracking up. She has a nice laugh.

I rest a moment on the couch. It's quarter after seven. Do I go over early to see how they're living, or do I arrive on time? If I arrive on time, I prove to Dewey that at least one of us can be punctual. If I arrive early, I might seem too eager. But . . . I'm curious. I gotta see how they're living. Hell, I'm dressed like a black cat—might as well go *be* one.

I leave the apartment and am almost down the stairs of the porch when I hear a voice. "Mornin'."

I turn and see Fred. "Why you out here so early?"

He twists the jar on his ear. "Better reception. 'Sides, somebody took a shower at an ungodly hour this morning. Damn pipes woke my ass up. You ought to get them pipes fixed."

"Yeah. Well, I'm off."

"Where you off to lookin' like you goin' on recon?"

"On what?"

"Recon. Put a little paint on your face, and you could be a marine. Except for them stripes. Y'all need a better dryer."

The sun ain't even up, and you can see the stripes on my sweats? Geez. "Were you a marine, Fred?"

He nods. "Two tours in Nam." Daa-em. One tour would be enough for anybody. "I'll guard the place while you're gone."

"It doesn't need guarding, Fred. There ain't nothin' inside worth stealing."

He screws the jar firmly into his ear. "That ain't what God tells me. Never know who might do some trespassin'." He winks. "You go on out on your date now."

I take a step and stop. "How you know that?" And it ain't a date . . . Is it?

He taps the glass with an index finger. "And make sure you watch the little arrows and not the pins. That's the key."

I cannot believe this. "God told you all that?"

He cocks his head like he's listening. He nods a couple times. "And don't worry about the weight of the ball. Just find one that fits your fingers."

"I will." *Lord, are You hearing what Fred's telling me that You said? Why didn't You just say it to me and cut out the middle man?* "I gotta go."

He holds up one finger, nods once, and smiles. "Take your time. They ain't ready. The littlest one is havin' a fit."

"Dee?"

He puts the jar down. "That boy needs your help, Ruth Childress."

I have so many chill bumps my skin feels tight. How does Fred know all this? "How you know my name? And don't tell me God told you."

"Okay." He blows in the jar and sticks it back up to his ear. "I won't tell you."

He doesn't say another word. "I'll see you later," I say, and I practically jog the four blocks to Dewey's apartment as the sun becomes an orange ball in the sky. I tap on the door till Tee opens it.

"Good morning, Miss Jones."

She looks at my shoes, her little nose twitching. Shit, I sprayed too much. "Hi, Penny. C'mon in."

I step inside the apartment . . . and am almost out of it. This ain't no shotgun apartment; it's a little pistol no bigger than the size of my sitting room. An old joke finally makes sense to me: "Your apartment so small, when you put the key in the lock, you break the back window." A two-seater sofa hugs the left wall. Probably a sleeper for Dewey, but I don't see how he can fit in it. The back wall is the kitchen with only three cabinets, a single sink, a skinny, two-burner electric stove, and a noisy Kelvinator fridge from back in the '50s. Some stools sit in front of a skinny counter. Not much of a dinner table. To the right is the only other door, most likely to the bathroom. A bunk bed, neatly made, and an enormous antique dresser with a mirror cover most of the space to the right. A small, dusty TV sits on the dresser.

"Daddy and Dee are in the bathroom," Tee says, sitting on the couch.

I sit next to her, realizing that I'm sitting on Dewey's bed. *And we haven't even kissed yet!* "Everything all right?"

She shakes her head. "Dee peed himself again."

"Again?"

She nods. "Daddy says it's the medicine." She points at the bunk bed. "I sleep in the top bunk."

I look at the bottom bunk and see plastic sticking out from the mattress. Poor child is peeing his bed, too. "How long they been in there?"

She shrugs. "A long time. Dee's taking another bath."

Maybe it was more than pee. "Did, um, did Dee throw a temper tantrum this morning?"

"Uh-huh. He doesn't want to go."

"I thought he liked bowling."

"He does." She puts her hand on mine. "But when Daddy told him you were goin' with us, Dee fell out on the floor and started kicking his legs."

"What?"

"Wanna watch TV? Cartoons are on."

"Yeah, sure."

She leaps from the couch and snaps on the TV.

Dee pitched a fit when he heard that I was going? What'd I ever do to him? The last time I was with him, he drew those pictures for me. Dee "spoke" to me . . . And the very next day, he's off to the psychiatrist. He can't blame me for that, can he? *I was trying to help him, Lord. Make that child understand!*

The door to the bathroom opens, and Dee, wrapped in a towel, comes shivering across the room to his bunk where he sits. His eyes are sunken into his head, his lips permanently frowning, his shoulders hunched. There doesn't seem to be any life in him at all. Dewey follows a few moments later with a bottle of lotion. "We'll be ready in a few minutes, Ruth," he says, and he begins lotioning Dee's legs.

I stand. "I can do that if you like."

"It's all right," Dewey says without turning to me. "I'm getting pretty good at it."

I see a stack of clothes on the dresser and go to them, unrolling a pair of almost-white socks. When Dewey turns, I hand the socks to him and look at his eyes. This man has not slept at all, and he's looking older than me. He takes the socks with a nod, and I turn to the stack again. Staring up at me are a pair of underwear and some plastic underpants, the kind kids wear when they're potty training. *Lord Jesus, why are You lettin' this happen to this boy? What did this child ever do to You?* I hand Dewey the underwear and the plastic pants, and he slides them up Dee's legs. Dee barely moves at all. It's almost like Dewey's dressing a doll. I shake out Dee's jeans before giving them to Dewey, and the sound jolts Dee, making him look quickly at me. *You little devil!* You're here, all right. You're just playin' a little game.

"It's okay, it's okay," Dewey whispers to Dee. "Stand up." Dee slides off the bed and steps into his jeans, looking, as far as I can tell, at absolutely nothing again. This child is a pretty good zombie, but I've seen better staring at me from my own bathroom mirror.

Dewey removes the towel from around Dee and lotions his little bird chest and back while I pick lint off Dee's little maroon sweatshirt. I stretch out the neck opening and make my move, stepping between Dewey and Dee when he turns to take the sweatshirt from me. "I'll do it," I say, slipping the sweatshirt over Dee's head.

"Thanks. I'll, uh, wash my hands."

I have to hold Dee's arms up to get them into the sleeves, and Dee's eyes never leave that nowhere place he's so fond of. I look up and see Tee leaning over to watch. I smooth my hand on Dee's chest. "Looking good, Mr. Dee. Where are your shoes?" I see them peeking from under the bed and grab them. "Sit back on the bed, boy." He doesn't move. I put my eyes as close to his eyes as I can. "I said, sit back on the bed, boy." Dee's eyes dart to the side; then he backs up and sits. "Give me your right foot." His feet stay still. I lock eyes with his. "Your right foot, Mr. Dee." He shoots it out faster than I can move away, his big toe digging into my knee. I know it hurt him more than it hurt me, so I don't react at all . . . though the little boy needs to have that toenail trimmed. Tee laughs from her perch above us, but I ignore her. I slide the shoe on but don't tie it. "Your left foot now, Mr. Dee." This time I back away before he can nail me, and I slip the left shoe on. I duck my head under the top bunk and sit next to him. "Now tie 'em up."

"He won't do it," Tee says.

"Wanna bet?" I say to her. "Tie your shoes, Dee."

Dee doesn't move, his legs still sticking straight out.

I put my lips right next to his ear. "You ain't foolin' no one, little boy," I whisper. "There ain't a thing wrong with you a switch couldn't fix. Now tie 'em up or I'll take a switch to your ass." He turns his face slowly to me. "Saw a nice switch on my way over; think it mighta even had a few thorns on it." He tries to jump off the bed, but I haul him back on. "I ain't kiddin', boy. Tie 'em up. Now."

Dee starts to shake, his little face turning red. He takes a huge gulp of air and closes his mouth.

"Uh-oh!" Tee yells.

"I know this game," I whisper, and I pinch Dee's nose tightly for good measure. Dee's eyes pop open, but he won't take a breath. "You want to play this game right, you got to cut off all the openings. Otherwise you might cheat."

Dewey comes out of the bathroom wiping his hands on a towel. "What are you doing?"

Dee starts to swoon. "Winning a little game that me and Dee are playing," I say. "He thinks he can hold his breath so he won't have to tie his shoes."

"He's holdin' his breath?"

"Uh-huh. He holds it long enough, he gonna pass out."

"Let go!" Dewey yells, taking a step toward me.

I shake my head and put out my hand. "Watch."

In a matter of seconds, Dee's eyes flutter, he falls over, I let go of his nose, and he takes an enormous breath. He starts shaking again.

"Scared you, didn't it?" I say.

Dee nods. *Thank You, Lord. The nodding boy is back.*

"And you ain't gonna ever do it again, are you?"

He shakes his head.

"And you're gonna tie those shoes, right?"

His hands fly to those shoes, and though he has trouble with the loops, he ties 'em up just fine.

I duck out from under the bunk and put my hand out to Dee. He takes it without any commands from me—*as he should.* His mama must have schooled him on switches. Tiffany Jones didn't play that, and neither will I. "We ready."

I can tell that Dewey doesn't know what to say because he doesn't say anything. He lifts Tee off the bunk and carries her to the front door. He holds it open for Dee and me, and we walk out to the truck, Dewey running around to the passenger side to open that door. Two doors in one day! I put Dee in ahead of me and slide in, fitting just fine on the bench seat. I like me some truck, yes sir. Plenty of room in a truck for us big-boned women, though I don't like the fact that it leans to the right when I finally settle in. I pull Dee close to me, Tee slides in from the driver's side, and Dewey gets in, tilting the truck back to his side. *Lord Jesus, thank You for making a man on this earth who is bigger than me.*

Dewey backs out, turning the wheel with those massive arms of his, and we're off to the bowling alley. And little Dee doesn't let go of my hand the entire way there. Dewey lets Tee fiddle with the radio dial, but she doesn't find anything since the truck only has an AM radio that brings in mostly all-news stations.

"Rides nice," I say.

"Yep," Dewey says. "Got over two hundred thousand miles on her."

Her? Why is it that a truck is a "her"? For that matter, why is a ship called a "she"? What are men trying to say about us women?

"Yep, Gert and me been together for ten years now."

"Gert?"

Dewey smiles. "Just always called her that."

"Short for Gertrude?"

"Nope. Just . . . Gert. Seems to fit her."

"Nanna calls her truck Betsy," Tee says. "She say, 'C'mon, Betsy. Get me up the hill, girl.' "

"Truck's older than Mama," Dewey says. "Still runs like a dream." The truck or Nanna?

But this scene . . . is a dream. I'm finally with this man, his children in between us, going out and away from Vine Street, and we're making conversation. About trucks. Hmm. Long as he don't start talkin' about NASCAR, we might just get along.

The parking lot at Mountainside Lanes is almost full when we arrive. "Kids' league," Dewey says. "But they always have a few lanes open."

When we get inside, I hear the glorious giggles and shouts of children and see half the bowling alley filled with dancing, jumping . . . white kids. Ain't a black person in here besides me, Tee, and Dee. We follow Dewey to his locker, he gets his ball bag, and we go to the front counter.

"Need a lane, Charlie," he says to the bearded man behind the counter.

Charlie looks us over and presses a button on a computer. "Lane forty. Y'all need bumpers?"

"Yeah."

Charlie picks up a microphone. "Bumpers on lane forty." He puts the microphone down. "Y'all need shoes?"

"Yeah." Dewey bends down and looks inside one of Tee's shoes, then inside one of Dee's. Man doesn't even know his own children's shoe sizes. "A two and a thirteen," he says to Charlie.

Charlie gets the shoes and looks at me. "A woman's twelve," I say softly.

"Man's nine, okay?" Charlie asks. "They run kinda big."

This is embarrassing. "Sure."

We carry our shoes to the other end of the alley away from the kids' league and sit on the bench in front of the last lane. Tryin' to keep us as far away from the white folks as possible, huh, Charlie? My red-and-blue shoes don't quite fit—my feet may be long, but they ain't wide enough—but I lace them up tight, checking and tightening Tee's and Dee's shoes. Another alley dude lays these long plastic tubes down each gutter. Dewey shines his ball with a towel. "Find yourselves a ball," he says to us, pointing at a rack of colorful balls.

Tee races to the rack and tries to lift a purple ball with enormous holes. I take her hand away from it. "That's a bit big for you, girl."

"I'm only gonna push it, Penny."

"Oh." I put my fingers in the purple ball and find that they fit pretty well. "I'll use this one, too." Fifteen pounds? Geez. I'm in men's shoes about to use a man's ball.

Dee picks out a red ball, and we carry the balls to the circular rack. Dewey has already entered our names on the big blue computer screen, Dee's name first. "Y'all ready?" he asks. Dee nods, and Tee says, "Yeah!"

I don't say a thing. No, I am not ready. My hands and knees start to sweat. *Lord, please keep me from making a fool of myself.*

Dewey carries Dee's ball to a spot behind a line. Dee squats over the ball and holds it on the sides, rolling it back and forth before pushing it down the lane. It starts out straight, then rolls left into the bumper before straightening out and heading right down the middle. The pins don't do a whole lot, falling over one by one like real slow dominos, but only four are left standing.

"Way to go!" Dewey shouts, and Dee almost smiles, backing away from the pins to the ball return. Dee's second ball knocks down three more, and he returns to his seat beside me.

"Almost got 'em all," I say, and I put my arm around him. He stiffens and looks at my hand on his right shoulder, but I don't let go. This is my child today.

Dewey helps Tee with her ball, and Tee obviously likes to keep folks in suspense, rolling that ball back and forth between her legs for the longest time before pushing it down the lane with a loud "Whoo!" She squats and mumbles, "come on, come on" nonstop till the ball hits the pins. Only four fall. "Shoot," she says with a snap of the fingers. Her next ball misses everything, but she doesn't seem to care, skipping back to us. "I'm just gettin' warmed up," she says.

And now, it's my turn. I slide my fingers into the holes and center myself on the little dots at my feet. "Don't look at the pins; look at the arrows," I whisper to myself. I step forward with my right leg, do a little pitter-pat, throw the ball out behind me, and rocket it forward staring at those little arrows. That ball . . . daa-em . . . hauls some God-honest *ass* down that lane and knocks them all down. *Lord Jesus, thank You, oh, my God!*

I try to remain calm, but I do a little dance back to my seat. Dee's eyes are wide, and Tee's yelling, "Strike!"

Dewey smiles and nods. "Looks like I got some competition."

"Just lucky," I say.

He stands and picks up his ball. "You have nice form."

Whoo, my heart! "Thank you."

He wipes the ball only once, does his little routine, launches that ball, and only knocks down nine, the one in the very middle left standing.

"Ah, Daddy, you missed the booty pin!" Tee shouts.

Dewey's face turns red.

"The what?" I whisper to Tee.

She points at the lonely pin. "That's called the booty pin."

I am not about to ask a six-year-old why . . . so I ask Dewey. "Why's it called the booty pin, Dewey?"

His face gets even redder. "Um, if I don't knock it down, um, I don't . . ." He grabs his ball and turns before finishing his sentence. He don't get no booty? Daa-em. Hope he makes it, for my sake.

He approaches the pin slowly, releases a little more smoothly, and turns his back on that lonely pin, closing his eyes. Tee and I look around him to see the ball just barely slide by the pin.

"You missed the booty pin, Daddy!"

"Yup," he says, his face nearly as red as some of my freckles. He sits next to Tee.

I look at the scoreboard, and I'm actually winning. I push Dee off the seat, and the two of us go to get his ball. I hand it to him, and he cradles it against his chest. "Want you to do the whole thing, boy," I say.

He carries the ball to the line and sets it down, pulls it way back, and rolls it to the right. It bounces off the right bumper, the left bumper, and the right bumper again before taking out six pins, two pins left on either side with a big hole in the middle. Dee turns to look at me with scrunched-up lips.

"It's okay," I say. The ball squirts out of its tunnel, and I hand it to him. "Just knock down as many as you can."

His second ball is another pinball off the bumpers that ends up right down the middle and misses everything. Dee pouts.

"What you poutin' for, boy?" I say. "You just kicked a field goal."

I hand the purple ball to Tee. She has some difficulty getting that heavy thing to the line and drops it with a bang. "Oops," she says. She flops to her butt and pushes the ball down the lane with her feet, knocking down eight without hitting either bumper.

I carry the ball to her this time. "Pretty good, girl."

"Thanks." She takes the ball, lines it up with a thumb, and kicks it down the lane . . . missing everything. "Oh, well," she says.

"Good try," I say, helping her up. "Use a little more right foot next time."

I stand at the ball return with my hand above the little fan. "Dewey, I have a confession to make."

"What?"

I pick up my ball. "This is the first time I have ever bowled in my life."

"You're kidding."

I shake my head. "So if you can give me any help, I'd surely appreciate it." And if you want to touch me, position my hips, say, you go right on. And if your hand should slip, oh, onto my ass, well—

"Just keep doin' what you're doin'."

I knew he was going to say that. Men and their "don't fix it if it ain't broke" mentality. The second ball I've ever bowled goes right down the middle leaving two pins far apart. "What do I do now?" I ask.

"Just try to get one," he says. "Seven-ten splits are nearly impossible to get."

I get my ball, take smaller steps, don't throw it as hard—and throw it straight down the middle. I turn and smile. "Got a field goal, too, Mr. Dee."

Dee smiles. *You brought smiling boy back, too, Lord. Thank You.*

For the rest of my first game, I throw it consistently down the middle, get another strike, two spares, and the rest? Splits. Lots of splits. "How do I keep from gettin' them?" I ask Dewey as he removes the scores from the screen. He won with a 189, and I had a 119. Dee and Tee tied at 84.

He points to the dots at the beginning of the lane. "Just stand a little to the right or left of the center dot. Your ball will hit the pocket more often." He looks over at a little clock on the wall. "Time for Dee's medicine." He pulls a bottle of pills from his shirt pocket.

Dee, who perked up steadily during the game, looks at me with those huge brown eyes of his. He doesn't want his medicine, and I don't want him to have any either. "I can give it to him," I say, and I hold out my hand to Dewey.

"It's okay."

I leave my hand there. "I have to use the ladies' room anyway."

He puts the bottle in my hand. "Just give him one with a little water," he whispers. "Just a tiny little bit of water. You understand?"

"Sure."

I take Dee's hand, and we walk into an empty ladies' room, going to the farthest stall and shutting the door behind us. I sit on the toilet seat and face him. "Dee, I have to tell you something. You see these pills?"

He nods.

"These pills are bad for you, you know that?"

Dee shrugs.

"They make you sleepy, don't they?"

He nods.

"They make you cranky, too, and I ought to know. I used to take pills like these, but I don't take them anymore." I open the pill bottle and drop one pill into his hand. "I'm not gonna make you take it, Dee. If you want to, you can just drop it into the toilet."

He looks at the pill, then drops it into the toilet.

"Feel better?"

He shrugs.

"Tell you what, any time you don't want to take these, you put it in the toilet. But if your daddy or Nanna is watching, you just put it under your tongue, and when no one's looking, you throw it away in the trash or something. Understand?"

He nods.

I rattle the bottle in front of him. "Sometimes medicine makes you sicker, Dee, makes you a zombie." I scrunch up my face and cross my eyes. "You don't want to be a zombie, do you?"

He shakes his head rapidly.

"Good. Now let's go out there and knock us down some pins."

During the second game, I get Dewey to help me position my feet. He doesn't touch me, but just having him standing behind or near me ... joy! I can't explain it. A man is staring at my ass, my legs, my feet, and he ain't grimacing or looking away. Though I don't bowl anywhere near my weight, I have a much better game, even getting two strikes in a row, and end up with a 165. Neither Tee nor Dee breaks 100; but they have so much fun, and I even catch Dee smiling up at me a couple times.

The whole "date" only costs Dewey ten bucks, and on the ride home, both Tee and Dee fall asleep between us.

"I loved the cake," Dewey whispers.

"Loved? Is it gone?" He nods. "I'll have to make you another."

"I'd like that. Um, did you really mean what you said in that note?"

"Yes."

He smiles. "I'm real new to all this. Tiffany raised them by herself, and, uh, I just don't know enough. I don't know what they like to eat, what clothes they should wear, when to bathe them. I'm learnin' somethin' new every day."

"You're doin' all right."

"I hope so."

We're quiet for a spell, and I fight like hell *not* to ask him about Tiffany Jones, though his silence gives me the perfect opening. I can think *Why didn't you do right by Tiffany?* but I can't get that thought to my lips. I mean, I hardly know this man, and I'm gonna bust out and ask him why he did another woman wrong with that woman's children right here beside me? Sure I want to know. I sort of have to know so I don't make the same mistakes that she made. But what if I don't want to hear his answer? Maybe Tiffany was too fat or ugly. Maybe she was too rough 'n' stuff with her Afro puffs. Maybe she beat his ass, though I can't see that happening to Dewey. The man's ass goes all the way to his shoulders. Man's gotta lot of back back there ... Or maybe *Tiffany* had too much back and he couldn't handle it. Not many men know what to do with a big booty.

I watch him watching the road for a few moments, his massive

hands wrapped around the steering wheel. No. Dewey knows what to
do. He gave her two children. Bet he could slap him some booty with
them hands. I don't know, maybe Tiffany was fat and sloppy and ate
too much (like I used to do), or maybe she couldn't clean or cook or
keep house. Maybe she didn't even like sex or liked it too much or
used sex as a substitute for love. Hell, maybe she snored too loud,
picked her nose in public, had pierced nipples and a nose ring, had a
sixth toe, and sported a tattoo of another man on her ass. Whatever the
reason, I'll let Dewey tell me about it when *he's* good and ready.

As long as he's ready to tell me soon, like tomorrow.

Dewey turns to me at a stoplight. "Well, Ruth, I'd appreciate any
kind of help you can give me. Mama tries to help out, but she's got a
farm to run down in Pine County."

"What kind of help you need?"

"Any."

So many possibilities. "How 'bout if I walk them home from school
on Tuesdays and Wednesdays? I'll be at Avery those days anyway.
That will give you a couple extra hours to work so you won't have to
work so late on Fridays."

"Tee told you."

"Yep."

He sighs. "What *hasn't* Tee told you?"

"Not much."

"She knows too much."

"Yep. And I can mind them till you get home either at the playground or at my place on Vine."

"Deal," he says as we turn onto Vine.

That was a quick decision. "You ain't gonna think no more about
it?"

"No." He smiles. "I'd be a fool not to take you up on this. If I put in
two more hours those days, I can get home at a reasonable hour on
Fridays. Can you mind them till, say, five?"

I could mind them much longer, Mr. Baxter. "Sure."

"Great. Where should I drop you off?"

I direct him to the apartment, Fred still in the same spot. "Are y'all
free to go to church tomorrow?" Dewey doesn't answer, leaning up
and squinting through the windshield. "That's just Fred. He's a friend
of mine."

"Oh."

"So . . . Are y'all free to go to church tomorrow?"

"Which one?"

"Antioch Church. I play the organ there."

Dewey blinks. "Um, I don't think so."

"You'll be my guest, Mr. Baxter."

"I'd feel out of place."

And the congregation at Antioch would help him feel more out of place. "Well, can I at least take your children? They'd like Sunday school, and I'd even let them sit with me at the organ during the service."

"I don't know."

"You'll get to sleep in. They'll be with me from nine to one at least."

He taps the steering wheel. "I'll think about it, let you know."

I open the door. "Don't wait too long this time, Mr. Baxter. Sunday school starts at nine-thirty sharp."

"Oh, yeah. I'm sorry about callin' you so early."

"Don't be. I had fun. Call me tonight, okay?"

"Okay."

I get out and shut the door. Dee stirs inside, yawns, and looks at me. I wave. He puts his little hand on the window, and I add mine. "Bye," I say, and I walk up the sidewalk as the truck rolls away.

"How was your date?" Fred asks.

I stare him down. "You tell me."

He closes his eyes. "Something about . . . a booty pin."

I laugh. "Better clean out that jar, old man."

"What's a booty pin?"

I smile. "Ain't no such thing as a booty pin. God's pullin' your leg."

"He wouldn't do that to me."

No, I think as I climb the steps to the porch, He wouldn't. But I might.

Fifteen

I'm almost sound asleep for a badly needed nap when the phone rings.

"Good morning, Ruth," Naomi says.

"Mornin'."

"What are you planning for today?"

"Nothin'."

"Want to go shopping or something? We could hit some outlet malls."

Oh, joy. All day in a car to watch Naomi spend money. "Not today."

She's quiet for a spell. "Say, I was looking at today's paper, and I happened to look at the personals section."

Not this shit again. "Just happened?"

"Um, yeah, and I saw one that looks promising."

She reads these to me occasionally, and though it sounds like they're for her, they are really for me. "Is this one for you or for me?" I ask this time.

"For you, of course." Of course. "Want me to read it to you?"

"No." I roll over and get more comfortable. "But go ahead."

"Okay. 'Single black male, forty-five, dependable, honest, thoughtful, nice, never married, tall, serious, Christian churchgoer, nonsmoker, nondrinker, enjoys walking, spending quiet evenings at home, seeks single black female for friendship and hopefully a lifetime of passion.' He sounds so right for you, Ruth."

"Naomi, what are you tryin' to do?"

"Do? All I did was read—"

"I know you don't like Dewey. You've made that perfectly clear. Now stay out of my business."

"Don't take it the wrong way."

"How many other ways are there to take it?"

"I'm just saying that there are black men out there for you."

"Yeah right. First of all, a man has got to be desperate to put one of those ads in the paper." Naomi doesn't respond. What'd I say? Wait a minute. Naomi the Beautiful has an ad running in the personals?

"He might not be desperate," she says softly. "He might be shy."

Naomi's kinda shy . . . hmm. "Come on, Naomi. Anyone who brags that much on hisself has to be lyin' if he's a real Christian. And I don't want to spend quiet evenings at home no more. I want to get out, go out. Shit, why don't *you* call him up or write him or whatever you do with those ads."

"I just might."

"Well, go on, then."

"I will. Goodbye, Ruth."

Click.

Daa-em. I can't take a nap now. I have to get to Hood's to get me a newspaper to check the personals for Naomi's ad. I grab some change and dash out to see Fred reading a newspaper. "Is that today's, Fred?"

"Yep." He folds it twice and holds it out to me without a word. I take it and find that it's open to the personals. "Third one down on the left," he says. "And the booty pin is the one in the middle."

Fred is one spooky man. I scan down the page and see Naomi's personal ad:

> *Christian SBF, 35, no kids, n/s, n/d, likes attending church, working out, playing cards, bowling ISO SBCM for friendship first.*

Her age is off by three years. It's just like a woman to lie about her age, but Naomi don't lie. Naomi never lies. Oh, my God! The ad in front of me has been running for *three* years? That's so sad.

But it ain't too sad to call Tonya about.

"You through with this, Fred?"

"Yep," Fred says. "You gonna need it anyway."

I rush inside and call Tonya with the news. "You know what our friend Naomi has been doing for the last three years?"

"Coloring her hair?"

"She has?"

"I don't know. You're her hairdresser. I was just taking a guess."

"You might be right, but did you know she has had a personals ad running in the *Calhoun Times* for three years?"

"Yes. I got one in there, too."

What? "No way, girl!"

"Sure. It's probably two columns over from Naomi's by now."

I trace a finger over two columns and find Tonya's:

SENSUOUS Ebony Goddess, 29, ISO SWM (25-40) who is healthy, financially secure, romantic, and has no kids, for the time of your life GUARANTEED.

"You ain't twenty-nine, Tonya."

"But I look twenty-nine, right? I want me a young stud with money so I can quit my job and lie around the house looking beautiful. And there ain't no black man in this town who's gonna give me that."

Two of the prettiest women I've ever known resort to this . . . *impersonal* method of meeting men? "I never thought you had any trouble getting men, Tonya."

"I don't. I just like to keep all my options open. Even got an ad out on the Internet. I might get lucky."

"I prefer to make my own luck."

"Dewey call yet?"

"Yep. Today, and I already been out on a date."

"It's only . . . ten-thirty."

"We went bowling." I describe the entire event, even mentioning the three booty pins Dewey missed.

"You must make him nervous, Ruth."

"I hope."

"And you bowled a one-nineteen and a one-sixty-five?"

"Yeah. Surprised myself."

"You on our team now, girl. Shoot, we might just win a game this week. Have you told Naomi?"

"No. She was too busy this morning tryin' to get me a hookup with a single black male."

"Age forty-five, likes to go walking?"

"Yeah."

"She tried the same shit with me last night. Heifer needs to get herself a life."

"And I need to get myself some rest. I used some muscles today I haven't used in years."

"You doin' anything tonight?"

"No. Dewey's supposed to call."

"I'll probably be home alone myself. Give me a call if you're bored."

"Okay."

I'm drifting off to sleep a little later when the phone rings again. "Hello?"

"The kids will be ready at nine," Dewey says.

Thank You, Lord. "Will you be going, Mr. Baxter?"

"Some other time."

"I'll hold you to that." And if you let me, I'll hold you to *me,* and then we'll see if your pin can knock my booty.

"See you tomorrow."

"Bye, Dewey."

I'm too excited to sleep after that, so I cook up some greens, pinto beans, and corn muffins to have me a country lunch. I jump a little rope while the water boils, and halfway through "Cinderella" I hear a knock at the door.

I open it and see Fred, jar in hand. "Don't tell me. God told you to come to lunch."

"No. Smelled it. This building needs replacement windows."

"You wanna eat it here or in the basement?"

He looks at the jar in his hands. "Nice day for a picnic."

"It ain't but fifty degrees outside."

"Won't have no ants, then." He looks up. "Greens taste better outside anyway."

So . . . Fred and I have a picnic, me wrapped in a blanket, him in only that windbreaker. I never thought I was that good of a cook, but Fred makes every bite seem like it's the best he's ever had.

"Corn bread's just right," he tells me.

"It's from a box," I tell him.

"Good brand, Jiffy." He holds up a muffin in the sunlight. "Ain't it nice how somethin' so simple as a muffin can make your day?" He takes a bite. "Yeah, it's just a muffin, but when you make somethin' with love, it just tastes better. You love him, Ruth?"

Where's this coming from? "Which 'him' you referring to?"

"The white man."

I wipe my lips with a napkin. "Don't know. I hardly know him."

Fred laughs. "There's a lot there to love. Man's as big as a bus."

"He ain't that big. He's a country boy, and they grow 'em bigger in Pine County."

"He got a big heart, too," Fred says as he sips his tea. "Just never really opened it up before. His children are workin' on it, though. Yeah, children can really open up a heart."

The man is righter than right. I look at his empty plate. "Want some more?"

"No. Gotta watch my weight."

We sit in silence for a while. "Fred, how do you know so much?"

He shrugs. "It's a gift like any other, I suppose. Didn't have it all my life. Sort of developed it after Nam. Ain't the kind of gift I'd give to someone else, though. Don't like what I hear most times." He smooths the grass beside him. "But ever since I been sittin' here, it's all been good."

"You'll tell me if something's wrong, won't you?"

He cocks his ear. "Phone's ringing."

"For me?" He nods. "Who is it?"

"Good news and bad news."

I rush inside and grab the phone. "Hello?"

"Ruth, it's Jonas."

Well, if it isn't Mr. Bad News himself. But Fred said there was some good news comin', so I decide to be civil. "Hello, Jonas. Did Junie tell you that I—"

"Yes, yes," he interrupts. "But that Myers boy is not playing."

Junie told him? I didn't think she had the guts. Good for her. "Why not, Jonas?"

"I do not want a beggar playing at my wedding."

This coming from the man who chose Junie. There will already be one beggar at the church. "Kevin's no beggar. In fact, he has a steady job at Diana's now, playing inside off the street. He's really quite good, and—"

"He won't play at my wedding."

I take a breath and count to five. "Then, I won't either."

"Fine."

Fine? Just like that? Junie's gonna be pissed. Maybe this is the good news? "Anything else?"

"I'm tired of you embarrassing me."

"*Me* embarrassing *you?*"

"Yes."

"How have I embarrassed you, Jonas?"

"Having that degenerate in your front yard, feeding him your scraps." Jonas has spies. "And today you have a picnic with him in broad daylight?"

"Fred is a remarkable man, Jonas."

"I'll bet he is."

Do I hear jealousy? From Jonas the narcissist? "Fred is a wonderful man. But anyway, how is loving my neighbor embarrassing to you?"

He doesn't answer right away. "You still have my last name, Ruth. When are you going to change it?"

When the right man comes along, I guess. When keeping it loses its effect on the congregation at Antioch. Two Mrs. Borums in the same church—I just have to see what confusion that causes. "I may never change it, Jonas."

"Why?"

"I don't have to give you my reasons."

"Ruth, for the sake of the church, you must change your name once Junie and I are married."

"Why?"

"You want me to look like a polygamist?"

Hadn't thought of that one. "*Are* you a polygamist, Jonas?"

"I knew talking sense to you was a waste of time."

"You're right. Guess I'm still just a little mentally unbalanced, huh?"

"You can say that again. Going out in public with that white man, the very same white man who made a fool of himself in our church. Have you no shame?"

Jesus! Jonas has white spies, too? "Guess I don't, Jonas. Must have lost my shame in the settlement as well. Least I had me some shame before the divorce, huh? Always good to have a marriage with at least one shameful person." He doesn't respond, but I bet he's grinding his teeth. "Oh, by the way, I'll have his children with me at Antioch tomorrow."

"What?"

"Don't worry. They're black, and they still have a sense of shame."

"Ruth, you just can't—"

"Can't *what?*" I interrupt. "Can't bring children to the house of the Lord?"

I hear him take a massive breath. "You are just bound and determined to hurt me in every way you can."

"I'm bringing two wonderful children to church. If that hurts you, you should get out of the preaching profession. 'Suffer the little children to come unto Me,' right?"

He doesn't speak for the longest time. "So you and the white man are serious?"

"His name is Dewey Baxter, and yes, I'm gettin' serious." Not too sure about Dewey bein' serious back, but I'm workin' on it.

"I don't know who you are anymore, Ruth."

"What you talkin' about? You knew I was half white when you married me. I've tried one half of me and got you. That was a mistake. Now I want to see how my other half lives."

"Dr. Holt needs to increase your medication."

"Haven't seen Dr. Holt in months."

"You haven't?"

So Jonas *doesn't* know everything. "No. I'm completely me now."

"Well, that will change some things."

"Such as?"

"How much spousal support I have to give you."

"From the pittance I get now, you might as well cut me off entirely." What am I saying? Oh, yeah. I don't want to have anything to do with this man, and that measly little check hurts my pride.

"I'll see my lawyer."

"Good." Dag, we're talking *and* being civil. Is *this* the good news? "Jonas, I have to know something, and if you don't want to tell me, you don't have to. Did you marry me because I'm light-skinned? It wasn't because I was beautiful."

"I married you because God called me to."

"You must not have heard Him right. Did God call you to marry Junie so soon after our divorce?"

"As a matter of fact, He did."

"You got to get your ears cleaned out, Jonas. You still got a whole lot of shit up in there. I'll get Fred to loan you his Mason jar so you can hear God more clearly."

"I don't have to listen to this," Jonas barks, and he hangs up on me. But I'm not mad.

Wait a minute. I'm not mad. What is wrong with me? I should be mad. He had no right to say any of what he said, yet . . . It just doesn't matter anymore. I don't give a shit what Jonas thinks anymore. *Thank You, Lord.*

I return to Fred with the goofiest smile on my face. "You were right."

"What was the good news?"

"I don't have to play at my ex-husband's wedding."

"Hmm. And the bad?"

"I've pissed off my ex-husband."

Fred nods a bit. "You sure you ain't got 'em mixed up?"

"What?"

"Maybe not playin' is the bad news, and pissin' off your ex is the good news."

I shake my head. "No, I think I got it right."

He empties the rest of his tea on the ground and dries the jar with a napkin. "I'll let you know."

"You don't have to, Fred. It's pretty obvious to me."

But of course, I have to think about it the rest of the day. Not playing is *bad* news? Naomi will certainly be happy, and I won't have to see the man who I used to love marrying someone else. But I won't get any closure, and Kevin won't get a big audience. And pissing Jonas off is *good* news? When that holy man's really angry, he can do some unholy damage. I lost so many friends during the divorce . . . but I'm making many more. And in a wicked way, I want him to be angry, even afraid of me. He knows I can ruin him for life, and though that makes me feel powerful, I don't intend to exercise that power. Yet. Besides, an angry Jonas might just self-destruct on his own without my help.

I can't help but humming "Ain't-a That Good News" off and on through the afternoon and evening, even adding the line: "I've pissed-a off the good reverend, ain't-a that good news?"

Sixteen

Bright and early Sunday morning, I collect Tee and Dee and march them to Antioch. Dewey was barely awake, kissing each on the forehead and winking at me before shutting the door.

That single wink . . . Damn, that's better than coffee to start my day. I don't need me no caffeine—I need winks from a cute man with dimples.

Dewey has done a decent job of dressing them. Tee wears a frilly dark purple dress with white tights and black shoes, and Dee sports a gray suit and red tie. Both look scrubbed and polished, and neither seems reluctant to go to church with a penny-colored lady wearing a black dress with a white collar. Jonas had said that I looked too "Catholic" in this dress and forbid me to wear it, and that's why I am wearing it today. I want that man to notice me more today than when we were married. I have this feeling deep down in my bones that something wonderful is going to happen today.

We get us some double-takes going into Antioch, let me tell you. I hear some fine whispers like "Isn't that—" and "Will you look at—" as we skip down the sidewalk and go in the side door to the basement. I lead "my children" through a maze of folding chairs to the back corner where Mrs. Robertson's room is, smiling at anyone who stares open-mouthed at us.

"Got some new additions to your class this morning," I tell Mrs. Robertson, a sweet, smiling woman who was my Sunday school teacher thirty years ago and is one of the few people from the old days who still speaks to me. "I'd like you to meet Tee and Dee Jones."

"Tiffany Jones's children?"

"Yes."

"My, you two have grown. I remember when you were so tiny."
She shows them to a table full of smiling children. "Miss Ruth, I'd like
you to stay with us this morning. I think you'll like the lesson."

"I wouldn't miss this for the world." I don't want to be away from
Tee and Dee for a single second today. I don't know how any mother
can bear to be away from her children during church. There just seems
to be something so . . . holy about sharing the service with them.

I sit in a folding chair behind Dee, just in case the lesson reminds
him of his mama.

After we sing a few songs, Mrs. Robertson pulls out this hideous,
hairy puppet and wears it on her right hand. "This here's Goliath," she
tells them. "Anyone know who Goliath is?"

"He a giant," one child says.

"You're right. He was a big ol' giant who no one could beat. He
was the champ, and everybody was afraid of him."

"Everybody?" Tee asks.

"Everybody. They say he was eight or nine feet tall."

"He coulda played basketball," a little girl says.

"Right," Mrs. Robertson says. "One day, ol' Goliath starts challeng-
ing some folks to a fight." She holds the puppet out and growls,
"Which one of you is brave enough to fight against me?"

Tee raises her hand. "I am!"

Mrs. Robertson doesn't miss a beat. "But you're so small. You
wouldn't stand a chance against me!"

"Wanna bet?" Tee says, and she jumps to her feet.

"Tee," I whisper. "Sit down. It's only a puppet."

"Oh," Tee says. "Sorry."

"The folks who were afraid of Goliath needed someone to fight for
them, but who were they gonna find who was gonna be brave enough,
and strong enough, and smart enough to fight for them?" She winks at
me.

Daa-em, she's been talking about Jonas as Goliath the entire time,
and I ain't been listening. Am I supposed to be David? Hell, *this* David
is twice the size as Jonas, and Jonas ain't nearly as hairy as the puppet.

Mrs. Robertson puts Goliath down and pulls out a smaller puppet,
a curly-haired David, and puts him on her left hand. "This is David.
He's a shepherd boy. Can this little shepherd boy beat Goliath?"

"No!" the children cry, but Dee . . . The boy's nodding.

Mrs. Robertson notices and talks with the puppet to Dee. "Dee, do you think I can beat that ol' giant Goliath?"

Dee nods.

"I think I can whip that ol' giant and I won't even need any armor or even a sword. All I will need are five little rocks." Mrs. Robertson reaches into a pouch tied to the puppet's waist and pulls out five tiny stones.

"How can five little rocks kill a big giant?" Tee asks. She is so curious. I'll bet that's why she gets in so much trouble at school. Tee is no dummy. She's just a very active learner who wants answers, and I'll bet her teacher, Miss Freitag, ignores her questions. I'm gonna have to straighten that. "A little rock can't kill a giant," she says in her grown-up's voice.

"I'll just use my slingshot." Mrs. Robertson removes a tiny slingshot looped around the puppet's shoulder. She places a tiny stone in it and holds it with the puppet's arms. "Now, where's that ol' giant, Goliath?" She slides her right arm back into Goliath. "Here I am. Who are you, little man?" She holds David out to Dee. "You want to be David, Dee?"

He shakes his head.

"All you have to do is put him on. I'll say all his parts."

Dee takes the puppet and slides it on, the tightest little smile on his face. Dag, I feel a rush of pride because *my boy is the star!*

"I'm David, you big bully, and I'm gonna knock your block off," Mrs. Robertson says. The children giggle. "And then, David used that slingshot and threw that rock and bonked ol' Goliath right on the head." She drops the Goliath puppet on the table, and a few children shrink back.

"Is he dead?" Tee asks.

Mrs. Robertson nods. "A little boy not much bigger than all of you used his brain to beat a giant. You don't have to be big; you don't have to be strong. As long as you use your brain, you can do anything."

After that, we make David puppets out of brown paper bags (I'm sure David had a tan, being a shepherd and all); then each child "talks" to Goliath. Most of the children repeat what Mrs. Robertson said, but not Tee. "I got you, you ol' bully, you!" she says with glee. "I'm the champ! I'm the champ!" This child will one day be an actress.

Dee only moves his puppet's lips, but that's more than I expected. I wonder what he said to Goliath. I need to speak to Fred about Dee.

We leave Mrs. Robertson's class a little early so I can play the prelude upstairs. I sit on the bench at the organ, Dee on my right, Tee on
the left, and play "God Still Answers Prayer" as folks stream in, many
of them singing along. Tee asks a zillion questions about the stops, the
words on the stops, the white keys, the black keys, the foot pedals, the
pipes . . . and I whisper as fast as I can, but I can't keep up with her.
I'm beginning to pity Miss Freitag. I glimpse back to the congregation
when I can and see Kevin way up in the balcony with his mama. I feel
the need to impress him, so I play "Still Have Joy" with all the stops
pulled out. Tee and Dee cover their ears, but I don't care because the
song is so true.

At precisely 10:30, Jonas enters and takes his place on the little pew
to the right of the pulpit, and Cedric Lee, the choir director, opens the
service with a rousing, foot-stomping rendition of "He's Able." Jonas,
as usual, doesn't sing, turning and kneeling in front of the little pew to
pray. But he ain't prayin' today. He's looking up at us. I smile at him,
and when I do, I see Sam's bald head bobbin' down the center aisle following Angie and Paulette. *Thank You, Lord!* During the opening
prayer, I keep my eyes open and check out Deacon Rutledge, who also
has his eyes open. He's whispering something to Sam, and Sam's smiling and whispering back, and all the while Jonas stares at me with
daggers in his eyes.

This is gonna be one *helluva* service!

Tee and Dee are curious children, but once I stop playing, they
don't turn their little heads to look at the congregation for nothin'. I
can only imagine what folks are thinking. The soft-hearted ones will
see me with two children. The hard-hearted will see me with two children *that I couldn't have.* Who cares what they think—at least they're
thinking *something* for a change.

I take Tee and Dee to a little pew to the side during the sermon and
unwrap two mints as slowly as I can. *Crinkle crinkle crinkle.* Jonas can't
stand the sound of crinkling wrappers during a sermon and waits till
I've put a mint in each child's mouth. *Crinkle crinkle crinkle.* He sighs
deeply before taking off his watch and laying it on his Bible. I think
we—Jonas, me, and the children—now have the undivided attention
of the entire congregation. That's right, y'all, look upon me and these
children and your preacher and wonder some more. Wonder how I
have two beautiful children up here when I ain't married to your
preacher. Think hard now. Figure it out.

"I have been led of the Lord to change the topic of my sermon this morning," Jonas says, "so please turn with me to Ezra, chapter nine." Guess my old John 3:1–16 sermon will have to be recycled for another Sunday. I flip to Ezra and see a bunch of puzzled folks in the audience. He's never done this before, but I'm sure he has a reason.

Me and the two children beside me.

Deacon Rutledge stands to read the verses, but Jonas waves him down. "They can read it for themselves, Deacon Rutledge."

Two changes in tradition in *one* service at Antioch Church? *Jesus, You ain't comin' back today, are You?*

"Today's sermon will cover the sinful practice of intermarriage with *heathen*."

Oh no he *didn't!*

"The Israelites, God's *chosen* people, were guilty of mingling their *holiest* of holy races with the *heathen* blood of others, and Ezra was *appalled* and *ashamed* and *disgraced*."

I hope Junie's readin' between the lines on this one, because she's about to mingle her blood with the biggest heathen in the church. I see her marking in her Bible. Think it through, girl! Make the connection!

"The Lord, Who had delivered them out of *bondage*, Who had delivered them out of abject *slavery*, Who had brought them to the *promised land*, Who had saved them from *shackles* and the *whip*—the Lord God forbade these marriages, yet . . . They happened."

Oh, now he's trying to get racial. Since when have black folks been Jewish? We about as Jewish as the Pope, Jonas! I can't let this go on much longer, and I feel something stirring deep inside me.

"They intermarried with *corrupt, detestable* people—"

"Amen!" I shout, and Tee and Dee cringe beside me. I have never done this before. Never. I'll join in, but I have never started an "Amen!" in my life. No one else, however, seconds me. My "Amen!" dies with a tiny echo.

"And . . . and . . . They intermarried and showed *no* shame!" Jonas shouts. "They were *drowning* in sin!"

"Drowning in sin!" I shout. "Yes, Lord! Hallelujah! Heading straight to the bottom of the ocean of sin!"

You can hear a hairpin drop it's so quiet. Jonas turns to me, and I get ready to charge. If he says just one little thing to me, I'm gonna rebuke his ass in front of all these people, try to shut his ass up for good. But he turns away. Chicken. I want to flap my wings at him.

"The, uh, the solution to this *filthy intermarriage* was the *putting away* of these *foreign* wives!"

Putting away? That's KJV for divorce. "Divorce, Lord! Yes, Lord! Divorce was the only solution! Put 'em away, Lord! Yes, Lord!"

"And . . . and the great theologian John Wesley says that verse forty-four of chapter ten implies that most of these *foreign* wives were *barren*, and that those who had children, those children were *illegitimate!*"

Well shut my mouth. Our marriage is in the Bible, right there in Ezra 9 and 10. But calling Tee and Dee illegitimate like that in public? I have to stand up for my children this time. I slam my Bible on the pew and jump to my feet. "Praise the Lord for *miscarriages* caused by weak *sperm!*" The word "sperm" echoes a bit before dying down. *Forgive me, Lord. You know that it had to be said.* I sit and squeeze Tee's and Dee's hands.

I hear Sam chuckling and see Deacon Rutledge turn to shush him. Sam don't play that and stands. " 'Scuse me, Reverend Borum," Sam says in that golden baritone voice of his, "but what *precisely* are you talking about today? Are you talking about the Lord God of Israel and his dealings with the Hebrew nation around about four hundred B.C., or are you talking about you, the Lord God of Antioch Church, and your dealings with your ex-wife and those two children around about . . . oh, today?"

"Amen!" I hear from way up in the balcony. Thank you, Kevin. I think I've embarrassed myself enough for one day.

"I am talking . . ." Jonas pauses and stares at Sam. "Please sit, sir."

"After you've answered my question," Sam says.

"I will tell you once you are seated."

Sam smiles. "Pretty smooth. That'll give you more time to think up an answer."

Deacon Rutledge stands and turns to Sam. "Sit down."

Sam turns to the rest of the congregation. "Brothers and sisters, this is truly a holy moment, a blessed event! The good Deacon Rutledge has finally spoken, after nearly seven years, to the father of his daughter's baby, his grandbaby Angie! Can I get a hallelujah?"

"Hallelujah!" rings from all over the place, and I mean, *all over the place*. From the choir, from the sanctuary, from the balcony. I don't know what's going on, but I like it, oh, yes, I like it a lot!

Sam turns back to Jonas as Deacon Rutledge sits his narrow ass down. "You gonna answer my question now?"

Jonas gulps, drops his eyes, and instead says, "Let us pray."

Let us pray? I check my watch, and I ain't the only one checking. I even see a few fools shaking their wrists like their watches have stopped. It's twenty minutes to twelve. I lead Tee and Dee back to the organ bench where I'm supposed to play "I Surrender All" during the last prayer. I ain't surrendering a damn thing today, so I play "Get Right With God" instead, playing it louder than usual to drown out Jonas's weak-ass, mumbled prayer. When Jonas finishes, I pull out all the stops and crank up "Total Praise" for folks to walk out to, only today they're practically running out.

When the sanctuary is finally empty, I let Tee and Dee play a bit. They pull out the stops, dance on the pedals, and generally make joyful noises to the Lord.

"Y'all hungry?" Two happy nods. "There's a potluck dinner downstairs with tables just bursting with good food." And I want to get down there to hear what folks are saying about the service while it's still fresh in their minds.

I walk with *my* children through the line, sitting with *my* children, and no one will speak to me. All conversations seem to come to a stop when we pass by. They stare, though, and I make sure to keep a broad smile on my face when I stare back. I don't see Sam and family or Kevin, but that's okay because I got me my own family here today.

Naomi stops by but doesn't sit with us. "Are you proud of yourself, Ruth?" she whispers.

I look at Tee and Dee destroying a plate of wings and mashed potatoes. "Yes."

"Junie ran out of the service before it ended," Naomi hisses. "Are you proud now?"

"She did? Good for her." I look around. "Is that where Jonas is now?"

She leans down. "No, Reverend Borum is meeting with the deacons right now in his study. Guess who they're talking about?"

I put my hand on my chest. "Little ol' me?"

She shakes her head. "Don't you even care what happens?"

"Sure I do." I wipe a speck of mashed potatoes off Dee's lip. "Long as the truth comes out."

"Girl, they're probably thinking of a way to remove you from this church."

"I'd like to see them try," I say. "Want some more milk, Dee?" He nods. I hold out Dee's empty glass to Naomi. "You mind getting Dee some milk?"

Naomi sighs, scowls, and walks away. I guess that was a "no."

"Who was that mean lady, Penny?" Tee asks.

"You don't remember her?"

"No."

I stand. "That was one of my best friends, Tee." And after today, Naomi might be one of my ex-friends. Hmm. It'll hurt like hell, but I think I can handle it. But Naomi and I have been through too much for it to end over this. She'll stew for a few days, then call and apologize. Or should I call her this time? I'm gonna have to pray about this one. "You want some more chicken, Tee?"

"Uh-huh."

While I'm loading up another plate with wings and getting Dee some milk, Mrs. Robertson touches my elbow, whispers, "Goliath has fallen," and continues on. Goliath has fallen. What did David do next? He chopped off that ol' giant's head. Hmm. Don't know if I can do that yet . . . but I'm willing to try.

When I return to the table, I see Deacon Rutledge sitting in my spot. So soon? Dag, the board reached a decision in less than a month. I place Dee's milk in front of him and put the wings in front of Tee. "Deacon Rutledge," I say, sitting in a chair opposite him.

"The board would like a word with you."

"Just one?"

He growls. "You know what we mean, Mrs. Borum."

"Who is we? I only see you sittin' here." I touch his bony arm. "I know what you mean, Deacon Rutledge, but I'm afraid I'm just too busy today. I have these children to look after."

"It will only take a moment."

"We got us a moment right here. Tell me now."

Deacon Rutledge eyes Tee and Dee. "The board is waiting for us upstairs."

"You're the head deacon, right?" He nods. "So you speak for the board, right?"

"It's, um, a little more complicated than that."

Tee has cleaned her plate again. "Y'all through?" Two nods. "Wipe your faces with your napkins." They do. I turn to Deacon Rutledge. "I'll be free this afternoon. Why doesn't the board drop by my apartment, say, around three."

"Mrs. Borum, the board—"

"Will have to come to *me* this time," I interrupt. "C'mon, y'all," I say to Tee and Dee. "Let's go for a walk."

We walk nice and slow out of Antioch, skip across Vine, and go up to my apartment where I give them a tour. It's a short tour, but it gives Tee and Dee a chance to use the bathroom. I let them explore on their own for a few minutes till Tee comes into the sitting room holding my jump rope.

"You jump rope, Penny?" she asks.

"Sure. Who doesn't?"

"Can we go outside and jump rope with you?"

For the next half hour in front of my apartment on Vine Street, a rope turned by two precious children, this forty-year-old probably soon-to-be-former member of Antioch Church dances in the sun, still in her dress, laughing and giggling. I give them each a turn, and there are moments . . . when I want to cry for joy. Hearing Tee shouting out a rhyme, her velvety dress flashing in the sun. Seeing Dee's little red tie flapping up and down, the biggest smile on his face. This is what I've missed, and I know I don't want to miss any of this anymore.

I want this, all of it. Now. I'm gonna have to make a move on their daddy. Today.

At two, I return them to Dewey. It's a sad walk for me—I want to keep them with me all day so badly!—but Tee's constant chatter and Dee's smiling face help me through. When we get to the apartment, we see Dewey's legs sticking out from under the truck. Oh, Lord, he's wearing cowboy boots. Is that snakeskin? "Can we help, Daddy?" Tee says.

Dewey slides out, his clothes covered with grease, and is that a bulge of tobacco in his cheek? My man dips snuff? That shit's nasty! "Sure. Go change your clothes." They tear inside. He squints up at me. "How was church?"

"Memorable," I say. "Wish you were there." But not with that shit in your mouth.

He reaches into a pocket . . . and pulls out a bag of black licorice. "Want some?"

"No thank you." At least it's not tobacco. But sucking on a wad of black licorice?

He separates a piece and bends it a couple of times. "I would have gone to church with y'all, except—"

"It's okay. I remember your entrance a few months ago. Were you mourning for Tiffany then?"

He looks away. "Yeah."

He says it without hesitation, so Dewey might have loved her. Hmm. "Were you also mourning that you had to be a real daddy all of a sudden?"

He sighs. "Yep. I was kinda mourning over that, too."

That's probably closer to the truth of why he was crying. "And Antioch was the first church you ran into, huh?"

He turns back to me. "I wasn't thinkin' very clearly that day."

I want to tell him that I think God led him to me, but I don't since I don't know how religious he is yet. "Well, Mr. Baxter, the man who consoled you that day was my ex-husband." Dewey's eyes widen. "But I still play the organ at his church because I have to. I have a gift that has to be given." I take a deep breath. Time to make my move. *Lord Jesus, please give me the words.* "I like being with your children, Mr. Baxter. And, I like being with you." Is this me, shy Ruthie Lee, saying all this? It is. Where has this woman been? *Thank You, Lord.* "I've got my eye on you, Mr. Baxter. You got your eye on me?"

"I, uh . . . well." He stands and looks me in the eye. "Ruth, I don't know if I'm, um, ready for—"

"Yes you are," I interrupt, and I plant a kiss on his greasy cheek. In broad daylight. On Sixteenth Street. In Calhoun, Virginia. And I feel so light! It's like I've broken some spell hanging over this neighborhood. "I know you're ready for me, Dewey Baxter."

"But I—"

"And I don't care a lick why you didn't marry Tiffany." Though I really really do care, and if you look into my eyes, Dewey Baxter, you'll see that I have to know cuz tomorrow has come. I gave you a whole day to answer my unasked question; now it's your turn to come through. This is where you tell me every damn thing.

He squints. "You really don't care why Tiff and I never got married?"

Of course I do! This shit's called reverse psychology, Mr. Baxter, and you ain't doin' it right! "Not a bit. You had your reasons, and I don't need to hear 'em." When he doesn't answer right away, I step closer to him and bite my lower lip. "Unless . . . you, um, want to tell me why."

He looks away. Damn. He ain't gonna tell me today. "It's just . . . so complicated."

Complicated? From what Naomi told me, Tiffany didn't sound like a complicated person. What could be so complicated—Gulp. Maybe I don't want to know right now.

"You see, um, Tiff—"

"It's okay," I interrupt. "I mean, it's really none of my business, right?" He doesn't look back at me . . . which means that *he* thinks it's none of my business. This shit ain't complicated. It's conflicted. I have to make the best of this. "Tiffany, uh, obviously wasn't the right woman for you, right?"

He nods, but he still won't look at me.

I reach up and turn his face to mine, putting my nose a hair from his. "But I know that I am the right woman for you." I put a finger on his soft lips. "See you tomorrow." I kiss him on his other cheek. I am amazing myself. "You need me, Dewey Baxter, and if you think long enough on it, you'll see that I'm right."

I leave him standing there and feel so . . . scared. I have just made my intentions known to this man, and now it's all on him. What if he doesn't respond? I turn to look and see him still standing in place, a lost look on his face, two of my lip marks showing through the grease on his face. Is a confused response acceptable, Ruthie Lee? I smile and wave.

He smiles back.

Now, that's better. A smile is not a confused response. A smile requires thought. He's thinking about me right this second. Wait. *He's thinking about me right this second!* Should I go back? I could spend the day with him, leave the board hanging, get me some more less-greasy kisses. No. Dewey's got to want me on his own; he's got to come to me next. It's his turn not to be shy. Besides, I can't wait to hear what the board has decided about li'l ol' me.

Who said divorced life wasn't exciting?

I decide to meet the board on the porch with Fred sitting in the yard, that shiny glass jar to his ear. The board is just gonna love seeing him. "You got any news for me, Fred?"

"Storm's comin'."

"There isn't a cloud in the sky."

"There's different kinds of storms, Ruth. This one comin' in a dark swarm, like locusts."

I shiver. Locusts. That is one accurate description of the church board. "Am I in danger?"

He stares at me for the longest time. "No."

"Well, you just keep both ears open."

He smiles. "Always do."

There aren't enough lawn chairs for everyone if the whole board shows up, but that's okay. I don't mind standing to face my accusers.

"The storm has arrived," Fred says, and I look a little ways up Vine. The board marches almost in step in a tight formation, like they're marching to Zion—or a funeral. Every one of them is wearin' black. A few folks out raking leaves stop and stare. They probably think the eight wrinkled men and women are Jehovah's Witnesses or something. They march by Fred without even a glance his way and climb the steps, the three ladies sitting on the lawn chairs, the five men leaning against the porch rail.

"Where's Jonas?" I ask.

"Reverend Borum," Deacon Rutledge says, "is comforting Miss Pruett."

"As he should, Deacon Rutledge," I say. I get a few of the old biddies to nod along with me. "Have you comforted your daughter and granddaughter yet, Deacon Rutledge?" The biddies stop nodding, but I've made my point.

Deacon Rutledge clears his raspy throat. "We are here today to strongly suggest that you cease and desist from your efforts to upset the sanctity of the church."

I let that mess roll around in my head for a bit. "The sanctity?"

"Yes. The purity, the holiness of the church."

There's holiness at Antioch Church? "And y'all are only suggesting that I cease and desist?"

"*Strongly* suggesting," Deacon Rutledge says.

I squint at the other members of the board, all mute in the presence of Deacon Rutledge. Such stupid sheep. "So y'all ain't *telling* me to stop, then?"

"You are a member of our church, Mrs. Borum. The board can only suggest at this point. We expect a certain decorum from a member of Antioch Church. You did not display such proper decorum today."

"Really? I said amen and hallelujah, right? Isn't that proper decorum?"

"You said these things at inappropriate times."

"I did? You mean there are inappropriate times to praise God? What if the Holy Spirit moves me to say these things?"

Deacon Rutledge scowls. "You interrupted the sermon, Mrs. Borum."

"I spoke the truth, Deacon Rutledge. Hmm. Proper decorum means you can't interrupt a sermon with the truth. I'll try to remember that."

Deacon Rutledge's voice rises. "Mrs. Borum, you were sharing your private business with the congregation."

"So was Jonas." I stare down Mrs. Finn. "Feel free to speak any time you want to, Mrs. Finn. Be part of the action." I turn to Deacon Rutledge. "Did you tell Jonas to cease and desist, too?"

"We cannot tell Reverend Borum what to or what not to preach on. As you'll recall, he said he was led of the Lord—"

"And you can accept that?" I interrupt.

"Yes."

"You sure?"

"We are sure."

"Ain't no 'we' talkin' up here on this porch. Just you, Deacon Rutledge." I drift to a corner, then turn suddenly. "So if someone says he was led of the Lord, you'll accept that?" Nods all around. They all share the same diseased brain. "Okay." I pause, close my eyes, and start humming, shaking my right leg furiously. "Oh, Lord!" I shout. "I feel led of the Lord . . . Oh, I feel the holy power! I feel led of the Lord . . . to tell you all to get the hell off my porch!"

If the old biddies were Catholic, they would have crossed themselves. "We are not leaving," Deacon Rutledge says, "till you give us your guarantee that—"

I start shaking both legs, throwin' in a little shimmy for good measure. "The Lord's leading me to warm up my feet for some *powerful* kick-ass! Oh, I feel the power!" I take two giant steps toward them, the biddies scurry down the stairs, and all the men except Deacon Rutledge back away.

"You are a *disgrace*, Mrs. Borum," Deacon Rutledge says with clenched teeth. "You are in danger of being excommunicated."

This is new. "Excommunicated? We ain't Catholic!"

"You are guilty of causing a schism in the church."

"A what?"

"A rift, a split in the church. You are sowing discord among us."

"I am? Folks are taking sides?"

"They are."

Now *this* is good news. "Well, it's about damn time."

Deacon Rutledge sputters a bit. "You're actually *proud* of the trouble that you caused today?"

"Least folks are thinking for themselves for a change. And I didn't cause any of this. Jonas did, and you know it. You're just too thick-headed and hard-hearted to admit it. I pity you, Deacon Rutledge."

He has trouble breathing for a moment. "Do you *want* to be excommunicated, Mrs. Borum?"

I smile because in a way, I've already been excommunicated. The divorce has already put me out to pasture. "How would excommunication work exactly?" He doesn't respond. "I want to know."

"The church members would vote whether you were to stay or to go."

"As in go, never to come back, never to play the organ again?"

"Yes."

"Hmm. Does it have to be a unanimous decision?"

"No. A simple majority is all that's necessary."

"To ruin a church!" Fred yells.

Deacon Rutledge leans over the rail. "What did you say?"

Fred winks at me. "I said that a simple majority is all that's necessary to ruin a church."

Deacon Rutledge waves his hand at Fred. "I do not listen to degenerates."

I stand inches from Deacon Rutledge's faded black suit. "Who you callin' a degenerate? You, who have excommunicated your own flesh and blood and turned your back on your own daughter and granddaughter. *You* should be ashamed of yourself."

His jaw flaps up and down. "They sinned."

"The child, too? What's Angie ever done to you?"

"She was born from sin."

"As were we all," Fred says from the bottom step in a deep voice. Dag, it made me jump more than Deacon Rutledge. Fred sounded like the very voice of God. "The Bible says there ain't *none* righteous, no not one." Fred comes up on the porch and puts a finger in Deacon Rutledge's chest. *"No . . . not . . . one."*

Deacon Rutledge looks fit to be hog-tied. "We'll be paying close attention to you, Mrs. Borum."

"Good," I say. "I want you to. I like the attention. And while you're doing that, Deacon Rutledge, maybe you can pay closer attention to God."

Without another word, Deacon Rutledge tries to sidestep Fred, but Fred, that jar stuck up in his ear, blocks his path. It is the funniest dance I've ever seen. A skinny, wrinkled man in a suit is doing a two-step with a skinny, wrinkled man in rags holding a Mason jar to his ear. I burst out laughing as Fred lets Deacon Rutledge pass.

Fred shakes his head and sits in a lawn chair. "That man's heart ain't but an itty-bitty speck of dirt."

"Yep," I say as I sit next to him. "God tell you anything about him?"

"Too much. Gonna have to wash out the jar."

The Deacon been bad? "What you mean?"

"That is one evil man, Ruth," Fred says. "Tells the government he's tax-exempt cuz he's a deacon, reads The Song of Solomon to get a rise out of his . . . you know, picks his nose during prayers and puts his boogers under his pew. How'd he get to be a deacon?"

"I have no idea. He's just always been the head deacon for as long as I can remember. And now he wants to get me excommunicated."

Fred laughs. "I'll vote your way."

"Thanks, Fred, but only church members can vote."

He winks. "Like I said, I'll vote your way."

Say what? "You're a member of Antioch?"

Fred nods. "Got baptized there a long time ago. Know a lot of folks still probably on the rolls. Most of 'em in the jail or at shelters round about. I'll let 'em know, be with you at the vote next Sunday."

A jolt rushes from my toes to my nose. "Next Sunday?"

He nods. "And watch out for dead folks."

"Huh?"

He points at the jar. "It's saying somethin' about dead folks, Ruth. I don't interpret. I just inform."

"Oh." Dead folks? "What you think it means?"

He shrugs. "All I know is that it's important." He stands. "I'll let you know if I hear any more."

"Where you goin'?"

He looks at me like my mama used to, his forehead dippin', his eyes focused and mean like I've asked the wrong question. "Out."

I look away. "I . . . just worry about you is all."

He smiles. "Thank you. But for the next seven days, you just worry about yourself." He leaves the porch and heads up Vine.

And I start to worry.

Seventeen

As a rule, a Monday at Diana's is fun: full house, lots of juicy week-end gossip, and not much cutting or styling since the ladies are really only there for the dirt. An hour or two on Monday morning at Diana's is a good way to get caught up on news, births, deaths, and scandal without opening a newspaper. And since all the other salons are usually closed on Monday, Diana's has a lockdown on gossip.

But today is not fun, and it's dragging like a lead weight.

"Where is everybody?" Diana asks me at nine. We usually have folks waiting by now, the dirt flyin' every which way.

"Don't know." I look at Kevin. "You know?" He shrugs and continues playing something almost classical on the guitar. "What you playin'?"

"Somethin' I made up," he says.

"Sounds nice. What you call it?"

"No name. I just play it."

"How 'bout callin' it 'Kevin's First Symphony'?"

"Cool. I like it."

And Kevin's symphony is all we hear till Mildred bangs through the door in her wheelchair at eleven. "Hey, Mildred," I say with a smile. I get my brushes ready.

"Mornin'," Mildred says to Diana, but she only scowls at me. What's this? "Diana, I want you to do my hair this mornin'." Mildred wheels herself next to Diana's chair and continues to make faces at me. What's going on?

"Everything okay today, Mildred?" I ask.

"Diana," Mildred says, "you tell that person over there to leave me alone."

"Excuse me?" I ask.

"Diana, you tell that person over there that she needs to learn when to speak and when not to speak."

I march over to her chair. "Don't play that with me, Miss Millie. I been doin' your hair for free for far too long to put up with this shit. What you talkin' about?"

"Diana," Mildred says, "you tell this person that the house of the Lord is no place to talk shit."

"What did you say?" I ask.

"She was talkin' shit in the house of the Lord yesterday," she says to Diana. "Surprised you let a person like that work here."

Oh, this is too much! "You weren't even there!" I shout.

"I heard a few things last night, Diana. Wicked, sinful things. You tell that person she should be ashamed of herself. You tell her that she needs to get right with God."

"I ain't ashamed of anything I said because it was all true," I say, trying to catch Mildred's eyes. She's not very good at dodging them. "Who'd you hear this from?"

Mildred finally turns to me. "Mrs. Finn. She said you threatened to kick her ass."

"I did no such thing!"

"She said it, I believe it, that settles it." Mildred folds her arms in front of her.

"I said that I *felt* a kick-ass in my legs. I didn't kick anyone's ass. I just wanted them off my porch."

Mildred rolls her eyes. "You threatened her, and Mrs. Finn is older than me. Threatenin' an old woman. Don't know what this world is comin' to." She blinks her eyes at Diana. "You gonna plait my hair or what?"

Diana starts to loosen Mildred's plaits. "Soon as you're done bad-mouthin' my friend, I will."

"If I was you, she wouldn't *be* my friend," Mildred says. "She's gonna cost you some business. Mrs. Finn has been busy, let me tell you. Nubian Designs is open today." Nubian Designs is *never* open on a Monday. "Folks is goin' to Nubian Designs this mornin', saw a whole lot of them marchin' in there together." Oh shit. I'm the reason business is slow. I am the gossip target. Again. The gossip target cannot be present for gossip to begin. It's a tradition as ancient as hair-styling. Mrs. Finn and the board have been busy lining up folks against me, and they've even gone so far as to open up a salon to do their dirty work. I'm already being excommunicated, and I'm costing me and Diana a small fortune! My hands go cold. "Where your customers at, Diana?"

"You're here," Diana says.

"Nubian Designs was gonna charge me ten bucks for this. Y'all will do me for free."

Diana pulls out the last of Mildred's plaits and cuts her eyes at me. "Not anymore."

"What?" That's what I would have said, too, but I can't get my mouth to work. Every part of me is going numb.

"You gonna keep badmouthin' my friend?"

"I'm just tellin' you what I heard, Diana."

Diana sighs. *"You* need to learn when to speak and when not to speak, Mildred Overstreet. You got five dollars?"

"You know I don't."

"Oh, well," Diana says, and she walks away from Mildred's wheelchair.

Mildred looks fit to be tied. "Wait till I get over to Nubian Designs and tell them about this shit!" She starts to wheel away.

"I'll do it," I say.

She stops but doesn't turn to look at me. "For free?"

"Yes."

She sits a minute rolling her chair back and forth. "Can't go out lookin' like this. I guess I can let you do it this one *last* time." She locks her wheels in place near the door. "And tell that boy over there to stop playin' that dreadful music."

I approach her. "It ain't dreadful, Millie," I say. "Would you prefer something else? He takes requests."

"I'm requestin' that he stop."

Ain't nothin' workin' right this mornin'! I turn to Kevin. "Play some Etta James or some Muddy Waters for us, Kevin. I could use me some blues."

Mildred squints. "He know Etta James and Muddy Waters?"

I grasp Mildred's hair and start to brush. "Yep." Kevin plays a little "Rolling Stone," a song that matches my mood. I should be a rolling stone and roll on up out of here. "You want to hear the whole story now?"

"What whole story?"

"*My* whole story. The whole truth and nothin' but."

"I'm listenin'."

For the next half hour, I tell Mildred Overstreet the entire story of fifteen years with Jonas, of the last few months alone, of the last few weeks with Dewey, Dee, and Tee. I leave out nothing, mainly because telling the story is good for me, like I'm flushing out my system or something. During my story, Kevin plays softer, Diana sits in her chair and acts like she's not listening so I know she is, and Mildred nods every once in a while. When I'm through, Kevin plays his symphony again, and Diana drifts to the back.

"So now you know everything," I tell Mildred, clipping the last plait in place.

"You expect me to believe all that shit?"

"Believe what you want," I say. "It's the truth."

"As *you* see it."

"As I *know* it. Least now you have my side of it." I stand in front of her. "See you next Monday?"

"Maybe," Mildred says.

"I hope I do," I say. "Can't start my week without you. Your hair gives me a good workout, warms up my hands."

Mildred fumbles with her hands a moment before grabbing her wheels. "If you see me, you see me."

"I can accept that." I smile. I watch her bang out the door, and instead of turning right to go home, she rolls to the left. Maybe she's going to Nubian Designs to straighten things out, but whether she is or isn't, I have to leave for Diana's sake. "Gonna take the rest of the day off, Diana," I call out.

"What for?"

"Not feeling too good," I say, and it isn't a total lie. I don't feel well. I feel achy all over, like I got the flu comin' on. It's probably just my body's reactions to all this shit.

"You don't have to go, Ruth," Diana says. "They'll be back. Nubian Designs charges way too much."

"It's all right." I get my coat. "You can call me if business picks up." I pause at the door. "Oh, and I won't be in tomorrow or Wednesday. I'm workin' over at Avery, remember?"

Diana walks toward me. "Ruth, they'll be back. I remember when Nubian Designs opened. I only lost them for one day."

I shake my head. "It's okay, Diana. See you Thursday."

The walk home is ice cold, and the thoughts in my head are colder, tears dripping from my eyes. *Lord, they're messin' with my job now! Lord Jesus, what Your people can do when they put their simple minds to it. I can't lose that job; I mean, what else am I gonna do? Where You leadin' me? I would go back as a full-time aide at Avery, but that pay's barely above minimum wage, I won't have no summer work, and Mrs. Holland says there's no funding anyway! What am I gonna do?*

When I get to the apartment, I hear Fred humming a song from his spot on the grass. It sounds so familiar, but I'm just not sure what it is. I wipe a tear away. "What you hummin', Fred?"

"Old song," he says. "Good old song. It'll come to you, Ruth." He hums louder, but I still can't place it.

"Just tell me."

He shakes his head. "Let it come to you, Ruth."

I leave him, walk up the stairs, open my door, close it gently behind me, and have a good old weeping session right there on my kitchen floor. *Lord Jesus, I'm hurtin' here. Only thing holdin' me up just now is the linoleum on this dusty floor. I ain't got but a few friends left, I got no family, and I might not have a job or a church soon. I might not be playin' the organ no more. I ain't got much left to hold on to. Give me something, anything to hold on to.*

And then Fred's song comes to me . . . and the pain bleeds away as I hum "Hold On," the ancient words going through my head:

> *Hold on, jus' a li'l while longer*
> *Hold on, jus' a li'l while longer*
> *Hold on, jus' a li'l while longer*
> *Everything will be all right*
> *Everything will be all right*
> *Pray on, jus' a li'l while longer*
> *Pray on, jus' a li'l while longer*
> *Pray on, jus' a li'l while longer*
> *Everything will be all right*
> *Everything will be all right*

I wipe my tears on a paper towel and throw open the window to hear Fred singing out the last, triumphant verse of that old spiritual:

> *"Fight on, jus' a li'l while longer*
> *Fight on, jus' a li'l while longer*

Fight on, jus' a li'l while longer
Everything will be all right
Everything will be all right."

The phone rings. I clear my throat and answer. "Hello?"

"Ruth, girl, you gotta get back here quick!" Diana shouts.

"Why?"

"They all came back, and, girl, there's lots of hair to fix!"

Thank You, Jesus! "I ain't been gone but half an hour."

"Millie hauled ass to Nubian Designs. Now get *your* ass down here!" *Click.*

I don't say anything to Fred, and he doesn't say anything to me as I'm leaving the apartment. He merely tips his hat and smiles.

Everything will be all right.

When I walk into Diana's, the only voice I hear is Mildred's. "And after that ho, he started messin' with a *man.*" The ladies look at me, eyes wide, hands on chests, little sighs escaping. "That's when *she* divorced *him.*"

"You poor dear," Mrs. Phillips says. I want to thank Mrs. Phillips, but I'm afraid I'll start laughing. Someone at Nubian Designs colored her white hair yellow, not blond, and that is one color that just does not belong on a dark black woman. She looks like a black candle.

"I told 'em everything," Mildred says, wheeling over to me. "And we'll all be at the church come Sunday."

"I will be in the front row of that church cuz what they tryin' to do to you is just plain wrong," Mrs. Thompson says. And what Nubian Designs did to her hair was wrong, too. It's been colored bright red and stacked in a triangle to a point about ten inches above her forehead. She looks like an upside-down yield sign.

"Thanks y'all," I say. "I'll need all the help I can get."

Mrs. Wilomena Monroe busts through the door a split second later, and no one seems to breathe. Her poor hair! Someone has added light brown extensions that snake off her head to two long ponytails hanging down to her bubble butt while her natural jet-black hair sticks straight up, the tips frosted white. Dear Jesus, they put an Indian headdress on her! "Can y'all please help me?"

With a pair of hedge trimmers, maybe.

"She can go in front of me," Mrs. Thompson says, looking away and giggling. "She need some emergency treatment."

"I can be a blonde a little longer," Mrs. Phillips says with a smile.

For the rest of the day, the topic of gossip—me—repairs a dozen heads of hair while the gossip *about* me rages on all around me.

And I don't have to say a single thing.

Everything will be all right.

Eighteen

I rise with the sun the next morning and don't have to struggle to get out of bed like I used to. Guess I'm gettin' more country tryin' to get me a country man. During my shower, I get two glorious minutes of lukewarm water and hope that the water wakes Fred since I need to speak to him about Dee. If anyone on this planet knows anything about that boy, it will be Fred. I dress in jeans and a white sweater, throw on a ratty coat, and head out the door.

Fred is in his usual spot, but today he looks more ragged than usual. "Good morning, Fred."

"It would be a good mornin' if you didn't have to take a shower so damn early, woman," he growls. "Why you take so many showers?"

"You know what they say about cleanliness, Fred."

He sniffs under his arms. "I prefer godliness. God don't take no showers. God is in the earth, you know. He only showers when it rains." He frowns as he screws the jar back to his ear. "You woke me up for a reason. What is it?"

"Um, Fred, you hear anything in that jar about Dee Jones?"

"The little boy?"

"Yes."

"What you need to know?"

I'm afraid to ask. "Will Dee . . . Will he ever speak again?"

"Yes," Fred says with no hesitation.

Thank You, Jesus! "That's wonderful! When?"

"When you least expect it."

Oh, that was helpful. "Will it happen soon?"

"You want it to happen?"

More than you'll ever know, Fred. "Oh, yes."

"Then, it ain't gonna happen."

"Why not?"

"Cuz you're expectin' it. A watched pot—"

"I know," I interrupt. "A watched pot never boils. You soundin' like my grandma, Fred." I pout. "It'll be a quiet day, then, huh?"

"Just listen with your heart, Ruth, and you'll hear an earful today."

"I'll try." I take a few steps and stop. "You feelin' okay this morning, Fred?"

"Yeah. Why you ask?"

"You, uh, look more . . . " He raises his eyebrows. "You look more worse for wear."

"Didn't get enough sleep. The pipes woke my ass up."

"Oh, yeah. Sorry about that."

"It's all right. Folks sleep more than they need to." He smiles. "Go on. Ask the next question."

"What question?"

"The one that's been eatin' at you to ask me."

"You answered the question. It was about Dee."

He shakes his head. "No it wasn't. You wanna know if God tells me things about myself."

"Well, I am kinda curious. Does He?"

"Sometimes."

I walk back to him. "What does He say?"

"He doesn't say anythin' exactly. He just kinda . . . moves me from place to place."

I get chill bumps. "Like you're in His hand?"

"Something like that."

"And you're in His hand now."

"Yep."

That must be the best feeling! "How long you gonna stay here?"

"Don't know. I like it here. But . . . " He sighs. "But whenever I like a place, I get moved. Might not be here much longer."

Not yet, God! Since this man has been here, my life has changed for the better! "Well, when I get back, I'll make you some biscuits."

"I'd like that." He screws the jar tighter onto his ear. "But I won't like 'em that much, okay?"

"Okay."

He tilts his head to the sky. "Wouldn't want Anyone up there listenin' to think I actually *like* it here!"

"God heard you, Fred."

He drops his chin to his chest. "I know." He narrows his eyes. "You goin' to see the little girl's teacher today?"

Dag, the man can even read my thoughts from days ago. "Hadn't planned on it today."

"Go. But be careful. She a hard-headed somethin' somethin'."

"Tee or the teacher?"

"The teacher. Thinks she knows every damn thing. You gots to set her straight."

"I'll try."

He eyes me from head to toe. "You're wearin' the right clothes today."

"For what?"

He winks. "You'll see."

"Be here when I get back, Fred."

"I'll try. Wish I had me an anchor."

I mist up a little. "Fred, *you* have been my anchor these last few days."

He looks away and flexes his nose like old men do when they don't want to cry in front of you. "Go on, you gonna be late."

I step over to him, bend down, and kiss him on the forehead. "Thank you for everything, Fred."

His eyes well with tears. "I'll be gone for sure now, woman. Why you gotta do that?"

"God told me to."

He grunts. "That Man talk too much."

I kiss his forehead again. "Hope you're here when I get back."

"I hope so, too."

On the way to Avery, I think about Fred. To anyone walking or driving by, he's a crazy old stank man with a jar at his ear, just another crazy Negro. What they don't know—what they *should* know—man's tuned in to WGOD every day. Dag, I get chill bumps just thinking about that.

I also wonder what I'm going to say to Miss Freitag. Hi, I'm not Tee's mama, but I got a bone to pick with you? Hello, I'm Tee's temporary baby-sitter who's in love with Tee's daddy, and we have a few things to straighten out? What right do I have to say anything?

I sign in before even Mrs. Holland arrives and slip around to Miss Freitag's room. I peek inside and see Miss Freitag sitting at a table full to bursting with stacks of paper. She's hard at work grading papers, and this obviously ain't a good time. But Fred said to talk to her, so . . .

"Good morning."

Miss Freitag looks up. "Yes?" she says in that mousy voice of hers.

"Is this a bad time?"

She folds her hands deliberately and forces a tight smile. "What can I help you with?"

I move into the room. "I'm Ruth Borum, and I'm here to talk to you about Tee Jones." Miss Freitag's little knuckles whiten. Dag, all I did was say Tee's name. "I think I can help you out with her, Miss Freitag."

"You can?"

That's what I said. "Yes."

She motions me to a tiny-ass chair where I sit, both my butt-cheeks hanging over the sides. "You volunteer here, right?"

"Yes. I work mainly with Tee's brother, Dee."

"You do?"

She must be hard of hearing. "Yes."

"And you think you can help me with Tee?"

All this rat-faced wench does is ask questions! "Yes. You see, I think—"

"Are you Tee's mother?"

"No, but I mind her after school, and—"

"Then, we shouldn't be having this conversation."

Hard-headed? This girl is hard-hearted! "What conversation, Miss Freitag? All you doin' is interruptin' and askin' questions." I stare the bitch down. "If you want Tee to behave, you'll listen to me without interrupting or asking any more questions."

She rolls her eyes. "I'm listening."

"No you ain't!" I stand. "You're just waitin' for me to say my piece and get out."

"You're very observant, Mrs. Borum."

What a smart-ass! And they let this rat-faced, squeaky-voiced ho teach here? I take a deep breath. "Miss Freitag, you *need* my help."

She smiles. "I do?"

I have had enough. "You don't want my help, fine. I hope Tee kills all your damn fish."

"Excuse me?"

"You heard me. Just cuz you don't know how to teach a little black girl—"

"How dare you!"

"How dare *me*? How dare *you* treat her like shit! Tee is a very bright girl."

"You think so?"

If the bitch asks one more question, I'm going to whump up some kick-ass, and with her, I'll only need one foot, tiny as she is. *Hold me back, Lord. Keep me from punting this wench across the room.* "Look, I *know* Tee is a bright child, and so *should* you. She asks lots of questions, right?" Miss Freitag looks at her hands. "She does, doesn't she? Drives you right up the walls. I know all about that, and I sympathize with you. Am I right?"

"Yes. She doesn't know when to shut up."

"And that's a bad thing?"

"It is when you're trying to teach twenty-four other children."

Now we're cookin'. I return to my seat. "Tee Jones is just a curious girl who craves attention, Miss Freitag. She's gonna be an actress someday, I just know it. You ever let her do anything in front of the class on her own?"

"Never."

"Why not?"

"She'll take over, Mrs. Borum. I have to keep her under control."

I roll my eyes this time. "How you know she'll take over? How you know what will happen unless you let it happen once?" She doesn't answer. "Y'all still do the Pledge of Allegiance, right?"

"Yes. So?"

"You ever let Tee lead it?"

"Of course not. That's a privilege a student must earn."

"Why?"

"Why? It's one of my main rules. You get privileges if you earn them. That's the way it is in real life."

Dag, it's gettin' thick up in here. "It is? What privileges you earned so far workin' here at Avery?"

She sighs. "Not many."

She's weakening. "Isn't saying the Pledge the right of every American?"

"Yes, of course. Tee says it along with the others. Loudly."

Tee would. "Bet the windows rattle."

She smiles. "Yep."

I'm beginning to like this woman. "Miss Freitag, could you maybe put Tee in charge of something?"

"Like what?"

I look around the room. "I don't know." I focus on a board displaying the day's weather. "Let her give the weather report. Let her pass out paper. Hell, she's practically sitting at your desk anyway. Save yourself some walkin'. Let her run errands for you. Let her do something, let her be useful, give *her* some control. You know about her mama, right?"

"No. I've never met her."

She doesn't know? That explains a bundle. "It's cuz she died a few months back."

Miss Freitag closes her eyes, and we're quiet for a few moments. "I didn't know that. Tee didn't say anything about it."

"Why would she? Every time Tee speaks, you put a red mark on that sign. I wouldn't tell you my business either." Miss Freitag opens her eyes, and they're lookin' right sad. "But I don't think Tee would tell you anyway. She hardly talks about it to anyone, even me. I think she's so busy trying to *be* her mama that she hasn't found time to cry over her mama. She's practically raising her brother all by her six-year-old self." A bell rings, and Miss Freitag looks like she's about to cry. "I didn't mean to ruin your day. Really. I just want to help." I stand. "I better be goin'."

I'm almost to the door when Miss Freitag says, "Wait." I turn. "I know exactly how Tee feels. My mother . . . My mother died when I was nine. I had a horrible time in school then, too. I should have recognized the problem, seen myself in Tee."

I smile despite the sadness welling in my heart for my own mama. "My mama died when I was ten. But . . . six, nine, ten—I don't think it matters when it happens. It's going to mess you up some way, somehow."

The first cute little kids come in, backpacks strapped on. "Thanks for stopping by," Miss Freitag says, scooping stacks of paper from the table.

"I'll be around Tuesdays and Wednesdays if you need me."

"Okay."

Instead of going to Mrs. King's class, I return to the office to pick up Dee, my "class" for the day.

"Is he here yet?" I ask Mrs. Holland.

"Not yet. What y'all gonna do all day?"

I shrug. "Don't know. Y'all still have that resource classroom upstairs?"

"Sure."

"Guess we'll go there."

"Supposed to warm up later today," she says with that crafty smile of hers. "Might even get into the sixties. Dee's missing gym today, so . . . "

Yep. I'm dressed to go to a park all right. "I understand."

I keep looking at the doorway to the office. I can't help it. It's like I haven't seen my son for weeks or something. At a little after nine, Dee slip-slides in, a bright blue backpack strapped on, his face blank. I squat in front of him and remove his book bag. "You ready?"

He nods.

I stand, he takes my hand, and we head upstairs to the resource room, which is really a closet with a table and a few chairs. We spend most of the morning practicing numbers and letters using some blank sheets of paper, and I say as little as possible. I write a letter or number, and he copies it in long strings.

I hand him a blank sheet. "I want you to draw me now. I want something I can hang on my refrigerator."

He blinks and roots around in his book bag for something, pulling out an orange-red crayon.

"Is that the color you think I am, Mr. Dee?"

He shrugs.

I slide my arm across the table. "Check it out, boy. Put your crayon on my arm." He does. "Now, does that match?"

He shakes his head and opens his mouth. *Lord Jesus, he's about to speak!*

But nothing comes out but a little yawn.

I laugh. "You sleepin' okay?"

He shrugs.

"You ain't takin' that medicine, are you?"

He shakes his head.

"Good." I gotta wake this child up. "Let's get out of here. You can draw me some other time. We're going to the park, Mr. Dee."

I let Dee guide me through the park, and we're the only ones there. We pass some slides and a jungle gym glistening with melted frost and walk till we come to a scruffy-looking tree missing most of its leaves. He stops and looks up. "You wanna climb it?"

He nods.

I look around to check for nosy bodies. "Go on, then."

He jumps for the lowest branch, grabs on, swings his legs up . . . and gets stuck. I want to wait for him to ask me for help, but I don't want him to fall. I turn him so he's on top of the branch, and in seconds, he's climbing like a squirrel till he's at least twenty feet up the tree, balancing on a branch no thicker than his leg.

"You be careful now."

He ain't hearin' me at all, his face one bright smile. The boy's just enjoyin' the view. Wish I could join him.

"What you see up there, Mr. Dee?"

No response.

"You see the ocean?"

He shakes his head.

"You see the mountains?"

Another shake.

"You see the school?"

Another shake.

What's left? It doesn't matter, I guess. Just to see anything different, get off the ground, climb out of a rut, look at the world in a new way—that's enough. Climb a tree and get away from your troubles.

"You okay up there?"

He nods.

"You hungry?"

He nods and climbs down, my heart catching on his every step. *Lord, keep Your angels on standby, okay?* When he gets to the lowest branch, I reach up for him, but he jumps off instead, landing on his feet. Climb a tree, solve your troubles, land on your feet—I ought to send that to *Reader's Digest* myself.

He takes my hand. "Thank you, Penny."

"You're welcome, Mr. Dee."

Wait a minute.

He spoke.

Dee Jones, the nodding boy, spoke.

My nose tingles, the tears not far behind.

Oh, my Lord, my Lord! And I didn't expect it! I try to blink my eyes so the tears don't come, but a few slip out anyway.

"You okay, Penny?"

I nod this time.

"You hungry?"

I nod again.

"Me, too."

I want to weep for joy, but I don't want to scare this child. What would he think if folks cried every time he spoke? To think that God, in His infinite wisdom, allowed this scrawny tree to stand here for maybe forty or fifty years till the day it would help a little boy to speak! *Lord, thank You for this tree!*

"Think they got chicken nuggets and fries today," I say with a sniff as we begin to walk.

"Yuck."

"Yuck?"

"It ain't real chicken like we ate at church."

"No, it isn't. Maybe they'll have something better."

He rolls his eyes. "They won't."

And they don't. Dee eats half a sloppy Joe and a few limp fries, washing it down with a carton of chocolate milk, chattering about his daddy, his sister, his teacher, a cartoon show, some creature that can change into a space ship—everything but his mama. I don't eat a single bit of my food because I don't want to miss a single, blessed word. He takes both our trays to the trash cans and leads me back upstairs. On the way, we pass the gym and find it empty.

"Wanna play some basketball, boy?"

"Uh-huh."

For the rest of that afternoon, Dee Jones, formerly the blank-faced boy, becomes the giggling boy, shooting and making most of his shots to the basket, which is only about six feet off the ground. I lift him a few times so he can dunk the ball, and he even challenges me to a game of horse, which I gladly lose.

"I'm terrible, aren't I?" I ask him.

"Yup," he says just like his daddy.

"Guess I should stick to bowling, huh?"

"Yup."

A bell rings to end the day, we get his backpack and coat from the resource room, and we return to the office where Tee is waiting on the bench. "And how is Miss Jones this fine day?" I ask.

"Okay."

I sit next to her, Dee leaning on my legs. "How was school, girl?"

"Okay."

"Just okay?"

"Uh-huh."

I see Mrs. Holland edging toward the counter. "What color did Miss Freitag put on the board today, Tee?" she asks.

"Green."

Yes! I smile at Mrs. Holland, and she winks. "You had a good day, girl," I say, and I hug her.

"So did I," Dee says.

Little Tee's whole body shakes, and it doesn't look like she knows what to do. She stares at her brother, at Mrs. Holland, at me. "Penny, did Dee just say something?"

"Uh-huh," Dee says. "C'mon." He takes Tee's hand. "Let's go to the playground."

Tee leaps off that bench, and the two of them race out of the office. *Great God in heaven! Thank You for watching Your sparrows today!*

"You had a good day today, too, Ruth Childress," Mrs. Holland says.

"Yup," I say. I stand. "Gonna go cross the monkey bars now."

"The what?"

"Gonna cross the monkey bars."

"Okay, you do that."

I catch up to Tee and Dee outside and stride right over to those bars. I climb the ladder, reach out both hands to the first bar, and swing out without falling. I look down and see Dee looking up at me.

"You goin' all the way across, Penny?"

"Gonna try."

"Be careful, Penny."

He's so cute! "I'll try."

I take one swipe with my right hand and reach the second bar, gripping it tightly. I'm still holding on!

"You can do it, Penny," Tee says from the top of the sliding board.

I grip tighter with my right hand and release my left, watching my hand float by my face to the third bar as I twist in the air. I latch on. My heart's goin' a million beats a second, I'm sweating, my arms ache, my hands hurt, but I ain't lettin' go. Four more bars to go.

"I'll catch you if you fall, Penny," Dee says.

Damn. Here come the tears. "Thank you, Mr. Dee." I grip harder with my left, release my right . . . and drop to the ground, but this time I land on my feet. "Almost made it." Whoo! Halfway. I made it halfway.

"You just need more practice, Penny," Tee says, and she flies down the slide.

"You gonna try again?" Dee asks.

"Maybe tomorrow."

"You did good," he says.

I go to the bench and sit. "Thank you, Mr. Dee."

"You look wore out, Penny. You need to rest."

"Thank you. I will. Y'all go on and play now."

For the next two hours or so, I watch them playing, their combined giggles and shouts soothing my aches away. A few other children from the neighborhood show up without their mamas, and they chase each other around, playing those made-up games children are famous for. Naturally, Tee controls the action, making (and remaking) the rules for a game she calls "Catch." I won't explain the rules since they change every five minutes, but it looks a lot like tag. At five, we say our good-byes and leave for the apartment.

"I get to read the weather report tomorrow, Penny," Tee says on the way. "Think it'll be cold and rainy?"

"Might be."

Dee pouts. "I won't be able to climb the tree if it rains."

I squeeze his hand. "We'll find something to do."

When we get to the apartment, we see Nanna sitting in her rusty truck. She leaps out and runs to Tee and Dee as the children race to her, Dee shouting, "Nanna!"

She hugs them both, then holds Dee's face, kissing him on the nose and smiling as wide as her little face will let her. I feel so much joy right now that I can't contain myself, like I'm about to burst. I can't wait till Dewey gets home!

"Y'all go in and get washed up," Nanna says. "And Tee, you do your homework."

"Bye Penny," Dee says.

"See you tomorrow, Mr. Dee. And Miss Tee, you practice that weather report."

"Okay."

They disappear into the apartment leaving Nanna and me at the back of her truck. "Isn't that amazing? He's speaking again!"

"Yup."

"We were just climbin' trees when—"

"Where y'all been?" she interrupts, and with an attitude, too. What's bitin' her in the ass?

"At the playground behind the school."

"Well, I've been worried sick."

Uh-oh. "Dewey didn't tell you that I was mindin' them?"

"No."

"It's only for Tuesdays and Wednesdays, the days I volunteer."

Nanna nods, her lips tightening. "What you doin'?"

"Doin'?"

She crosses her arms. "Nice what you've done for Dee, but what you *really* doin' here?"

I don't like the sound of her tone. "I'm mindin' your son's children."

"Uh-huh."

"I am."

"That ain't all, is it?"

"What you mean?"

"Bakin' a cake and actin' all neighborly when you ain't my son's neighbor, puttin' that note in with all them words underlined, goin' bowlin' with 'em, volunteerin' at their school. And you're just mindin' the children? You think I'm that stupid?"

I feel an empty space growing in my stomach. Everything was going along so well, and now this. "You're right, Mrs. Baxter. There is more to this."

She shakes her head. "Here we go again."

Here we go again? "Here what goes again?"

"This has Tiffany Jones written all over it."

"No it doesn't."

"The hell it don't!"

"I am not Tiffany Jones, Mrs. Baxter."

"No. You the one who divorced the preacher." Even white people know? "My son sure can pick 'em. First a whore, and now you." *Lord, the shit gettin' holy now! You best cover Your ears for a spell.* "You after my boy or his kids or both?"

My heart is thundering in my chest, and I want so bad to cuss her out. I swallow and say, "Both."

"You're as crazy as they say."

"Or in love," I say, and it slips out before I can catch it. Why am I pouring my heart out to this woman?

"Now I *know* you're crazy. I even hear you're playing at your ex-husband's wedding. What self-respecting woman does that?"

This is happening way too fast. "I'm not playing at his wedding."

"You were gonna, right?"

"Yes, but now—"

"And you're still callin' yourself Mrs. Borum like it means something anymore. You ask me, it don't mean shit. If you know what's good for you, you'll stay away from my Dewey. His plate is full enough without you addin' to it."

How can I make her know that I *can't* stay away? "The only thing I'm addin' to his plate is cake, Mrs. Baxter. I'm trying to lighten his load, not add to it."

"Horseshit. Anyone can make a decent cake. You're just trying to find you a man to pay your bills. Just like Tiffany."

"No, I'm not. I don't have any bills." Okay, I owe a couple thousand on some credit cards. "And I was going to play at that wedding because playing the organ is what I'm called to do."

"More horseshit."

"It ain't horseshit, Mrs. Baxter. Really. Playing the organ is my calling; it's my gift."

She rolls her eyes. "Your gift? Right. Well, I'm that boy's mama, he's my only son, he's *my* gift, and I am *called* to look out for him."

She got me, but I can't let this go. "He's a grown man, Mrs. Baxter." I take the deepest breath of my life. "And I intend one day to be your son's wife whether you like it or not."

"What? My boy will never marry you."

"Dewey ain't no boy, Mrs. Baxter. He's a man."

She cackles. "He's a boy to me, and he *ain't* gonna marry you, girl. So you just quit your tryin'."

"Why? Why ain't he gonna marry me?"

"Tiffany Jones was after my boy for six years. *Six* years, and he didn't marry her. Here you come along all of a sudden expectin' him to pop the damn question." She snaps her fingers. "It won't happen."

"Why?"

"I just told you. Are you deaf *and* crazy?"

I take a deep breath. "Why won't it happen? I think I already know, but I want to hear it from you."

"You wanna hear *what* from me?"

"I wanna hear you say it won't happen because *you* don't want it to happen."

"Course I don't want it to happen. Whites and coloreds ain't supposed to be mixin'. It's in the Bible."

Now we're gettin' right down to it. "In Ezra nine and ten, right?"

"Shit, I don't know. I just know it's in there."

Lord, why You let ignorance create racism? "Well, it ain't in there, Mrs.

Baxter. Ain't nothin' in the Bible that says I can't be mixin' with your son, and I oughta know. I was once a preacher's wife, and I've read that book cover to cover so I could write his sermons." I step closer, putting her in my shadow. "Say it."

"Say what?"

"Say what you mean, Mrs. Baxter, and don't you bring God or the Bible into it. Why won't Dewey marry me?"

She looks away. "Cuz I won't let him."

I step back, my heart sinking a little. Naomi was right about Dewey's mama. "Thank you for your honesty, Mrs. Baxter. Now, I'm gonna give you some honesty of my own. I intend to marry your son, and if I have to ask *him* to marry *me*, I will. There are some forces at work here that even I do not fully understand, but I'm goin' with the flow. Your son, his children, me—*we* are meant to be together." I smile. "And there ain't a damn thing you can do about it, so *you* shouldn't even try."

"There ain't?"

"There ain't."

"We'll see about that, Miss Penny. We'll just see about that."

"What God has brought together, no man or woman can tear apart."

She starts to walk toward the apartment door, then stops, turning slowly to me. "I ain't just any woman, Miss Penny. I am my son's mama. You ain't never been a mama, have you?" I don't answer. "You don't know that a boy's mama is the most powerful person on earth. I talked him out of hitchin' up with that whore for six years. This little thing you tryin' now ain't *nothin'* I can't handle."

I can't think of a thing to say because I just can't think! I wanna cuss, I wanna cry, I wanna break shit, but I can't. Okay, so the bitch has had practice at this, but I've been through much worse shit with Jonas. I get my breathing under control and stand taller. "This ain't no little thing, Mrs. Baxter. When Dewey gets home, and he gets to talk to his son again, you're gonna have a lot to handle."

"You takin' credit for that?"

Am I? I know it was God and that tree, but I was there! "No, Mrs. Baxter. God gets all the glory for this. But Dewey . . ." I leave that hanging in the air.

"But Dewey what?"

"Think it through, Mrs. Baxter. Think it through. Don't really matter what either of us thinks, does it?"

Her face scrunches up for a moment, but then it relaxes into an evil smile. "I can handle that."

Bitch is gonna lie about it. "You gonna lie, right?"

"Sure am."

I nod. "And he'll believe you cuz you're his mama."

"Damn straight. You're catchin' on. You're pretty smart for a loony-toon."

I sure am. Crazy like a fox, and this fox has an idea. "So you gotta lie to keep your son's love, huh? I pity you."

That smile vanishes. "Now you just—"

"Oh, it's time for Dee's medication," I interrupt. "Got to give it to him like clockwork if you want him to keep talkin'. And you gotta make sure he swallows. The boy is gettin' in the habit of spitting it out when you ain't lookin'. Caught him today just before he spoke for the first time tryin' to spit it out in a trash can. And don't let him into the bathroom. Caught him tryin' to flush one the other day." *Forgive me, Lord, but I gotta do what I gotta do.*

"Goodbye, Mrs. Borum," she says, running to the apartment door.

"This ain't goodbye, Mrs. Baxter. We'll be seeing each other again soon."

Though I want to wait on Dewey to get home, I'm too angry. Why she gotta ruin my perfect day? I got a silent boy to make lots of noise, helped Tee's teacher to really see her for the first time, and this is my reward? I gotta get home to get the lowdown on Dewey's mama from Fred.

But when I get home, Fred's gone from the yard. I check the laundry room, don't see him, and walk wearily up the steps to the apartment. Maybe he's just out somewhere, or maybe he got hisself arrested because it was pressed turkey night at the jail. I don't want to think of God's hand lifting him out of my yard right now, so I go ahead and make the biscuits, checking the window every few minutes for Fred.

He never shows.

The biscuits go cold.

Dewey doesn't call to thank me for getting his son to laugh again. And I can't sing "Hold On," cuz everything will not be all right.

Nineteen

It rains somethin' awful the next morning, and I'm late getting to Avery since my umbrella keeps folding up on itself, leaving me drenched right down the middle of my back. Serves me right for buying a three-dollar umbrella from a big bin at a check-out line. I shake off outside the office and see Dee sitting on the bench.

Staring into space. Staring at nothing.

Oh shit. He's back to being a zombie. What have I done?

I walk in, sign in, and reach out my hand to Dee. He doesn't take it. I take his hand, and we walk up to the resource room, my heart getting heavier and heavier. I close the door and help him out of his coat. He won't look at me. He just stares at that nowhere place in front of him.

"Have a seat, Mr. Dee," I say, but he doesn't move. I pull a chair behind him and help him sit. "What you wanna do today?"

He doesn't even shrug.

"You could draw that picture of me. You wanna do that?"

Dee doesn't seem to be breathing.

I root around in his book bag, looking for crayons. I only find a lunch bag, a few pieces of brown crayon, and a drawing. I hold the drawing up to my eyes and see . . . me and Dee. It's me, all right. I'm penny-colored, tall, freckled, and I'm wearing a hat and standing near a tall tree. High up in the tree is Dee, a smile on his beige face.

"When did you draw this?"

No response.

"Did you draw this for me last night?"

No response.

He had to have drawn it last night. "Thank you, Mr. Dee. It's beautiful." I'm not, but the picture is. "Please speak to me, Dee. When did you do this?"

He finally looks up at me. "After Nanna went to sleep."

I sigh, my heart getting lighter. He's been faking all this time? "She stayed with y'all last night?"

"Uh-huh. She kept tryin' to make me take my medicine cuz *you* said to."

Ouch. "Well, Dee, you see—" How do you explain this to a four-year-old? I decide to tell the truth. "I was tryin' to get back at your Nanna for bein' so hateful to me, Dee, and I hope you pitched the worst fit you ever pitched."

He smiles. "I did."

"Good! So you didn't take the medicine?"

"Nope. It tasted yucky."

I smile. "So how long you been fakin' bein' a zombie?"

He smiles. "Since you and Nanna started fussin'."

So that means . . . Nanna didn't get a peep out of my Dee! "You were listening to us fuss?"

He nods. "It was Tee's idea, and we fooled everybody. Nanna, Daddy, even you, Penny."

"Yep, you got me." Both Tee and Dee should be in the movies. "But you didn't even speak to your daddy?"

"Nope."

"Why not?"

"Cuz Tee said I couldn't talk till Nanna was gone."

"Is she *still* there?"

"Uh-huh. She's supposed to pick us up after school."

To keep me away from Dewey, and she's putting her whole farm on hold cuz of li'l ol' me? "Did Nanna try to get you to talk?"

"Uh-huh. But I didn't say anything."

Bet that frustrated the bitch somethin' awful. I take his hand. "But wasn't your daddy sad?"

"I guess."

"You don't want your daddy to be sad, do you?"

"No."

We could call him right now and beat ol' Nanna to the punch! "Wanna call him on the phone?"

"Okay."

I race him down the stairs to the office, lifting and setting him on the counter. "Mrs. Holland, Dee would like to speak to his daddy on the phone."

"Is it an emergency?" Mrs. Holland asks.

"No," I say. "Dee just wants to say hi."

She rifles through the file cabinet and pulls out Dee's file, showing me Dewey's work number. "You may have to leave a message."

"That's okay," I say as I dial the number.

"Calhoun Steel, Vicki speaking."

"This is Ruth Borum from Avery Elementary School. I'd like to leave a message for Dewey Baxter to call the school concerning his son, Dee."

"Is this an emergency?"

"Yes," I lie. "And the sooner the better." I give her the number.

"Might be a bit," Vicki says. "He's out in all that mess out there, but I'll be sure he gets the message."

"Thank you." I hang up and look deeply into Dee's eyes. "What you gonna say to your daddy, boy?"

He shrugs. "Don't know."

"I'm sure you've thought about it."

"Yeah."

I get right up in his face. "So?"

He bats his little brown eyes at me. "I know what to say, Penny."

"Okay, okay." I back off. "I'm just curious. You don't want to tell me, fine." I wait him out, but Dee doesn't say another word. Tough kid.

The phone rings several times—all false alarms—then Mrs. Holland's eyes light up. "Yes sir, Mr. Baxter. Ruth Borum would like to speak to you."

I take the phone, my heart pounding. "Hi, Dewey."

"What's wrong?"

I decide to play with him a little. "Dee's, um, well, had an interesting day."

"What happened?"

"Well . . ." Dee grabs for the phone, but I pull it away.

"Is he hurt? Is he all right?"

Dag, I'm scarin' the man. "He's fine, and he's not hurt."

"Then, what was the emergency?"

I smile. "Ask him."

"Huh?"

"I'll let *Dee* tell you all about it."

"What?"

I give Dee the phone, and Dee says, "Hi, Daddy." So much for advanced preparation. But . . . that would be enough. Just to hear my child say "Hi, Mama" would make me melt. A full minute later, Dee whispers to me, "He's crying."

And now so am I. "Talk to him," I whisper.

"Daddy? Penny is crying, too. " Dee listens a bit, then turns to me. "He's coming here!"

"He is?" A date at an elementary school? This just keeps getting better and better!

"Uh-huh." He listens a bit more. "But you better bring your own lunch, Daddy." He hands the phone to me. "He wants to talk to you."

I yank that phone from Dee. "Hello?"

"Thank you, Ruth. Thank you!"

Those are two right beautiful words, Lord. Thank You for creating them. "I didn't do it, Dewey. God did."

"Right."

"I just happened to be in the right place at the right time." I'm good at that lately. A good Penny is turnin' up all over the damn place. "And Dee's right about lunch, Dewey. You might want to pick up something on the way."

"I will. You want anything?"

Just you, Dewey. Just you. "You buyin'?"

"Yup."

"Just get four of whatever you're havin'."

"Four?"

Man's already forgotten he has a daughter. "You want Tee to eat with us, too, don't you?"

"Oh, yeah. I'll be there as soon as I can."

"See you soon."

I hang up and pull Dee to me, his little arms around my neck. "We better get ready, huh? Gotta get your sister out of class."

Mrs. Holland holds up a piece of paper. "Already wrote the pass for Tee."

"We'll have us a picnic, then."

"Where?" Dee asks.

"Upstairs in the resource room," I say. Just wanna keep it cozy. "Mrs. Holland, can you send Tee and Mr. Baxter up to us?"

"Sure."

While we wait, I can't keep my feet from dancing I'm so excited. A family picnic! Sure the room's small, windowless, and stuffy, but . . . daa-em, a picnic in a closet! But Dewey will smell like wet dog. Hmm. Might need some air freshener.

"Dee, why did you speak all of a sudden yesterday?"

He frowns. "Just did."

"C'mon, boy. You had to have a reason. What, four months without saying a single word, and out of the blue you start chatterin' like a squirrel?"

"Well . . ." He smiles a little. "Mama and me was goin' tree climbing that day. But it was raining. Like today." He takes my hand and turns it over, smoothing his hand on my palm. I am a human chill bump. Is this what he did to his mama's hand that day in the car? Did he hold her hand one last time? "And then yesterday . . . you took me."

A sob rises in my throat, and I have trouble swallowing it. "If it wasn't raining today, you know we'd be out there again."

"Tee says it's supposed to rain till Saturday."

"Maybe we can go climbin' on Saturday."

"Yeah. At Nanna's. We're goin' there on Saturday." He rests his little head on my hand. "Will you go with us?"

"I'd love to, Dee, but I don't think your Nanna likes me very much."

He closes his eyes. "She don't want you gettin' with my daddy." The child *did* hear everything. He lifts his head and looks at me. "You gonna get with him anyway, right? Tee says you will."

Daa-em. Tee *does* know too much. "What you know about gettin' with someone, boy?"

"Mama wanted to get with Daddy in the worstest way." His eyes cloud over. "She was . . . goin' to see him 'bout that when it happened."

More chill bumps. She was going to see Dewey to force the issue. I can see her driving and saying something like "Gonna go get that man to do right by me." Driving too fast. Tiffany was on her way to do what I've been tryin' to do . . . and it killed her. Tiffany Jones died loving that man. What about me? *Am I goin' too fast, Lord? Got me a speed bump with Nanna yesterday and stumbled a little bit, but I don't want to slow down.*

"What do you want to happen, Dee?"

"I want you to be my mama."

I blink. "Just like that?"

"Uh-huh. Tee wants the same thing."

"What about your daddy?"

He shrugs. "Tee says it ain't up to us 'bout that. It's all up to you."

It sure is. "How am I doin' so far?"

He smiles. "Daddy liked your cake."

"Anything else?"

He giggles. "Tee said not to tell."

I stare him down. "You want me to be your mama?"

He stops giggling. "Yes." The child has manners when you scare him, sayin' "yes" instead of "uh-huh." I'll have to remember that.

I raise my eyebrows as high as they'll go, making my eyes as big as I can. "Then, you have to tell me everything."

"Everything?"

"Everything. That's the rules. Now, what did Tee say?"

"Tee said that . . . that Daddy be starin' hard at your booty when you was bowlin'."

Oh, my God! "He was?"

Dee nods. "Probably why he kept missin' that booty pin."

The man likes my cake *and* my booty. I've won his stomach *and* his pecker. "What else can you tell me that you ain't supposed to?" Like, does he call out my name in his sleep?

He shrugs. "Don't know."

Tee appears in the doorway. "Hi, Penny. Where's my daddy?"

And that's the only question anybody has for the next two hours. It's almost one-thirty by the time Dewey shows up with two soggy bags of fast food. He fills the doorway to the closet, smelling like all outdoors, dripping wet.

"Sorry I'm late," he says as he slaps the bags onto the table. "Rain's backin' everythin' up down there." He smiles at Tee and lifts Dee. "How's my little man?"

"Okay," Dee says. "Hungry."

"Me, too," Dewey says, holding Dee to him, his body shuddering with sobs. *Lord, this is joy.* Forget that definition in the dictionary. This picture should take its place.

I feel a sob rising into my throat, so I pick up the bags. "I'll find a microwave for these."

I don't think Dewey hears me, but it doesn't matter. He has his little man back. I leave them hugging on each other, find a microwave in the teacher's lounge, and attempt to rescue four soaked cheeseburgers and four orders of barely cooked fries. By the time I get back, they're giggling and laughing and carrying on—and I suddenly feel left out. I ain't part of this family yet. I ain't neither child's mama, and I ain't even the daddy's girlfriend. I look at the bags in my hands. I'm just the waitress. Damn, why I got to depress myself? I put the food on the table.

"Looks good," Dewey says.

"Y'all eat up," I say, and I start to leave.

"Aren't you gonna eat with us?" Dewey asks.

"Uh, I have some work to do," I say softly. "Besides, there ain't enough room." Dewey fills the right side of the closet, the children the left. Unless I sit on the table, there isn't enough room for all of us.

"We'll make room," Dewey says. He leans over the table and picks up Dee, placing him on his lap. "How's that?"

"I can sit on your lap, Penny," Tee says.

"Thanks, but there ain't enough food to go around either. You can't get through the day on just one little cheeseburger, Dewey."

He smiles. "I'll make it." Then he holds out his hand to me. To *me!* "Please join us, Ruth."

My head wants to stay, but my feet are taking me in the other direction. *Why, Lord, why? You know that I want to take that man's hand worse than anything in my life! Why am I hesitating?* "Thanks for the offer," I hear myself saying, "but y'all have a lot of catchin' up to do."

I watch his hand slowly return to his son's shoulder. "Okay. Um, you bowlin' tonight?"

"Yes." At least I think I am. I doubt Naomi would want me there, but at least Tonya might give me a ride. I may have at least one friend left.

"Need a ride?"

"No." What the *hell* am I saying? I'd *love* to ride in this man's rusty-dusty truck instead of Tonya's cramped little car! "I'll catch a ride with someone."

"I could pick you up around six."

"That's okay, Dewey."

His eyes drop. "I hope to see you there."

"Yeah."

I'm not ten feet from the resource room when I cannot stop the tears, stumbling into the first bathroom I come to, which turns out to be a little girls' room. I slide into a tiny stall and close the door, wadding up toilet paper and blowing my nose. I am such a fool. I was invited to his table, and I turned him down. I was offered a ride, and I turned it down. Why am I doing this? Is it because I don't want to be like Tiffany and end up driving too fast? Or is it because I'm scared to death that I'll get rejected by him? Or is it—

A jolt of electricity shoots through me.

Oh shit.

Or is it because I am truly, hopelessly in love with someone for the first time in my life?

Holy Jesus, I have fallen in love with this man, and now I'm afraid of what might happen!

I grip the tops of both sides of the little stall to keep myself from falling headfirst into the toilet. "Lord Jesus," I whisper, "this is Ruth Lee Childress Borum, another one of Your little pennies, here in the toilet. I'm at a crossroads or something, Lord Jesus. You gotta help me, Man. You gotta help me through this."

The door to the bathroom swings open, and a little girl no taller than my knee enters. I get more chill bumps because God has sent another child to rescue me! But when she sees me—standing head and shoulders above the top of a stall—she stops moving. "You in the right bathroom, honey," I say. Must look funny to see a woman standing like a man in a stall. She doesn't move. "Really." I step out of my stall. "I was just blowing my nose."

"Oh," she says in the tiniest voice. She blinks at me. "I wasn't sure." Then she tears into the stall next to mine and slams the door behind her. For some reason, it is the funniest thing I have ever seen, and as I hunch down to look in the little mirror to dry away the last of my tears with a paper towel, I get the giggles so bad that I have to hold on to the little sink to keep from falling out.

The little girl flushes and comes out. "What's so funny?" she asks with the nastiest little attitude.

"Everything," I say. "Everything on God's green earth is funny."

She frowns. "You need Jesus, yo."

I get the giggles something fierce then, and the little girl flies from that bathroom. I recover and look in the mirror at this strange woman I've become. "Too late, child," I say. "Too late."

Twenty

By the time I leave the bathroom, the resource room is empty except for the smell of greasy fries and one stank man. I go to the office to look for Dee.

"You lookin' for Dee?" Mrs. Holland asks. I nod. "Mr. Baxter took 'em out of school for the rest of the day."

"Oh." They just ate and ran.

"They all looked so happy, Ruth. I'm proud of you."

"Thanks."

When I get home, I call Tonya and leave a message for her to pick me up. I check outside every now and then for Fred but don't see anything except coarse yellow grass where he used to sit. Then I just sit and wait.

And think.

A man reached out to me over fifteen years ago, and I held on to him for dear life . . . and got the worst hurtin' I've ever had. Another man, a very different man in every respect, is reaching out to me now . . . and I'm runnin' away. *I want him, Lord, I really do, but I can't get hurt like that again. Like they say so many times in the movies, I'm gettin' too old for this shit.* I laugh. *Sorry I curse so much, Lord, but I've had a lot to curse about.*

I mess with my hair for a spell, and even my hair seems to be running away from my brush. Dag, I should have taken Dewey up on his offer, and he probably wouldn't have been late picking me up since it's his bowling night. I would have been able to walk in with him, would have walked in a with a smile, would have had (damn!) the eyes of four hundred bowlers on me and him. As scary as that sounds, I'd like to see that, like to see their reactions, like to feel their eyes. We make a nice couple, Dewey and me. We fit together. We ain't matching book-ends, but we both got freckles, big hands and feet, young faces, and some fat, some insulation. Add his children, and we make us a hand-some family. Big Penny, her shiny nickel white man, and her little pen-nies. There's something almost . . . right about the whole thing. It ain't right to run away from something so right.

I hear a horn blow outside and see Tonya's Mustang at the curb. I throw on a coat, skip down the stairs, and get to sit in the front seat for a change.

"How you been, girl?" Tonya asks.

"Better," I say.

"Haven't seen you in a couple days. What you been doin'?"

I fill her in on most of the previous three days' activities, and she's strangely silent. "So, what you think about all this, Tonya?"

"I'm jealous," she says as she turns into the parking lot at Mountainside.

"Why?"

"I don't think I've ever been in love, I mean, really in love."

"Be thankful," I say as I get out. "Cuz it scares the livin' shit out of me."

We walk in and find Naomi poring over a piece of paper on lane thirty-eight. I take a deep breath and say, "Hey, Naomi."

"Hey," she says, but she doesn't look up.

"I'm, um, here if y'all need me to bowl tonight."

"Uh-huh." She looks up at me with a tight little smile on her face. "But everybody's supposed to be here, so . . ."

Naomi don't want me to bowl, and suddenly I want to bowl in the worst way.

Tonya rolls her eyes and grabs my arm. "C'mon. Let's get you some shoes and a ball. Just in case."

Tonya pays for the shoe rental, and I find a purple ball like the one I used with Dewey, placing it on the ball rack. An announcement comes on, all garbled and full of static, and our side of the bowling alley fills with the sound of practicing bowlers. I back away to a table behind lane thirty-eight, but Tonya pushes me back to the lane where Naomi's already throwing a practice ball.

"Throw a few," she says. "Show Naomi what you got."

I stand in line behind a distinguished black man with a ready smile. "You bowlin' tonight, Mrs. Borum?"

"Don't know," I say. "I'm just a sub."

"I'm Ernest." He steps aside with the nicest little bow. "After you."

"Thank you." A *polite,* older black man at this meat market? I pick up my ball, line up my feet, and imagine that the pins are all little Naomis with bad attitudes and tight-lipped smiles. A big step and some pitter-pats and I launch that purple ball down the lane knocking the living shit out of every pin. And the sound is *loud,* as loud as a head-on car wreck. I turn to look at Naomi waiting in line behind Ernest, but she's looking away.

Ernest gives me some dap. "You'll be bowlin' tonight."

I see Yvonne and Bill come through the door, but I get in line on the other lane anyway because I need all the practice I can get. If Mike shows, I'll just sit down and watch or drift down to Dewey's side. No big deal. Hell, I only threw one strike. But when I throw another strike on my next ball, the sound just as deafening, I decide that I have to bowl tonight. I see Tonya talking to Naomi, waving her hands and rolling her neck like only Tonya can. Naomi ain't havin' it, shaking her head slowly and looking toward the door. Ho wants Mike to come roll his measly ninety.

I pick up my ball for my third practice ball, and an announcement comes on as I'm lining up my feet. The bowlers to either side of me put down their balls, and the whole alley becomes silent. Not me. I don't care if shadow bowling is over. I intend to make a statement. A loud one. I rocket that ball down the lane as hard as I can and hurt those pins so bad that one even flies out so far on the lane that the guard-thing can't collect it. If my right hand was a gun, I'd be blowin' the smoke off it. I turn and stare a hole in Naomi's head as I stalk toward her.

"Am I bowlin' tonight?" I ask her.

"Mike's supposed to be coming," she says.

"He'll be late," Tonya says. "C'mon, Naomi. Let Ruth bowl. She's on a roll."

"We'll wait for Mike," Naomi says.

"Naomi—" Tonya starts to say, but I silence her with a hand.

"It's okay, Tonya," I say. "I wouldn't want to beat Naomi, you know, embarrass her in front of all these people."

"Excuse me?" Naomi says.

I put my fat nose an inch from hers. "I would kick your tight little ass tonight, Naomi."

"You really think so?"

"Up one lane and down the next."

Another crackly announcement starts the balls flying again. "We'll see about that." She rushes to the little computer and plugs my name in for Mike, who bowls last. Tonya gives me a little dap, and Naomi's and my grudge match begins.

For whatever reason, everybody *but* Naomi has a good game. Tonya doesn't wiggle as much and puts a bunch of spares together. Bill gets several strikes in a row, and Yvonne doesn't fall, picking up several tricky splits. Me? I bowl my damn weight, a one-ninety, my best game ever, and I beat a fussin' and cussin' Naomi by thirty pins. And even though the team wins by forty-seven pins, Naomi is pissed, and because Mike has arrived, she tries to put him back up on the blue screen for the second game.

"Nah, girl," Tonya says to Naomi. "Once a sub bowls for someone, the sub bowls every game. You know that. You want us to forfeit? Besides, Mike drunk as a brewery. Didn't you see him stumblin' in here? Ruth has to stay up there."

Naomi blinks at Tonya. "But Mike is an official member of this team, Tonya, so we should make every effort to—"

"You want to win?" Tonya asks.

"Of course, but—"

"If you don't want us to forfeit, you have to keep Ruth up there."

Naomi wrinkles up her lips. "Ask Mike if it's all right."

"What I got to ask him for? Ruth subbed in, so she got to stay." She looks at Mike, who is swaying in his chair. "Boy can't even sit up straight. He probably be pukin' by the end of the evening."

Naomi sighs and punches my name back into the computer with deliberate slowness.

I don't bowl as well the second game, and Naomi has a better game, beating me by a bunch. But the team wins again, and Naomi seems more relaxed, almost giving me dap a few times before remembering.

Till Dewey drops by in between games.

"How you doin'?" he asks me, his hands deep in his pockets.

"A one-ninety and a one-fifty-something," I tell him. "How 'bout you?"

He shrugs. "Off night. We just finished and lost every game."

"Too bad."

"Um, can I get y'all anything?"

All this competition has made me hungry. "Two hot pretzels and a large Coke."

He smiles. "Okay."

"And don't forget the mustard."

"Sure."

He turns to Tonya and Naomi. "Y'all want anything?"

"No thanks," Tonya says, and Naomi walks away with a scowl.

During the last game, I match Naomi strike for strike, spare for spare through the first nine frames, and NYTBM is crushing the other team. Dewey delivers the pretzels, and I sit next to him in between turns. Though I get dap from both teams, gettin' dap from Dewey is a little more, well, sensuous. I hold on to his warm hand a little longer each time, and even squeeze it. I can't believe I'm flirtin' with him using dap, but it seems to be workin'.

"Shouldn't you be gettin' home?" I ask him.

"Mama's watchin' the kids," he says.

"And you're watchin' me."

His face turns a delicious shade of red. "Yup."

I squeeze his hand under the table. "You thinkin' bad thoughts about what you see, Mr. Baxter?"

He nods.

"How bad?"

He gulps. "Real bad."

"Good."

He squeezes my hand. "Are you, uh, thinkin', um—"

I put my lips next to his ears. "Think of the wickedest thing you can and multiply it by infinity."

"Oh . . . shit," he whispers.

I stand to bowl the last frame, releasing his hand slowly. "Now double it, Mr. Baxter."

I leave him nodding and gulping and lean over Tonya. "Dewey's givin' me a ride," I say with a wink.

She doesn't catch my meaning right off, but then she smiles. "You gotta tell me everything, okay?"

I shake my head. "No I don't. You'll just have to use your imagination." I look at the scores. "What I got to do to beat Naomi?"

"You gotta strike out. You get two strikes and a nine, and y'all will tie at one-ninety-nine. Three strikes and you get a two hundred."

Three strikes in a row. I started the evening that way; I can end that way. First ball: strike. Second ball: strike. I pick up the ball and rub on it. That's all I do—really—but it's enough to get me thinkin' about what's to come later with Dewey. I mean, I got my fingers in a *purple* ball about to knock down some *thick* pins standing *erect* at the other end of an oily *alley . . . Sorry, Lord. But bowling can be a sexual sport.*

I line up my feet, watch the arrows instead of the pins, release the ball, see an explosion—but I leave one pin dead center in the middle. The booty pin. I laugh, and when I turn, I see Dewey laughing, too. So I tied with Naomi, big deal. I look around and don't even see her. Wench didn't even stay around to congratulate me for helping her team finally sweep a night of bowling.

"Roll one more girl," Tonya says.

I point at the screen. "Game's over."

"I know," she whispers, "but you can't go home with Dewey and leave that pin there. It ain't good luck."

"What if I miss it?"

"Don't."

I pick up my ball, go through my routine, and roll that ball as slowly as I can down the lane. Instead of watching the ball, I turn to watch the expression in Dewey's eyes, but damn if he ain't lookin' right back into mine. He ain't lookin' at the ball—he's lookin' at me. Maybe he's really seeing me for the very first time. I hear the pin drop behind me.

I'm gettin' me some tonight, oh, yes.

We don't get any stares as Dewey and I leave Mountainside, probably because the parking lot is so dark. He opens my door and waits till I'm settled before closing it. Such a gentleman. On the way to Vine, I take his hand, keeping him from shifting into fourth gear.

"Dewey, how come you ain't tried to kiss me yet?" I ask.

"Well, I—"

"Well, I nothin'. You gonna kiss me or what?"

"Now? While I'm drivin'?"

"Hell yes. I got your son to speak, I got your daughter to behave, and I got you starin' at my ass. I deserve more than a kiss, Dewey Baxter, but I'll settle for one. Now."

He pulls into a church parking lot, an empty Presbyterian parking lot with very straight white lines. Bet it didn't take them six months to decide to paint those. "This okay?"

"No." He starts to shift into reverse, but I bump the gear shift into neutral. "The place is okay, but it ain't okay that you ain't kissin' me yet."

"Oh."

And then . . . We do us some necking and play us some tonsil hockey. Like everything else about him so far, his tongue is huge and very tasty. The damn gear shift keeps getting in the way of my leg, but we manage to swap a whole lot of juicy, wet, loud kisses, his hands pressin' all over me, my hands explorin' all over him. Whenever I come up for air—which ain't often—I check out the windows fogging up around us. We puttin' out some heat!

I reach up and touch his face, and he stops tickling my teeth with his tongue. "Why don't you wear cologne?" I ask.

"Never have."

"I'll buy you some." Why am I thinkin' this shit at this moment?

"Burns my skin."

"Well, you need something. You smell too . . . plain." I smile. "We'll find you something nice." I take a deep breath and say what I have never said to anyone in my life: "Wanna go back to my apartment?"

He nods, but he says, "But I should be getting back to the kids."

Damn. "Yeah."

"Mama has a long drive."

Why'd he have to bring that wench into this warm, steamy truck? "You know that she hates my ass, don't you?"

He laughs, but he doesn't let go of me, caressing my shoulders. "Mama really don't like anyone."

"Cuz she's a racist."

Dewey shakes his head. "I don't think you can call Mama a racist."

Yes you can. "She told me just the other day that whites and coloreds shouldn't mix."

"She said that?" I nod. "Mama will say anything to make a person mad."

"It worked."

"She used to push Tiff's buttons, too, saying that at least her children are halfway intelligent."

"Now, that's racist."

Dewey shrugs. "Maybe."

"Maybe? Dewey, that is extremely racist!"

"Not if Mama was really referring to the black half of my children as being intelligent, right?"

I smile. "True, but that's not how I'd take it if I was their mama."

He nods. "Tiff didn't take too kindly to that kind of thing either, and she used to go off, let me tell you, especially when Mama would be sweet to her one day and contrary as a hedgehog the next day." Maybe Dewey's mama is one of them manic-depressives or got that bipolar disorder. "Fact is, Mama likes pushing everybody's buttons. And what she said to you—she's just lookin' for the button to set you off."

"Well, she found it. And it *sounded* racist."

"Believe me, my mama ain't no racist. She's just mean. A racist is supposed to hate one race and say their race is the best, right?" I nod. "That ain't Mama at all. You should hear her cuss white people. Cracker this, and cracker that. Believe me, Ruth, my mama hates everybody."

"She can't hate everybody." Can she? Dewey's mama is a *human* racist?

"She sure is trying to."

"But why?"

"Mama's always been ornery as a snake, but when Daddy died, she became completely hateful to everyone, even me sometimes. She spent that first year after Daddy's death sayin' everybody was goin' to hell, even told a few folks right to their faces." Nanna sounds almost like the average preacher! "Mama don't have many friends left." He squeezes my hand. "She's just testing you, Ruth."

Am I passin' the test? "Why she gotta test me?"

"Cuz she can." He kisses and nibbles at that little dip between my neck and my shoulders, and I close my eyes. Please, just end this conversation and keep doing that! But he stops nibbling. "In a way, her bein' hateful to you is a good sign."

"How is her bein' hateful good?"

He kisses that spot again. Thank you! "Mama wouldn't test you if she wasn't worried that you might steal me away." He sucks a little on the space under my earlobe; then he whispers, "You must be gettin' to her."

And this man is gettin' to me. I want to know more about Nanna, but I am just too moist to be doin' anythin' but some humpin'. You can't sit and chat when you're juicy, and once you start you some foreplay, you got to finish the job. That's in the rule book, I'm sure. "Please come to my apartment. Just for a few minutes."

"I don't know, Ruth. I'm liable to do something I shouldn't."

"Really? Like what?"

He turns red. "You know."

"Then, drive me to my apartment, and when we get there, take me inside"—I put my hand on his leg, dragging my nails across his jeans—"and do you some you know on me as best as you know how."

There must be a little NASCAR in every white man because Dewey breaks every speed record getting us to Vine. He parks the truck with a jerk and leaps out before I can even get the seat belt off. This boy wants some, too! He's halfway up the porch stairs before he remembers to come back and open my door. I step out and take his hand, and he practically pushes me up all those stairs, his hand wandering to my ass by the time we get to the top.

Once inside with the door closed, he slams me against the door, removing my blouse with fast fingers and an even faster tongue. This ain't gonna be just a few minutes, no sir. And my nipples are about to fly off and break them some windows.

I yank off his Steelers jersey and get a look at his titties. Lord, they're bigger than mine! Shit, what he do? Fertilize them or something? I reach out and squeeze, but they ain't flabby. Boy got him some rock-hard titties, and a quick glimpse down shows me he got a rock-hard somethin' else, too. This boy is packin' a concealed weapon, and I intend to frisk that bad boy out of him.

He buries his head on my titties and works his way down to my stomach, but instead of skipping it and getting to my pants zipper, he kisses all over my fat stomach, holding it, squeezing it like it's the best piece of flesh he ever had. When he puts his tongue in my belly button, I nearly fall out my legs are getting so weak.

"Dewey," I whisper. "Take off my pants."

The zipper comes down; then he goes down down down down down on me. We still haven't left the door, and the doorknob is gettin' right fresh with my ass. If any of my neighbors come by just now and stand on the other side of the door, they'll be getting an earful of slurping, moaning, and "Oh, yes!"-ing.

"Let's go to the bed," I say. He stands. "I wanna see what you got."

Instead of me leading him there, he sweeps me into his arms and carries me, sucking hard on my neck. *Lord, bein' airborne is nice!* He eases me onto the edge of the bed, and I unzip his pants and remove his underwear. What falls into my hands is like sculpture, and the only thing runnin' through my head, I swear, is *Some elephant is runnin' around in Africa with a tusk missin'.*

I slide back on the bed, but I don't let go of his booty pin, and unlike Jonas, Dewey knows exactly where to put it and how to use it. He finds a rhythm with that booty pin of his, and he splits my alley till I'm thinkin' *STRIKE STRIKE STRIKE!*

The phone rings during my second orgasm. Yes, the Lord has a strange sense of humor, and no, I'm not answering it, and no, you don't have to stop massaging my back, and yes, you're hard again, and oh, yes we goin' bowlin' bowlin' bowlin' . . .

"It's about time you came around, Dewey," I whisper to him while he spoons me afterward. I like this feeling, too—his massive arms around me, his hot breath on the back of my neck. I don't feel any guilt, despite all the time I've spent in church. I know premarital sex is wrong, but if you ask me, some *marital* sex is wrong, too. "You know you gotta marry me now, right?"

"I do?"

"See there? You're already practicin' for the wedding. I like me a man who thinks ahead."

"Now, uh, just wait a minute, I—"

I slam my booty back into his stuff, which is still sort of hard. His stuff should be illegal. "I am not the type of woman who sleeps with a man without a reason. I want to marry you, Dewey."

"I know, but I—"

I squash his stuff again, and it feels even harder. "You want this again?"

"You keep doing that, I'll have to do something about it."

"Then, give it up, boy. Work that thing." He gets himself in position, but I knock him loose with a hand. "That didn't hurt, did it?"

"No."

Damn near bruised my hand! I ain't swattin' his stuff away again. "So you gonna marry me?"

"Can I think about it?"

"You have to think about it?"

"Well, yeah. There's so much to think about."

I grind on him a little. "Like what?"

"Like a lot of things."

I put his hand on my tittie. "Like what?"

"Like . . . the kids."

I turn over and straddle him, putting my full weight on him. He doesn't even flinch. I never even attempted this position with Jonas. Might have killed him. "I love your children, Dewey. You have to know that by now. I'd raise them as my own." I kiss his narrow nose. "And maybe we might have one of our own. I ain't that old."

"I don't know, Ruth," he says. "Mama—"

"Don't you bring her in this," I interrupt. Shit, boy, you gonna dry up all my juices you keep talking about her. "I ain't marryin' your mama, and you shouldn't let her decide who you can marry."

"Is that what you think happened between me and Tiff?"

"Is it?"

"No." He doesn't say anything for an entire minute; then he sighs. "Do we have to be talkin' 'bout marriage right now?"

I feel his stuff rising, oh, yes, it's rising! "I just want you to know how serious I am about you, and I want you to be serious back."

"I care about you, Ruth, but—"

I put him inside me. My alley has only been vacant for five minutes, but that's five minutes too long. "Go on." I start me a little ride. Lord, this is what sex is supposed to be! "What were you sayin'?"

"Oh, Ruth," he groans.

I scratch his chest and ride him harder. "That's my name, boy, but that ain't what you were about to say. Now finish what you were sayin'."

He tries to sit up, but I keep him flat on the bed, riding him harder than before. "Can I . . . oh shit . . . Can I tell you after this?"

I'm gettin' right close to coming my damn self. "Do you love me at least?"

He starts thrusting up as I plunge down. "Yes. Yes, Ruth."

"So you might marry me?"

He pulls me down to him, and while he chews on my ear and I get happy like a tent meeting revival in the pouring July rain, he whispers, "If I ever marry anyone, Ruth, it will be you."

Thank You, Jesus! I cry all over that man's face after that, kissing away my own tears as he rolls me over and finishes, pumping me, filling me, holding me, loving me.

And when we're through, I get all up in his business. I gave him some; now he got to give me some important information.

"You gonna tell me about you and Tiffany Jones now, Mr. Baxter?"

He goes limp inside me. "Yeah. I guess I should." He rolls to his side of the bed. Where'd my sculpture go? Bring it back! "I had every intention of marrying Tiff. I really did. And I would have except . . . except for the . . . people she hung out with." He closes his eyes. "Those . . . people ruined her."

I almost don't want him to go on, but I have to know. "What people?"

He shakes his head. "Her so-called friends. Tiff was the sweetest girl when I met her. She told me the first time we met that she had just gotten out of jail but that she was changing her life around. And I believed her. She was a wonderful mother to Tee at first. But when her old friends started coming around, the ones she used to run with that got her put in jail, Tiff became someone else. She drank heavily. She got high. She started running the streets again, staying out all night with who knows who. She even . . . She even forgot she was Tee's mama cuz of the . . . cuz of that little glass pipe."

Whoa. Naomi didn't tell me about this side of Tiffany. I'll bet Naomi didn't know. "I get the picture, Dewey. You don't have to tell me any more."

"No, I do, cuz of what it has to do with Mama. You see, Tee been raised almost as much by my mama as by Tiff. I can't tell you how many times Mama went over to Tiff's apartment to find all sorts of insanity goin' on, and there was Tee holdin' an empty bottle wearin' a dirty diaper and howlin' in her crib. If it wasn't for Mama, Tee might have been taken away from Tiff and put in foster care a long time ago."

Which explains more why Tee don't miss her mama as much as Dee . . . and it also explains that Nanna is more protective of her *grandchildren* than her son. She's lookin' out for a good mama for Dewey's kids; she's just thinkin' about *her* babies—like me. We both want the same thing! All I have to do is convince her that we think alike.

"I sent money to them, but I shouldn't have stayed away like I did. I know it was wrong, but I just . . . I didn't want to be caught up in all that. I didn't fit in. I didn't belong. I was afraid of gettin' arrested or even becoming what Tiff became."

"That's no excuse, Dewey. Tee was *your* child. She needed you, not just your money."

He nods. "I know. I know I should have done more, but as it was, I got to see Tee right often anyway, just about every weekend."

This is getting way too complicated now. "Well, if Tiffany was so messed up, why you go back to her?"

Dewey sighs. "I thought she had changed. Her place was clean. She started taking better care of Tee. Mama didn't have to 'baby-sit' nearly as often. She went to church every Sunday. She was holding a job for more than a month. Her friends stopped coming around. Fact is, her friends were either in jail or in worse shape than she was, a few even in detox somewhere."

"Did she ever get any treatment?"

Dewey shakes his head. "Just church once a week."

Even I know that ain't enough for any addiction. Tiffany's attendance at church would have been enough for Naomi, though. What was it Naomi said? That Tiffany had gotten her act together? That Dewey had ruined this girl? Tiffany Jones ruined her damn self six days a week.

"And the day she died, I think Tiff was going across town to . . . to get hooked up again."

Tiffany wasn't coming to see him? What did Dee say? Something about wanting something in the "worstest" way? "Dee said she was coming to see you at work."

He sighs. "She was coming to me for more money. She started doin' that more and more near the end. Said she was gettin' the kids new clothes or shoes, but Mama and I never saw them. Half my paycheck just wasn't enough for her."

The phone rings again, fifteen times before quitting.

"It's probably Mama," he says.

"Thanks for tellin' me all that, Dewey." I kiss his forehead.

"I wish I could stay."

"So do I, but you better be goin'." I sniff the air. "You wanna take a shower first? Your mama gonna know you been doin' this."

He squeezes my ass. "I want her to know."

"Really? She ain't gonna be happy about it."

He smiles and pulls on his underwear. "She'll get over it." He slides into his jeans. "But . . . I won't."

"Neither will I." Shit, my coochie bruised. I pull my covers around me. "You weren't lyin' to me about marrying me, were you?"

He pops his head through his jersey. "No."

"You sure?"

He returns to the bed and holds my face in his hands. "I'm sure. Tonight was . . . magic or something. Kinda like a real live miracle."

Daa-em. I can't speak.

He puts on his boots, tucking the laces inside. "I ain't much of a religious man, Ruth, but . . . You've been a blessing to me and my family. I wanna do right by you."

Oh, yes, Lord! "Then, ask me to marry you."

He stands. "I will. When the time is right."

"And tonight isn't right? You just said it was a miracle."

He reaches out his hand, and I take it, my heart bouncing around in my chest. Is this it? Is this the moment he asks me? He pulls me out of the bed, the covers falling away till I'm naked. He kisses me, hugs me, and looks into my eyes. "I don't have a ring for you yet, right? I can't make it official without a ring, right?"

Oh, yeah. A ring helps. "You'll get me one?"

He compares his pinkie to my ring finger, and they're pretty close in size. "Might."

I swat him on the ass. "You might?"

He kisses my forehead. "If I say I definitely will, it won't be a surprise, will it?"

"I've had enough surprises in my life, Dewey Baxter, believe me. I want something real." I guess that's all I've *ever* really wanted. Something real.

"So do I, Ruth. So do I."

We kiss one long last time, I walk him to the door, kiss him once more, and close the door behind him. The phone rings again, and this time I answer it.

"Hello?"

"Is Dewey there?" Nanna asks.

"No, Mrs. Baxter," I say, and I ain't lyin'. "He just left. How you doin' this evening?"

"Why you ain't been answerin' the phone? I just called a few minutes ago. What if there was some emergency with the children?"

My heart skips a beat. "Are they all right?"

"They're fine, not that you'd care."

"I do care, Mrs. Baxter."

"Uh-huh. Right. Anything you say."

Calm down, Ruth. She's just trying to press some more of your buttons . . . But I can't let this shit go! I got more self-respect than that! I'm gonna give her a dose of her own hatefulness, see how she likes it. "I didn't answer the phone, Mrs. Baxter, because I was busy with your son," I say.

"Busy?"

"Busy. Very busy. You understand what I'm tellin' you?"

Silence on the other end.

"Mrs. Baxter?"

Click.

I think she understands. Oh, yes, my Dewey's gonna walk into that apartment smelling like me, and Nanna gonna know she is messin' with a real woman this time, a sober woman, a woman addicted only to God now. I ain't gonna fade away because she wants me to. I ain't gonna ever lose sight of those children. My friends ain't into none of that shit. No. Nanna is gonna see that we think alike, so much so that whenever she looks at me, she gonna see herself staring back. Whenever she hears me speak, it'll be her own voice comin' at her. I'm in it to win it, and I think that I've already won.

I want to call Tonya and tell her everything, but . . . Tonight was too special for that. I'm just going to treasure all these things in my heart.

And I am gonna sleep directly on the wet spot because I earned it.

PART FOUR

What the Lord Has for Me, It Is for Me

Twenty-One

The phone wakes me at six the next morning. This had better not be Nanna again. "Hello?"

"Good mornin', Ruth," Dewey says. "How you doin'?"

I could get used to his voice every morning, country as it is. "How am I doin'? I am sore." My alley all busted up, and I will be cringing as I style hair today. "Other than that, I'm good. Everything okay there?"

"Yup."

"You ain't sore?"

"Nope."

That ain't fair. He should at least be chafed or something. "Your mama's mad, ain't she?"

"Yup."

"She still there?"

"Yup."

"And she's right there listenin' to this call."

"Yup."

I smile. We're gonna play us a little game. "Dewey Baxter, I love you."

Now's the time to say it, boy. Now's the time to put it in your mama's face. Now's the time to make things perfectly clear to that wench. "Same to you," he says instead.

I roll my eyes. "You were supposed to say it back to me."

"I know."

"Why didn't you?"

"I'd rather show you."

Oh, yes, I would much rather that he showed me—in about a

month. My coochie gonna have to be rehabilitated. Almost feels like I've been through another birth. "When am I gonna see you again?"

"How 'bout tomorrow night? I'm taking the kids out to ride the go-karts."

Joy. Exhaust fumes, video games, and bad pizza. "What about tonight?"

"Thought I'd give you a rest."

That's better. Nanna is probably clutching at her turkey neck right now. "I need it. You wouldn't believe how sore I am."

"I'm sorry."

"Don't be. I'm sore in a very good way."

"Oh."

"When will you pick me up?"

"Probably around six, but it may be a little later."

I'll count on later. "I'll be ready at six."

"Bye, Ruth."

"Bye, Dewey. Thanks for callin'. Have a good day."

With his mama listening in, a man has called me the morning after outstanding sex. He didn't say he loved me out loud, but he certainly made it clear to his mama that I was a force to be reckoned with.

I smell my body and turn up my nose. "And my funk is a force to be reckoned with, too," I say, easing out of bed and going into the bathroom. I check out my neck and see a few love-bites, find a huge love-bite on my left tittie, turn and look at my ass and see another. When did he do that? And *how* did he do that? Oh, yeah. I was just too busy examining his "tusk" to notice.

I take a fairly warm shower, dress in some loose sweats and a turtleneck, and head for Diana's. The pain in my coochie is wonderful! Dewey and I are gonna have to do it often till I'm used to it, and I'm gonna have to keep walkin' and jumpin' rope so I can keep up with him. I'm gonna lose me some weight while I gets me some lovin'. *Lord Jesus, thank You for inventing sex!*

My first client at Diana's is, of all the people on this planet on this particular morning, Junie Pruett. She never comes into Diana's, so she must be here to talk. Kevin plays softer, and Diana stops clipping Mrs. Simpson so loud.

"What you want done, Junie?"

She sits in my chair. "Oh, just comb it out, style it whichever way."

"You sure? I could edge you up, trim a bit."

She smiles. "Uh, no. I'll get all that done the day of the wedding."

Had to remind me, huh? But her bringing up the wedding doesn't bother me that much as it used to. Maybe I'm ready to fully let go. "Who you gettin' to do that for you?"

"Nubian Designs."

Of course. They'll probably color her hair to match her wedding dress. I comb for a bit, Junie saying nothing. We're back on the porch again.

"Um, Ruth, I didn't really come in here to get my hair done," she says. "I came to ask you to play at my wedding next Saturday."

Hmm. This could get pretty tricky. "Jonas said I wasn't playing."

She takes the deepest breath I've ever seen her take. "Well, Jonas is wrong. You are playing at my wedding, and damn it if Jonas can't handle it."

You go, Junie Pruett! "Okay."

"We'll rehearse with the tone-deaf soloist and the mechanical heifer organist he's picked out from Central Baptist, but you and Kevin just show up the day of the wedding and do your thing. Jonas can't say no then because I'll say no to him at the altar if he makes a fuss."

Wouldn't *that* be something! "You sure, Junie?"

She turns to me with a look of determination, her eyes two round pieces of coal. "I'm damn sure, Ruth. Damn sure."

I look at Kevin. "You know 'The Wedding Song' yet?"

"Yes, ma'am."

"Good."

"Um, you won't be listed in the program at all," Junie says, fumbling with her hands. "Hope that's all right."

That solves the two Mrs. Borums problem. "It's fine, Junie. I'm sure everyone there will know who I am."

Junie and I go over the order of the service from the processional to the recessional, she pays me with a crisp fifty (!), and she leaves.

I look at Diana. "None of this leaves this place, hear?" Mrs. Simpson, the silent one, nods. Kevin nods. Diana . . . smiles. "Diana, you can't tell *no one* any of this."

"Why not?"

"Cuz it ain't right."

"Girl, this about the juiciest gossip I've ever heard. There's gonna be a showdown at a wedding. That is some juicy shit, and you want me to keep quiet about it? I have a reputation to preserve. If it gets out that I held this shit back, folks will stop comin' by. This is my establishment, and I own any and all gossip told here. I have a right to tell it all, Ruth."

"Just this once, girl, keep it to yourself. Please. If Jonas finds out, there'll be hell to pay."

"She got that right," Mrs. Simpson says in a deep, gravelly voice.

I blink at Mrs. Simpson. I have never heard her speak before. "And I won't be able to get my revenge," I plead.

"That's right," Mrs. Simpson says with a nod.

"How come you speakin' all of a sudden, Mrs. Simpson?" Diana asks.

"I finally got something to say," Mrs. Simpson says. "I been invited to that wedding, and for once, I'm actually gonna pay attention. Might even sit down front, bring me some popcorn to throw at that preacher." She winks at me. "Kick his ass, Ruth Childress. Kick that two-timin' faggot's ass."

After Mrs. Simpson leaves Diana with a dollar tip (Diana says she's gonna get the dollar framed), Tonya rolls in for a wash and perm. She ain't in here for that either, but I don't mind. I have to tell someone how magical last night was.

"You got some, right?" she asks as I wet her hair in the sink.

"How you know I got some?"

"You wearin' a damn turtleneck, that's why. He tear your shit up or what?"

"I might just be wearin' a turtleneck cuz it's cold as shit outside."

"Right. You got you some."

"Shh," I say. "We on gossip lock-down today."

"Why?"

"Swear you won't tell another living soul first."

"I swear."

"Cross your heart or something." She draws an X on her chest. "I'm playin' at Jonas's wedding."

She blinks. "No shit?"

"No shit." I smile.

"Daa-em. I'm gonna be there."

"Good."

She stares at me for the longest time. "And I know you got you some. You lookin' like you been callin' out Jesus's name all night."

"I did."

"You did?"

"Yesssssss." I massage in some shampoo. "And you can't be tellin' no one that either. Especially Naomi."

"I won't." She giggles. "I'm so happy for you. Was he good?"

I nod. "So good I cried, girl."

"Oh shit. That's good. That's real good." She chews on her bottom lip. "His mama know?"

"Uh-huh, but I got it handled. She ain't gonna be a problem." I hope. I rinse out the shampoo. "Dewey even called me this morning."

"He did?"

"Yep."

She frowns. "No man ever did that for me. Course, I ain't never done that for no man either. He's gettin' serious then, huh?"

"Yep. And we got us a real date tomorrow night."

"Y'all goin' out?"

I squeeze the water out of her hair. "The kids are goin', too. Be kind of like a family outing."

I wrap a towel around her head, and she sits up. "Everything's comin' together, huh?"

"Yep." Should I tell her the next part? I have to. "And . . . I might be gettin' me a ring."

Her eyes become little soup bowls. "A . . . ring?"

"Yep."

She sighs. "Daa-em. Can I be your maid of honor?"

I help her out of the chair and get a little misty. "You're my only choice, Tonya."

She hugs me. "Thank you." She hugs me again a little longer. "Girl, you got you some huggable titties."

"Say what?"

She hugs me *again*. "Wish I had me some of these. They the kind that makes a man wanna come to mama."

I push her away, spin her around, and point at my chair. "Get your little ass in that chair, girl. And don't you say a damn thing about what I told you."

For the rest of the afternoon and all day Friday, Diana's is the quietest hair salon on planet Earth, so quiet that I think some of our customers *must* know something's goin' down. I can see it in their raised eyebrows and darting eyes, hear it in their hurried whispers, feel it in their warm hands as they overtip me. No one talks bad about no one, no one talks about the wedding, no one talks about the miserable rainy weather outside, no one talks about their upcoming plans for Halloween, Thanksgiving, or Christmas, no one even talks about the vote at Antioch on Sunday, something I had almost completely forgotten about. I've just been so busy that I haven't had time to think about it. God has certainly filled my calendar this week. Yet the chairs are full all day Friday. We even get a few new customers, refugees from Nubian Designs, who sit and listen . . . to absolutely nothing since Kevin has a doctor's appointment.

Once we're down to one customer waiting, I leave Diana's at quarter to six to prepare for my date. There's no need to change, and when six o'clock becomes six-thirty, there's no need to hurry. I play with my hair some but decide to let it go its own way. "Lookin' kinda wild," I whisper to the woman in the mirror. "You must have got yourself some."

A little after seven, I hear a tiny little rapping on my door. "Who is it?" I call out.

I hear a giggle.

I get my coat and stand by the door. "Is it the po-lice?"

I hear two giggles.

"Hmm. I know who it is!" I throw open the door and see Tee and Dee, each holding a rose out to me. I squat and look at *four*, not two, beautiful flowers. "Those are beautiful. Are they for me?"

Dee nods and hands me his. Tee doesn't look so sure. She wants a rose from her daddy, too.

I slide my rose into a button hole on my coat. "I only need one, Tee. You can have that one."

She smiles. "Thanks!"

We walk out to the truck where Dewey has the door open for us. I help Tee and Dee get in and kiss Dewey's cheek before I slide in. "Thanks for the rose."

"You're welcome."

We ride out to the county to Race 'n' Play, an indoor go-kart and video palace set up in an old warehouse. As soon as we hit the door and Dewey gets ten dollars' worth of tokens, Tee and Dee disappear, their pants pockets jingling. Dewey orders a pizza and drinks, we find an empty table between Ski-Bol and some basketball-shooting game, and we sit.

And say absolutely nothing.

And it doesn't bother me one bit. We watch Tee and Dee flitting from game to game and smile a lot. Two nights ago we made love, and today we're shy. Damn, we're cute. When the pizza arrives, Tee and Dee materialize, devour several slices, and vanish again.

This place is *real* cheap daycare.

"Gonna ride the go-karts with us, Ruth?"

I had tried years ago on an outing for the youth group at Antioch when Race 'n' Play had first opened, but I couldn't squeeze into the go-kart. "Maybe."

"Maybe? They're a blast! Dee can't stop talkin' 'bout how you and him are gonna whip our tails."

"I've never driven a go-kart."

He leans closer. "It's the same as drivin' a car."

"Never driven one of those either."

He sits back. "You're kiddin'."

"No." Neither Mama nor Grandma owned a car, and I've never had enough money for one myself.

"Never?"

I shake my head. "You gonna have to teach me."

"I'll take you out for a lesson at the farm tomorrow."

I lick my lower lip like Tonya does. "What kind of lesson, Mr. Baxter?"

He turns red. "A drivin' lesson."

"Ooh, I like it when you talk dirty."

He laughs. "A *drivin'* lesson. In the truck."

"Ooh, boy, you makin' me hot," I whisper. "We gonna do it in the front seat or on the bed? Cuz if it's on the bed, you gotta bring me a blanket."

"I'll . . . make sure you have a blanket."

Whew, it's gettin' hot up in here!

Dee returns with a pout, bouncing his little chest off Dewey's knee. "I need more money, Daddy," he says, and he shows Dewey his empty pockets for proof.

"Why don't we ride the go-karts now?" Dewey asks.

"Yeah!"

"Go find your sister and meet us at the track," Dewey says. Dee runs off as Dewey stands. "You goin'?"

"I guess." I groan and stand. "I ain't promisin' nothin', now. You got insurance on Dee?"

"Yes." We walk toward the track. "And you can't get hurt. They're built so they don't tip over."

Like me.

Tee and Dee join us in line, Dewey pays the man ten dollars, and after squeezing into the go-kart, I am holding on to the wheel of a vehicle for the first time in my life, Dee strapped in beside me, my knees squashed up to my titties.

"Go real fast, Penny!" Dee shouts.

"I'll try," I say. *Lord, keep us alive, please. I don't know what I'm doin'.*

I can't see the pedals at my feet, but I figure them out soon enough. The right one shoots us forward with a snap, the left one stops us with a slide. Steering the go-kart is kinda tough, but I manage to get us in line behind Dewey and Tee.

"We gonna stomp y'all!" Tee yells.

"No you ain't!" Dee yells back.

A light at the start line changes from red to orange to green, and we're off. Sort of. I get confused and hit the brake instead of the accelerator, and the go-kart behind us bounces into the back of our go-kart. I press the right pedal, and in no time, we're roaring down the track . . . straight into a bunch of rubber tires.

"You forgot to turn, Penny!" Dee yells between giggles.

"Oops."

One of the attendants comes over and pulls the front end of the go-kart free. "Start your turn 'bout halfway down the straightaway."

"Okay."

When we finally get rolling again, we are way behind Dewey and Tee, and after a few shaky laps, I'm gettin' the hang of this thing. Driving ain't as hard as I thought it would be, and I even drive one-handed for a spell, the smoky air blowing through my hair. Dee keeps whipping his head from one side to the other looking for his daddy, but I know we'll never catch him. "They're gonna win!"

"Only this time," I yell in his ear. "Once I get more practice, we're gonna smoke 'em."

"I wanted to win *this* time!"

After twenty laps or so, the go-karts stop by themselves. I get out and unbuckle Dee, who runs to catch up with Dewey and Tee. Little boy's mad at his Penny. I'll have to teach him about losing the right way. I have a degree in that.

Tee and Dee play Ski-Bol for the rest of the evening till Dewey's wallet is empty. They take their tickets to this little booth and get cheap little toys, but they hold those toys like they're the best presents they ever got. Dee picks out a detective's kit complete with magnifying glass and badge, while Tee gets a bunch of rubber critters all designed to scare the bejeezus out of someone.

She will not be allowed to take these critters to school.

Instead of taking me home, we ride to Dewey's apartment where we sit on the couch in front of that little TV and watch some silly cop show till both children are purring away, Dee fast asleep and clutching my neck, Tee snoring and laid out on Dewey's lap. Dewey nods toward the bunk bed, and we carry them across the room, tucking them in for the night.

Then we go back to the couch . . . and *don't* watch the eleven o' clock news or *The Tonight Show* or even some old reruns of *M*A*S*H* because we are far too busy swapping hands and squeezing flesh.

"How you sleep on this?" I ask between deep soul kisses.

"Badly," he whispers. "I've missed you for the last two days."

"I've missed you, too."

We're halfway into a wonderfully wicked position when I look over and see both children sitting up in bed. I pick Dewey's head off my chest and turn his head toward the bed.

"Go to sleep, y'all," he says.

Tee slumps back to her mattress, but Dee turns on his side and wraps his covers over his head, his little forehead and eyes visible.

"Dee, go to sleep," Dewey says.

"He's just curious," I whisper. "And I really should go." I can't be doin' this with the children watching anyway. "When y'all comin' to get me?"

Dewey pulls my sweater down and sits up. "A little before sunrise."

"Dag," I say, "that's only in a few hours."

"Yup."

I snuggle up next to him. "Maybe I should just stay, huh?"

"Yeah."

"But no grindin'," I whisper. "I don't want to put that child back into therapy."

"Neither do I."

For the rest of the night, Dewey holds me, snoring softly in my ear, while Dee and I make faces at each other.

Twenty-Two

The next morning, Dewey rushes us out the door, the kids still asleep, me still dreaming about elephants. No breakfast, no brushing teeth, no washing faces, just let's get on out the door. "What is the rush, Dewey?" I ask.

"We gotta get there before Mama leaves."

"Where she goin' on a Saturday morning?"

"The farmer's market at Pine."

"Oh." Where else do farmers go? "Well, at least let the kids brush their teeth or something."

"No time."

Tee and Dee wake only briefly out in the cold but fall back to their purring as Dewey races away from Vine Street to some country road I have never been on before. "This will take us most of the way there. Might want to put on your seat belt cuz it's a real curvy road."

He isn't kidding about that, and I'm glad I haven't eaten. Country roads are about as straight as a snake, with sudden hills and hairpin turns thrown in. We are definitely not in the city anymore. Forests, fields, and dirt fly past us in the mist. We've only been traveling for twenty minutes or so when he slows to a crawl and takes this muddy gravel road through what looks like an apple orchard guarded by gray board fences.

"Are we there yet?" I ask.

"Yup," Dewey says, shifting into four-wheel drive. "This here's our truck farm."

"Your what?"

"Mama runs a truck farm."

"What does that mean?"

"Means we grow strawberries, raspberries, blackberries if we have a wet spring. You saw the apple orchard. We even got a hive for honey, and we sell it all up in Pine on Saturday mornings at the farmer's market."

"You do all that and only sell it one day a week?"

"Yup."

That don't sound right. "Y'all make any money?"

"Enough. Land and house are paid for, the truck, too. Taxes are pretty low, and Mama don't need much else."

We bump over some ruts, and Tee and Dee wake up. "Y'all ought to pave this road."

"It ain't a road, Ruth. It's our driveway."

Daa-em. A driveway as long as Vine Street? "Then, y'all ought to pave your driveway."

Dewey stops the truck in front of what looks like an old railroad tie, and a farmhouse with a wide rocking-chair porch breaks through the fog in front of us. It has a single front door, two wide windows on either side, and real shutters that close up on all the windows. It looks like a Vine Street four-square, only it's plainer with fewer windows on the second story and a tin and tar-paper roof instead of shingles.

"This is where you grew up?"

"Yup."

Dag, Dewey must have been lonely.

Tee and Dee crawl over me and disappear into the fog to our left. "Where are they goin'?"

"To see Myron."

"Who?"

"Myron, Mama's pet pig. Wanna meet him? He's practically tame, knows his name and everything."

How nice. "I'm stayin' away from pork, thanks, and I don't want no pig near me that knows his own name." He might get sweet on me or something. I get out and stretch my back. Dewey's gotta get us a real bed, like a king size. Two big people should never sleep spooning on a love seat sleeper sofa. Surprised I didn't fall off. Least he doesn't snore. "Where's your mama?"

"Probably loadin' up her truck over at the barn." He takes my hand. "Come on."

We walk for about fifty yards on a narrow muddy path, huge pine trees shooting up around us, until a faded red barn appears out of the mist. I see Nanna's old dented truck jutting out, its short bed loaded with boxes, Nanna tying down a blue tarp over the bed.

"Mornin', Mama," Dewey calls out.

Nanna takes a short look at us and continues tying. Bet you never expected to see me here, Nanna. I look down at my hand and still see Dewey's hand in mine. And I bet you never expected to see your son holding my hand.

"You need any help today, Mama? Truck looks pretty full. Gonna be a clear day once this fog lifts, probably have a nice turnout."

"I don't need no help," Nanna says. "Been doin' it for forty years. What I need help today for?"

Dewey squeezes my hand. "What?" I whisper.

"Why don't you help her?"

Say what? "She said she don't need any." And I don't want to. I aim to climb me a tree today.

"Ain't polite to whisper," Nanna says. She ties down the last corner. "See y'all at lunchtime."

Dewey looks hard at me, nodding his head toward the truck. Oh. I get it. We rushed here so I could rush off to make nice with Nanna. Like that's gonna work. I walk over to her anyway. "Mrs. Baxter, I'd like to go with you."

"You would?"

"Yes."

"What for?"

To get to know you, to let you get to know your future daughter-in-law, to get you to be less hateful to me. "To help."

"Don't need it and don't want it."

"Then . . . Let me tag along. I won't get in the way."

Nanna shoots a look past me to Dewey, then attempts to stare a hole in my head. "You can't make me like you," she whispers.

"It ain't polite to whisper, and I ain't tryin' to get you to like me."

"Bullshit."

"Really. I'm just tryin' to get you to *respect* me."

Nanna chews on her cheek, and her staring eyes wander to my feet. "It ain't gonna be no fun."

Don't I know it. "I got nothin' better to do."

"Hmm." She nods her head. "Get in. Let's get there so we can get back."

I wave at Dewey, he winks, and I get into the truck. *Lord, I don't know where all this is leadin', but I am in Your hands. Help this woman warm up to me, and keep my tongue as quiet as this ride's probably gonna be.*

We bump and lurch out to the road, go up the road a piece, crawl over some train tracks, creep up a long hill, and take a right onto a cart-path driveway. Ain't no one in the country got a paved driveway? My back is killing me!

"Gotta pick up somethin'," Nanna says as we bottom out here and there till we're stopped in front of a one-story wooden shack, smoke billowing out of a stone chimney. I help Nanna collect several large boxes containing Mason jars full of preserves, jams, and jellies from some stone steps, load them carefully into the bed of the truck, and we're off again. I don't ask no questions because it seems to be part of her routine.

Out the cart path, back on the road, up the rest of that long hill— and I see Pine Lake shimmering in the distance. As close as Calhoun is to Pine Lake, I have never been there, and it's breathtaking. You emerge through a cloud of fog at the top of the hill, and there's a sparkling lake way down below you. Almost makes me feel weight- less. Almost. "Lord, that's pretty," I say.

"You wouldn't say that if that was once your farm," Nanna says.

Damn it, why can't I keep my mouth shut? Yes, Nanna is speaking to me, but it sounds like she wants to argue. Do I want to argue back? Hmm. I'll ask questions instead. "It hasn't always been there?"

"Nope. About sixty years ago, the government bought up and flooded the land to make that lake."

"Looks like it belongs there."

Nanna scowls. "Good land gone so rich folks would have some- place to play, make noise, and throw shit in the water. Not every farmer sold out, though. Old Bill Winters stayed on his land up till the last second, and ain't no one ever seen him since."

"No shit?"

"No shit. Hear tell that folks out fishing can see lights moving up under the water. That's just old Bill tendin' to his cows."

There's a ghost in Pine Lake?

She cackles a bit. "And the fishermen have been catching rooster weathervanes and tractor tires for years."

"What?"

"That's right. Got at least four towns up under that lake with roads and stop signs and everything."

I am never swimming in Pine Lake.

We ride down the center of the town of Pine on Pine Street (what else?) till we get to the farmer's market. It's already crowded with pickup trucks, and folks mill around thirty or forty stalls. Nanna parks behind an empty stall, and after she lays out an old quilt on a long folding table, we unload the truck. We set out bags and baskets of green and red apples and Teddy-bear-shaped containers of honey on the quilt, but the boxes we collected from that shack go under the table.

"Why we don't put them up top?" I ask.

"Shh," Nanna says.

Shh, yourself! Apples and honey. That's it? I look at the other stalls and see price lists, free samples signs, bushel baskets of corn, pumpkins, squash, jams, jellies—and we got apples and honey, no lists, no signs, no variety. We ain't gonna sell shit.

Nanna pulls a stool out of the truck and sits at one end of the table. "Don't have a stool for you cuz I didn't expect any company."

"That's okay. I'm used to being on my feet."

She stares at me. "You weren't on your feet the other night."

I blush a little. "No, ma'am, but neither was your son."

She nods. "Why I'm mad at the both of you."

I smile. "But mainly at me, right?"

"No. It's about even. Far as I can tell, you don't have a mind, and that boy's done lost his."

Ouch. "Least we're compatible," I say, and I look away.

I hear her cackle. "You two, compatible? Hmm. Gonna have to think a spell on that one. You get tired of standin', you can sit in the truck."

Which I may end up doing. Ain't nothin' happenin' at Nanna's stall. She ain't talkin', and neither am I. A few customers come by, browsing, fingering the apples, holding the honey up to the light. A wrinkled prune of a woman wearing a shawl holds up an apple and asks Nanna, "These fresh?"

Nanna nods.

"Can I have a sample?"

"No," Nanna says. Wrinkled Prune Woman sets the apple down and continues on.

Nothing more happens for the next *two hours.* And Nanna's been doin' this for forty years? She don't know shit about sellin' stuff. Dag, we should be puttin' out these preserves. I walked around and looked at what other folks had to sell, and none of their preserves looked half as good.

Around ten, swarms of white women stream in wearing clothing too fashionable for a farmer's market, gold bracelets dangling from thin wrists, expensive long coats probably bought in New York. They browse the stalls, chat with whoever latches on to them, gossip in clumps, squeeze and smell everything their hands touch, and munch on samples—but not at Nanna's stall, and Nanna ain't doing a damn thing about it.

"Maybe if you gave out free samples," I suggest, but Nanna only shakes her head.

"I know what I'm doin', Ruth," she says.

"Sorry."

Half an hour later, Nanna's eyes brighten as a huge white woman, who has to be six feet tall and six feet wide, moves down the center of the market. She carries a handbag, if you can call it that, the size of a potato sack. Yep, it's a burlap bag. Heads turn, bodies scatter, and the hum of conversation stops. Lord, that woman is twins who didn't separate at birth. She gotta weigh at least four hundred, maybe five hundred pounds. Dag, if I stood next to her, I'd look like one of them anorexic models in the magazines.

"Who is she?" I ask instead of what I really want to ask: "Who are *they?*"

"That's Sue," Nanna says. "Sue is a dear old friend of mine."

Sue stops in front of Nanna's stall, sweat streaming down her face, her odor strong, her breath coming in huge heaves. "Meg," she says. Nanna is Meg, short for Megan? That's such a . . . nice name for a witch. Bet she got called "Nutmeg" as a child.

"Sue," Meg says. I'll never think of her as Nanna again. "What you need?"

"Four."

"Strawb or rasp?"

Sue leans a flabby hand on the table, and I catch a strong whiff of . . . a fireplace? Geez, I hope it ain't her flesh sizzlin'. "Two of each."

Meg pulls four Mason jars out of a box and slams them on the table. "Two of each."

Sue hands Meg a one-dollar bill and drops the jars into her burlap sack. "See you soon," she says, and she moves away, her surplus flesh rippling through the rippling crowd.

"See you," Meg says, folding the dollar and slipping it into her shirt pocket.

One dollar for four jars of preserves? A *quarter* a pop? What, Meg feels sorry for super-heifer Sue? What the *hell* is going on?

"Get ready, Miss Penny," Meg says out of the corner of her mouth.

"For what?"

"Money."

I look up and see a swarm of folks heading toward our stall, hands jammed into purses and handbags, some with five- and ten-dollar bills waving in the air in front of them. In seconds, I am handing jar after jar of jelly, jam, and preserves at *five* bucks a pop to some of the greediest, grabbiest white women I have ever seen. It's like I'm at one of those early-morning sales after Thanksgiving with all the snatching and grabbing going on. In less than twenty minutes of furious selling, every jar is gone. The apples disappear as well, and after the crowd fades away, we're down to one little Teddy bear of honey.

"That was amazing!" I say, fanning the money in my hand.

"We did okay," Meg says, and she begins tossing the empty boxes and bags into the truck.

"Okay? Girl, you made at least five hundred dollars in less than half an hour!"

"About average," Meg says. "Didn't sell it all, though."

I dig in my pocket for some money and only come up with a crumpled dollar bill. "I'm a little short."

Meg shrugs and takes my dollar. "It's enough. Come on. Let's get back."

The truck seems faster on the ride out of Pine, and once again, Meg turns off the long hill onto that cart path, stopping at that little shack. "Only be a sec," she says. I watch her go to the door and knock.

Super-heifer Sue opens the door.

Holy shit! Meg just pulled herself a little flim-flam! That scheming, wicked . . . *smart* old lady!

Meg splits the roll of money with Sue and gets the four jars Sue "bought" in the process. When Meg gets back in the truck, I can't contain myself. "You gonna explain what just happened?"

"You're pretty smart. You explain it to me."

"The preserves are obviously Sue's."

"Yup."

"Sue, um, has trouble getting out and about because of her, um—"

"Sue is fat," Meg snaps. "Been fat all her life, gonna die fat."

But Sue is in a whole new category of fat. Sue is super-size fat. She could have a country named after her, and I bet she'll have to be buried in *two* plots. "You picked up her preserves and jams and held them back because you knew they'd sell like hotcakes."

"Yup. Best stuff on earth."

"But . . . In order to sell your apples and honey, you needed a stampede. You had to get folks to think that if the preserves are good, the apples must be good, too."

"That's how it works."

"So Sue shows up, which is rare or somethin'."

"She don't get out much. Maybe once a month."

I didn't see a truck at Sue's shack, so that means Sue walked all that way? Dag, girl probably lost fifty pounds! That *was* her flesh I smelled burning! But if she walked there, how'd she get back so quick? "How did Sue get to the market?"

Meg smiles. "Horse."

"A horse?" As in just *one?*

"Big one. Clydesdale."

Whoa! That poor horse! But I can't even imagine Sue being able to get up on a horse without help. She must have to step off the roof onto the horse . . . but how does she get up to her roof? I don't pry any further into that. "And when folks see Sue, they know she came for a real good reason because she's so, um—"

"Fat."

I just cannot say that word. "And then Sue buys her own preserves."

"Which I get as payment at the end of the day for my trouble."

It's a perfect setup. "And the rush begins."

"Yup."

"And no one's figured it out yet?"

"Nope. Rich city folks are stupid, comin' way out here to get shit they could get at the farmer's market in Calhoun."

I am not offended because I ain't rich. "I figured it out."

"Cuz I let you in on it, and cuz you got some redneck in you."

"I do not!"

"You had my Dewey, didn't you?"

Oh, yeah. I had me a big ol' redneck inside of me. Is this Meg being nice to me? "Well, it's all pretty slick, Meg."

Meg shrugs. "It's a livin'."

"You don't mind if I call you Meg, do you?"

"Not at all. What you want me to call you?"

Your daughter? "Ruth, I guess."

We ride by the farmhouse where I don't see Dewey or the children, and Meg parks the truck in the barn. I open my door, but Meg touches my arm. "We should talk, Ruth."

I close the door. This moment, in an ancient pickup in an antique barn with a wrinkled woman who I still cannot figure out—this one conversation could be the most important in my life.

"I was . . . a little harsh to you the other day," Meg says.

"And today."

"Yup. Today, too. Sorry about that. I always been protective of Dewey, and not just cuz he's my only child. He's been my only family since Mitchell passed goin' on twelve years ago. Mitchell was my husband."

"I'm so sorry for your loss," I say, and for once, I really, truly mean it.

"Thank you. He was quite a man." She smiles. "And Dewey is just like him, just like him."

"Mr. Baxter was a big man, too?"

Meg shakes her head vigorously. "Nope. Mitchell was my size. Don't know how we made Dewey so big; I mean, when Dewey was born, he barely weighed six pounds. Squirted on out of me before I even knew he was out. He was so scrawny for most of his life till he hit twelve, thirteen . . . and then he ate us out of house and home and barn and field. We had to milk the cow two, three times a day to keep up with that boy."

"Y'all have a cow?"

"Not anymore. Sold her ages ago cuz I couldn't keep up with her no more. Nothin' worse than an unmilked cow's moaning, let me tell you."

Oh, how I know the feeling.

"You know I been testin' you, right?"

I nod. "I had a feeling."

"Tested Tiffany Jones, too, and for the most part, that child passed with flying colors. She shot the shit back at me faster than I could shovel it at her most times. The girl had a very quick tongue. Cussed more than she should have, but I respect that. You're pretty good at it, too."

"Thank you."

"Not as good as me, now, but you do all right."

"You'll just have to teach me."

She nods. "You're never too old to learn, right?"

"Right." I take a deep breath and sigh. "So you didn't really hate Tiffany, did you?"

She sighs. "No. I liked Tiffany."

"You called her a whore."

"She weren't no whore. She was good company, had the prettiest smile, was almost as good a cook as me. Almost, I said. She was kind of like the daughter I never had." She sighs. "But when that crack got a hold of her and she started forgettin' she was Tee's mama . . . I couldn't stand by and watch. Had to do something about it. Broke my heart, it did."

"Dewey said Tee has spent a lot of time with you."

She nods. "Yup. And that's probably why Tiffany started hating me. She'd go on one of her sprees, I'd collect Tee . . . and a few days later, Tiffany would be on the phone hollerin', 'Where my baby at, bitch?' I can't tell you how many times I asked that child to get help, but she didn't think she had a problem. 'I can handle my own damn business,' she would say. If only I had dragged her butt someplace, she might still be alive today."

"You can't blame yourself for what she did to herself, Meg. God helps those who help themselves, right?"

"He's supposed to. But Tiffany didn't want nobody's help." She rolls her eyes. "And I didn't think I needed nobody's help either till you started comin' around. One day I'm Nanna, and the next day you turn me into just another old woman. You replaced me in the space of a few days. I wasn't prepared for that."

"I don't want to replace you, Meg."

She smiled. "It's what you're supposed to do, Ruth. You're supposed to take my place. You're supposed to steal my boy and my grandchildren away from me."

What do you say to that? I keep quiet.

"Dewey seems happy enough, and the kids like you." She sighs. "Bet they even love you. Not as much as they love me, now."

"No, ma'am."

"And you is one *persistent* somethin'." She pats my hand. "I like that in a person, too."

"Thank you."

"You know my Dewey's intentions?"

"I think he's planning on asking me to marry him."

She chews on her cheeks again. Guess it's how she keeps from saying the wrong thing. Maybe I ought to try it.

"About time that boy settled down." She looks at me, and a tiny smile breaks through the crease in her lips. "And he ain't chosen too awful badly this time."

I roll my neck a little. "What you mean 'too awful badly'?"

Meg laughs. "Girl, you the ex-wife of a preacher who is still crazy enough to keep his name and play the organ at his church. You have to be touched in the head."

"I ain't crazy."

She winks. "Sure you are. You're about as crazy as me. I like crazy in a person. Keeps life lively."

"Thank you." I'm starting to mist up. She calls me "crazy," and I get emotional? Maybe I *am* crazy. I have to look away.

"You know how to flat-foot?"

River dance? "No." Though my feet are flat.

"I'll teach you. Nothin' to it. Just got to keep up with the music. How are you with canning?"

I smile. "I know a thing or two about Mason jars."

"Just a thing or two? You got a lot to learn about Mason jars, then." She opens her door. "Let's go eat us some lunch."

I get out and block the path. "Thank you, Meg."

"You ain't gonna hug on me, are you?"

"I'd like to."

"You don't have to."

I step closer. "I want to." Cuz you need it, Meg.

She rolls her eyes. "Y'all is some huggin' people." She frowns. "Well, get it over with. Dewey and the kids are probably hungry."

I pull Meg to me and squeeze gently, kissing her softly on the cheek. "Thank you."

She looks away. "For what?"

"For giving me a chance."

She turns and stares at me. "That ain't what you're thanking me for."

"No, really, I am."

"No you ain't. You thankin' me for not breakin' when you just tried to squeeze the life outta me."

"I didn't hug you too hard."

"Yeah, you did. I'm an old woman. Save your hugs for Dewey and my babies, okay?"

I smile. "Okay."

We eat the best peanut butter and jelly sandwiches I have ever eaten at a huge oak table in Meg's kitchen. I even eat two: one thick with strawberry jam, the other oozing with raspberry jam. Tee and Dee suck down their milk and inhale two sandwiches each before zipping off.

"I thought farm life was supposed to be slower," I say.

"It is," Meg says. "It's just a little more of an intense slow than the city."

Dewey smiles. "How was Pine, Mama?"

"Sold out," she says.

"Good. How's Sue doin'?"

"Fine, fine." Meg removes our plates. "Y'all want to make yourselves useful, you can walk the fence."

Dewey groans. "Today?"

"Ain't gettin' fixed on its own," Meg says. " 'Sides, y'all look like you could use some exercise."

"A walk sounds fine to me," I say.

"It ain't much of a walk," Dewey says.

He ain't wrong about that. Walking the fence involves loading up the truck with fence posts, planks, and nails, and driving around the fence line to repair every dangling board, every leaning post, every missing section. And even though I'm wearing heavy leather gloves, I still get blisters from pounding so many nails.

"When's this damn fence end?" I ask.

"It doesn't," Dewey says, positioning another piece of board and hammering it into a post. "Guess everything went okay at the market with Mama, huh?"

"Went much better than I expected."

"Good." He massages my shoulders, and I nearly pass out. "You know that you're the first girl I've ever had out to the farm?"

"First girl? You are massaging a woman, and if you stop, I will hammer a nail into your head."

"Why don't we, um, get more comfortable?"

"For what?"

He kisses my neck. "I brought the blanket."

Hot damn! But I am still sore from the other night. "Maybe later. Let's finish this up. I promised Dee I'd let him teach me to climb a tree."

"Nobody around for miles," he whispers.

"Dewey, please. There's still all that wood in the back of the truck. I ain't gettin' any splinters that I can't explain to your mama." Like in my ass. How you tell a doctor about that?

He puts his nose in my ear. "I'll put the blanket on the ground, then."

I turn to him. "You want me now, here, and on the ground?"

He nods. "I do."

"This a country thing, Dewey? I ain't never done it outside. We city folk prefer beds." Although the thought of going buck wild in the wild excites me, it also scares the shit out of me. "What if someone should come by?" Like, when we're coming? Or worse, what if some bull-cow should come sniffing by looking for love in all the wrong places?

"That's the risk we'll just have to take."

I blink at Dewey. "You that hard up, boy?"

He puts my hand on his stuff. Oh, my! "And gettin' harder."

I'm gettin' right moist myself. "But I'm all sweaty, Dewey." And you is a *stank,* stank man. "Why can't you put a leash on that thing till we get home?"

He shakes his head. "I want you now, Ruth. I want you here, and I want you now."

Daa-em. No man ever wanted me this badly. Then again, no man ever truly wanted me period. "Get the damn blanket."

For the next half hour, I look out for cows and watch clouds drift by while Dewey makes love to me. The wind chills my coochie juices something awful, the ground smells all musty, I get grass all up in my hair, he stinks, I stink, we stink . . . And it's the *best* lovin' I've ever had. We're two people alone in a world of sky and earth and sun and clouds lying on a quilt a hundred years old in a field of brown grass. It ain't quite Eden, but it is paradise enough for me.

"Get that ring yet?" I ask as we ride back to the farmhouse. Just bein' persistent, right?

"Maybe."

"Now, what kind of an answer is that? Either you got the ring or you don't got the ring."

He raises his eyebrows. "Or I've bought it and I'm having it sized, and it ain't back at the jeweler's yet."

Oh, yeah. Wait. He's already picked it out? Without me there to make sure he picked out the right ring? What was he thinkin'? "You bought it already?"

"Maybe."

"What? Either you bought it—"

"I'm paying on it, Ruth," he interrupts.

I blink. "You got my ring on layaway?"

"Somethin' like that."

My ring is on layaway. That ain't romantic. "You better not be payin' a dollar a week on it, boy."

"I ain't payin' a dollar a week, Ruth."

"Good."

"Fifty cents is all I can afford right now."

"What!"

He stops in front of that smelly railroad tie. "I'm kiddin', Ruth."

"You *better* be."

"Geez, why can't you just let it be a surprise?"

"I want a sure thing is why. I don't like surprises, Dewey. In fact, I have never liked surprises. I've had too many surprises in my life, and most of them were bad."

He takes my hand. "You love me?"

"Yes."

"Doesn't that surprise you?"

I stop and think. He got me. I never even looked twice at a white man before Dewey. No reason really. I just thought that if black men weren't interested in me, white men wouldn't be interested in me either. "Yeah. I never thought I'd love a funky-smellin', rusty-truck-drivin' country boy who'd have the nerve to put *my* ring on layaway." He laughs. "Go on and laugh. See if *you* get a ring anytime soon."

"You buy it yet?" he asks.

Shit. Ain't no room on any of my credit cards, and rent comin' due. "Maybe," I say with attitude, "and don't you be askin' me any questions about it or it won't be a surprise."

"Okay."

I squeeze his hand. "You really went and picked it out?"

"Yes."

"That mean you love me?"

"Yup," he says. He kisses my cheek. "That means I love you, Ruth."

I feel so light! I throw open my door. "I got to go find me a tree to climb," I say as I get out.

"Huh?"

"It's a city thing," I say. Have some sex, listen to a man say he loves you, climb a tree. "Which tree does Dee usually climb?"

"Don't you want to have your first driving lesson?"

"I already did, boy. In fact, I've already had two, and we weren't in the truck either time."

He blushes. "Yeah."

He takes my hand and leads me through a maze of trees to *the* tree, a massive oak that has to be close to a hundred feet high with branches reaching fifty feet out in all directions. A steep hill rises behind it and shades the tree. I see Dee already way up in the tree, Tee about halfway up.

"You let them climb up there without you bein' around?"

"Yup," Dewey says. "They been climbin' since they could walk." We move toward the lowest branch. "Need a lift?"

"You already given me a lift, boy," I say. "I gotta do this all by myself."

He steps back. "If you fall, I'll catch you."

I kiss his chin. "You already did."

I stand in front of the branch which is about as round as I used to be, the bark dark and hard as an old scab. I try to lock my arms around it, but the branch is too fat. I look back at Dewey, who has settled himself against the trunk. "Gonna have to jump for it, I guess," I say. "And don't you laugh at me if I miss."

"You won't miss, Ruth."

I look up at the branch again and see Tee and Dee peering down at me like two little squirrels. "I'm comin', I'm comin'."

"Be careful, Penny," Dee says.

Be careful. Spent my whole life bein' careful, and it didn't get me anywhere. Bein' careful got me a triflin' husband. Bein' careful got me fat. Bein' careful left me lonely.

I fall a little short on my first jump, my hands sliding off the branch. I examine the scrapes but don't see any cuts. There's got to be a trick to this.

"You're just warmin' up, huh, Penny?" Tee asks.

"Right. Just warmin' up."

I take a few steps back and run at the branch, jumping and latching on. I work my elbows up to the top and pull myself onto the branch while Dee and Tee cheer. I feel like an opossum, my arms and legs hooked around the branch.

"You gonna stand up?" Dee asks.

One embarrassing moment at a time. "Soon as I catch my breath, Dee," I say. I look down at the top of Dewey's head. "You need another haircut, boy."

He doesn't answer.

"Dewey?"

I see little shoes dancing on the branch in front of me. "Daddy's asleep," Dee says.

Yep, Dewey's chin is bouncing off his chest. Bet he didn't even see my leap. I give him some, and he's worn out. Come to think of it, so am I. "What do I do next, Mr. Dee?"

"Stand up," he says.

Stand up. That's all. Just unhook my legs and arms and stand. I just have to let go of this branch to get vertical, gotta let go to get up. *Lord, You never stop teaching us, do You?* "Stand back, Mr. Dee." The dancing shoes disappear. I hunch myself up to my knees, my hands never letting go of the branch. Now I'm a cat posing in a tree. Where's my fireman to save me? Oh, he's sound asleep below me cuz I gave him some. I crawl on the branch a few feet until I'm looking at the trunk. I walk my hands from the branch to the trunk, kick out one foot, then the other . . . and I'm standing on a branch in a tree six feet off the ground for the first time in my life.

"You did it!" Dee says from somewhere above me.

"Yep." I sure did. With the Lord's help. *Lord God, You have some strong hands.* The view isn't that much different, but I hug the tree any-way.

"What you doin'?" Tee asks.

"Thanking the tree," I say.

"You think it would break or somethin'?"

I smile at her. A few months ago, it might have. But now, with my man below me and my children—*my children!*—above me, ain't nothin' gonna let me down again. No matter what happens at Antioch tomorrow, I'm still gonna live my life six feet off the ground. The air's a little thinner, the wind stronger, but it certainly ain't ordinary. I ain't never gonna be plain Ruth again.

"You goin' any higher?" Dee asks.

I smile at him. "This is high enough for now."

Because this is exactly where I want to be.

Twenty-Three

The next morning I walk Tee and Dee to Antioch with Dewey promising to be there in time for the morning worship service. As sleepy as he looks, I doubt I'll see him.

"Please come," I say. "This is a big day for me."

"I'll try," he says with a yawn.

"Be there."

Mrs. Robertson's Sunday school lesson, the parable of the lost talents, hits home with me. A man gives some money (the talents) to some folks. One invests it and makes money while another hides it and eventually loses it all. "You can't be hiding your talent under a bushel," Mrs. Robertson tells them. "You have to let it shine, let it shine, let it shine."

The children make a list of all the things they're good at, and Tee says that she's good at talking. "Lots of folks talk for a living," Mrs. Robertson says. "You could be a teacher or a lawyer or even the president." So glad she didn't say preacher.

"I could be the president?" Tee asks.

"Sure. God gives us talents so we can be anything we want to be."

Dee tells everyone that he's good at climbing trees "and figuring out stuff." Mrs. Robertson tells him he could be a famous mountain climber or a great scientist one day. Then she turns to me. "So, Miss Penny, what are you good at?"

"I'm good at playing the organ."

"Too loud," a little boy says.

"I'll play softer today."

But when I get to my bench, Tee and Dee on either side of me, I don't feel like playing anything soft. You don't play soft music on a battlefield, right? I start off with a soulful version of "Onward Christian Soldiers" and blend it into "The Battle Hymn of the Republic" till the whole congregation is marching and singing "Glory, glory hallelujah!" by the time Jonas enters and kneels in front of his pew. He glares up at me, then pinches his bony fingers on the space between his eyebrows and bows his head. Folks in the sanctuary probably think he's prayin' hard. He ain't. It means he's got a headache. Good. My "cannons" have upset the general's mind.

I have set the tone for this service.

After that, I wait for the vote. It doesn't happen after the opening song, after the announcements, after the prayer, after the testifying, after two choir numbers, or after the reading from the Bible. And when it doesn't happen before, during, or immediately after the sermon, I think it ain't gonna happen at all. They couldn't have forgotten, but maybe Jonas and the board have decided that it would be more trouble than it's worth—which it is. Maybe they've come to their senses.

Jonas pronounces the benediction, folks start to get up, and then Jonas taps the microphone. My stomach leaps into my throat, then settles back down. They haven't forgotten. Here we go.

"At this time, I have been led of the Lord to hold an important members-only business meeting," Jonas says with a smirk my way. "If you are a nonmember, please leave the sanctuary as quickly and quietly as possible. I'd like the board to join me in the front."

Not too many people leave, and I gather Tee and Dee to me. They may not be members of the church, but they are members of my family. I look to the back of the church and see Dewey—*thank You, Lord!*— wearing that same awful suit but looking like an angel, sitting in the last pew. When did he sneak in? An usher approaches him, and Dewey stands. They're kicking him out! Don't leave me, Dewey—but he does.

"Where's Daddy goin'?" Tee asks.

"He'll wait for us outside," I say.

The ushers close and guard the back doors, but I can still see Dewey's face in the little window. At least his eyes are on me. *Lord, You got Your eyes on this, too, right? I know You're here, and I hope You don't like what You're seein'. This kind of thing just shouldn't happen in any church.*

Jonas takes the microphone from the podium and walks down front to join the board in front of the altar. "Members of Antioch Church, we have a difficult question to put to you today. The board and I would like you to vote on whether a member of our church should or should not remain a member of this church. That member is Ruth Childress." Couldn't say Borum, could you, Jonas? Wouldn't want to associate yourself with me. Nah, that would only confuse folks. "The board has deliberated long and hard on this matter, and I want each of you to pray about this before you decide."

After the shortest moment of silence in the history of Antioch Church, Jonas holds up a sheaf of paper. "This is a list of the members of Antioch Church. There are five hundred and twelve names listed here. Miss Childress needs a majority or two hundred and fifty-seven votes to remain a member here."

Wait just a damn minute! There are only maybe four hundred folks in the sanctuary today! I should only have to get half of *these* folks to stand! Oh, this is dirty! And my supporters, not my enemies, have to stand up in front of the prune-lipped board and Jonas? Oh, this is about as unholy a thing as I've ever heard of!

"All those in favor of Miss Childress—"

"Hold on, Jonas," I interrupt. "Don't I get to say anything in my defense?"

He smiles with all his skinny little teeth. Oh, he has never been a pretty man. "The church bylaws forbid it."

"Well, then, what are the charges?"

"This isn't court, Miss Childress." He smiles at the congregation. "And I think everyone here knows you very well." A few heads nod here and there. "All those in favor of Miss Childress remaining a member—"

A disturbance at the doors in the back makes nearly every head turn. "What's going on back there?" Jonas asks.

The doors open, and *Fred* (Praise Jesus!) leads a slew of folks down the aisle, most of them wearing tattered clothes, dirty coats, and untied shoes. *Lord, keep me from cryin'!* Fred marches right up to me while the others fan out into the pews, and the folks in the congregation make lots of room for them.

Fred takes off his hat and bows a little. "You can kiss me now."

I grab Fred's head and kiss him on his rusty, coarse cheek. "Thank you, Fred."

"Wouldn't have missed this for the world." He winks. "This is gonna be fun." He walks down the steps, nods to Deacon Rutledge, and sits in the first pew.

"Penny, what's that smell?" Dee asks.

White Lightning, I think, but I shush Dee.

"What is the meaning of this?" Jonas demands.

"We heard there was a members' meetin'," Fred says, his voice booming out as loud as thunder. "And we are all members of this church."

"All of you can't be members," Jonas says.

"We are," Fred says. "Every last one of us."

"I have never seen any of you before," Jonas says.

"Sure you have," Fred says, and he winks at me. "You just ain't been lookin' hard enough."

Deacon Rutledge and Jonas exchange a few quick whispers, and Deacon Rutledge approaches Fred. "May I see some form of identification?"

Fred scowls. "My name is Frederick Douglass Carter, Jr., and I've been a member of this church for over fifty years." Dag, that's a lot of names. Frederick Douglass? That's a name I'd be proud to tell folks.

"We'll need to see some identification," Deacon Rutledge insists.

"You ID us, you got to ID everybody here," Fred says. "You gonna do that?" He stands and addresses the congregation. "How many of y'all brought an ID to church?" He turns to Jonas. "Ain't a one in here a number or a picture to the Lord God."

Deacon Rutledge returns to Jonas's side, and I hear Jonas whisper, "Let's just get on with the damn vote." Gettin' testy, are you, Jonas? Things just ain't workin' out for you.

Jonas taps the microphone again. "All those in favor of Miss Ruth Childress retaining her membership in Antioch Church, please stand."

And then . . . They rise. They don't leap to their feet, but they rise. Fred and his crew stand, a few of them swaying and having to hold on to the pews in front of them or the terrified folks next to them. Mrs. Robertson and a few of the old-timers jump to their feet. The ladies from Diana's all stand together, their hair perfect of course. Tonya (when did she sneak in?) stands and waves. I count roughly a hundred folks, mostly women, and start to get nervous. It never entered my mind that I might lose. Never. *Lord, I'm gonna need a miracle here. You still do them, right?*

Then Junie Pruett stands, her bony shoulders straight, her jaw set and pointing at Jonas, and everyone in the sanctuary hears her . . . growling? Growling! Junie Pruett, that quiet woman, is growling! I have created a monster. When folks who haven't stood yet see and hear Junie, row after row of women and a few men stand . . . but not

Naomi. She sits in the third pew, her head bowed. That hurts, but I can deal with it. She got a right to her own opinion, wrong as it is. She got as much a right to be stubborn as I do. *But, Lord, does this mean that our friendship has just ended?* I don't want to think about that, so I look at Jonas. Dag, his hands are trembling, and his lips are moving; but nothing is coming out. Just like one of his sermons. He instructs Deacon Rutledge to make the count. Fred follows behind Deacon Rutledge and does his own count. There they go a-dancin' again. Fred is gettin' to be the booger that Deacon Rutledge just can't flick.

After several tense minutes, Deacon Rutledge announces, "Two hundred and twenty-four." I see Fred nod, so the number must be right. I've fallen short by thirty-three votes.

Jonas is beaming. "Two hundred and twenty-four is not enough for a majority, so I'm afraid, Miss Childress, that your tenure here as organist and member of Antioch Church must—"

"Wait a minute!" I yell, because I have just remembered what Fred warned me about a week ago. "What about the dead people?"

"The what?" Jonas asks.

"Y'all stay here," I say to Dee and Tee. "Mama's gonna go straighten this out." I bust off my pew and go right down to Jonas. "Gimme that list."

He holds it away from me. "Why?"

"Cuz there are dead people on it!" I look at Fred, and he gives me an okay sign. Then he puts that jar up to his ear, right there in the front row! Bet he can hear God *real* well now. Hope that jar don't break. "Dead people are not active members of this church anymore, Jonas."

"But they're still members," Jonas says.

"How can they be members if they're dead, Jonas? Dead folks can't vote or tithe or take up space in the pew! Give me the list." He drops the list into my hands. I read down the list and call out quite a few names of dead members. "A lot of these folks have passed, Jonas. You even did many of their funerals right here where we're standing." I turn to Fred. "Count up the names as I call them out, Fred."

"Seventy-seven," Fred says.

"Seventy-seven?" I say.

Fred nods. "Two sevens, one right after the other."

If Fred says it, I believe it. I do the math in my head. "That leaves . . . four hundred and thirty-five living, active members." I smile. "And I only need two hundred and eighteen votes my way." I turn to Jonas. "Reverend Borum, I won by six votes."

Jonas snatches the list from my hand and gives it to Deacon Rutledge. "Add up the number of dead—um, the number of those who have passed on to glory, Deacon Rutledge."

Deacon Rutledge goes through that list three times, little sweat beads forming on his gray head, and each time it adds up to seventy-seven. "It's . . . seventy-seven, Reverend Borum," he says in a small voice. "Seventy-seven."

"Just like I told you," Fred says.

Jonas tears the list from Deacon Rutledge's hand. "It can't be, it just can't be!"

Most of the folks in the sanctuary are up and headed toward the door. There's no applause, no cheer, just folks leavin' church like usual. The show's over, the final buzzer has sounded, and I have won by knockout, technical though it was. I collect Tee and Dee, and we walk hand-in-hand to Jonas. "See you next Sunday, Reverend Borum."

But in my head I'm saying, *See you next* Saturday, *Jonas. Same spot, too. Right down here at the altar.*

Lord, it's nice to have something to live for.

Twenty-Four

My phone rings off the hook all week long! The folks who stood up for me call to wish me well. "I gotta come to church more often," Tonya tells me. "I never knew there was so much drama there."

"What made you come?"

"My friend needed me."

Oh, this child does my heart some good. "Have you spoken to Naomi?"

"Girl, weren't you listening? I said my *friend* needed me."

"Y'all didn't have a fallin' out, did you?"

"Hell, yes. I called that bitch up the second I got home from church and ragged her ass till she hung up on me."

"Why you do that?"

"She had it comin'. Sittin' on her hands instead of standing up for you."

"She was just voting her conscience, and even if she stood, I would have only won by seven votes. So whether she sat or not, I still would have won."

"She did you dirty, Ruth, and I cannot forgive that."

"I can."

"How?"

"Cuz . . . She's still *my* friend. Naomi will always be a friend of mine."

One person, though, calls me late at night on Monday to wish me hell. "You're ruining our church," a squeaky male voice says.

I recognize the voice immediately and decide to play along. "Who is this?"

"It doesn't matter who this is. You just stay away from Antioch, you heathen. Quit coming or else."

I start to laugh and have to cover the mouthpiece on the phone. He said *heathen?* What a dead giveaway. "Or else what?"

"Or something bad is going to happen to you. Just quit coming."

"I just can't quit comin' . . . *Jonas.* Dewey makes me come with just a single kiss. He whispers in my ear, I come. He merely winks at me, I see stars. Dag, I'm about to come just thinkin' about it."

Click.

What some people will do when they can't sleep.

Of course, Dewey also calls me all week—"tucking me in," he calls it—and we get right nasty.

"What you wearin'?" I ask.

"T-shirt and boxers," he says.

"Oooh, boxers." Never understood the concept of boxers. Are men so lazy that they don't want to unzip or unbutton something down there? Them things have to be drafty. "Is your stuff peekin' out?"

"Might be. What you wearin'?"

"Just my soft, silky skin." I wrap my ratty robe around me. I just have to get this phone moved into my bedroom so I can roll around with my pillow when he calls.

"Nothin' else?"

"Oh, just a smile. Your stuff peekin' out now?"

A pause. "Sure is."

"How far?"

I hear his breath coming in short bursts. "Pretty far."

"What you doin'?"

He takes a deep breath. "Imagining you here."

"What am I doin' to you?"

I think I'll stop here. The things that man has me doing to him just cannot be repeated in polite company. Let's just say that I enjoy what he says I'm doing to him, too.

What some people do when they can't sleep *together.*

Why can't we sleep together? For one thing, he's working extra hours because it's the holiday season, and the trains are fuller than usual. But the main thing is my job. Diana's overflows all week! So many folks come to hear the play-by-play from the showdown that I can't get home at a decent hour. I also can't get away to Avery to work with Dee on Tuesday or Wednesday. But now that he's back to "normal" (whatever that is), he's back in the regular classroom and doing well, and the tips I'm making are going toward Dewey's ring, and—

I don't normally gush like this, but I've got a lot to gush about. I am an oil well that's just sprung loose, and I ain't about to be tapped any time soon.

Instead of bowling, I have Kevin over to my apartment to hear him play "The Wedding Song." And after hearing it only once, I decide that I won't have to sing it, chant it, rap it, or even accompany it because Kevin has a golden voice, and that song is far too beautiful to add a huge pipe organ to it.

"I want you to sing and play it all by yourself at the wedding, boy."

"I don't know," Kevin says. "I ain't never sung in public before."

"There's always a first time."

He shrugs. "I might."

"You will."

On Friday night, I finally have a chance to see Dewey and the kids for more than a few minutes because I have been invited to dinner. It isn't much of one—Dewey picks up a box of chicken and some home fries from a convenience store—but the dessert is wonderful: strawberry shortcake with Sue's strawberry preserves and a heap of real whipped cream. A thousand calories a bite at least. I am halfway through, barely tasting each delicious bite, when I feel three sets of eyes on me.

"What?"

"Nothin'," Tee says quickly.

They haven't touched their desserts yet. Where are my manners? "Sorry," I say, and I wipe my lips with a napkin. "This is just so good."

I wait till they begin eating theirs before I dig my spoon into all that deliciousness and—

Clink.

I'm using a foam bowl, and there's something—*clink*—metal at the bottom of my bowl. I'm eating soft, mushy, sugary food, and there's a hunk of metal—*clink*. I look at Dewey, my heart beating faster, my pulse racing. "What else you got up in here, Mr. Baxter?"

He shrugs. "Special ingredient."

I can't swallow, I can't breathe, I can't move. "Is it . . . golden?"

"Uh-huh," Dee says with a giggle.

"And is it round?"

"Sure is!" Tee yells.

Oh, Lord Jesus, to find a ring at the bottom of a foam bowl of strawberry shortcake—Of course, You already knew about this, right? What a script You have written for my life!

I move a bit of shortcake and a large strawberry aside, and . . . There's the ring! Sweet Jesus! It's gold, and round, and plain, and covered with strawberry syrup, and it's more beautiful than a sunrise and a sunset combined! Instead of digging it out and rinsing it off first, I look hard at Dewey. "You're supposed to put it on me, Mr. Baxter."

"I am?"

Oh, yeah. He's new at all this. "Yes."

"Okay." He reaches across the table and digs his hand into that goop, lifting the ring out of the bowl. I will *not* be finishing my dessert tonight.

"Yuck!" Tee cries.

I shoot out my left hand. "Ain't nothin' yucky about a wedding ring, girl."

Dewey smiles and cups his other hand under the ring, strings of syrup dripping down. "Ruth, will you marry me?"

"Oh, yes." He slides it on, strawberry goo oozing out all over my finger.

"Eww!" Dee cries.

I lick the syrup off. "I am never taking this off," I say. "Never."

"How am I gonna put it on you at the wedding, then?"

"You ain't. This is my ring forever." I take Dewey's slimy red hand with my right. "Thank you, Mr. Baxter."

He leans over the table and kisses me. "Thank *you*, Mrs. Baxter."

Mrs. Ruth Lee Childress Borum Baxter. That's too much of a mouthful. Ruth Lee Borum Baxter? Ruth Lee Childress Baxter? Maybe I'll just be Penny Baxter. No. Sounds too white. Ruth Baxter? Sounds like a TV name from way back in the day.

"A toast!" Dewey hollers, raising his plastic cup of milk. Tee and Dee raise their sipper cups. "A toast to the future Mrs. Baxter."

I sip my milk, but I ain't in the mood for making a toast. "So . . . When we gettin' hitched, boy?"

"Soon."

"How soon?"

"Soon, Ruth, soon."

I don't press him for an exact date, though I really should, tardy as he is about everything. "I don't want no long-term engagement, Dewey."

"It won't be."

"Promise?"

He sighs. "I knew this would happen."

"Knew what would happen?"

"I knew that the second I put that ring on you, you'd want to get married."

I sit back. "So if you knew, why'd you give it to me?"

He looks at his hands and shakes his head. "So you'd know that my intentions are good, that's all."

The apartment's too small and it's too cold outside to have the children leave us to our conversation. "We'll have to reserve Antioch quick. Lots of folks there like to have Christmas weddings."

He rubs his eyes. "Yeah. We'll have to do that."

Dewey ain't soundin' too serious. "You think I'm kiddin'? Black folks in Calhoun been jumpin' the broom around Christmas since slave times." Might have something to do with taxes, too, but I'm not real sure. "Now, are we gonna be married by Christmas or ain't we?" I look over at Tee and Dee, who are watching this conversation very closely. "Be a nice Christmas present for your children, right? You'll be gettin' them a mama for Christmas."

He reaches out his hand to me, but I ain't takin' it. Not till he says we're gettin' married by Christmas. "Okay."

"Okay what?"

"Okay, we'll get married by Christmas."

While the children cheer, I go over and sit on Dewey's lap, praying that the stool will hold us while I kiss the hell out of him. The stool holds, Dewey holds me, and two warm and wonderful children join in, kissing and hugging me. I slide off the ring and put it in Dewey's hand. "I trust you with this, boy. Don't lose it."

"I thought you said—"

I put a wet, sloppy kiss on his lips. "I know what I said. I was just kidding. But understand this: when you do put it on me for real that first time, it ain't never coming off. And neither will yours." I stand. "Now, I got to get me some sleep cuz I got a wedding to do tomorrow."

"Will we see you tomorrow?" Dewey asks.

"Doubt it. I intend to participate all the way in this wedding, and I probably won't be back till late."

Dewey pouts. "We'll miss you."

"You better." I hug Dee and Tee to me. "I'll pick y'all up for church nine o'clock sharp on Sunday morning." I dig a finger into Dewey's chest. "And you, Mr. Baxter, will go with us."

He smiles. "Okay."

"And *puh-lease* wear something decent this time. Go out tomorrow and get yourself a suit from *this* century, okay?"

"Okay."

I go to the door and put on my coat. "Call me later?"

He nods, his hands jammed into his pockets.

"Kiss me."

He pecks my cheek and looks down at the floor. "Bye."

I lift his chin. "What's wrong?"

"Nothin'."

Nothin'? Uh-huh. "Then, kiss me properly."

He drapes his arms around me and kisses me hard on the lips. "Have fun tomorrow."

I hug him tightly. "You know I will."

But will Jonas?

Twenty-Five

I call Tonya early the next morning. "I'm gonna need your help today."

After she cusses me for waking her, she asks, "What you need me to do?"

"I'll tell you when I get there."

I bust up into her house ten minutes later, don't find her downstairs, and have to literally pull her out of bed in her upstairs bedroom. I look around at all the mirrors and melted candles. If these walls could talk. "Time to get up, Miss Lewis."

"Leave me alone, Ruth!" she says, and she tries to crawl back into bed.

I drag her back to the floor where she tries to snuggle up with her comforter. "We got work to do, girl."

"It's my day off. I ain't doin' a damn thing today."

"The hell you ain't! We got us a wedding to get ready for."

She blinks. "Whose wedding?"

I almost say "mine," but that can wait. "Junie's."

She buries her head in the comforter. "That ain't till seven o'clock tonight, wench."

I yank on one end of the comforter, spilling her out onto the floor. "Get up, Tonya."

"Why?"

"Cuz you gotta make me the most beautiful woman there."

She sits up. "How am I gonna do that? How can just one person make you beautiful?"

I act like I'm gonna hit her and sit on the bed. "I need a new dress."
She stands and stretches her back. "Get one, then."
"And shoes."
"So buy some, dag."
"Don't have no money."
"Oh."
"And I'll need you to do me a makeover, fix my hair, put the makeup on right."
She sits next to me. "You should have come by a week ago, girl. We ain't got enough time to do all that today."
I punch her hard in the arm. "Get dressed. We goin' shoppin' with your credit card."
Instead of going to the mall and most of the stores I used to shop at—the plus-size places with the skinny salespeople—Tonya takes us downtown, parks in an alley, and hustles me down the sidewalk to stop in front of Silhouette's, a chic little boutique.
"I ain't never been in here," I tell her. I check out a silky maroon pantsuit on the mannequin in the window. "They ain't gonna have my size."
"They will," Tonya says.
We stand there a few more moments. "Ain't we goin' in?"
"We are. I'm just workin' up the proper attitude."
"Huh?"
"You'll see."
And I do see—and hear—Tonya Lewis, who grew up in the 'hood, turn into a diva with a white voice.
"Tonya, darling," a pale, dark-haired woman says as soon as we hit the door. She leaves her glass-topped counter and extends both arms. Tonya must be a regular.
"Greta, darling," Tonya says, and she kisses Greta on the cheek. I ain't doin' that. I don't know Greta that well. Tonya steps back. "You look wonderful."
"So do you," Greta says with some strange accent. She German? What she doin' in Virginia?
Tonya pulls me by the elbow to stand next to her. "I am not here today for me, Greta. I am here for my friend, Ruth. She needs our help."
Thanks a lot, bitch!
Greta walks around me, touching me on my back, my ass, my shoulders. What the hell?

"And what is the occasion?" Greta asks.

"A wedding."

"Ahh," Greta says.

"Her *ex-husband's* wedding."

Greta clucks her tongue. "And we wish to look better than the bride, yes?"

At least Greta ain't dumb. "Yes, ma'am," I say.

"Call me Greta, Ruth. We are going to get to know each other very well." Long as you don't touch me on the ass again, we might. "Come, come," she says, and we walk down a hallway into a larger room where three mirrors almost surround a little pedestal. "Take your coat off and stand there," Greta says, pointing at the pedestal.

I look at Tonya. "She serious?" I whisper.

Tonya nods.

I ain't never been up on a pedestal before. I toss my coat on an armchair and take my place, checking out my ass in the left and right mirrors. Even though I'm in a pair of faded jeans and a green sweatshirt, I ain't lookin' too shabby. Got to get me some mirrors like this at the apartment. Dewey might like them, too.

For the next ten minutes, Greta and Tonya sit in matching blue armchairs and stare at me, whispering things back and forth like "princess-line, empire, or a-line?" They have me turn to one side, then the other, and spend a whole lot of time looking at my ass. Then Greta starts draping different colored fabrics on me, stepping back, crossing her arms, turning to Tonya and shaking her head. In a matter of minutes, I look like a damn Maypole, fabrics snaking off me every which way.

" 'Scuse me, y'all," I say. "Is there a point to all this?"

"We are seeing what colors are best for you," Greta says, removing orange, red, and yellow and leaving me with burgundy, dark brown, and black.

"The burgundy, I think," Tonya says.

"Yes." Greta removes the dark brown and black. "Yes. Burgundy is you."

I think they're finished, so I step down. They ain't finished. For the next excruciating half hour, Greta measures the hell out of my body, writing everything down in centimeters on a yellow legal pad. I hate the metric system. My chest is eighty-eight centimeters, and my waist is ninety-something!

"You may step down now," Greta says. "I will have it ready in two hours."

"Have what ready?" I whisper to Tonya as we walk out.

"Your dress."

"She didn't even ask me what I wanted."

"I know. Isn't that neat?"

We walk out of Silhouette's and head toward the center of the city. "Neat? Girl, she don't know what I like to wear. She don't know my style."

"You ain't got a style, Ruth. Greta will give you a style that will amaze you."

"How a, what, German white woman know what looks good on me?"

Tonya laughs. "Greta a Cajun, girl! Shit, she at least a quarter black."

I look back. "Her? She was pale as a ghost!"

"She's only a shade lighter than you, Ruth."

True. "Um, is Greta, uh . . . you know."

"She go both ways," Tonya says.

"How you know?"

"How you think?" My mouth drops open. "Come on, Ruth. Let's go eat."

Tonya pushes me into a crowded little dive called Melki's, the chairs and tables so close together that folks eating at one table could eat off the plate of someone at another table.

"What we doin' here?" I whisper.

"Grubbin'," Tonya says, and she directs me to a booth where two white men in fancy suits sit in front of empty plates, one talking on a cell phone, the other writing something in a leather-bound folder. They must be lawyers or something. "Y'all almost through?" she asks. How rude!

"Excuse me?" the man on the phone asks, but he doesn't ask it with attitude like he should.

"I asked if y'all was almost through." Tonya smiles and winks at the man writing.

"Uh, yeah," he says, sliding his golden pen into his suit jacket. "Let's go, Tom."

A few seconds later, we're sitting in the booth. "That was rude," I tell Tonya.

"Don't tell me you wanted to wait till they finished on their own," she says, waving at the waitress, an ancient woman with gray-blue hair and, dag, a moustache?

"That woman got a moustache," I whisper.

"And a bad temper," Tonya adds. "Don't piss Marcella off or you'll never see your food."

Marcella stands in front of us, wiping her hands on an already dirty apron. How nasty! "What?" she says in a gruff voice. She ain't gettin' no tip, talkin' like that. This is Calhoun, Virginia, not New York City. Waitresses around here say, "How y'all doin'?"

"Two specials," Tonya says, "and put the house dressing on the side."

"Yeah, yeah," Marcella says. "You want water?"

"Please," I say. Somebody gotta be polite at this table.

Marcella stares at me. "You want ice in your water?"

"Yes, please." I smile. "If it's not too much trouble."

"So you want *ice* water," Marcella says. "A lot of ice, a little, what?"

Bitch is pluckin' my nerves. "Whatever you think is enough," I say.

She shrugs. "Don't know what I may be thinking by the time I get your water. You tell me. You are the customer."

I bite my tongue. "I'll have a Coke, then. In the can. Cold. Unopened."

Marcella smiles. "She learns quick, eh?"

Tonya smiles. "Yes, Marcella. And don't forget to put—"

"Dressing on the side," Marcella interrupts. "I won't forget." Marcella rolls her eyes at me. "Welcome to Melki's." She shuffles away.

"Um," I say, "what did you just order for me?"

"You'll love it. It's a Greek salad with feta cheese, black olives, green olives, ham, chicken, beef, hot peppers, onions, tomatoes, lettuce, carrots."

"All that?"

"Oh, and enough pita bread to make you sick."

A Cajun white woman who likes to touch my ass and, apparently, Tonya's ass and everything in between, a Greek woman with a terrible attitude and a moustache, and now a salad containing food I'm gonna poot all day—I'm having the strangest day, and it ain't even noon.

The salad, though, is delicious, the pita bread hot and full of flavor, unlike that shit you get at the grocery store that tastes like paper. Neither of us says much while we're grubbin', and Marcella brings us each a slab of baklava. "I didn't order this," Tonya says.

"On the house," Marcella says. "No one is buying it today." She smiles at Tonya and takes her empty plate, and I notice two of Marcella's top front teeth are missing. "You looked hungry."

Tonya opens her mouth, but nothing comes out. She slides the baklava toward Marcella. "No thank you."

Marcella slides it back. "You insult me. I made the baklava."

I take a forkful and slip it into my mouth. It tastes *so* good, but at a thousand calories per square inch, it had better. I put my fork down and pat my lips with a napkin. "It's good, Tonya."

"I've had better," Tonya says.

Marcella looks hurt and drifts away.

"Why you do that?" I ask, digging into my baklava.

"Ho insulted me! Sayin' I looked hungry."

"You cleaned your plate, Tonya."

"I know." She slides the baklava back to her and sneaks a bite when Marcella isn't looking. "But she didn't have to say that. That's why I never tip her ass."

"That ain't very nice."

"Well, neither is she."

"How often you eat here?"

"One, two times a week."

I roll my eyes. "Why you think you get such bad service, then?"

She nods toward the cash register. "When we leave, look at her tip jar. It'll be empty. She mean to everybody."

When we get to the cash register and I see Marcella's nearly empty tip jar, I make Tonya get two more slabs of baklava to go. Marcella can't help it if she never learned any manners. Marcella leans around me to look at our table, then looks at Tonya with that screwy gap-toothed grin. "You like my baklava, then."

"No," Tonya says. "It's for my cat."

Marcella's eyes pop, and so do mine. "She ain't got a cat, Marcella," I say, putting a dollar in the tip jar. "She's just messin' with you."

"Oh, that's right, Ruth," Tonya says. "The cat ran away. Guess I'll just use your baklava for a doorstop, Marcella."

I add two more dollars and grab Tonya's arm. "Come on, Tonya."

Tonya locks eyes with Marcella. "If I got a hundred of these, I could build me a damn house."

Marcella's mouth drops open, and I dig deep into my purse,

pulling out and stuffing a five-dollar bill into Marcella's tip jar. "Don't listen to her, Marcella. Your baklava is delicious."

"You," Marcella says, pointing at Tonya, "you not come back." Marcella turns to me. "You come back any time."

On the walk back to Silhouette's, I try to get Tonya to talk to me, but she's in one of her legendary moods, the kind of mood only an entire pound cake can cure.

"What man done you wrong now?" I ask while we sit on the blue armchairs in the fitting room. But if what she said about her and Greta is true, it might not have been a man?

"What makes you think a man did me wrong?"

"The way you're acting."

"And how's that?"

I blink. "The way you're acting and using that tone of voice on me."

"What tone is that?" she asks with a roll of the neck.

Dag, maybe she's just on her period. "That one."

"I am buying you a damn dress, Ruth, ain't I?"

"Yes. Thank you." I chew on my cheek like Meg does, and the shit works. Can't say nothin' bad when you're chewin' on your cheek.

She jumps up from her chair and goes into the boutique part, returning a minute later with tears streaming down her face. Here we go.

"What's wrong, girl?"

"Gene."

"Ain't he the—"

"Yes. He was the white man who wouldn't get a divorce to be with me. And guess what? He got his damn divorce, and now he's hookin' up with someone else."

"Who?" I wince, because that's the wrong question to ask.

"Skinny, light-skinned bitch with blue eyes and a weave. Tramp can't be more than twenty." She buries her head in her hands. "Ruth, I'm gettin' old."

"No you ain't."

"I turn thirty-eight next week."

"So, you cryin' cuz you gettin' old or cuz you ain't gettin' any?" She sits up. "Cuz I'm gettin' old."

"Liar. I think it's cuz you ain't gettin' any. You gettin' to be just like Naomi. You need yourself a good, stiff dick. Bet you'll find yourself one at the wedding tonight."

"It's an old folks wedding, Ruth."

"Reception's at the Hotel Calhoun. Lots of well-hung young studs bussin' tables there."

She laughs. "Oh, so now you're the expert on well-hung young studs?"

"Uh-huh. A man who's hung will keep you young."

She laughs so hard that she nearly falls out of her chair. "Ruth, girl, you have changed."

"I know. Ain't I the shit?"

Greta comes through a door a few minutes later, a velvet burgundy dress folded over her arm, a box in her hands. "Please remove your clothes," she says to me.

I can't take my eyes off the dress. "Ain't you got a dressing room?"

"You're sittin' in it," Tonya says.

Daa-em. After a few hesitant moments, I'm in only my bra and bloomers up on that pedestal. Tonya helps Greta lower the dress over me . . . and it fits like a glove. It's a little snug in my waist, but it ain't tight enough to cut off the circulation. I look down at my titties staring back at me. I will not be able to bend over in this thing. I look behind me and see a V-shaped slice of my back, the dress hitting me about midcalf. The sleeves end just below my elbows, and my shoulders are kind of puffy. Greta opens the box, and I step into a pair of matching velvet shoes that are surprisingly comfortable for high heels. I look in the mirrors, turning slowly around. Dag, I've just become Cinderella. I can't help the tears sliding out of me.

"I think she likes it," Greta says.

"Yes," I say. "I love it."

She steps behind me and runs her hands over my shoulders. "I broadened your shoulders slightly. I hope you don't mind."

"I don't."

She runs her fingers down the V-slit on my back. "I have high-lighted your beautiful back."

"And her huge front," Tonya says.

"Turn," Greta says, and I turn to her, her chin inches from my tit-ties. "You will be the most beautiful woman at this wedding."

"Thank you."

After Tonya pays for the dress, a slip, a bra, some nice hose that don't come in a plastic container, and the shoes—"You taken care of for the next ten birthdays and Christmases," she tells me—we go to her house for a makeover. She sits me in front of her kitchen window, which looks directly across the narrow space between her house and Naomi's house into Naomi's kitchen.

"Why we gotta do it here?" I ask.

"Want Naomi to see what she could be helpin' me with."

"You think she'll come over?"

"No. She ain't allowed in my house no more."

We don't talk any more about Naomi, and Tonya tackles my hair first. She washes and conditions it before cutting away a bunch of stray hairs. "Gonna frame your face first," she tells me like a seasoned stylist. "Then I'm gonna layer it, and then I'm gonna add some burgundy highlights."

"You can do all that?"

She combs through a particularly stringy patch of hair and snips the ends. "Been doin' all that on Naomi since we was little." She yanks the comb through another unruly section of hair. "Bitch gonna have to find herself someone else now."

I wince. "You gotta take her out on my hair?"

She steps back. "Am I pullin' too hard?"

"Yes."

"Sorry. Your hair is spaghetti, Ruth. How you ever become a hairdresser?"

"I got divorced."

"Oh, yeah."

She streaks the tips of my hair burgundy, a fairly good match on the dress, lets it set, then washes my hair again. While Tonya blowdries my hair, I see Naomi walking back and forth in her kitchen, her hair pinned up, a phone stuck to her cheek. She occasionally faces us with a big smile and a laugh.

"She certainly looks happy," I say.

"She fakin'," Tonya says.

"How you know?"

"Watch." She picks up her portable phone and dials. I hear the tinny ring of a phone and see Naomi pressing a button on her phone. Tonya clicks off her phone and stands in front of the window. "Told you."

"Don't she have call-waiting?"

"Yeah. But the phone don't ring with call-waiting, right?"

"Oh, yeah."

Naomi frowns and closes her kitchen curtains. That's the last we see of Naomi.

Tonya returns to me. "You want a 'fro or some curls?"

"What you think will look better?"

"You ain't got enough hair for a full 'fro, so . . . Let's go with curls." She picks up the largest curling iron I have ever seen. "Got this one at Sally's."

"You ever use it?"

"Nah."

"So why you usin' it on me?"

"Cuz I want to make you some sexy curls, girl. You gonna have coils comin' down that gonna bounce . . . gonna turn some heads."

"My hair don't curl well, girl."

"It will, Ruth. I know what I'm doing."

"But my hair don't."

Half an hour later, Tonya gives up on the curls because I look like a freckled, beige Shirley Temple. She scrunches up her lips. "That didn't work. Does your hair straighten at all?"

"Some. But you gotta sneak up on it."

She removes the curls using a smaller Golden Hot, and it's nearly three o'clock by the time she has twisted large chunks of my hair from my forehead to the center of my head and lifted them with a rattail comb. She pins these twists with tiny hairpins and combs the back straight down behind my ears to my shoulders. I check her work in a mirror and smile. I can see my entire face and both ears.

"I like it."

"You better. Only idea I had left was some pigtails."

I ignore her. "I'm gonna need some nice earrings."

She rubs my earlobes. "You got sexy ears, Ruth. You won't need 'em."

I rub at my freckles. "What am I gonna do about these?"

She holds my face in her hands. "They about to disappear."

And they do. Tonya darkens my face, neck, chest, and back with a mixture of cream foundation and the Bronzing Stick. "You gonna look black tonight, girl." Then using a collection of creams, shimmers, and concealers, Tonya highlights my eyes to blend in with my hair.

"I can't believe that this is me," I say, looking in a hand mirror. I really look black.

"It's you, but I ain't done yet. You got some tricky lips. They ain't full enough, so . . . We gonna have to trick folks into thinkin' that they are."

Ten minutes later, I'm looking at lips I didn't know I had. They're kind of plum-colored and glisten, and though I know they're thin, they look thick.

"You could do this on the side, Tonya," I say.

"Y'all need someone down at Diana's?"

I squint. "You ain't quittin' the phone company, are you?"

"I might."

"Cuz of Naomi?"

"Yep."

"You're gonna throw away a sixteen-year career over her?"

"Might." She washes her hands. "Tired of that place anyway." She looks at me a long time. "You've always been beautiful, Ruth."

"Go on."

"Really. It's just been under the surface."

I blush, but the face in the mirror remains black. "And you brought it out."

She shakes her head. "Nah. I just dressed it up a bit." She checks the clock. "We better be gettin' to the church, right? Get dressed. I'll be down in a minute."

"Right. Don't you have to do your hair and makeup now?"

She walks out of the kitchen. "I said a minute, I mean a minute."

I slip on all the new clothes, and it feels like a birthday or a Christmas that I never had. Everything I'm putting on is new—except for my bloomers. I got to get me something sexier than these. I slide on the silky slip and hose, a very sexy bra, and as I'm putting the dress over my head, Tonya returns to the kitchen.

"Ready?" she says.

I pop my head through the top of the dress and look at her. She's plain Jane with her hair pulled back, very little makeup, and a simple jade green dress and matching shoes. "You goin' to a wedding lookin' like that?"

She pulls down on my dress to hide the slip. "This is your night, Ruth. I didn't want to take away from your glory."

"You might find you a man, girl."

She winks. "But boys got some good imaginations."

I'm almost out the door when I remember Kevin. I call his mama's apartment and get no answer. "He's probably already there," I say. "Let's go."

I don't stop traffic or nothin' like that on the short walk to Antioch, but I feel like I could. Tonya and I walk up the main steps, open the doors, and . . . Jesus, somebody puked lavender and gold all over the damn place! I'm gonna stand out for sure now.

"Ka-CHING," Tonya whispers as we enter the sanctuary.

"Ka-gaudy," I whisper back.

Lavender and gold bows hug the ends of every pew, and lavender and gold ribbons intertwine and snake all over the place. Jesus, if Junie's wearin' lavender, will Jonas be wearin' gold? Little biddies, some of them board members, run to and fro attaching and reattaching fallen ribbons while Jonas's family keeps to its gray self in the corner.

"Flowers don't match," Tonya says, pointing at the garden around the pulpit. "Pale yellow roses and gold ribbons. Very tacky."

Dag, Junie's dowry must have been a big one. There's more money tied up in those flowers than in my entire wedding.

Tonya nods toward my bench. "Time to regulate."

I see the tiniest little woman on my bench. Girl can't possibly reach the pedals. I look all around for Kevin, but I don't see him anywhere. "You got my back?"

"Always," Tonya says, and we march up to the munchkin on my bench.

"Excuse me," I say.

Miss Munchkin turns and stares at me through some very thick glasses. "Yes?"

"You're sittin' on my bench," I say.

She squints. "I'm playing for the wedding."

"Not anymore," I say. "Go talk to Junie."

"I have already," she says. "I've been rehearsing for weeks."

Tonya steps closer. "You're bein' replaced."

"I don't understand," she says.

"You been paid?" I ask.

"Yes."

"Then, get lost."

"But—"

I slide onto the bench and bump her to the other end till she slides off. "Enjoy the wedding," I say, and I start pulling out stops.

Miss Munchkin's little jaw pumps up and down, and she storms off down the aisle to the back of the church.

"One down," I say. And where is Kevin? I tell Tonya Kevin's number, and she goes off to call him.

I warm up with a few choruses of "He's Able" till a tall, skinny black man approaches and taps my shoulder. "Where's Darlene?"

This is the soloist? I don't stop playing, but I have the courtesy to push in a few stops. "She's been replaced. By me."

"You know the songs I'll be singing?"

"You won't be singing."

"Excuse me?"

I hear the back doors open and turn, seeing Kevin out of the corner of my eye. *Thank You, Lord.* "You won't be singing."

"I won't?"

I turn to the black beanpole. "You deaf as well as tone-deaf? You've been replaced, now git."

"Who's singing, then?"

Kevin, in a badly fitting blue suit with a loud red tie, stands beside him. "Kevin is."

"Him?"

Kevin smiles. "Yeah, me. You got a problem with it?"

Beanpole jumps back once he gets a complete look at Kevin's scarred face. "No."

Beanpole vanishes.

"Had me worried, boy," I say, beginning the prelude as folks start to stream in.

"Me, too," Kevin says. "Broke a string last night and had to get out to the mall to get another."

"You tune up while folks get a good long look at us."

Kevin smiles. "I hardly recognized you till I got right up next to you, Mrs. Borum."

"Call me Ruth," I tell him. "Call me Ruth from now on."

I am completely amazed that no one—no board member, no Jonas, no Deacon Rutledge—has attempted to remove me from my bench. Maybe no one recognizes me for real. Jonas's family barely glanced my way, but they've always been like that. I turn and look at the thickening crowd, Tonya in the second row. We got us a full house all right. I shrug to Tonya, she smiles, and I keep playing.

At around seven the lights dim, and the ushers light the candles. This is so romantic! I've always liked candles. Think we only had a unity candle for our wedding. A unity candle. Two candles burn as one. Guess Jonas and I had short candles. I see Jonas and Deacon Rutledge enter (the good deacon is his best man?) and nod at them. Jonas nods back, looks at the crowd . . . then bolts directly up the stairs to me, leaving Deacon Rutledge alone in front of the altar as some wrinkled, robed minister enters from the side door.

"What are you doing here?" Jonas hisses.

"Ask Junie," I say.

"I'm not supposed to see her!"

"Ask her afterward."

He grabs my arms. "If you ruin this wedding, I'll—"

"I won't ruin this wedding like you ruined ours."

"How'd I ruin ours?"

"You showed up." I blink at him. "Don't worry, Jonas."

He scowls and storms away, and the wedding begins. All in all, it's a standard, conservative wedding straight out of the little black book Reverend Otis Woodson's trembling hands hold on to. Kevin's song is beautiful, and as I watch the folks watching and listening to him, I realize that I, too, have always believed in something that I've never seen before—love. I've always believed in love. Jonas and I weren't in love, we weren't a match made in heaven . . . and we weren't quite a match made in hell either. We just didn't have love.

When Reverend Woodson begins saying, "If there be any among you who know of any just cause . . . "every single eye in the church is on me. Jonas and Deacon Rutledge form two of the meanest pairs of eyes I've ever seen. Junie, though, has the craftiest little smile as if to say, "We messin' with him, ain't we?" I chew on my cheek a bit, but I never intended to say anything. I nod at Junie, then smile at Jonas, who's lookin' so sweaty his ring will probably slide off. Poor Junie! He'll probably slide right off her tonight, too. No, his pajamas will soak it all up. Hell, she's pruney enough to soak him up!

I watch the kiss, and when Reverend Woodson presents Junie and Jonas as "Mr. and Mrs. Jonas Borum," I don't feel a thing. I'm Ruth Childress again, like some spell on me is broken forever. I'm plain Ruth again, and it feels wonderful. I play the recessional with the same joy I used to have way before Jonas even came to Antioch, and once the pews are empty, Tonya comes up and gives me some dap.

"Whew, that was some wedding."

"Pretty boring if you asked me." I push in the stops and stand.

"Boring? Geez, girl, you have no idea how much tension was out there. Folks all around me were on the edge of their seats waitin' for something to happen."

"You think anything was gonna happen here, in church?"

She smiles. "Somethin' gonna happen at the reception?"

"You know it."

The reception in the Culpeper Room at the Hotel Calhoun is wall-to-wall glitz and glamour, like a society wedding or something. Kevin plays requests in a corner in front of a very receptive audience while a live jazz band plays in another. Folks dance, eat, gossip, and toast the bride and groom, and it's everything my wedding wasn't. I'm kind of glad, though. Jonas and me would still be payin' for this one.

Tonya and I chow down on some wonderful food, drink some expensive champagne, and dance with all sorts of men, most of them married. An hour into the dancing, Tonya slides over to me and whispers, "Cut in on Jonas."

"Didn't bring my razor."

She laughs. "Go on. I'll make sure the photographer gets a few good shots."

I thank my partner, some overly drunk man waving a linen napkin above his head, and slip through the crowd to Junie and Jonas. "May I dance with your husband?" I whisper to Junie.

"Certainly," she says with a smile. "I need a rest." She joins my hand with Jonas's, and we start to move.

"Smile, Jonas," I say. "You should be happy."

"I'm not."

"Why?"

"You should know."

I shake my head. "Tell me."

"You're embarrassing me again."

I look down at my feet. "I'm keepin' up with the music."

"It isn't that, Ruth, and you know it."

I pull him closer. "We never danced like this, did we, Jonas?"

He tries to pull away, but my grip is much too strong on his bony shoulder. "You have embarrassed me for the last time."

I roll my eyes. "You're right. I'm gonna remove your name from mine forever."

He squints. "You are?"

"Yep. Bad luck." I move him toward the bandstand. "I didn't ruin your wedding, did I? I could have, you know. You shouldn't be ashamed of me." He doesn't speak. "I am, after all, the prettiest woman here. And while I'm thinkin' on it, I forgive you, Jonas."

"For what?"

"For everything." My body feels light, and now my heart feels light. Forgiveness is the shit. *Forgive me, Lord, but it is.* "I'm all through hating you, Jonas."

"Thank you, Ruth."

I smile. "Oh, and Dewey and I would like to be married at Antioch before Christmas." His eyes bulge. "Think you could swing it? No, don't give me an answer now. I can't blame you for not answering. Just take it to the Lord in prayer, Jonas. You can't have a wedding unless it's at Antioch, right?"

The song ends, folks clap, and I leave Jonas by himself on an empty dance floor. I go to the head table and smile at Junie. "He's all yours, girl."

"Thank you," she says. "I've got your number on speed dial."

"I'll be at the other end." I kiss her cheek. "You had a beautiful wedding, Junie."

"Thanks to you, Ruth."

Then Tonya and I close that wedding down. I drink just enough champagne to give me a nice hum, not a buzz, and when I get home, me and Dewey have us some down and dirty phone sex.

I'm gonna have me a beautiful wedding, too, but right now, talking to Dewey on the phone, I ain't thinkin' a damn bit about that.

Twenty-Six

I wake up with the sun without a hangover and call the Hotel Calhoun to try to wake up Jonas. "Reverend Borum, please."

And they connect me! Jonas didn't leave a "do not disturb" message? What a crummy wedding night. "Hello?"

"So, have you thought about it?"

"It's Ruth," he says to Junie.

I am such a pest. "Well, have you?"

"Yes."

"And?"

"You cannot expect me to join the two of you in marriage."

Like I'd even want that. "I don't want you to marry us, Jonas. I'll find someone else to do the hitching. I just want to be married—again—at Antioch, just like you."

"I don't know if that's such a good idea, Ruth, you see—"

"I got a right," I interrupt. "I'm a member of the church."

"By only six votes."

Rub it in, why don't you. "Whatever. So, can we do it or not?"

"I don't think it's a good idea. He's a nonmember, and—"

"You really mean it ain't a good idea cuz he's white."

"Well, that would certainly be a first for Antioch, and like you told me all those years ago, things don't change too fast at Antioch."

Bastard! Of all the things he forgot—like his marriage vows—*this* he remembers. "It ain't up to you alone anyway, Jonas."

"You're right, Ruth. As a matter of fact, the board has decided that all future marriages must be voted on by the church membership."

I don't think I like the sound of that. "No shit? When did they decide that?"

"Last night at the reception."

Figures. "Before or after we danced?"

"After."

Of course. "So . . . We'll need to take another vote?"

"I'm afraid so."

"I ain't afraid." If the same folks stand up as before, I'll win again. But will they? And will Fred and his crew be in attendance today? I'm sure they will. Fred has to know there's going to be a vote. "Go for it."

"Are you sure, Ruth?"

"Positive. And I want the vote done today."

"So soon?"

"Today, Jonas." I slam down the phone. *Lord, I've forgiven that man, but it don't mean I got to like him.*

I put on a conservative black-and-gray outfit and walk over to Dewey's. And miracle of miracles, they're all ready to go. Dewey wears a nice, dark brown suit and matching tie.

"I picked out the tie," Tee says.

"You done good," I say, and I kiss Dewey on the cheek. I sniff. "Aftershave or cologne?"

"Aftershave. Old Spice."

I grimace. "We got to get you some cologne."

We walk to church as a family, and, damn, we make us a nice-lookin' family. A day ago, I didn't turn any heads crossing Vine. Today, the four of us turn us some damn heads on the street, on the steps, and inside the church. We drop Tee and Dee off at Mrs. Robertson's door like any other parents and go to the adult class in the main sanctuary like any other adults. We share a Bible and hold hands under it, and when Sunday school is over, we collect our children like any other parents.

We belong up in here.

The children sit with Dewey in Junie's pew at Junie's insistence, and for the first time in a long time, I'm a little scared. Keeping my membership was one thing, but this is an entirely different animal. If I'm voted down on this, I don't know if I can ever come back here. I'm about to break a whole bunch of rules that I didn't make and never liked. I hope they see past Dewey's skin to that big ol' heart he has pumpin' inside.

To calm myself down, I play "Hold On" at a steady, even pace till some of the older ladies join in. Jonas enters, and instead of praying at his pew like always, he goes directly to the pulpit and taps the microphone. I stop playing abruptly with no fade-out.

This is it. Good thing I don't have high blood pressure no more, or I'd probably spring a leak.

"Brothers and sisters, I'd like to thank those who attended my wedding yesterday," he says, nice and smooth. Sure. Thank the folks so they'll vote your way. "It was truly a glorious event, and Junie and I are grateful for all the lovely gifts."

They got gifts? Oh, yeah. Two tables were crammed full of gifts in the Culpeper Room last night. All we got was a four-slice toaster and some towels way back when. I hope they got themselves ten toasters.

"At this time, I'd like to explain a change the board has made concerning future weddings at Antioch. The board has voted that all weddings to be held within these walls will be voted on by the church membership. The board considered this prayerfully—"

For about five minutes between shots of champagne.

"—and you can see the logic behind the board's decision. Marriage is not something to go into lightly. It is a holy thing, and a holy people must bless any union before that union takes place."

I can't believe what I'm hearing, and I hope no one falls for this load of shit. At this rate, ain't no one gonna want to be married at Antioch. Who'd want to be shot down like that? And at this church, *someone* is gonna find fault with *every* marriage. Jonas is lucky they put this in effect after his wedding. It would have been my pleasure to sit down against him.

"So today, we have someone who would like to have her wedding here at Antioch." Jonas turns to me. "Miss Childress, would you like to say a few words?"

Oh, I couldn't say anything last week, but today I can? I leave my bench and walk past Jonas to the floor in front of the altar. I don't need no microphone because Antioch is quiet as a tomb. "How y'all doin' this mornin'?" I hear a few mumbled words of encouragement, but this crowd is lookin' tore up. Many of the folks in front of me closed down the wedding last night, too, and they was some hard-drinkin' folks. At least twenty men are already on the nods, and the service hasn't even begun.

"My name is Ruth Childress, and I've been your organist for over twenty years now. I been coming here since I was a little girl and got baptized here by Reverend Hamlin almost thirty years ago." Just establishing my qualifications, lettin' them know I've been a member a long time. "I was once married to Reverend Borum, and now I wish to remarry here at Antioch just like he did yesterday." I been here longer, y'all, and if JonASS can do it, so can I. "With your blessing, of course." I motion for Dewey and the children to join me in front of the altar. As Dewey rises, all the eyes in the church leave me and focus on him. A few even half stand to see him better. Don't know why. He's big enough to see from all over the church. Dewey stands to my right looking so nice, and the children lean back against my legs.

Lord, help me out here. I am really nervous. Open some hearts, please, and don't let me put a foot in my mouth.

"I'd like to marry this man and become the mama to these precious children." I look at all those faces, but they still ain't lookin' at me. They're hard starin' at Dewey. "Uh, the board says we need to vote, so we're gonna vote. New rules for a new millennium, huh?" I squeeze Dee's shoulder. *They still ain't lookin' at me, Lord. What am I gonna do?* "Um, last Sunday, a whole bunch of y'all stood up for me, and I've been meaning to thank you for that. It was truly a blessing to me. And today, I need y'all to stand up for me again." They still don't see me. "Thank you." I look behind me at Jonas. "I'm through, Reverend Borum." And they are still starin' holes in Dewey. *Oh Lord, what have I just done?*

"Thank you, Miss Childress. All church members in favor of this marriage, please—" he starts to say, but I cut him off with a look. He clears his throat. "All church members in favor of these two holding their *wedding* here at Antioch, please stand."

A few folks stand immediately. Junie's up. Mrs. Robertson's up. A few older ladies including some of Diana's customers stand. Kevin and his mama are standing and waving from the balcony. A few seconds pass, and no one else stands. Fred and his crew aren't here. Not a single man is standing. *Make 'em stand, Lord Jesus! Get 'em off their asses!* Tonya jumps up from her spot in the middle of the sanctuary, but only a few of the younger members join her. I check out Naomi in the third pew. She still sits, tears streaming down her face. She looks at me and mouths "I'm so sorry." I fight back my own tears, then let them loose when I see Tonya's eyes overflowing.

"C'mon, y'all," Tonya says with a moan. "Get up!" She whirls around. "These two is in love, y'all, just look at them."

They have been lookin', I want to tell her, and that's why they ain't standin'. They've been looking at a white man, not a man. I cannot believe that this is happening at my church, and I cannot believe that I am blubbering like a whale in front of them.

No one else stands, and a few folks who had been standing sit down.

"Any others?" Jonas asks with a smile. "I count only . . . fifteen, no fourteen in favor—" I cut JonASS off with another look.

I stare down every person who has the gall to finally look at me, and I chew on my cheek till I taste blood. Stones. These folks have stones for hearts. This is how it is? Times they ain't a-changin'. Older folks I can understand, but the young ones? They ain't *from* the past, so they shouldn't be livin' *in* the past. I dry my tears and take Dewey's left hand in my right, Dee's little hand in my left. Tee takes Dewey's right. I walk them to the center of the aisle and wipe my shoes on the carpet. I do it nice and slow so everyone will notice. Matthew 10 says that if anyone doesn't receive you or listen to you, you are to leave that house or city and shake the dust from your feet, and I shake me some dust off my shoes. Then we walk out, my head high, my shoulders broader, and we collect Tonya, Mrs. Robertson, and the rest of the others who stood up for me, including Junie. I bust through the front doors and fly down those steps till I'm on the sidewalk when it finally hits me that I'm never stepping foot in that church again.

I've just said goodbye to Antioch Church.

"When's the wedding?" Mrs. Robertson asks me, but I can't speak just yet.

"Soon," Dewey answers for me.

"Make sure we're all invited," Junie says as she and Mrs. Robertson walk away together.

"We will," Dewey says.

I find my voice, but it's so small. "Y'all go on ahead."

"You sure?" Dewey whispers.

"Yeah. I'll catch up to you."

Dewey takes Dee and Tee across Vine, and only Tonya and I are left standing in front of the steps.

"Damn, it's quiet," she says.

"Yeah."

"Choir gonna have to sing along with the piano for a while."

"Yep."

She hugs me. "I'll call you."

"Okay."

Then it's just me alone on that sidewalk looking up at the church, the only church I've ever attended, the only church that I've ever called home. Too many memories are flooding into my brain . . . Mama holding my hand up these slippery steps, the concrete pitted like acne then . . . singing in those Christmas pageants, loud, proud, and way off key . . . Mama's funeral . . . Grandma in the front row at my baptism, her cane at the ready to pull me up if I stayed down too long or to hit Reverend Hambone if he forgot to bring me back up . . . my first Sunday playing the organ, my hands playing one thing, my feet playing another till my feet caught up with my hands . . . Grandma's funeral . . . my wedding . . . last week's vote. I'll never forget that. They wanted me then, but they don't want Dewey and the kids and me now.

They don't want me now . . . because of Dewey.

Lord, help me to hold on to the good memories and let the bad ones go. From out here it may only look like a building of a million bricks, but it's Your house, Lord, and You better get in there and clean up that mess, better fix the bricks sittin' in them pews. You been gone too long.

I look up at the steeple one last time, and when my eyes come to rest on the double oak doors, I see Naomi looking out, her face all puffy.

"Ruth, I don't know what to say."

"Then, don't say anything, Naomi. Don't say a damn thing."

I walk down Vine a little ways and stop in front of Jonas's house. I look up in the tree and smile because the iron's still there. Good. Even if the ignorant sheep at Antioch forget me and my name, I don't ever want that man to forget me. Whenever he looks at my empty bench, I want that man to tremble.

Lord, help me to understand what just happened. All those people . . . have turned their backs on me. Why, Lord? What good can possibly come out of this pain I'm feelin'?

Twenty-Seven

Instead of going to Dewey's apartment, I walk aimlessly around Vine Street looking at rundown buildings, resting on grafitti-encrusted park benches, watching rusty cars go by. I give my feet some horrible blisters, burst into tears every other block, and scare the shit out of every pigeon or stray cat I come across. By the time I get to my apartment, I don't want to do anything but sleep, so I disconnect the phone and take me a power nap.

I am hard asleep when I hear some awful banging at the door. I throw on my robe and open the door. Dewey stands there looking pitiful.

"Where have you been?" he asks as he steps past me.

"Come on in," I say to his back.

He turns. "I've been lookin' everywhere for you, Ruth."

"Really?" I shut the door. "If you looked everywhere, you would have found me."

He sits on the couch and doesn't answer right off. He hasn't seen this side of me before. Come to think of it, I ain't seen this side of me either. "I was worried about you, Ruth."

"What for? I'm a big girl." I walk past him to my bed, slip off my robe, and slide under the covers. Now, where was I? Oh, yeah. Power nap. Close eyes. Count folks standing up for me and Dewey. One, two, three—no, that's Naomi sittin' on her hands, so two—

The bed sags. "I thought something bad had happened to you."

"Something bad did happen to me," I say without opening my eyes. "I got dissed by my church and disgraced in front of my church because of you, but don't let that concern you, Dewey, cuz you ain't really concerned about me."

"I am, Ruth."

"Uh-huh. You just mad that I wasn't where I was supposed to be."

I hear him sigh. "Okay, I'm a little mad, but mostly I'm sad. I don't like to see you cry. And I was kinda lookin' forward to gettin' married there. It's such a beautiful church."

I sit up. "Only kinda?"

He reaches for my hand, but I hide it under the covers. "I'm still gonna marry you, Ruth."

"Where? Where we gonna get married now? You got a church you go to that will marry us?"

"I'm workin' on it."

I stare him down. "You workin' on it right now at this very moment?"

"Well, no, but—"

"Then, we ain't got nothin' to talk about. Get out."

He looks away. "I'm, uh, I'm tryin' to talk to you. I'm tryin' to comfort you, Ruth."

"I don't need comforting, Dewey. There ain't no comfort for what I've just been through. Where are Tee and Dee?"

"Waitin' in the truck."

"Well, go on out and comfort them." I pull the covers over my head. "I need some sleep."

"You sure?"

"That I need sleep? Hell, yes!"

"No, I meant . . . Are you sure you don't want me to be with you?"

I pop my head out of the covers. "Bein' with you got me into this mess; now get the hell out."

I slump to my pillow and don't say another word. The door eventually opens and shuts, and I'm alone.

Again.

I sleep through most of Sunday before I connect the phone again. As soon as I do, it rings.

"What?" I say.

"Ruth, it's me, Naomi, and I—"

I disconnect the phone again. She could have stood up for me. Sure, I still would have lost, but not to stand up for a friend you've had for twenty years *twice in seven days?* Who needs a friend like that? It just proves how shallow she is.

I sleep through most of Monday before briefly connecting the phone and calling Diana's. "I won't be in today," I say.

"I figured that already," Diana says. "How you doin'?"

"I ain't. Y'all busy?"

"No."

Because of me. The word is out, the gossip has got to be flyin' about me and Dewey, and ain't no one going to hear it at Diana's. What they afraid of? It ain't contagious! "Well, I won't be in the rest of the week."

"Just come back when you're ready."

"I ain't never gonna be ready, Diana. Just send me whatever you owe me and hire someone else."

"You ain't quittin', are you?"

"You ain't busy, right?"

"C'mon, girl. It's Monday. We're sometimes slow on—"

"No we ain't, and you know it. Everybody who is anybody comes in to gossip on Monday. They ain't gonna come if I'm there, Diana, so I ain't comin' back. Spread the word."

"They'll come back, Ruth."

"No they won't. Haven't you heard? I'm marrying a white man."

"So I've heard, but I don't see what that—"

"See you around, Diana."

"Wait, Kevin wants to talk to you."

I don't need this shit! A moment later, Kevin says, "Mrs. Borum, I mean, Ruth?"

"Yes, Kevin?"

"I just wanted to thank you for gettin' me to do that wedding. I gave my number to all sorts of folks at the reception, and some have already called. I'll be doin' three weddings, a couple anniversaries, a birthday—"

"That's great, Kevin," I interrupt. "See you around." I hang up and disconnect the phone.

I set the kid up to play at a wedding—which turns out to be the last time I play the organ for an entire service at Antioch—and now he's going somewhere while I . . . I don't have a place to play anymore. *Oh, that's fair, God. Thank You so much! Jump-start him, and ruin me.*

Tuesday I connect the phone, but I don't answer it when it rings. It could be Tonya or Dewey, but then again it could be Naomi calling to apologize, or Jonas calling to gloat, or Diana calling to get my ass back to work. Least folks are concerned.

Now, if only I was.

On Wednesday I shower and dress, but I still don't leave the apartment. I put a kitchen chair next to a window and watch the world go by. *Look at me, Lord. I'm just another woman who can't afford cable sittin' at a window. How much more pathetic can You make me?*

A knock at the door wakes me from a mininap in the chair. "Who is it?" I call out.

"Dewey."

I don't get up. "What you want?"

"I brought you dinner."

From a convenience store, probably. "I'm not hungry."

"Could you at least open the door?"

"Why?"

"I want to see you. I want to talk to you. Please open the door."

I get up and lean heavily on the door. "Where are the children?"

"Down at Mama's."

What? What they doin' there? "On a Wednesday night?"

He doesn't answer right away. "It's Thursday, Ruth."

Huh? Where'd I lose a day? I ain't on medication no more. Have I been sleepin' that long? "It is?"

"Yeah."

Dag, I been holed up for four days. "You been callin' me?"

"Yes."

"Well, why didn't you come by when I didn't answer?"

"I did stop by, but you didn't come to the door." I been sleepin' that hard? "I've been tryin' to tell you that we've been movin', and we just finished packin', and—"

"Did you say movin'?" My feet turn to ice.

"Yeah. I, uh, I withdrew Tee and Dee from Avery, and they're goin' to school in Pine County now. Enrolled them just yesterday."

I open the door a crack. "You ain't shittin' me, are you?"

He shakes his head and looks at his shoes. "Um, I'm movin' back down there, too. There's a lot more room at Mama's house for the kids. It was gettin' kinda crowded in that apartment."

I've lost an entire day somehow, and now I'm losing my future family? *Yes, Lord, You can lay someone low in a hurry. I'm a modern-day Job. You obviously ain't through makin' me pathetic.* "How am I gonna see you, Dewey? How am I gonna see Tee and Dee?"

"I can see you after work, and you can come down weekends."

Wonderful. He'll be stank, sweaty, and tired after work, and I'll be stank, sweaty, and tired after working on the farm. Dewey's feet are gettin' as cold as the weather outside. "You turnin' your back on me, too?"

He takes a step toward me, but I shut the door in his face. "I'm not turnin' my back on you, Ruth."

"Sounds like it. You just moved your ass far away from me, right? You just turnin' tail and runnin' away. *Again.* That somethin' you do to black girls, Dewey Baxter? Wished I had me some kids of yours so you could send me money and I could come crawlin' to you for more money on my way to get a fix." What would I spend the extra money on? Fish sandwiches at Dude's? Grease can kill you if you suck down enough of it. And it even comes in a brown paper bag like a forty-ounce of beer. Yeah, I'll just sit on the curb and suck me down some greasy fish till I die.

"Please, Ruth. Just let me in, and I'll explain."

"You don't have to explain shit to me. You've made it very clear, Mr. Baxter. You just gonna run out on me like you ran out on Tiffany and your children. All I am is the sequel to Tiffany Jones."

"Please open the door, Ruth."

"I am not opening this door. You only gonna bring more hurt inside."

His voice cracks. "I won't, I promise. I love you."

"You love Tiffany, too?"

"I don't know. Maybe."

"Maybe? And *maybe* you love me now?"

"I do love you. I might have loved Tiff back at the beginning, before the drugs, but—"

"So your love ends when the goin' gets rough?"

"No."

"Sounds like it."

"Ruth, please, all this been rough, ain't it?" I don't answer. "I'm still tryin', right? I'm still here. I'm right here outside your door. I'm not running away. And I'm still trying to find us a church."

"You find us one?"

"No, not yet."

"Terrific."

"I've called all over."

"Sure you have."

"I have. I called all over Calhoun for a church to marry us by Christmas, and I even called a few churches in Pine; but they're all booked up."

"You call white churches or black churches?"

"Mostly black churches. Tonya helped me, and—"

"You tell 'em we were interracial?"

"Well, yeah."

What a dumbass! "Of course they're booked up, Dewey! Shit, soon as you tell 'em you're white and I'm black, they gonna be suddenly booked up. No one marries salt and pepper shakers around here."

"But there's an interracial church over in Sutton County, and the pastor says he'll be glad to marry us."

Really? Never been to one of those. "When?"

"Well, the pastor says we gotta complete an eight-week couples course first, but then—"

"I am not waiting eight weeks, Dewey." Eight weeks? Who gets married in January? "You promised me that we'd be married by Christmas."

"I know I did."

"Your promises ain't worth shit, are they? You go on and give up. I don't give a shit anymore."

"I ain't givin' up, Ruth. Look, I called that little chapel, you know, the one that only does weddings, and they can marry us the day after Valentine's Day. I signed us up for six o'clock."

Oh no he didn't! "You signed us up to be married at a wedding chapel at night? Shit, boy, just get us out to Vegas while you're at it."

"It was that or just gettin' the license and gettin' married at the courthouse in front of a judge. I wish you'd open this door so we can sit down and talk about it."

"I ain't havin' a courthouse wedding, boy, and I ain't openin' this door."

"Well, I don't know any other alternative. I don't know what to do." That makes two of us. "I need your help, Ruth."

"This is all on you, Dewey Baxter; so you had better figure something out quick, and you can't be doin' it talking to a damn door."

"You could open it."

"I could, but I won't. In fact, I ain't gonna open it till you got us a place, understand?"

I hear his hand slide down the door. "I understand, Ruth."

I listen to his footsteps fade away, and my heart sinks so low as I sink to the floor. Nothing is working now. Fred's gone. Naomi's there, but I don't want to hear her. My church simply isn't my church anymore, and the folks there are all gone in the head. Tee and Dee are gone. And now, Dewey's gone to do the impossible in Calhoun, Virginia. Ain't no one gonna marry us nowhere. I could make a few calls, but it'd only end up the same. Too many folks know me. Who's left that I can talk to now?

I scramble to the phone, connect it to the wall, and dial Tonya's number. I let it ring seven times, and then her voice mail picks up. "I can't come to the phone right now," she says in that sexy voice, "but you know why. Leave an interesting message, and maybe I'll call back." I listen to the beep . . . and hang up.

Now everybody's gone.

Fuck 'em. I been alone before. I can handle it. Hell, I was alone for the last six years of my marriage. I don't need them. I don't need anyone.

I grab my jump rope and start jumping, no square of carpet under my feet to soften the sound, my robe flapping around me. I make the floor shake and the glasses in my cupboards rattle by landing on my heels. BOOM . . . BOOM . . . BOOM . . . like a little boy's fists and head hitting a door. After ten minutes, I feel the blisters forming, growing, and burning on my hands—but I don't care. I hear my neighbors pounding the walls, the floors, the door—but I don't care. The phone rings and rings and rings because I forgot to disconnect it again—but I don't care.

I don't care. I'm alone, and I don't care.

Wait. If I don't care, what the hell am I jumping this damn rope for? I stop, open a window, and toss the rope outside. The pounding on the walls stops. The fool at my door goes away. The apartment is silent except for the pounding in my chest, the rapid pulses in my temples, the drip of my sweat hitting the linoleum, the phone ringing and ringing.

"God, You and me gotta talk. Meet me at the playground in half an hour."

I bet He don't show, the wuss.

I don't put on a coat, don't even lock my door behind me, and go out into the night. I pass by leafless trees where beautiful houses used to stand, trip over uneven sidewalks still stained with blood, and walk under street lights that have been broken since I was a little girl. Bet God's too scared to come here. He ain't from the 'hood. I move into that playground at Avery and stand under the monkey bars.

"You got a lot of damn nerve, God," I say as I climb the ladder at one end. "You took away my mama, and you took away my grandma. What'd they ever do to You?" I lean out and grip the first bar with my right hand. "You blessed me with a marriage made in hell and provided me with a minister who probably still ain't quite sure what to do with his pecker." The cold bar cools the blisters on my hand, and I swing out. "You took away one of the best friends that I've ever had, and You even gave me a gift that I can't give anymore." I reach for and grab the next bar with my left. "You let my children, damn, You *took*, You *stole* my first four children, and now You're hiding Tee and Dee from me. You ain't nothin' but an Indian giver." I latch on to the next bar with my right and rest. "You let this world go to hell, God. Red and yellow, black and white my ass. Ain't no one precious in no one's sight down here." I reposition my right hand away from an open blister and swing forward. "Why didn't You make everybody all one color? This racial shit ain't holy at all." I take a deep breath and swing my left hand for the last bar, grip it, and swing my legs onto the ladder at the other end. "And now . . . I've made it across these damn bars hating Your holy ass, only there ain't a soul to see it cuz . . ." I start to cry. "Cuz You've now taken the man You led me to . . . You led me to Dewey, and You've taken him far away from me. Thanks for nothin', God."

I wander around Vine till I get to Tonya's and sit on the porch when no one answers the door. I see lights on at Naomi's, but I don't want to see her. I wait at least an hour, realize that I'm freezing my ass off, and walk home.

But it ain't home because I really don't have one anymore.

As soon as I shut the door behind me, I fall to my knees. Why I do this on the cold kitchen floor and not on some nice warm carpet, I don't know, but here I am praying in the kitchen again. Must be something I inherited from Mama and Grandma.

Lord, I'm sorry, but I'm not. I know the Bible says to be thankful for everything, but my list just ain't that long anymore. Thanksgiving is only a few weeks away, and I ain't even sure where I'm gonna spend it. I may end up spending it alone with a slab of pressed turkey. What do I have to be thankful for now?

I cry for a bit and let my tears mix with the drops of sweat on the floor. I know it's a damn pity party, but I just can't help it. "WHY?" I cry out, and that only leads to more tears.

I take a few deep breaths and close my eyes. *Okay, Lord, I'm thank-*

ful that I'm thinner, and though I'll probably wake up with a nasty cold, at least I have my health. For now. I saw what You did to Mama, saw how You crippled Grandma, and I know You could take me at any time, but . . . Thanks for keeping me alive. If I only knew for what! Thank You for Dee, too. And Tee. But no thank You for takin' their mama away, as messed up as she was. That was cruel. I know I probably wouldn't be in the picture if Tiffany was alive, but . . . Why You got to hurt her kids like that?

I make two fists, then relax them, some of my tension easing away. *Let's see . . . Thank You for Tonya and Mrs. Robertson and Junie and Fred and Kevin and anyone who stood up for me and—Naomi. Yeah, even her. She has helped me through a lot of shit for twenty years, but . . . Why'd You hold her down in her pew? Why didn't You lift her up?*

I tap my fingers on the linoleum. *Okay, okay, I have a lot to be thankful for, Lord, but You got a lot to answer for when I finally get to heaven. You've put me through some changes, and You even helped me make a few on my own. I've held on to my sanity and my faith—for the most part—and the only thing now is this hurt inside me which You can take away with a snap of Your fingers . . .* "Now, Lord," I say aloud, "I'm askin' that . . . I'm askin' that You snap Your fingers and take away my hurt."

Nothing happens. I still feel a burning in my chest, and the tears start up again. "Did you hear me, Lord? I'm tired of the hurt; now take it away right now." More nothing happens. "You gone, too?"

God's gone, too.

I *am* alone.

Twenty-Eight

Three weeks pass like a bad dream. I don't go outside because I don't want anybody's eyes on me. "There go the woman who wants to marry the white man," they'll say. "She actually expected her church, a black church, to bless her marriage with a white man. Imagine!" I barely eat, shower only when I can't stand my funk, listen to the phone ring, and keep the door shut. I talk to Tonya and Dewey through the door, but I don't open it. I can't. I don't want them to see me. Tonya asks me to come over and eat popcorn, play some cards, go out to eat. "No," I say. "But thanks for the offer." Dewey just wants to hold me, and I want to hold him, too; but . . . I can't open the damn door. There's just too much shit out there to step in. He's had no luck in finding us a church, and I've taken that as a sign from God that Dewey and me weren't meant to be.

Even Naomi comes to my door, but I don't speak to her. I can't. I have nothing to say to her. Nothing nice, anyway, but I listen to her. "I'm praying all day long for you, Ruth," she says, "all night, too." I want to tell her that I tried that, and that the shit didn't work. Three people comin' to my door, sayin' their piece, and goin' back down the stairs. Dag, it's like my door is a shrine or something, but it ain't gonna be my door for much longer. I'll have to use Dewey's ring money to pay my rent this month, and there won't be any extra for my electric . . . or my phone . . . or my credit card bills.

So what do I do all day while I'm waiting to be evicted and join Fred with a Mason jar on my ear? I look out my kitchen window and see the stubbornest leaves clinging to trees, the coldest rain dropping from gray skies, and the stubbornest gray people goin' on with their lives while mine . . . stops . . . cuz God is gone; God is gone away. Oh, sure, He leaves signs everywhere, but they all say "Do Not Enter" or "No Exit" or "Wrong Way, Go Back."

On Thanksgiving Day, I'm in the apartment with half a package of crackers and a few shiny slices of ham for my big meal. No turkey, no corn bread stuffing, no mashed potatoes (the real ones with all the lumps that you make yourself), no corn pudding, no green beans with bacon and fatback, no greens, no chitlins, no deviled eggs, no brown gravy, no sweet potato pie. Crackers and old ham. I ain't alone, though. Got at least one rat tryin' to chew its way into my empty cupboards. Probably one of the rats my "medicine" fucked up this past summer. "Ain't no food here," I tell it, poking the walls with a broom handle, but still it scratches and claws. Damn, even rats are tryin' to get in to see me. I expect Jonas will be by sometime soon cuz he's the king of the rats. I should use the ham in my hands as bait for the smaller rat. Hell, the scent of it alone would probably kill him, and I know it's a male rat. A female rat wouldn't go to all this trouble. Nah, she'd take a sniff, smell nothin' tasty, and be on her way. Wish the roaches would do the same. It's like walking in a movie theater in here some nights, and I don't always remember to wear socks.

Phone's been ringin' nonstop for the past few hours. That is one persistent someone, all right. Fifteen rings should be the maximum allowed by law, but that phone has rung at least a hundred times in a row. Is it Tonya? Nah. She got a life. Probably got someone over for dinner with her as the dessert. Might be Naomi, but I doubt it. She usually goes visiting all her relatives at Thanksgiving. Dewey? Hmm. Maybe. Wonder what he has to say. Probably the same old shit: "I haven't found us a church, Ruth, but I'm tryin'."

I decide to pick it up. "Hello?"

"Ruth, it's Meg. Dee's stuck up in a tree and won't come down for anyone but you."

Dee's . . . stuck in a tree? "What you mean, stuck?"

"He's gone too high this time. He's way up near the top, Ruth. Dewey's too big to climb that high, and everyone in the Pine volunteer fire company is eatin' turkey. You gotta get down here!"

No, I don't. "He'll come down when he's ready, Meg. He just bein' stubborn like before. He just after a little attention."

"But an ice storm's movin' in, Ruth, and it's gettin' dark."

Ice storm? What ice storm? I look out the window and see nothing but clear skies. "We havin' an ice storm?"

"They callin' for it down here, and the clouds are rollin' in."

Daa-em. Ice storms are a mess around here. "What time is it?"

"Past three, now, are you comin'? He's callin' for you and you alone."

Somebody's callin' my name. A little boy is callin' my name. "I have no way to get there, Meg, so you'll just have to—"

"Can't you call a friend?"

I only have one left. "I could, but—"

"Make the call."

"I don't know. It's Thanksgiving Day and all, so—"

"Please, Ruth."

I look out the window again. Sure enough, the horizon is darkening up with some ugly black clouds. "I'll try."

"Please hurry!"

I hang up and dial Tonya's. After seven rings, I get her voice mail. I hang up and stare at the phone. I ain't callin' Naomi. She probably ain't there anyway. No, Dee will be all right. He's just tryin' to get himself a little attention. He'll come down when the first cold rain and sleet hit him. He ain't dumb. No, I'm stayin' out of this little drama cuz it ain't my show no more.

The phone rings again. I pick it up. "Couldn't get a ride, Meg. Sorry."

"Ruth, it's Naomi."

"Oh." I take a breath. "Thought you were somebody else." I start to hang up.

"You say you need a ride somewhere?"

Don't I always? "Yeah, but it's okay."

"Where you need to go?"

"Pine County, but it's okay."

"I can take you, Ruth."

"No, that's okay. Little Dee is supposedly stuck in a tree and won't come down, but I know he ain't stuck. He's just after a little attention."

"I don't mind driving you, Ruth. Really."

"Ain't you got relatives to visit?"

"Already did. I'll be by in a few minutes."

"That isn't necessary—" *Click.* Dag, two persistent women in a row. I gotta stop answering that phone.

I slog through the clothes lumped on the floor in my bedroom and look for tree-climbing pants. I find some jeans and a sweatshirt that don't smell too bad, grab my coat, and stand at the door. I haven't left this apartment in almost a month, and here I am about to leave. I

watch my hand touch the doorknob, watch my hand turn the doorknob, watch my hand pull the door back, and watch my feet step outside.

I chuckle because I don't step in any shit and smile when I see the
flowers. Dewey left me flowers, roses, on my doormat. Right wilted
now, but . . . There they are. My door *has* become a shrine.

I drift down the stairs to the porch . . . where *Fred* sits in a lawn
chair, my jump rope in his hands. What's Fred doin' here . . . now?
And why wasn't he at the church to stand up for me? My heart races a
whole lot faster.

He hands me the jump rope before I can go off on him. "You better
hurry, woman. That boy needs you."

I take the rope. "He's really in danger?"

"What you think, woman? You think I'd come over here when I
could be eatin' turkey and stuffing at the jail? Of course he's in danger." He stands and stares up at me. "Now get your ass down there."

I see Naomi's car flyin' down Vine. "Will I need the rope, Fred?"

He nods. "Sure will."

I swallow hard. "Thanks for coming."

He turns me toward the stairs to the sidewalk. "Now go. You got a
life to save."

I take two steps and turn back. "Thanks for everything, Fred."

"Yeah. And by the way, Ruth Lee Childress, God ain't gone. God
ain't never been gone. *You* the one who is gone from Him."

I nod. "I know."

"Well, woman, if you know, then go find Him! Get your ass in
gear!"

I trot down the sidewalk and open the passenger door of Naomi's
car before the car stops. "We have to hurry," I say, and she does a
squealing U-turn across Vine and floors it. "You know the way?"

"To Pine County? Sure."

I look at the streets whizzing by. "Dewey took some side street, but
I'm not sure which one."

"I know the way." She smiles. "I'll get you there, Ruth. What's the
rope for?"

"Don't know. Fred says I'll need it."

Naomi finds the curvy road without any trouble, and as we pass
the "Welcome to Pine County" sign, sleet starts pinging off the hood.
Naomi slows down, her windshield wipers flying, her windows fogging up.

"Can't you go a little faster?"

"It's getting icy, girl. You know I don't like going out in this kind of weather."

"But Dee's hands could slip."

She slows to a crawl and wipes the windshield with her hand. "We need to get there in one piece, Ruth. Just tell me where to turn."

It's getting too dark, and the windows are too foggy to see anything outside, much less a dirt driveway, and Naomi slows down even more. I can't see a damn thing because the sleet is getting so thick and it's so dark and I'm about to shred this jump rope in my hands all to pieces and—

"There!" I shout, and I point at a dented red mailbox.

"Where?"

I roll down the window, sleet flying into the car. "There! Turn there! At the mailbox!"

"I don't see a mailbox, and that isn't a road, Ruth!"

"It's their driveway!" I pull the wheel toward me, and the back end of Naomi's car slides to the left.

"Let go, Ruth!"

I let go. "Turn here," I say in a small voice as I roll up the window. "At the mailbox."

"I'm turning already!"

We bump and bounce down the dirt driveway to the farmhouse, mud spraying all over the car, and before Naomi can park the car behind Dewey's truck, I'm out and running over the slippery ground through the little forest to *the* tree, my jump rope whipping back and forth. The air burns my lungs, the sleet stings my eyes and face, and I slip and fall several times, mud caking on my knees and elbows. Couldn't have done this a few months ago. I race to the base of the tree and look up, calling, "Dee! Dee! I'm here! It's Penny!"

I don't see him, and my heart flutters. Did he fall? *Dear Jesus, help him!*

"Penny!"

I turn and see Tee about halfway up the steep hill on the other side of the tree. "Where's Dee?"

"We took him inside the church."

"Church? What church?"

She points up the hill where I can just make out a flickering amber glow and the outline of a small building. "That one."

There wasn't a church there before, was there? I start up the hill be-hind Tee. "Is Dee hurt?"

"He's awful quiet, Penny. Come on!"

I try to keep up with her, but she's much too fast and nimble. I slip and fall several times, skinning my hands and knees. *Okay, Lord, You made the ground soft for my feet, but this is ridiculous!* By the time I reach the church, which is really a square barn with a little steeple and plas-tic sheets for windows, I am soaked, muddy, bleeding, and scared out of my mind. I bust through the door calling Dee's name—

And see candles, lots of candles, all lit, all smelling like strawber-ries.

I see Meg, and Kevin, and Mrs. Robertson, and Junie, and Diana, and Mildred, and is that Sam? It is! And Dewey's in overalls down front with Dee, and Tee's dropping flower petals down the aisle, and everybody's standing because there ain't no pews on the floor that's thick with sawdust—

My God, Dewey done built us a church! He couldn't find us one, so he built it for us! That's why he moved down here. My man built me a church and set up our home!

I hear Tonya to my right whispering something, and Naomi is smiling at me and saying something; but I can't hear them because I'm at my own wedding in the church my Dewey built and it's beautiful and I'm weeping, and *Holy God, I've found You!*

You ain't been gone, God. You've just been waiting for me in Pine County. Thank You for comin' to my wedding.

I turn to Naomi. "Did . . . Did you know about this?"

"It was her idea," Tonya says. "It was all her idea, Ruth. Except for this drafty building, that is. That was all your man."

I look down at my muddy jeans and see a tear at one knee. I laugh at all the mud at my elbows and feel sleet dripping off my hair and down my back. "But I'm not dressed."

"Sure you are," Tonya says, and she takes the jump rope from my trembling hand, replacing it with a bouquet of colorful wildflowers. "Look around, girl. You about as dressed up as anyone else."

Everyone is wearing jeans, flannel shirts, and boots, even Junie and Mildred. My wedding is lookin' like a hoe-down about to begin. "But I look a mess, y'all."

Dee leaves Dewey's side and takes Tee's hand. They skip up the aisle to me and take my hands as Kevin strums "The Wedding March."

This is really happening! I'm about to get married on Thanksgiving Day! "Come on, Penny," Dee says. "Let's go."

I let them lead me down the aisle, crying and laughing at the same time, smiling and crying and laughing at all the folks around me who are crying and laughing and smiling at me. The children stop me next to Dewey. Tee puts my hand in Dewey's, and I hold on to that hand with all my might.

"Surprise," he says.

I can only nod because I'm gonna like surprises from now on.

Sam stands in front of us. " 'Bout time you got here, Ruth," he says as he checks his imaginary watch.

"Yep," I say. And I never thought I'd be here. Never.

"I'm gonna skip all the dearly beloved stuff if y'all don't mind and get right down to it." Sam opens a tattered Bible and finds his place. "First, the Bible reading. I've chosen a passage that I've always loved, because it's all about love, the purest kind of love. Gonna read a little bit from the book of Ruth." I squeeze Dewey's hand tighter and feel all sorts of calluses. He built me a church with his own two hands!

" 'And Ruth said, intreat me not to leave thee, or to return from following after thee: for whither thou goest, I will go; and where thou lodgest, I will lodge: thy people will be my people, and thy God my God. Where thou diest, I will die, and there will I be buried: the Lord do so to me, and more also, if ought but death part thee and me.' " Sam closes his Bible, and chill bumps race up and down my arms. "Those were the original marriage vows, and they were spoken by Ruth to her mother-in-law all those thousands of years ago." He smiles. "I'm sure you'd rather say them to Dewey, though, right, Ruth?"

"Right," I say. I smile at Meg and see tears in her eyes.

"And since this is gonna be a marriage," Sam continues, "I want you to say your vows to each other at the same time. I want you to marry your words together."

While Kevin plays from his symphony, my grubby hands gripping Dewey's callused hands, we say our vows together: "Where you go, I will go. Where you live, I will live. Your people will be my people, and your God will be my God."

Dewey slides on my ring. "With this ring, Ruth Childress, I thee wed."

"But I don't have a—" I start to say, but I feel a ring in my hand and see Tonya sneaking away. Lord, she bought me that dress, and now the ring? I ain't gettin' a gift from her for the rest of my life! I look in my hand and see a ring that matches the one on my finger, only it's much bigger. I slide it onto Dewey's finger, and it fits like a dream. "With this ring, Dewey Baxter, I thee wed."

"I now pronounce you husband and wife," Sam says, and he steps away. "Y'all know what to do next."

I hold Dewey's face in my hands. "You built me a church, Mr. Baxter."

Tears roll out of his eyes. "I had to, Mrs. Baxter."

"I know." I wipe away some of his tears. "Thank you."

"You're welcome."

"Oh, come on now!" Meg yells. "Kiss each other for God's sake so we can do us some dancin'!"

Dewey and I crack up, kiss for one precious moment, and hold each other while the folks around us clap. I feel a tug on my arm and look down at Dee.

"What is it?"

He points at the jump rope stretched across the floor, Tee holding the other end. "Y'all gotta jump over it together now."

You're gonna need it, Fred said. *God, bless Fred something special tonight.*

Then . . . Dewey and I jump the rope, and for the rest of that blessed evening in that tiny church on the hill above *the* tree, we flat-foot the mud off all those boots (and the wheels of Mildred's wheel-chair) to the tunes rolling out of Kevin's guitar. And in the middle of all that joy and laughter (and some really bad dancing), I realize something: the life I have saved tonight, the life I've been saving all along, is my own.

Epilogue

P. O. Box 3473
Pine, VA 23789

Frederick Douglass Carter, Junior
Room 623
VA Hospital
Calhoun, VA 24555

Dear Fred,

Thank you for your letter. It really made my day. Sorry I haven't called or visited you at the hospital. I'm a newlywed, what can I say? You're more than welcome to come down for a visit once you heal up, but don't be surprised if Meg puts you to work. She's a hard-working something. Probably why she's so small. She's just done worked her flesh clean off. And so have I. You wouldn't recognize me. I am skinnier than Tonya now, and it won't be long till I'm skinnier than Naomi. And nowadays I don't care how many freckles I get. The Lord made me that way, and who am I to question Him?

So what have I been up to (as if you don't know)? Well, aside from tending to my children, who call me Mama (and mean it), I help Meg run her truck farm while Dewey commutes to Calhoun every day to play with the trains. I learned how to drive finally, but not Dewey's truck. The damn thing stalls out too much on me; so I drive Meg's old dusty truck, and we putt along fine. Just don't ask me to parallel park or drive when it's icy. Tee and Dee go to a good little elementary school down the way, and I volunteer when I can, which ain't often cuz Meg keeps me busy. Running a truck farm is hard work. I spent most of the winter canning, spent all of the spring cultivating, and I'm going to spend the summer pickin'. You should come down and help me. And bring some of your friends, too. Bet you could even get Diana out of the shop, too. They could all use the fresh air.

Lord, this is a growin' land. Tee and Dee are shootin' up like weeds. I think the air out here just makes 'em taller. They spend their days climbing trees, chasing Myron (he's our pet pig), helping out, but mainly, they're growing strong. Besides cutting their hair, I sometimes cut hair at the farmer's market. And when Meg's sick, I rake the money in alone, and I've even been workin' with Sue like your letter told me to. We're doing everything we can to get her out of that body. We tied two jump ropes together the other day, and Sue's up to seven jumps!

Thanks for the news about Antioch. I can't believe that they're still looking for an organist. I get the itch to sneak in there to blow the dust out of that organ every now and then, and you know what? I still got the key. I know it will work because the board is still too cheap to change the locks. If you see Junie, tell her I said hello. And if you see Jonas . . . just tell him good luck.

What do you think of Tonya's new man? I know you know all about him. Well, if you don't, he's divorced and white, and she's sounding serious. I mean, she caught the bouquet at my wedding, right? Doesn't that count for something? But what you told me about Naomi is just too hard to believe! She goes on walks around Vine Street with a man? My goodness! What's this world coming to? Tell 'em both I said hello, and if you see Kevin, tell him I'm proud of him.

Yes, Fred, I'm still playing the organ. I play a little pump organ at a little country church down the way every Sunday. It ain't one of them snake churches where they pick up snakes and dare 'em to strike. I already been there, done that with Jonas, right? It's just a little Baptist church, and I knew it was an all right church when they had James W. Johnson's "Lift Every Voice and Sing" in the hymnal. Yep, I'm losin' weight while I praise the Lord, and I'm even losin' weight while Dewey and I work on a little baby for me.

Yeah, that's right. We been right busy. Tonya asked me what I'd look like with three children under the age of seven. I told her that I'd look like the mother of three children, who would be happier than a pig slidin' in shit. I ain't gettin' too country, am I, Fred? Right now, at this moment (and please listen hard into that jar of yours), my period's late. I know I ain't too young to be goin' through *the change*, but I'm prayin' it's a child. Boy or girl, it don't matter. But no matter what I have, I'm gonna name him or her Penny cuz good pennies is always turnin' up.

Love,
Ruth—
Mrs. Ruth Baxter